MERSDALE

Loch Br..

Linnochmore

Milton of Clova

Adielinn

Wheen

Glen Clova

Ku...
and
Milton of Clova

Rottal

Whitehillocks

Braeminzion

Clachnabrain

Gella Ford

Glen Moy

Glen Moy

R. South Esk

Cullow

Glen Quiech

Dykehead

Cortachy

Prosen Water

Castle

Memus

N

R. South Esk

Caddam Woods

Kinnordy

Kirriemuir

TO CRY LOYAL

TO CRY LOYAL

HELEN B MCKENZIE

LOCHAR PUBLISHING **MOFFAT · SCOTLAND**

© Helen B. McKenzie, 1989

Published by
Lochar Publishing Ltd
7&8, The Holm
MOFFAT DG10 9JU

British Library Cataloguing in Publication Data
McKenzie, Helen B
  To cry loyal.
  I. Title
  823'.914[F]
  ISBN 0-948403-17-9

Typeset in 10 on 12pt Baskerville by Hewer Text Composition Services, Edinburgh
and printed in Great Britain by BPCC Wheatons Ltd, Exeter.

To my husband, Bill

Contents

Part One

I A STRANGE OMEN, AND A BLUNT WARNING

The Scottish summer seemed to have gone quickly that year as if aware that its sunny countenance was out of character in a sorely stricken land. Its all too brief visit had shown but little effect upon the icy armour with which the remote crags and corries of the Grampians had defied the wiles of spring, and now, even though autumn's colourful tints had scarcely reached the Braes of Angus, the winds blowing down from those wild mountain peaks held more than a hint of the next winter soon to come.

In that autumn of 1746 the onset of winter held a particularly daunting prospect for many Highlanders. Only a few months earlier the Battle of Culloden had ended in disaster for the Jacobites, and now those gallant clansmen who had rallied to the cause of Prince Charles Edward Stuart, and who had survived the butchery of the battlefield, were being hunted down like animals in their own country. Branded as outlaws, some of them grievously wounded and suffering from exposure, they lurked in forests and caves on the mountainsides, while their families, bereft of the breadwinners, and without even a roof over their heads, were turned adrift in an inhospitable climate to live the lives of beggars and tinkers.

As the chill wind swept over the lower slopes of Glen Clova the billowing clouds scudded across the sky, creating an ever-changing pattern of light and shade on the landscape below. The wind sighed through the branches

3

of the silver birch trees, and tugged at the tartan plaid and the red-gold ringlets of the young girl who stood beside the lichen-covered drystane dyke. Anxiously she scanned the nearby hillside. Then, with an impatient movement, she thrust the hair back from her brow. Pursing up her lips she emitted a piercing whistle.

'Sister Elenora! what a dreadfully unladylike sound!' exclaimed her companion, in mock reproof. 'Truly, that whistle would do credit to a goat-herd!' A tall dark-haired youth, some years her senior, whose tanned complexion bore evidence of recent contact with a tropical sun, leant casually against a tree trunk, holding his cloak closely wrapped around him to ward off the penetrating cold of the North East.

'You sound exactly like our stepmother,' retorted the girl, with a resentful flash of her grey-green eyes. 'I, for one, am heartily sick of all the artificial airs and graces that one is expected to affect at The Milton nowadays. What is wrong with behaving naturally? That's what I should like to know.'

The young man's smile widened into a broad grin.

'Still "the rebel maid", I see, Lora, in spite of advancing years,' he laughed. 'You seem to have grown up by leaps and bounds since my last visit home. Tell me, what age are you now?'

'That is not a question you should ask of a lady,' Lora replied, with a withering glance in his direction, 'and, as for being a rebel, had I been a man I should, most certainly, have been a rebel.'

'Had you been a man you would, most certainly, have had better control of that dog,' returned her companion, choosing to ignore the full significance of her latter remark. 'I haven't observed any response, so far, to your most inelegant whistle.'

Lora immediately emitted two further piercing blasts, and the offending animal – a long-legged, majestically-built dog, with the combined characteristics of the ancient breeds of Scottish Deerhound and Irish Wolfhound – at last hove in sight, with tongue lolling out, and showing signs of exhaustion after a series of strenuous hare hunts.

'Loyal! Loyal! This way!' Lora called, by way of guidance.

'What, in heaven's name was that you called the brute?' queried the young man, starting up from his reclining position against the tree trunk.

'I called him "Loyal" – L.O.Y.A.L., but my full name for him is "Loyal Highlander", if you want to know.'

'You must be mad! Surely you know better than to cry "Loyal" up and down the countryside at a time like this! No sensible person would deliberately try to arouse suspicion of Jacobite sympathies now! For Heaven's sake, Lora! Do you want us all thrown into prison?'

'Whom do you mean by "us", pray? I cannot see what my dog's name has to do with anyone else but myself, and I shall call him "Loyal" if I wish.'

'But to cry "Loyal" so loudly and deliberately is bound to attract unwelcome attention sooner or later! Don't you realise that? What point is there, anyway, in declaring to the world at large your adherence to a lost cause? Nothing *you* can say, or do, will reverse the situation. Have some sense, I beg of you, and think of all the other people you may implicate by your foolishness.'

'And who is to know which side *I* am loyal to?' argued Lora.

'That tartan plaid you are wearing could give the first clue I should imagine. Loyal subjects of King George do not sport the tartan at the present time.'

'If it comes to a question of clues, our stepmother's behaviour would provide all the clues necessary to prove which side The Milton adheres to now, whatever *my* personal inclinations may be. What you're afraid for, Paul, is your own skin! Go back to your sailing ships and your fine life in Edinburgh – which you obviously prefer anyway! Then you need have no fear of being classed with such as I.'

At these words anger flared in the young man, and, in two strides he had covered the space which separated them.

'How dare you!' he cried seizing her roughly by one arm.

His unexpected reaction took Lora completely by surprise. As she stared back into the angry eyes, which glared down at her from under the dark brows, she was intensely aware of the flame of resentment which her words had aroused. At that same moment a cloud obscured the sun, casting a shadow over the very spot upon which the young people stood. Lora shivered involuntarily. To her that shadow seemed like an evil omen – a strange foreboding of danger suddenly enveloping either, or both, of them.

Almost immediately the shadow passed. The day was bright again, and the uncanny premonition faded into nothing more than a figment of the imagination.

Paul's hold on Lora's arm had not relaxed, but her dog, with a savage snarl, decided to intervene.

'Let go, Paul! He'll bite you!' warned Lora, more concerned, if the truth be told, by the possible consequences to the dog than by the fear of any harm to the man.

Paul heeded her advice. He stepped back a pace or two and the dog placed itself in front of his mistress.

'You see! He *is* loyal!' cried Lora with evident satisfaction, 'Even *you* couldn't deny that now!.'

By this time, however, Paul had regained his normal composure and he had no intention of becoming involved in further argument.

'Have it your own way,' he shrugged, 'but remember this – whether you like it or not, the English soldiers have been sent to crush the Jacobite insurrection once and for all. Any act of defiance – however small – will be ruthlessly dealt with. So don't say I didn't warn you!' With that, he turned on his heel and strode off in the direction of the house.

Lora watched him go. Then she seated herself on the dyke and looked out over the glen. As far as the eye could reach, there were mountains and moorlands, hills, woods, and pasturelands, with the River South Esk flowing gracefully through the valley, and the little Brandy Burn tumbling headlong down the nearby hillside to join the river on its journey to the sea.

The road from Kirriemuir had branched left and right at the Gella ford near the foot of the glen, thereby giving access to the homesteads on either side of the river. Though picturesque, these roads were really no more than rough cart tracks, treacherous with loose stones on the braes and often slippery with mud in the howes. At The Milton of Clova the two roads converged, and, from there, continued again as a single track to the top of the glen and on into Glen Doll.

The Milton of Clova was an attractive little clachan, with its Laird's House sheltered by tall trees; a diminutive kirk; a smiddy; a water-mill; and a few thatched cottages, huddled by the roadside or dotted over the grassy slopes nearby.

From her vantage point, Lora could absorb the familiar sounds of the workaday life of the clachan – the plash of the mill wheel; the clang of the anvil in the smiddy; the voices of the men and women as they plied their sickles and scythes in the harvest fields; the clip-clop of a horse and cart heading up the glen; and the laughter of children playing by the burnside. These homely sounds, interspersed with the bleating of sheep and lowing of cattle; the varied calls of moorland birds and the cooing of wood-pigeons in the forest, combined to create a scene of peace and tranquillity. Yet Lora knew that underneath it all there was much sadness, and bitterness, and a growing sense of unease.

Glen Clova was nowhere near the scene of the battle, or of the route taken by the opposing armies, and none of Lora's immediate relatives had been directly involved, so their household had viewed the conflict with neutral eyes. Lora was a descendant of the clans Macrae and Cameron, however, and the Highland blood ran strong in her veins. Consequently she could not but feel a measure of involvement. She was also well acquainted with their laird's son – the young Lord Ogilvy – who had played a prominent part in the rebellion, and she thought sadly of him and of all the other men from Angus who had been 'out' in the 'forty-five', and were now running the hills.

Had her father been alive, Lora thought his sympathies might well have been with the Jacobites. Sadly, Ranald Macrae had been killed a few years earlier in a riding accident, and Lora's mother had died when Lora was a little girl.

Neither Lora nor her parents were natives of Glen Clova. It was Mr Macrae's interest in botany that had first brought them to the glen. Having once discovered the wealth of flora to be found in those hills he had been drawn as if by magnet and had decided he simply must spend part of every year there. From his friend the Earl of Airlie he had obtained a lease on the mansion house at The Milton – one of the smaller of the Ogilvy residences – and the Macraes had become regular visitors to the glen. Later, when Ranald Macrae lost his young wife he had felt an overwhelming need for the healing powers of peace and solitude. Thus it was that he and his small daughter began to spend more and more time at their mountain retreat. Soon Lora became so attached to the place she could hardly be persuaded to leave. So it had been decided to make the mansion house their permanent home.

When her father went to Edinburgh on business, Lora usually preferred to be left at The Milton in the care of their housekeeper Elsie MacLennan. Elsie had become something of a mother-figure to Lora and Lora was perfectly happy in the company of Elsie's friends and acquaintances in the glen.

A few years prior to his death Ranald Macrae had married again, his second wife being the widow of a wealthy shipping merchant from Leith. The new Mrs Macrae had brought two other members with her to join the Macrae household – her daughter Susan, by her first marriage, and her stepson Paul, the son of her first husband by his previous marriage. Lora had been convinced she would dislike the newcomers on sight, but, in actual fact she had liked all three.

Mrs Macrae was a social butterfly but her gaiety was infectious, and Lora had loved the way the older woman had made her father laugh again. Susan was a sweet-tempered girl, slightly younger than Lora. In no time at all they were firm friends. Paul was away most of the time, first at school and then in the army, but to Lora he had soon become the older brother she had never had. As time went by she had found herself counting the days to his school holidays and then to his army furloughs. During those welcome breaks the three young people had enjoyed some happy times together in the glen.

Ranald Macrae's untimely death had come as a dreadful shock to them all, and had, inevitably, brought changes. Mrs Macrae had left Clova soon after the funeral and had decided to live, henceforth, at the Edinburgh residence. Susan had gone with her mother. Paul was, by then, more or less permanently away from home in any case. He had given up the army and become involved in the shipping-merchant's business which his own father had bequeathed to him and which entailed much travelling to foreign lands. Lora, by her own request, had been left at The Milton with Elsie MacLennan in attendance.

This second bereavement had made Lora feel very much alone in the world, for she had no uncles or aunts on either side. Her only living relation was an aunt of her mother's – a Miss Riddoch – who lived in the Borders and whom she had met but once, on the sad occasion of her mother's funeral.

When the Jacobite rebellion had commenced, and the Prince's army had marched victorious into the Scottish capital, Mrs Macrae, along with the other society ladies of the time, had eagerly attended the royal functions and joined in the general celebrations. Alas, with the change in fortunes of the Highland army, so also had Mrs Macrae's loyalties changed. She was a woman who apparently desired comfort and security above all things. Hence her decision to leave Edinburgh and return to the comparative safety of The Milton whenever the news came that the Highlanders were definitely losing ground.

Once safely established in the glen, Mrs Macrae made no secret of her change of heart. Indeed, since the decisive English victory at Culloden she had even gone so far as to attend balls in the county town at which high-ranking officers of the Duke of Cumberland's army were honoured guests. In this, Lora had to admit, her stepmother had shown a considerable degree of cunning, for, by her unconcealed approval of the English presence, she had made the position of The Milton household virtually secure. Being a true Highlander herself, however, Lora had privately scorned such a turncoat attitude.

For Lora, the return of her stepmother had meant many other unwelcome changes. Mrs Macrae had frowned upon Lora's easy association with the country people and had disapproved of her close friendship with Elsie. She had repeatedly pointed out that Lora should behave according to her proper station in life and should cease forthwith to keep company with those whom the older woman chose to consider their 'inferiors'. Mrs Macrae also deplored Lora's evident lack of culture, and she had set to work at once to instil into her stepdaughter the manners and speech expected of an up-to-date young lady of society.

Sitting there on the dyke, Lora thought about all these things and sighed heavily. By now she was beginning to regret the scene she had precipitated between Paul and herself. She had looked forward so much to Paul's return. Then, when he had finally arrived, he had seemed so different from the old Paul – so aloof and superior somehow – that she had felt bitterly disappointed, almost cheated, in fact. Her disappointment had made her behave like a rebellious child. Now the previous pleasant relationship which had existed between her and Paul was probably spoilt forever.

After this reverie Lora felt disinclined for human company so she decided to go for a brisk walk before returning to the house. Accordingly, she adjusted the tartan plaid around her shoulders, gathered up her long sweeping skirts, and sprang nimbly over the dyke. Then, with the easy gait of the hardened hill-walker, she strode through the heather until she came to the bridle-path which crossed the mountains to Loch Lee and the Castle of Invermark, at the head of neighbouring Glen Esk.

Lora climbed the path for a bit, but it was extremely rough and stony so she turned aside to follow the course of the Brandy Burn which at that point led into a forest of birch and pine. The going was hard – uphill all the way. Soon Lora felt hot and thirsty, so she knelt down beside the burn and enjoyed a cool refreshing drink. Then she seated herself on a fallen tree trunk and began to drop withered leaves into the turbulent waters, idly watching the progress of her little 'boats' until they disappeared from view.

Overhead, the continual cooing of wood-pigeons acted as a soothing lullaby. Otherwise all was silent, except when the occasional snap of a dried twig, or a rustle of withered leaves, betrayed the presence of some shy little woodland creature. In this peaceful atmosphere Lora's vexation faded away as if by magic. She inhaled the pleasant scents of the pinewood and the heather, and revelled in the joy of solitude.

After a time Lora became aware of Loyal's prolonged absence. She whistled, but there was no response, so she set off in search of her pet, guided by the angry protests of a disturbed pheasant. As she made her way through the wood Lora called the dog's name loudly and imperatively and the hills echoed the call.

'Loyal! Loyal! Loyal!' seemed to reverberate in all directions and Lora laughed and called the name again and again, solely for the purpose of hearing the echo pass from hill to hill.

Suddenly she stopped short. There, on the edge of a clearing, and obviously watching her, was a tall gaunt-looking man. He was in Highland dress, but the kilt he wore was torn and bedraggled, and his boots were falling apart.

Becoming aware that Lora had seen him, the man doffed his cap and bowed slightly.

'Good afternoon,' he called out pleasantly. 'Pardon me if I startled you, fair maid,' and his cultured tones strangely belied the sadly neglected state of his person.

To Lora he was a complete stranger, but by his good manners and refined speech she judged him to be a gentleman who had fallen on hard times.

'That is quite all right,' she replied graciously. 'I wasn't so much startled as surprised. It is so seldom one meets anyone in this wood except perhaps an occasional shepherd or ghillie.'

'I can well believe that,' said the stranger. 'To tell you the truth, I was crossing the hill by the bridle-path when I began to hear cries of "loyal" echoing through the wood, and I simply had to see for myself what manner of person could be so bold as to cry "loyal" for all to hear. 'Tis a dangerous word these days, I am told.'

Lora was stunned by the realisation of her own foolishness. She had been so preoccupied by the echo that she hadn't stopped to think what she was doing. Paul's warning returned to her in full force, but she had no intention of betraying her discomfiture to this stranger.

'Then I hope your curiosity is satisfied, sir,' she replied calmly, 'but I fail to see why anyone's curiosity should be unduly aroused, simply because I choose to call my dog "Loyal". The dog is loyal to me, and I have named him accordingly.'

'Well spoken!' said the man. 'But I wasn't exactly aware you were calling to a dog. It sounded to me more like a shout of defiance, and I said to myself, "here at least is one brave Highland heart that is not to be cast down." Even now, on our short acquaintance, I would hazard a guess that it was the unquenchable clan spirit, and the loyal Highlander within you, that prompted you to choose such a deliberately challenging name for your pet. Is it not so?'

'Considering the very few moments you have spent in my company you have no right whatever to presume anything at all concerned with me,' protested Lora indignantly, drawing herself up to her full height. 'And, in view of the desperate plight of loyal Highlanders at this moment, I can only hope you won't make a habit of labelling everyone you meet as being in that particular category. Surely you have heard of Culloden Field!' With that, Lora turned abruptly away. 'Come Loyal,' she said, addressing the dog which now lay at her feet, 'it is time we went home.'

'One moment, please,' cried the stranger, starting forward. 'I beg your forgiveness if I have offended you, but, truly, I had to find out what manner of person you were. I am in need of help, and your cries of "loyal" came like an answer to my prayers when I had all but given up hope. You spoke just now of the desperate plight of loyal Highlanders. Such then is *my* plight, for I was a volunteer in the Prince's army. I fought on the battlefield of Culloden and I need help for a wounded comrade. We . . .'

'You mean you are a rebel soldier!' gasped Lora, interrupting him. 'Then you must not stay here! There is no refuge for rebels at The Milton.'

'Your people are against the Jacobite cause then? They favour King George?' queried the man, visibly shaken by this information.

'My father and mother are both dead,' Lora replied. 'It is my stepmother who favours the English, and you would be well advised to seek shelter elsewhere.'

'Believe me, I do not seek shelter on my own behalf. I have my health and strength and can fend for myself, but my young comrade urgently needs help. He was severely wounded in the battle but at first seemed to recover well. Unfortunately, the hardships we have suffered during our wanderings have taken their toll. He is now in a very weak condition and his wound has flared up again. Unless someone comes to our aid I fear he may die.'

'Were you in Lord Ogilvy's regiment?' queried Lora.

'No. We fought in Lord John Drummond's detachment.'

'Then why have you come all this way? Are you not strangers to these parts?'

'Although we are both of Scottish descent I'm afraid we are both strangers to Scotland. My young friend's home is in France, and mine in England, but his ancestors owned land in Glen Clova at one time. Tell me, is there an old castle called "The Peel of Clova" anywhere near here?'

'Yes there is. Just over the hill there, on the slopes of Ben Reid,' said Lora, indicating the direction, 'but it has been a ruin for many years.'

'Yes. We knew it was a ruin, but, when my friend sailed from France, his father told him, if he should ever be in dire need, to make for a place called "The Peel of Clova" and to seek one by the name of Hamish MacCrimmon. Do you know of anyone by that name in this neighbourhood?'

'Yes, indeed I do. There is no one I know better than Old Hamish, and it will be him you mean, for there is no other Hamish MacCrimmon in the glen.'

The rebel soldier heaved a great sigh of relief. 'Thank God!' he exclaimed. 'At least we have got this far safely! Would you be so kind as to direct me to Mr MacCrimmon's house please?'

'Certainly. In fact I shall take you there myself,' said Lora impulsively.

The man hesitated, 'I am grateful for your kind offer, but it might be dangerous for you to be seen in my company. Are there any English Dragoons in the neighbourhood?'

'I haven't seen any in the glen during the past few weeks. But, on second thoughts, it might be better if you waited until after nightfall to visit Hamish. A stranger in the glen arouses much curiosity. I would have suggested that I bring Hamish here to meet *you*, but that would be difficult, even by moonlight, for his sight is failing. Indeed, I cannot imagine how Hamish will be able to help you at all. Was your friend given the name of any other person to whom he might apply for help?'

'He hasn't mentioned anyone else to me. His father gave him a sealed letter addressed to Mr Hamish MacCrimmon, and it is this letter that I am hoping to deliver.'

'If you will trust the letter to me I shall see that Hamish gets it,' Lora offered.

The man hesitated uncertainly.

'For myself, I would trust you,' he said, 'but I promised faithfully that I would deliver the letter into no other hands but Hamish MacCrimmon's.'

'Then of course, you must keep your promise,' Lora agreed. 'Where exactly did you leave your friend? Is he far from here?'

'I left him on the hillside, some little way back, in the shelter of a massive boulder. He was too weak to walk further.'

Lora thought rapidly. It was already evening, and further delay would mean that she would be late for the evening meal. Undoubtedly that would bring down trouble on her head, since her stepmother deplored unpunctuality, but further delay might also have serious consequences for the young soldier, so she made up her mind.

'Let me come back with you and speak to your friend myself,' she suggested. 'It is just possible he may have heard of someone else with whom his father was acquainted. In any case, once he has met me, he may be willing to trust me with the letter. I think it would be better if you were both to remain in hiding meantime.'

'I agree entirely with what you say. By the way, my name is Alistair Drummond.'

'How do you do,' said Lora, extending her hand, 'and mine is Elenora Macrae – Lora for short.'

They shook hands solemnly, then Alistair turned and led Lora back through the wood by the way he had come.

'Tell me,' he asked, 'have you heard if Lord Ogilvy survived the battle?'

'Yes he did. He and a number of his men got safely back to Clova within four days of the battle, but a company of Hamilton's Dragoons were lying in wait for them at Cortachy, so the rebels were warned to take to the hills.'

'They may be in hiding in these hills here then?'

'Yes. They disbanded in Clova but we have been thinking lately that Lord Ogilvy may have got safely out of the country. That would explain why we haven't had any patrols up this way recently. Lord Ogilvy would be the prize they were looking for.'

'Is it true that his lady was taken prisoner near Inverness? We heard some talk of that.'

'Yes. Lady Ogilvy apparently watched the battle, and afterwards she wanted to join her husband in his bid to evade capture, but she was persuaded against the long hard ride over the mountains. She remained with friends at Killihuntly and was taken prisoner near there a few days later. She was being held in Inverness but we recently heard that she had been escorted south to Edinburgh. I believe she arrived in the capital on the fifteenth of June and is now a prisoner in Edinburgh Castle.'

'I am truly sorry to hear of their misfortunes,' said Alistair sadly. 'Lord Ogilvy and I became acquainted early in the campaign, and I met his lady when we occupied Edinburgh, and later when she joined him again before the battle of Falkirk. They were fine people, and we spent some pleasant evenings together. God only knows what will become of us all now!'

As they toiled up the steep hillside, Loyal ran backwards and forwards just ahead of them, investigating various interesting scents. All of a sudden the big dog stopped in its tracks, head raised, ears pricked, and nose twitching. It uttered a low growl, then shot off through the heather with the speed of a cannonball.

Alistair and Lora swung round, with one accord, to see what had attracted the dog's attention. They were just in time to see a man rise up from the heather. For a moment his dark outline was silhouetted dramatically against the rosy glow of the setting sun, but he was visible only for that moment. Then he plunged out of sight over a shoulder of the hill – in full flight before the oncoming dog.

Lora heard Alistair swear under his breath.

'That's done it!' he groaned. 'Our presence in the glen will be no secret now.'

Almost at the same moment Lora heard an urgent voice, with a distinctly foreign accent, hailing them from some little way ahead.

'Alistair! Alistair! *Voilà! Voilà!* You have been under observation since ever you came out of the forest!'

'Soldiers?' queried Alistair anxiously.

'*Non!* One man only, and no Redcoat.'

'Did you see where he came from?'

'No! I was watching your progress up the hillside when I became aware of another observer.'

'He didn't see you I hope?'

'No! I do not think so, I kept my head well down.'

'Good lad! It's better they shouldn't know there are two of us.'

'Perhaps it isn't as bad as it seems,' suggested Lora. 'There's always the chance it was another fugitive like yourselves. Some of the remnants of Lord Ogilvy's regiment may be lurking nearby.'

'I suppose there *is* that chance,' agreed Alistair without much conviction. 'Anyway, what's done can't be undone.'

For a few moments all three remained silent, scanning the hillside for any further sight of man or dog.

'There he goes!' exclaimed Alistair at last. 'Look! Away down there to the right. By jove! He can run!'

It was impossible at that distance for Lora to identify the figure, but the cold clammy hand of fear clutched at her heart. The man was heading for The Milton. A rebel would have run back into the hills, or sought refuge in the wood. The man must either be a member of the glen community, or, worse still, a hired spy!

'Your dog is hard on his heels now. Will he bring the man down, Miss Macrae?' she heard Alistair asking.

'No. Loyal would only attack in self-defence or to defend me. For all his great size he is not a vicious dog. When he gets in front he'll start barking to try to keep the man from running further. I'd better call him back.' So saying, Lora pursed up her lips and gave her peculiarly piercing whistle.

Alistair stared at her in amazement. 'You *are* a powerful whistler! I can't say I've ever heard a woman whistle like that before,' he said.

'I don't think I could really claim to be a whistler at all,' replied Lora. 'I just make that noise by sucking in my breath and I certainly can't whistle a tune. Actually, I've already been told this afternoon that my whistle is most unladylike, but it is handy to be able to call the dog.'

'Well, no one could disagree with that,' confirmed Alistair. 'I can see your dog is coming back right now, and the man is still in headlong flight. I think we should say "thank goodness for your dog," Miss Macrae. I'd be surprised if that particular spy ever troubled us again.'

With that, Alistair turned towards his comrade. 'Good news, at last, Angus!' he called, 'The Peel of Clova is just over the hill from here.'

'*Grâce à Dieu!*' breathed the young man.

13

'You won't believe it,' continued Alistair, 'but this young lady actually knows your Hamish MacCrimmon!'

'*C'est un miracle!*' exclaimed Angus disbelievingly, peering past Alistair to where Lora hovered in the background.

'On my honour! I swear 'tis true!' asserted Alistair, obviously relieved to be the bringer of good tidings at last. Taking Lora's arm he drew her forward. 'This is – Angus Lindsay – Miss Lora Macrae,' he said, by way of introduction.

The ailing man lay amongst the heather, more or less concealed by the overhanging rock, and his pitifully thin body was covered by his own plaid and Alistair's. As Lora leaned forward to take Angus's outstretched hand she was struck by the look of suffering on the young face that was turned towards her. Angus's eyes were sunk back in his head, and, even to Lora's inexperienced eye, it was plain that he was in a state of near collapse.

Alistair briefly explained to Angus how Lora and he had met, and how she had offered to deliver the letter.

Angus listened intently. 'She is very kind – but do you think it wise to involve a girl, Alistair?' he asked, when Alistair finished speaking. 'After all, anyone who associates with *us* is taking a grave risk.'

'Don't worry about that,' Lora interrupted hastily. 'I know the Mac-Crimmons well, so there will be no risk involved in delivering the letter. It would be much more dangerous for Alistair to venture down there. I really think it would be best if you both remained in hiding – especially after what has just happened.'

'Perhaps we had better look for another hideout,' suggested Alistair.

'*Mon Dieu*, Alistair! I beg of you, do not ask me to go further this night,' Angus beseeched him. 'I simply could not move another step! My leg is hurting abominably. I wonder if you could adjust the bandage a bit?'

While Alistair was doing what he could to ease the pain in his companion's leg, Lora observed them both more closely. Alistair was the elder by a number of years – possibly in his thirties – while Angus appeared to be little more than a boy – probably not much older than herself. Both men had suffered severely from the hardships experienced during their wanderings, yet Alistair's lithe-looking body, his dark, wiry hair, sunburned complexion, and large, capable-looking hands gave the impression of a person who was normally healthy and energetic, used to living a full life, with many outdoor pursuits. Angus, on the other hand, was slight of build, almost fragile-looking, with a fair skin, and fair hair which at the moment hung in lank, neglected coils around his shoulders. But it was his fine, sensitive-looking hands which held Lora's attention most of all. Never had she seen such beautiful hands on any man. The long, tapering fingers looked as if they had never, ever, done a stroke of work. In fact, the contrast between the two men was so marked that Lora found herself wondering how a friendship had ever blossomed between these two, and what they could possibly have in common with each other.

As if in answer to her thoughts, Alistair turned towards her with a grin. 'We're remotely connected, young Angus and I, though you'd probably never guess by looking at us! We ourselves only discovered the relationship by chance, but it seems we're cousins – two or three times removed, as one might say! We fought side by side at Culloden so we decided to make our bid for freedom together.'

'To tell the truth,' interrupted Angus, 'Alistair saved my life. If it had not been for him I would have been butchered on Drumossie Moor along with the hundreds of other wounded men that the Duke of Cumberland put to the sword. It is also thanks to him that I have got this far. Had I been alone I would, assuredly, have lain down and died long before now.'

'Nonsense, man!' laughed Alistair, 'We Highlanders are not so easily finished off. There's too much of the devil in us!'

'How have you managed to survive as regards food?' Lora asked.

'Well, we were all right at first. Kind friends came to our aid and gave us food and shelter,' said Alistair. 'We were transported from one hiding place to another, hidden under loads of hay in farm carts and the like, but the Redcoats were getting too close for comfort. So, whenever Angus's wound showed signs of improvement, we took to the hills. Since then, I'm afraid, we've had a hard time, but we've met many helpful people on our travels – people who had little enough themselves but who were willing to share what they had with us. One ghillie showed us how to snare rabbits, another taught me how to guddle trout, and a shepherd in Glen Lethnot made a fishing rod for me. Then we had an abundance of berries to eat – blaeberries, cranberries, and even some wild mountain brambles or cloudberries – "avarins" I think you call them. By the way, there are some very fine trout in that loch back there!'

'You mean Loch Brandy?'

'Is that the name? Well we breakfasted right royally this morning – or perhaps it would be more truthful to say, *I* did. Poor Angus had no appetite for food today,' and Alistair cast an anxious glance at his friend.

'How does the bandage feel now, Angus? Any better?'

'*Oui! Merci.* It is more bearable.'

'Well then, shall we decide to give Miss Macrae the letter?'

'Yes, please,' Angus agreed.

'Your father didn't say you could open the letter yourself in the case of an emergency?' suggested Alistair.

'*Non.* My father requested me to bring the letter back with the seal unbroken unless it was opened by *Monsieur* MacCrimmon.'

'Did your father mention anyone else who might help?' asked Lora.

'My father spoke many times of his adventures in 1715 but I must confess I paid but little attention, and now I cannot recall any other name except the one written there,' said Angus rather wearily.

'Here is the letter, then, Miss Macrae,' said Alistair rising from his kneeling position beside the invalid.

'Please don't bother to address me as Miss Macrae. Lora will do nicely,' said Lora, as she took the letter and concealed it in the bodice of her gown. 'First of all I must go home, in case my prolonged absence is causing anxiety, but I shall deliver the letter to Hamish as quickly as I can, and I shall return with his answer tonight yet. When I bring Hamish's reply I shall also bring food. There will be a moon, so I shall easily find my way. I shall whistle to let you know I am coming.'

'I shall be watching and listening for you,' said Alistair, 'and I should like to say how much we appreciate the risks you are taking on our behalf,' and he clasped Lora warmly by the hand.

'I'm glad to think I may be of help to you,' said Lora simply. 'I promise I shan't let you down. *Au revoir!*' and, signing to Loyal who had by now returned and was lying quietly in the heather nearby, she moved off rapidly down the hillside, anxious to reach the fastness of the wood.

Normally unaffected by the lack of company, and having no fear of the dark, Lora was surprised to find that she was glad of the big dog beside her tonight in the deepening shadows. As she passed the spot where she had so recently sat dropping leaves into the burn, she was struck by the change which such a short space of time had wrought in her life.

'It must have been fate!' she said aloud.

And even as she uttered the words, Lora instinctively knew that the meeting with those two strangers would alter the whole course of her existence. In seeking to aid rebels she would surely become one with them – living a life of subterfuge – ever watchful against possible betrayal. And she shivered as she recalled the strange omen, and the dark silhouette on the skyline!

16

II MISTAKEN IDENTITY

As Lora approached The Milton she began to wonder what sort of mood Paul would be in, after their 'tiff' of the afternoon. 'Sulky, no doubt,' she decided. 'Anyway, they'll all have had their meal and I'll probably have to take mine in the kitchen as a punishment for being late.' Lora smiled to herself at the thought. Relegation to the kitchen was certainly no punishment to her, for she had often eaten in the kitchen with Elsie, to save the old housekeeper unnecessary work when the other servants happened to be out.

The silence in the house, after the reverberating sound of the heavy door closing had died away, struck Lora as rather unusual. She was even more surprised to find Paul alone in the hall. He was sprawled on a wooden settle by the fire studying a plan, or a map, and he didn't even look up as she entered.

Lora crossed to the fire and thankfully held out her hands to the blazing logs. Darkness had fallen before she had reached The Milton and the autumn night had grown decidedly chilly.

'You're a bit late aren't you, Lora,' remarked Paul at last. 'I had almost decided to dine alone, for it looked as if you were having the night out.'

'I'm afraid I went further than I intended,' Lora replied, 'But why didn't you eat with Aunt Gwyneth and Susan?'

Paul regarded her with eyebrows slightly raised. 'Aunt Gwyneth and

Susan? Surely you knew that they were to be dining at Lednathie tonight. I understood you were included in the invitation.'

Lora's eyes opened wide and her hand flew to her mouth. 'Good gracious!' she exclaimed, 'I forgot all about it!'

'I thought as much,' said Paul, with an amused twinkle. 'I'm afraid Aunt Gwyneth will never make a society lady out of you, Lora, but I must say Susan seems to be shaping well.'

'Personally I had no desire to be considered a "society lady",' replied Lora with a shrug, 'and Susan, at the moment, just seems to be dazzled by the grandeur of it all. She can't stop talking about Lady So-and-so's magnificent silks, and the fabulous jewellery of Lady Such-and-such. That phase will soon pass.'

'But surely it is natural to appreciate beautiful things, Lora,' Paul pointed out, and, as he spoke, his eyes rested contemplatively on Lora's clear-cut profile, her flawless skin, and the auburn hair gleaming like burnished copper in the glow of the fire.

'Oh! I suppose it is,' agreed Lora as she pushed a log back into place with her foot, 'But beauty is in the eye of the beholder – or so 'tis said – and I'm glad it's the beauties of the countryside that *my* eye appreciates. What I dislike most about the so-called "society" is the insincerity and artificiality of it all. But come, Paul, if we continue in this vein we are sure to end up having another argument. We've quarrelled once today already, and I'm truly sorry about that. Let's forgive and forget. Besides, I'm hungry,' and with that Lora turned and led the way into the dining-hall.

'I feel dreadful about the Lednathie invitation,' Lora remarked as they sat down to supper, 'but I shall be able to make my apologies to the Stormonths when we meet at Logie House tomorrow.'

'I'm sorry to disappoint you there, Lora,' said Paul, 'but, when Aunt Gwyneth left, she told me to convey to you her deep displeasure at your irresponsible behaviour. I have to tell you that since you could so easily forget about the first invitation, she would be much obliged if you would absent yourself from the second also. She and Susan are staying the night at Lednathie and going on to Logie from there. She said she would plead indisposition on your behalf at both functions.'

'Oh!' exclaimed Lora, quite taken aback.

'Did you want so very much to visit the Kinlochs of Logie then?' asked Paul, observing her closely from under his bushy eyebrows.

'Yes. I did,' replied Lora simply, 'I always enjoy going there. I meet many of our old friends. However, I suppose I deserved that punishment.' So saying, she pushed back her chair and rose from the table.

'I thought you said you were hungry,' remarked Paul, glancing at the food which had been left almost untouched.

'It must have been a false hunger created by my walk in the fresh air,' said Lora hastily, 'I don't feel so hungry now. Excuse me Paul, please,' and she slipped quietly out of the room before he had time to say more.

Once out of the dining-room Lora gathered up her skirts and literally dashed upstairs to her bedroom where she hastily donned a warm velvet cloak in a rich shade of green. It was a colour which enhanced her auburn hair and fair complexion, but Lora didn't take time to glance at herself in the mirror. She paused only long enough to make sure that the letter was still safely tucked in the bodice of her dress. Then she sped swiftly downstairs again, hoping to get safely across the hall and down the entrance stairs before Paul emerged from the dining-room.

Alas! as she descended the last few steps, Paul opened the door.

'Going out *again*, Lora?' he enquired with raised eyebrows.

'Yes. It's a lovely moonlight night, so I thought I'd go out with Loyal for a bit,' Lora explained.

'But you're only just in,' Paul pointed out. 'However, I suppose a dog of that size does need a lot of exercise. Would you like me to come with you?'

'Well – er,' Lora floundered awkwardly.

'You'd rather I didn't. Is that it?'

'Oh no, Paul – not really, but, you see, I – I want to pay the MacCrimmons a call – and the old folk are a bit "put out" by strangers,' Lora ended rather lamely.

'Well that's as good an excuse as any,' said Paul, 'but you forget I'm not exactly a stranger around here, Lora. However, I have no desire to spoil your *tête-à-tête* with the MacCrimmons. Do you wish me to call later and escort you home?'

'No thank you. There is really no need for you to come out at all. I am perfectly safe with Loyal beside me.'

'Don't be too late, then. When Aunt Gwyneth is absent, someone must assume responsibility for irresponsible females like yourself, so I presume that doubtful honour falls on my shoulders.'

'I shouldn't think I'd be late. The old couple go to bed early, but there's no need for you to wait up if you want an early night yourself, Paul. I think I'll go and ask Elsie for the remains of that pastie we had for supper. It would make a change for the MacCrimmons. Come along Loyal,' and Lora hurried off in the direction of the kitchen quarters.

To her relief the pantry door was unlocked, and none of the servants was in the vicinity, so she quickly availed herself of the opportunity to fill a basket with a generous share of every commodity the well-stocked Milton larder could provide. Concealing the basket under her cloak, she let herself out by the back door. Then, with Loyal at her heels, she headed across the stable yard.

Once clear of The Milton grounds, and over the footbridge spanning the Brandy Burn, Lora heaved a sigh of relief. The path was rough and steep, but the moon shone brightly and the glen was bathed in a silvery light. It was truly a beautiful night, and Lora's spirits began to rise. Everything was really working out better than she had dared to hope. Her stepmother's absence couldn't have been better timed.

On arrival at the MacCrimmons' cottage, Lora tapped lightly on the window-pane in passing. Finding the door unlocked, she lifted the latch and stepped into the tiny square of dark lobby, calling cheerily, 'It's just me, Mrs MacCrimmon – Lora Macrae!'

'Ye're late in the road, are ye no', Miss Lora?' said the little old lady as she opened the door leading into the humble, earthen-floored living-room, 'but come away in, my dear. We're real glad to see ye.'

Old Hamish was sitting by the fireside with his plaid round his shoulders, and wearing his blue tam-o'-shanter bonnet. He was busy, with his wooden 'brose-caup' and his home-made horn spoon, taking his supper of porridge and buttermilk, and he had neither heard nor seen Lora come into the room. His wife drew his attention by calling loudly, 'Here's Miss Lora to see ye, Hamish.'

'How are you tonight, Hamish?' Lora enquired, as she joined him by the fire.

'Fine thank ye, Miss Lora. How are ye yersel', lass?'

'I'm very well, thank you,' Lora replied. 'I'm sorry to disturb you at this late hour, but I have a surprise for you, Hamish.'

'A surprise for *me* lass? Whatever could that be?'

'It's a letter addressed to *you*, Hamish.'

'A letter to *me*!' exclaimed Hamish unbelievingly, 'I doubt ye're jokin', Miss Lora. I never received a letter afore in my whole life. Who could have sent it, think ye?'

Lora withdrew the letter from the bodice of her gown. Then she told the old couple of her meeting with Alistair Drummond and Angus Lindsay, and about the letter that Angus's father had given him before he sailed from France. The old couple listened attentively.

'That young man's father would be Dugald Lindsay,' said Hamish, when she finished speaking. 'I mind o' him fine. A handsome man he was. He ran the hills around here for a while after the 'fifteen Rebellion, and eventually escaped to France, but he never cam' back here. Open the letter and see what it says, Miss Lora.'

Lora carefully broke the seal, while the old man stirred the peat fire into a brighter flame, and the old lady fetched over the oil 'cruisie', and held it aloft, so that its flickering light might lend its somewhat feeble assistance. Kneeling down by the open hearth Lora withdrew the contents from the envelope – a single sheet of parchment wrapped round a smaller envelope, which was also sealed, and addressed to 'Angus Drummond Lindsay, Esq.' This she replaced in the bodice of her gown. Then she smoothed out the parchment. It bore the heading:

PARIS, 1745

To my right assured friend,
Hamish MacCrimmon of Linnochmore,
in the Glen of Clova

Lora read aloud:

Right Trusted Friend.

As my only son, Angus Drummond Lindsay, sets sail from the coast of France, to join our gallant Prince Charles Edward Stuart in His Royal Highness's courageous bid to replace the British crown on the head of his father (to whom it rightfully belongs), my thoughts wing back over the years to that autumn of 1715 when you and I, and our staunch supporter David McInnes (now departed this life) were fugitives together in the hills of Glen Clova and Glen Doll. We have the highest hopes that this expedition may be blessed with the good fortune which its predecessor lacked. But 'tis wise, whilst planning victory, to make provision also against possible defeat, and thus it is that I pen these lines to you.

Having benefited, as I most assuredly did, from your expert knowledge of the hills, and since it is you alone that has the secret of the entrance to the hidden chamber in The Peel, I am instructing Angus (should he ever find himself 'on the run') to seek you out with all possible speed, and to deliver this package personally into your hands. You will understand what it is I desire of you – to open the secret chamber and provide a refuge for my dear son, and any comrades he may have with him, until a safe passage back to France may be arranged. Angus will see you do not go unrewarded. If you fail me, or him, then you are not the Hamish MacCrimmon that *I* once knew.

Your assured friend,
Dugald Lindsay

PS: The enclosure to be given (unopened) to Angus himself.

It was not until Lora finished reading the letter that Hamish spoke, and then his words came as a tremendous shock.

'That letter is no' for me, Miss Lora,' he cried hoarsely. 'I'm no' the Hamish MacCrimmon that Dugald Lindsay means.'

'But – if the letter isn't yours, then whose is it?' gasped Lora. 'I know of no other Hamish MacCrimmon.'

''Tis my nephew – the son o' my eldest brother – that the letter is meant for. And he – more shame to him – is no' the Hamish MacCrimmon that Dugald Lindsay knew, either.'

'Where *is* this nephew of yours then, Hamish? Do you know anything of him?' asked Lora, anxiously.

21

'As far as I ken, he has a room in a lodgin'-hoose in Kirrie, but the last I heard o' him he was in jail. He's a disgrace to the name MacCrimmon – a good-for-nothing. That's what he is, that nephew o' mine. I doubt if he's really to be relied on for help.'

Lora scanned the letter again. 'Dugald Lindsay obviously thought very highly of him,' she pointed out.

'Aye. At the time Dugald Lindsay knew him he was ane o' the finest young lads in the glen.'

'Then what could have happened to change him so much?'

'That's what I'll probably never know,' said Hamish, staring into the fire. 'Young Hamish was Captain Lindsay's batman, ye see. He and Davie McInnes were wi' the Captain when he was in hidin' here. Eventually they got to the Port o' Leith, and Davie went awa' to France wi' the Captain but Hamish remained in Edinburgh. He was awa' from here for years, and when he returned he was a changed man. He must've got in wi' bad company in the big city.'

'And what about the secret chamber in the castle? Do you know anything about that, Hamish?'

'Aye. I know about it of course, Miss Lora, and I have heard there was an underground passage from the secret chamber that led oot on to the hillside. But, though I looked several times, both at the castle and on the hill, I never found either an entrance or an exit. The auld tower has deteriorated a bit since those days, of course. As for the exit on to the hill, I've heard it said there wasna' a mair cunningly concealed spot in a' the Highlands. Again, we've got to bear in mind that the openin' may have been lost forever under a rockfall. Thirty years can make a big difference. Time takes its toll on a'body, and a'thing.'

Lora felt quite shattered by Old Hamish's revelations. Never for a moment had she doubted that he was the man they were seeking.

'I just don't know what I'm to do about the two rebels in the meantime,' she mused. 'The younger one looked dreadfully ill. I don't think he'll survive many more nights in the open. But, as you know, there could be no refuge for rebels at The Milton nowadays.'

'Bring the laddies here, Miss Lora,' suggested the old lady. 'We'll gi'e them shelter till something can be done for them.'

'But think of the consequences, Mrs MacCrimmon! If you were found to be harbouring rebels your cottage would be burned down about your ears! You cannot take such a risk for the sake of two complete strangers.'

'Angus Lindsay couldna' be looked upon as a stranger exactly,' the old man interrupted. 'His father was often here in Linnochmore, in bygone days, and he was more than generous to my father and mither. He seemed to have plenty o' money and what he gave them helped to cushion their auld age. I could never forget that. We couldna' lie here comfortable in oor bed and think o' Dugald's son oot there on the hillside! Maybe we would be breakin'

22

the law, but surely we would be committin' a bigger sin if we were to desert oor fellow creatures in their time o' need. Bring the laddies here, Miss Lora, as Jeannie suggested, and we'll share what we have wi' them.'

Lora didn't argue further. 'I'll go at once,' she said. 'By the way, you won't need to worry about food. I have a basketful out there in the lobby.' Then she remembered about Angus's wounded leg. 'On second thoughts, I doubt if Angus will be able to walk this far. I'll have to go back to the stables for a pony.'

'Tak' oor auld mare, Miss Lora. It might well arouse suspicion if you were seen takin' a horse oot o' the stables at this time o' nicht. Bess is very biddable, and she's sure-footed on the hill, so she'll serve your purpose fine.'

Mrs MacCrimmon lit the stable lantern and went with Lora to the shed on the end of the house, which was shared by the pony and the cow. The old mare was very surprised at being taken out at that late hour, but she was a 'canny' beast and allowed Lora to saddle her without demur. In no time at all they were heading up the hill, with Loyal beside them.

The wind had fallen now, and the glen was hushed, except for the rhythmic gushing and gurgling of the little Brandy Burn. Down in the valley below Lora could hear the distant plaintive cries of the pee-wits and oyster-catchers, and the sudden screech of an owl, in the dark recesses of the wood, seemed to emphasise, rather than to break, the stillness. Overhead, the big harvest moon hung in the sky like a huge Chinese lantern, and the smooth stretches of the river reflected its golden light, while the surrounding hills lay silent, and shrouded in mystery.

At any other time Lora would have revelled in the beauty and peace of such a perfect moonlight night, but now an edge of danger had crept into her life with its attendant fears and anxieties. Perhaps at this very moment she was being shadowed! At the thought, Lora peered nervously around her, then she gave herself a mental shake. She had given a promise, and she must live up to it! This was no task for the faint-of-heart! From now on, she must concentrate on the matter in hand, and cease to unnerve herself with imaginary dangers. So she stepped out briskly beside the little mare. Nevertheless – having given her whistle as agreed – she heaved a sigh of relief when she actually saw Alistair coming down the moonlit slope towards them.

'Any luck, Lora?' he asked, almost as if dreading the answer.

'I'm sorry to tell you, we've got the wrong Hamish MacCrimmon,' and Lora quickly described the happenings of the evening, 'but,' she concluded, 'at least you will have food and shelter for this night. Old Hamish has lent me his pony to take Angus down to Linnochmore.'

Alistair hesitated. He was loath to involve the old couple in any danger, but the thought of what even one more night of cold and damp might do to Angus decided for him.

'You said there were no Redcoats in the glen, Lora, so we shall accept your friends' kind offer of hospitality, for this night at least. Perhaps by tomorrow we may think of some other alternative.'

With difficulty, and considerable pain, Angus was hoisted on to the pony, and the journey downhill began. It was, of necessity, a slow journey. Lora went in front leading the little mare, and Alistair helped to support Angus in the saddle. Loyal remained fairly close to his mistress.

They travelled in complete silence, only talking in low tones when they paused for a rest.

As they drew near to The Milton the tension increased with every step, and Lora kept torturing herself with the thought of a possible encounter with one or other of the glen dwellers. What excuse could she make to cover such a situation?

All went well until they were skirting the belt of trees along the northern boundary of The Milton grounds. Loyal suddenly stiffened, and his hackles began to rise. He growled ominously as he sniffed the air. Then he gave a sort-of yelp and plunged into the undergrowth.

Terror seized Lora at the thought of what discovery at this stage might mean. Her heart was beating so loudly she felt it must surely be audible to the others. But somehow she managed to move steadily forward, holding tightly to Bess's bridle, and the little cavalcade never faltered. Loyal reappeared a few minutes later.

'Thank goodness! A false alarm!' Lora breathed, quickening her steps. Soon they had crossed the footbridge and were on the steep path up to the MacCrimmons' cottage. The first sight of its rough whinstone walls and heather-thatched roof seemed to Lora like the Promised Land itself.

The old couple had wasted no time after Lora had left. They had fastened the wooden shutters across the windows, stoked up the fire, and laid out a meal for their guests. Besides the food that Lora had fetched, Mrs MacCrimmon had provided bowls of warm milk and oatmeal bannocks. No doubt, in the eyes of those weary half-starved wanderers, the humble repast seemed like a veritable banquet.

In the glowing light of the fire Old Hamish came forward with both hands extended to welcome Angus, as Alistair and Lora helped the wounded man into the room. 'It's an honour to ha'e the son o' Dugald Lindsay under this roof,' said the old man. 'Dugald was often here in days gone by, and ony friend o' his is a friend o' oors. Ye're baith welcome to share what we have.'

By the time Lora came back from stabling the little mare, the men were seated at the table. Angus was deathly pale, and had no appetite for food, but the old lady had persuaded him to swallow some of the warm milk with a little whisky and honey in it. They were discussing the contents of the letter, and Hamish was explaining about the mistaken identity.

As Lora looked at the two young men she was again struck by the contrast between them, and an idea suddenly occurred to her.

'D'you know,' she said, during a lull in the conversation, 'I think it would be a good idea if you were to dress up as a woman, Angus, and pose as Alistair's wife. Then, if anyone called, Mrs MacCrimmon could say you were a niece and her husband over on a visit from Braemar or Ballater.'

'I think that would be an excellent idea,' Alistair agreed enthusiastically.

'Perhaps it would also be wise if you were to pretend to be stone deaf, Angus,' Lora added. 'That way you wouldn't have to get into conversation with strangers. I fear your foreign accent would give you away, whatever your dress.'

'So be it. Necessity knows no laws,' said Angus, with a shrug, 'I shall do my best to appear deaf, *and* ladylike, but I cannot claim to have had much experience as an actor.'

'I shall fetch you both a change of clothes tomorrow,' Lora promised, 'There are plenty of my late father's clothes still in the house, so that will be no great problem, and I'm sure I have a dress that could be altered to fit you, Angus. By the way, Angus, your father enclosed a letter to you with the one addressed to Hamish MacCrimmon. Here it is.' And she produced the package and handed it to him.

'*Merci beaucoup!* Just open it and read it to me, Lora, *s'il vous plaît*,' said Angus.

The envelope contained a short note and a chart. Lora crossed to get the benefit of the firelight and read aloud:

My Dear Son,

When you read this I presume you will be in the company of my good friend Hamish MacCrimmon. I desire you, for your own sake, to study carefully the enclosed chart. By following the directions thereon, you should find a leather pouch of Louis d'ors and English guineas which I concealed in the secret chamber in the Old Castle tower in the year 1715. I trust the pouch may contain sufficient means to buy your safe passage back to France. Please reward Hamish for his loyalty.

God be with you, my son, and may you be blessed with true friends in your time of need.

Your affectionate father,
Dugald Lindsay.

'*Grâce à Dieu!*' exclaimed Angus. 'My father must have possessed the second sight, for, truly, I scarce have a guinea to my name. The mean fellow who struck me down also robbed me of my purse. Had I not had a little money concealed elsewhere on my person, I should have been left penniless.'

'As regards your father's hoard, don't count your chickens before they're hatched, Angus,' Alistair warned him. 'Remember, we haven't yet found the person who holds the secret of the Tower.'

'We must leave no stone unturned in our search for the right Hamish

MacCrimmon,' said Lora decisively. 'I shall ride to Kirriemuir myself tomorrow and try to seek him out.'

'Now Angus, lad, it's time ye were into bed,' Mrs MacCrimmon interrupted. 'I can see by your face that ye're near the end o' your tether. I've prepared some clean bandages for your leg and I think I may have an ointment that could soothe your wound, if ye'll just let me have a look at it.'

'You couldn't be in better hands, Angus,' Lora smiled. 'In the glen Mrs MacCrimmon is known as Dr MacCrimmon. She really is a wizard with her liniments and potions. Just wait till you see! She'll have you as fit as a fiddle in no time! I've never known her to fail yet! Well, I must be going, for the night is far advanced. I shall return in the morning before I leave for Kirriemuir. Good-night all!' With that Lora wrapped her cloak around her and let herself out of the house. In spite of the roughness of the path she ran every step of the way to The Milton, with Loyal close at her heels.

By now Lora had lost count of time – so many things had happened in the course of one afternoon and evening – but she was thankful to find the door of The Milton still unlocked. She and Loyal slipped quietly inside, and Lora closed the massive door with the utmost care. Then she proceeded to tiptoe up the stone staircase. As she did so the wag-at-the-wa' clock in the hall gave a solitary chime. It was one o'clock in the morning!

Paul was sitting by the dying embers of the hall fire but he passed no remark, and Lora thought perhaps he was asleep. Still on tiptoe, she crossed to where Loyal's bowl of food waited in its customary niche. She passed it down in silence. Then she took one of the candles, set in readiness on a stone shelf near the fireplace. As she did so, Paul obligingly sat up and stirred the embers into a blaze so that she could light a taper.

'Well, how did you find the MacCrimmons tonight?' he asked.

'Very well, thank you,' Lora replied.

'I thought you said they went early to bed?'

'They do as a rule, but they were waiting for their niece and her husband to arrive.'

'At this time of night! From where, may I ask?'

'From Braemar.'

'Oh! Are they Bootleggers?'

'What d'you mean?'

'I thought it was only the smuggling fraternity that came down over "Jock's Road" by moonlight!'

'You're trying to be funny, Paul, but you must remember the man would have to finish his day's work before they set out,' and Lora secretly marvelled at the ease with which falsehoods rolled off her tongue.

'Don't you want anything to eat?' Paul asked, indicating the food which Elsie had left for her in a covered dish.

'No, thank you. I had supper with the MacCrimmons.' This was also untrue, but Lora felt that food would choke her at that particular moment. 'I think I'll just get off to bed,' she added, 'I'm rather tired.'

'I'm not surprised at that!'

The tone of Paul's voice made Lora turn sharply, and the hot colour rushed into her face as she noticed the amused expression in his eyes. Without doubt he knew she was lying! Lora turned hastily away.

'Good-night, Paul,' she said, keeping her gaze averted as she bent to pat Loyal's head.

'Good-night, Lora. I'll just make sure that all the doors are locked and barred before I retire.'

But, as Lora climbed the stair, she noticed that Paul remained where he was, gazing thoughtfully into the fire.

Before she went to her room Lora paid a hurried visit to what had been her father's dressing-room. His clothes had remained virtually untouched in the hanging closet, so it was a simple matter to select various items that would be useful to Alistair and Angus. Her main fear was that Paul might catch her in the act, but in fact there was no need to worry. She had been in bed for fully an hour before she heard his step on the landing, and the click of his bedroom door closing.

'Dear God, don't let him think too badly of me,' she whispered, and her cheeks flamed in the darkness at the thought of the lies she had told, and of the lies she might yet have to tell, as she became more entangled in the web of camouflage. Where would it all end?

III AN EVENTFUL DAY

Lora spent a restless night. When she slept she dreamed, and the dreams became terrifying nightmares. When she lay awake, her imagination exaggerated her fears until they almost reached panic pitch. Fortunately, before morning, she drifted into a dream-less sleep from which she awoke surprisingly refreshed and quite prepared to face whatever the day might bring.

As she opened her bedroom shutters the pale light of dawn had already begun to wake the glen, and the birds in the garden below were piping out a chorus of welcome to the new day. Further afield she could see wisps of smoke curling up from cottage chimneys as the glen dwellers prepared to set about their early morning tasks. So far there was no sign of life around The Milton itself. Nevertheless, Lora knew the kitchen and stable quarters would already be swinging into action.

A pitcher of water sat on a marble slab in the bedroom, so Lora washed her hands and splashed the cold water over her face. Then she brushed her hair vigorously, and dressed herself in her outdoor clothes. Finally, she inspected the contents of her hanging-closet and selected such items as she considered most suitable for Angus Lindsay to wear in his rôle of niece to the MacCrimmons.

'I must get those things out of the house before Paul puts in an appearance,' she said to herself. So she wrapped all the clothes in a bundle and concealed the bundle under her cloak. Then she slipped quietly out of her bedroom and down to the hall.

AN EVENTFUL DAY

Loyal rose eagerly from his sleeping quarters beside the hall fireplace as he heard his mistress's light step on the stairs. In fact, he displayed such a boisterous delight at the thought of a walk at that unusually early hour, that Lora had difficulty preventing his wild enthusiasm from developing into a chorus of barking.

Once she had calmed the dog, Lora hurried down the entrance stairs to the outside door. She was surprised to find it already unbarred, but a quick glance showed that Paul's riding crop was missing from its usual hook on the wall. For a moment she hesitated, uncertain what to do next. Then she gave herself a mental shake. This would require only a little more caution to be observed on her part. Besides, if Paul was out for an early morning gallop, he could be miles away by this time. She was probably worrying unnecessarily.

There had been a touch of ground frost overnight and the air was sharp and keen as Lora stepped out over the threshold. For a moment she paused to inhale the fresh sweet scents of the garden before she hurried round the end of the house in the direction of the stable yard. There appeared to be no one about, but she had hardly taken a step across the yard when the door of one of the stables swung open and Paul emerged leading Nero, his big black hunter.

Lora looked wildly around for the nearest hiding place. A water barrel seemed to offer the best possible refuge, so, without hesitation, she threw herself down behind the barrel, dragging Loyal down beside her. She huddled there, with bated breath, expecting to hear at any moment the derisive laugh which would indicate that Paul had seen her undignified disappearance, but she could hear nothing beyond the stamping and snorting of the stallion. The next moment Paul had swung himself into the saddle, and, with a clatter of hoofs on the cobbles, and a squawking and fluttering of disturbed poultry, he had galloped out of the yard.

'Phew! That was a narrow escape,' Lora breathed, as she scrambled to her feet and proceeded to brush the dust of the yard from her dress. Then a low growl from Loyal announced the presence of a third party. Lora swung round to find one of the stable boys watching her with open-mouthed astonishment.

Inwardly, Lora felt quite embarrassed by the lad's untimely arrival, and she wondered uneasily just how much he had witnessed of the episode. Outwardly, however, she strove to appear completely in charge of the situation and greeted the boy in her normal friendly manner.

'Good morning, Jock. That's a fine bright morning. Looks like being a good day. I'd like you to get my pony groomed, please. I'm going out riding later this morning.'

'Rufus cast a shoe when we had him oot for a gallop yesterday, Miss Lora, so I'll need to tak' him to the smiddy first.'

Lora thought for a moment. 'I could take one of the other ponies, but no, I would prefer Rufus today,' she said. 'Ask the smith to give me priority please. I want to leave fairly early.'

'Aye. I'll see to that right away, Miss Lora,' and the stable boy went off whistling cheerily, while Lora headed for the path to Linnochmore, thankful that she had at least kept the bundle of clothes hidden under her cloak. As she approached the cottage, Lora could see Alistair, with shirt sleeves rolled up, carrying a pitcher of water from the well. He noticed her almost at once and gave a friendly wave.

'Good morning, Lora! You're early afoot. Isn't it a beautiful morning! Makes one feel good to be alive, don't you think?'

'Yes, I heartily agree,' smiled Lora, noting, rather uneasily, just how out of keeping Alistair's cultured voice sounded in those humble surroundings. It was difficult to imagine anyone accepting him as a nephew-in-law of the MacCrimmons.

'You know, Alistair,' she said, as they walked towards the house, 'I think it might be better if you didn't talk very much at all. Your educated voice would be sure to betray you to any stranger.'

'I suppose you're right,' Alistair agreed, 'but it will be a dreadful hardship to have to keep my mouth shut all the time.'

Lora laughed. 'Oh, you won't have to keep it shut all the time. You can always chat freely to us when you're within the four walls of the cottage, but when you're in the company of strangers, or even within earshot of other people, I think you might be better to sing dumb.'

'You are determined to have us both sorely afflicted, I must say,' grinned Alistair. 'My poor wife deaf, and me dumb! I think we'd better be very careful we don't overdo the whole thing, Lora, otherwise someone would be sure to smell a rat!'

'It's certainly not going to be easy,' agreed Lora, 'especially with Angus's foreign accent and his mixture of French and English. Perhaps it would be best if you were both to feign dourness, and avoid getting into conversation with any of the MacCrimmons' acquaintances.'

'Don't worry too much about us,' Alistair reassured her. 'After all, we are of the Scottish breed and have our share of good Scots common sense. We can't entirely change the way we speak, of course, but Angus was educated at the Scots College in Paris and he really has commendable fluency in English. It is only in moments of stress and excitement that he reverts to his native tongue. But I assure you we are aware of the dangers and shall keep on the alert.'

'How is Angus this morning?' asked Lora.

'He seems much improved in spirits, thank goodness. The warm bed and nourishing drinks have worked wonders already but the wound is another matter. Mrs MacCrimmon is trying some of her herbal remedies so we are just hoping she may have the cure. She'll be telling you all about it herself, no doubt.'

Old Mrs MacCrimmon met them at the door.

'Come away in, my dear,' she said to Lora. 'I didna' expect to see you so early this mornin', but ye're lookin' as fresh as a daisy in spite o' your late nicht.'

As soon as they were safely inside, Lora produced the bundle from under her cloak.

'Here are the things I promised for Angus and you,' she said, addressing Alistair. 'I think my father's clothes should more or less fit either of you, for he was tall and slim-built as you are, but the hem of my dress may have to be let down for Angus.'

'Thank you very much, Lora. I'd better go and help Angus to change his sex then,' and Alistair took the bundle and disappeared into the other room, smiling broadly.

Left alone together, Mrs MacCrimmon drew Lora over to the fireplace.

'I'm very worried about Angus's wound,' she said, keeping her voice low. 'We'll have to get a doctor, Miss Lora.'

'A doctor!' exclaimed Lora, quite aghast.

'Aye. There's no way out, I'm afraid. None o' my remedies could cure that wound.'

Lora felt as if her legs had turned to jelly. This was something she had never anticipated.

'B-but how can we bring a doctor into a situation like this?' she stammered.

'I think old Dr Elliott would help us, Miss Lora. He was a great friend o' your father's, so I think he would keep a still tongue in his head, if only for your sake.'

'Well, I can go to him when I'm in Kirriemuir today,' said Lora. 'I'll have to try and think carefully what I'm to say to him. I don't know whether he'd favour the Jacobites or not. We won't be able to pretend to him about Angus being a woman, either,' she added ruefully, 'I wish there had been some other way out!'

'I wish that too, Miss Lora, but unless we get medical help very soon, that young man will be in real trouble. As it is, he may lose that leg yet. I dinna like the look o' it.'

The door of the bedroom opened at that point and put an end to the conversation.

'Your presence is requested, ladies!' came the call from Alistair. After receiving their approval of his own change of raiment, he ushered them into the bare little room.

'Meet my lady wife – Agnes Drummond, Aggie, for short,' he laughed. Mrs MacCrimmon and Lora laughed along with him, but, to Lora, her own laugh sounded hollow in her ears, and indeed, the way she was feeling at that moment, she marvelled that she could laugh at all.

'The dress is just a little on the short side, I think,' Mrs MacCrimmon was saying.

'Yes, I thought Agnes was displaying just a little too much leg,' agreed Alistair, surveying Angus with his head on one side. 'I shouldn't like her to be thought of as a "loose woman", y'know.'

Angus pulled a face, and Lora smiled. 'No, that would never do,' she said, 'but I can easily put the matter right. In fact, if you give me the dress back with me now, I may be able to alter it this morning yet. I have to wait for my pony being shod. Apart from the length though, I think the dress is a perfect fit. Don't you agree, Alistair?'

'Yes I do. I think it should fool the glen dwellers all right, but the English are another "kettle of fish". It isn't easy to cheat them, I can tell you.'

'*Mais, mon Dieu*, Alistair! We must be out of here before the English come!' exclaimed Angus. 'Think what would happen to these good people if we were discovered under their roof!'

'Don't worry about that in the meantime,' said Lora, with a cheerfulness she was far from feeling, 'There are no Redcoats around at the moment so we're quite safe. And, if your father's friend Hamish MacCrimmon is in Kirriemuir I'm determined I'll find him and bring him here to open that secret chamber in the Tower. Then, when danger threatens, you can take refuge in there. Who knows, the man may also be able to help us smuggle you out of the country. After all, he would know how your father's escape was arranged. Meantime, Angus, don't worry about a thing. Just stay in bed until your dress is ready to wear.'

'He'll have to hide in his bed. That's for sure,' asserted Mrs MacCrimmon. 'He *must* rest that leg.'

While Lora waited for the dress, Mrs MacCrimmon sang the praises of her lodgers. 'They're two grand lads,' she confided to Lora. 'I'm very fond o' them both already, and I pray that it may be the Lord's will that they'll come through their time o' trial safe and sound.'

When Alistair brought out the dress, Lora carefully concealed it once more under her cloak before leaving the house. Mrs MacCrimmon and Alistair then walked a little way with her to discuss the matter of medical assistance for Angus's leg. They were all very perturbed, but unanimous that this new risk had to be faced.

'I shan't mention the doctor's visit to Angus,' Alistair said. 'He would never agree to it, for he is very worried already – as also am I – about the danger in which we have involved you all.'

Lora's heart was heavy as she continued down to The Milton. She could have done well without this extra duty, especially as she couldn't remember what kind of man the doctor was. If he disapproved of Jacobites the situation could prove awkward.

At the stables she paused to make sure that Jock had taken her pony to the smithy, and was relieved to learn that Paul had not yet returned. She had scarcely left the stables, however, when the sound of galloping hooves reached her ears and just as she arrived at the front door of the house, Paul came thundering to a standstill beside her.

'The top of the morning to you, Lora!' he cried, doffing his cap and grinning down at her as she turned to stroke the horse's head.

'I was just beginning to think you'd forgotten all about breakfast,' said Lora.

'Forgotten about breakfast! You must be joking! I feel as if I could eat an ox! You should've been with us, Lora. Nothing like an early morning gallop to give one an appetite! Wait till I return Nero to his stall and I'll show you exactly what I mean.'

Over breakfast, Paul announced his intention of going out for a day's deer-stalking in the hills above Braedounie. 'What are your plans, Lora?' he asked.

'I haven't exactly made up my mind, but I have some alterations to make to a dress first of all. Then I may go out for a canter.' While she was speaking she kept her eyes on her plate, but she was uncomfortably aware of Paul's questioning gaze upon her. 'The result of a guilty conscience no doubt,' she said to herself, but she was very glad when the meal was over and Paul had gone to prepare for his day's outing.

No sooner had she seen him heading up the glen in the direction of Braedounie than she hastened to change into her riding habit. Things couldn't have worked out better – first her stepmother and Susan out of the way, and now Paul. There was no one to interfere with her plans. Perhaps, after all, luck was in her favour!

Lora had quickly unpicked the hem of the dress while she sat by her window waiting for Paul to leave. Now she plied her needle with vim and vigour, keeping an ear open for the sound of her pony coming from the forge. Just as Jock appeared leading Rufus, she had the satisfaction of putting in the last stitch, and she hurried off to the kitchen quarters to ask Elsie to press the hem with the flat iron.

'Just lay the dress on my bed when it's ready please, Elsie. There's no hurry for it. I've decided to ride down to Kirriemuir. The dressmaker asked me to call for a fitting this week, so I might as well take advantage of the dry day.'

'Would ye no' like one o' the stable lads to go with ye, Miss Lora? It's a long ride on your own,' said the housekeeper a trifle anxiously, as she accompanied Lora to the door.

'No, thank you,' Lora replied. 'I'd really prefer to go alone. I don't need company. Look after Loyal, please, Elsie.' Then she bent to give the dog's head a farewell pat. 'Stay, Loyal,' she ordered, 'and be a good dog till I come back.' With that, she swung into the saddle and set off at a brisk pace down the short carriageway and out to the rough country road.

The bright morning had developed into a crisp autumn day. The sun shone from a clear blue sky, and the hill air was sharp and bracing. Every woodland glade seemed to be a blaze of colour, and the rowan trees by the roadside were rich with red berries, while the birds sang merrily amongst the whins and the broom. Rufus was raring to go, so Lora gave him his head, and they went down by the farms of Addylin, Wheen, and Rottal at a spanking pace. It was quite a long ride to Kirriemuir but certainly not a boring one. In the districts of Dykehead and Cortachy the landscape was delightfully varied, and with every bend of the road, a fresh panorama of beauty unfolded. To remain unaffected by such glorious surroundings was quite impossible. Lora's eyes were soon alight with interest, and her heart was singing with the birds.

At first they saw few travellers on the road. By the time they had reached Caddam Woods, just north of Kirriemuir, however, they had caught up with a stream of traffic – strings of hill ponies being led in single file; droves of sheep and cattle; horses and carts piled high with farm produce; bands of tinkers laden with heather besoms, scrubbing brushes, and pot-scrapers; whole families of country people, weighed down by heavy sacks and baskets. Even the youngest children were carrying rabbit skins, or braces of rabbits, pigeons, or crows. Lora had never seen such a varied parade.

'Where is everyone going?' she asked of one country woman.

'Most o' them'll be bound for the horse fair on the Hill o' Kirrie – the Muckle Market, ye ken! Surely ye must be a stranger if ye've never heard o' the Mucklie.'

'Oh yes, I *have* heard of the Mucklie but I've never happened to be in the town at the time of the fair,' Lora replied. 'How long does it last?'

'It lasts for four days. When I was young, like you, a' the lasses and lads for miles around met together at the market on the Hill. Aye, we had some happy times, as we did. But I'm no' bound for the Hill Market this mornin'. I sell my butter an' eggs at the weekly market on the Toon Square, and it'll be a busy place this day, I can tell ye. Folk come frae far an' near to the Muckle Markets, and eventually they a' congregate in Kirrie itsel'. There'll hardly be room to move in the streets – but it a' helps the trade,' she added, with a smile of anticipation.

This was bad news indeed for Lora. She couldn't have chosen a worse time to go in search of Hamish MacCrimmon, but there was no turning back now. She looked down at the old country woman whose back was bent double by the weight of her laden baskets. Normally Lora would have offered to help, but now she realised that her first priority must be to get to Kirriemuir as quickly as possible. So she bade the woman 'good-day', and spurred Rufus on.

Having passed the Caddam Woods, there were two approaches to Kirriemuir. Lora chose the western approach via the Glengate, as the other road – down the steep brae known as the Roods – was also the town's main access to the Northmuir and the Hill Common where the Muckle Market was being held. Undoubtedly the Roods would be congested with traffic today, so it was best avoided.

AN EVENTFUL DAY

The horses from The Milton were always stabled at an inn at the north end of the town, in St Malcolm's Wynd, so Lora headed her horse in that direction with all possible speed. On arrival she looked anxiously around for 'Auld Geordie', the head groom. It had been her intention to ask Geordie where she could find Hamish MacCrimmon, but the old groom was so harrassed she found it impossible to get into conversation with him at all. Being the main coaching inn for the town, the yard was a hive of activity, and Lora had to be content with leaving Rufus in the care of one of the stable boys.

Kirriemuir – or the Kirkton of Kirriemuir, to give the township its full title – was a quaint little place made up of steep braes, narrow pends, crooked wynds and closes, the houses being of varied shapes and sizes and set at odd angles. Handloom-weaving was the main occupation, but there were also two tanyards and a vast amount of brew-houses. Normally the click-clack of handlooms coming from almost every house, and the smell from the tanyards, gave evidence of the industry of the inhabitants, but today was quite different. It appeared that almost the entire population had decided to have a holiday, and the cobbled streets were crowded. The area around the tolbooth held various stalls, and the street vendors were shouting their wares above the din of the jostling crowds, while the music of a barrel-organ here, and the skirl of bagpipes there, had each attracted their own kind of audience, many of whom were hooching and dancing in the streets and on the pavements. It was very obvious that a great deal of strong drink had already been imbibed by both sexes. As Lora made her way from St Malcolm's Wynd to the Town Square, she realised that she would be wise to make her stay in town as brief as possible. The rowdyism would most certainly grow worse as the day wore on.

Fortunately for Lora, Dr Elliott's house and Miss MacLaggan's dress-making establishment were both in the Kirkwynd area, so she turned her steps in that direction, deciding to make Dr Elliott's her first port of call. The doctor's door was slightly ajar but the only answer Lora received to her repeated knocking was a series of loud snores. In some exasperation she stepped into the lobby and knocked on the inner door, but with no better result.

'May I come in?' she called, poking her head round the door, but the snores continued. The doctor was sound asleep and sprawled across his desk. Lora crossed the room and shook him by the shoulder, remembering as she did so the remark she had once heard Elsie pass, 'Ye couldna find a better doctor or a nicer man. His only fault is his liking for the bottle.' With some dismay she realised Dr Elliott had been drinking.

'Wake up, Doctor!' she called, giving him another shake. This time she was successful. With a particularly loud snort he opened his eyes and looked indignantly at her.

'What do you want?' he demanded, noisily clearing his throat.

'We need a doctor rather urgently,' Lora replied.

The doctor roused himself. 'Where?' he asked.

'At Linnochmore in Glen Clova.'

'Linnochmore? Linnochmore?' the doctor repeated, apparently struggling to recall the name. 'And what's the trouble at Linnochmore?'

'Mrs MacCrimmon's nephew has a bad wound in his leg. She says it needs skilled attention.'

'Well now, that's a change, if I'm thinkin' o' the same Mrs MacCrimmon! She usually has a cure o' her ain for a' the ills in Glen Clova.'

'Yes, Mrs MacCrimmon is very good at helping folk who are ill,' Lora agreed, 'but this injury seems to be beyond her.'

'What happened to the lad's leg?'

'I don't really know. I haven't seen the wound.'

The doctor rubbed his chin thoughtfully. He had a sharp-featured face with a keen, intelligent expression which gave him an exceedingly youthful look in spite of his silvery hair. His eyes were a penetrating blue and his eyebrows stuck straight out in front, giving a sort of craggy appearance to the face. Although she had met him before, Lora felt she had never really looked at him until now, but she liked what she saw. His countenance was kind and compassionate.

'Will you come, as soon as you can, please, Doctor?' she asked.

'Aye, I'll come in the mornin' but I was just wonderin', and here the doctor stroked his chin reflectively, and peered up at Lora from under his craggy brows. 'Mistress MacCrimmon's nephew wouldna' be one o' those wild Jacobites, would he? Is it a battle wound, do ye know?'

Lora was taken aback. She glanced nervously at the doctor but was reassured by the twinkle in his eye.

'Ye needna' answer my questions of course,' he said with a broad grin. 'Just regard them as the idle fancies of an old man. By the way, I *have* seen you before, haven't I?'

'Yes, I'm Lora MacCrae.'

'From The Milton? I remember now. Of course I haven't seen ye since your father died. I'm sorry ye had to find me "asleep" at my post, as it were, Miss Macrae, the Dominie and I were just celebratin' the Mucklie for old time's sake, and, as we get older, a wee dram takes more effect. Ye can tell Mrs MacCrimmon I'll be up tomorrow in the forenoon.'

Lora thanked him. As she closed the door on her way out, she wished she had had the courage to ask where she could find Hamish MacCrimmon but the doctor's remark about Mrs MacCrimmon's nephew being a Jacobite unnerved her somewhat. If he knew anything of Hamish MacCrimmon's past he might have 'put two and two together'!

'Perhaps Miss MacLaggan the dressmaker will be able to direct me,' she consoled herself, 'She probably knows evereyone in Kirriemuir. Anyway, my conscience will feel easier once I've been to her, considering I gave that as my excuse for coming to town in the first place!'

Dr Elliott's house was at the Marywell end of the Kirkwynd, whereas Miss MacLaggan lived opposite Grant's Pend, near the Tolbooth, so Lora had to retrace her steps. She half expected the dressmaker might also be out celebrating the Mucklie, but her knock was answered immediately.

'Ah, it's you, Miss Macrae! Come away in! No need to ask after your health. You are looking "bright and breezy", just as you always do. My, aren't the streets busy! The Mucklie seems to attract more and more people every year. Well, I'm glad to tell you your dress is almost completed. This will be positively the last fitting. I'm attending to another customer at the moment, so perhaps you'll be good enough to take a seat till I'm ready. This is Mrs McNeish, who helps me with the seaming. Have you met her before?'

Lora and Mrs McNeish agreed that they had met on a previous occasion, so, with much becking and bowing, Miss MacLaggan tripped away into the adjoining room and left them together.

'A fine day for the market, Miss,' remarked Mrs McNeish conversationally, as she stitched away diligently at her seam.

'Yes, isn't it,' agreed Lora. 'I have never seen the town so busy, but of course, this is the first time I've been in Kirriemuir during a Muckle Market.'

'Well, I can tell ye it's aye like this, unless the weather breaks doon, and that tends to spoil things. Of course the Mucklie is just a fine excuse for a drinkin' orgy, as far as some folk are concerned. And there's ane o' them, awa' past the window at this very meenute. Aye, the Dominie has had a richt royal time these past few days. The school bairns wouldna be learnin' much from him, I'm thinkin'.'

'Is that the schoolmaster that has his school down Grant's Pend?' asked Lora.

'Aye, the very same. He hasna' been sober since Tuesday. I saw him an' his boozin' crony, Dr Elliott, comin' oot o' the Gairie Inn just afore dinnertime. Like as no' they'll have had a sleep noo, an' they'll be ready for anither skinful. It's a blessin' for the Kirrie folk that Dr Elliott has got an assistant, that's what I say.'

'An assistant?' queried Lora. 'I didn't know Dr Elliott had an assistant.'

'Och, he hasna had him very long, of course. Somebody said to me that the young doctor was wounded at Prestonpans and had to leave the army. That's how he happened to settle in Kirrie.'

'Was he a Jacobite?' asked Lora, a trifle too eagerly.

Mrs McNeish looked at her in some surprise. 'I couldna' tell ye. That's hardly a question anybody would be askin' him at the present time,' she added pointedly, giving Lora a distinctly disapproving glance. 'But, whatever side he was on, he's a fine upstandin' lad, in spite o' his limp. I see his tall figure aroond the toon most days and I think to mysel' what a fine-lookin' sodger he had been, and what a shame it was that he should've had to suffer such cruel wounds, an' him no' even in the fightin' line!'

Lora would have liked to have asked more about the doctor's new assistant but decided it might be better to change the subject.

'Is this a general holiday today?' she asked instead.

'No. I hardly think it could be ca'ed a general holiday. The shops are at their busiest durin' the Market time, and the weavers sell a lot o' their claith to the traders that come in aboot. When I was young, though, we looked forward from one Mucklie to the next, just for the fun o' it.'

'You're a native of Kirriemuir then?' Lora asked with interest. (Surely this was a heaven-sent opportunity, to get the information she wanted about Hamish! Without doubt, it would be safer to ask Mrs McNeish than to broach the subject to the dressmaker. The latter would probably think her queries strange, and might even mention the matter to Mrs Macrae on her next visit to the fitting-room.)

Lora came back from her meditations in time to give a suitable reply to Mrs McNeish's next remark. Then she decided to 'take the bull by the horns' and ask the question uppermost in her mind.

'Do you know a Hamish MacCrimmon who lives in Kirriemuir, Mrs McNeish?'

Lora really thought the woman's eyes were to pop out of her head.

'Hamish MacCrimmon! 'Deed I do that, Miss Macrae, but what possible interest could a young lady like you ha'e in the likes o' him?'

'Oh, I have no personal interest in him,' said Lora hastily, 'but a relative of his lives near us in the glen and I have a message to deliver to Mr MacCrimmon. Could you tell me, please, where I might find the gentleman?'

'*Gentleman*, did ye say? I hardly think the word "gentleman" would apply to Hamish MacCrimmon,' declared Mrs McNeish in evident disgust. 'The last I heard o' him, he'd been thrown into the County jail for causin' a breach o' the peace. He may be there yet, for a' I ken, but there's one thing sure – if he's no' in the jail he'll be in ane or ither o' the drink hooses. That's aboot a' he's fit for, if ye ask me. The Gairie Inn is a favourite haunt o' him an' his cronies.'

'But where does he live, Mrs McNeish,' Lora persisted. 'Where is his home?'

'Hamish has nae hoose o' his ain, if that's what ye mean, Miss Macrae. When he cam' to Kirrie first, he lodged wi' the Widow McInnes in the Glengate. . . . I've heard it said Mrs McInnes only took him in because o' his friendship wi' her late husband, David McInnes, an' she didna' like to see Hamish withoot a roof o'er his heid. She was a kind-hearted woman, Widow McInnes, and she was good to Hamish, but och, she just couldna put up wi' him. Naebody keeps *him* lang. Afore he landed in jail, he was bidin' in Mrs Crichton's lodgin'-hoose in the Skinner's Close, jist aff the Dirt Wynd.'

'Where is the Dirt Wynd?' asked Lora, 'I can't say I've heard of it before.'

'Have ye no? You'll likely have heard o' the Burial Wynd though? Well, the Dirt Wynd leads off the Burial Wynd. No' a very desirable part o' the toon. An' I believe Mistress Crichton keeps a gey rough hoose. But what could ye expect! She's nothing more than a tink' hersel'. She had never lived in a hoose until that daft auld Crichton married her in ane o' his drinkin' bouts. Afore that she just lived in a tent,' and Mrs McNeish gave a sniff of disdain.

'The Burial Wynd is a continuation of the Kirkwynd, isn't it?' queried Lora. 'Coming from the Town Square, it branches off to the right at the top of the Bellie's Brae, almost opposite the Tolbooth?'

'Aye, that's it, but dinna tell me you're meanin' to go in that way on your own, Miss Macrae! It's no' a place for a fine lady like you, especially on a Market nicht! There's some gey queer folk bide round there, I can tell ye. If ye like,' she added, as an afterthought, 'ye can tell me your message to Hamish MacCrimmon an' I'll see he gets it. What was it ye wanted to say to Hamish?'

'Oh, there's no need for you to trouble yourself,' Lora answered, feeling slightly annoyed at the woman's bold curiosity. 'Thank you for the information you have given me regarding Hamish. I shall pass it on to his relatives.'

Luckily, at that moment the door of the fitting room opened and the conversation was brought to a close as the dressmaker bowed out her other customer and ushered Lora in for her fitting.

Miss MacLaggan was nothing if not particular. Lora thought the pinning and unpinning was never to end. As she worked, the dressmaker chattered, and Lora found it almost impossible to get a word in edgeways. She tried several times to explain that she was alone, and wanted to be on her way home before dusk, but to no avail. Miss MacLaggan either didn't hear, or didn't heed.

When Lora was at last free to step out of the fitting-room she was thankful to see that Mrs McNeish's chair was vacant. With a hasty word of farewell to the dressmaker she hurried down the dimly-lit staircase and out into the street.

'Thank goodness my time in there hasn't been entirely wasted,' she said to herself as she made her way round the back of the Tolbooth in the direction of the Burial Wynd. Mrs McNeish had been a fund of useful information. It was just to be hoped Hamish was no longer reposing in jail!

As she threaded her way through the crowds, Lora became aware of an uproar on the Town Square. Above the din of hurdy-gurdy music she heard the clatter of horses' hooves on the cobbles, the terrified screams of women and children, men's voices raised in anger, and the high-pitched whinnying of frightened horses. It sounded as if an army was charging down the street, and that was exactly what it turned out to be. The people in front of Lora were thrown backwards, and Lora herself was flung unceremoniously against the wall of the Tolbooth. With an effort she retained her balance, however, and gazed in horror as a party of Redcoats cut their way through the crowd. They were lashing out with their whips to clear a passage, and riding roughshod over all who stumbled across their path.

The sight of a helpless woman, with a babe in her arms, being trampled underfoot made Lora's blood boil. Tales she had heard of the massacre of the wounded after Culloden, and the burning of innocent women and children in their homes, took on a new significance, whilst the imminent danger of Angus Lindsay and Alistair Drummond, and the old couple who were sheltering them, struck Lora with renewed force. Men like those troopers would have no mercy! She must find Hamish MacCrimmon at all costs – and quickly!

The cavalcade of troopers thundered on down the Bellie's Brae at the full gallop, leaving behind a trail of grievous injury, and furious indignation. Lora thought of the two people who had spoken to her of their happy childhood memories of bygone Mucklies. 'Some children won't have many happy memories of this Mucklie,' she said to herself ruefully.

As soon as it was possible to get moving again, Lora hurried across the top of the Bellie's Brae and entered the Burial Wynd which led into the labyrinth of closes and pends known as the Crofthead. An old man, feeding some hens at his door, directed her to Mrs Crichton's lodging-house, which proved to be in a particularly foul-smelling alley. Here the roughly-built hovels were so closely packed together that their overhanging, and rotting, thatch almost prevented the daylight from penetrating to the lane at all. As a result, the unfortunate inhabitants were doomed to live out their days in a sort of semi-darkness, even at the height of summer.

Rats, of all shapes and sizes, seemed to be everywhere, and Lora hesitated to enter the gloomy depths, but the memory of the scenes she had just witnessed spurred her on. Drawing the hood of her cloak well down, she headed for the first doorway. The screech of a half-starved-looking cat, which sprang, hissing and spitting, from under her very feet, unnerved Lora somewhat, causing her to stumble over a stone step. As she pitched forward she collided with an old woman who sat huddled in the doorway smoking a clay pipe. The woman was as shocked as Lora was, and gave an unearthly shriek, followed by a string of oaths directed at Lora.

Thoughts of witches and warlocks flashed through Lora's mind, and, when the woman actually turned towards her, it was only with a supreme effort that Lora suppressed a scream. Never before in her life had she seen such an evil countenance!

'I – I b-beg your p-pardon,' she stuttered. 'I-I h-hope I didn't hurt you. Can you tell me, please, if a Mr Hamish MacCrimmon lives around here?'

The old crone screwed up her wizened, pock-marked face and peered at Lora. Then she removed the pipe from her mouth and spat into the gutter.

'Hamish MacCrimmon?' she echoed, 'and what would the likes o' you be wantin' wi' Hamish MacCrimmon, I'd like to ken?'

'I have a message for him – from his uncle,' Lora explained.

As they were talking, a door creaked within the darkness of the house and a harsh voice rasped out, 'Wha's that?'

'It's a young leddy wantin' Hamish,' replied the old woman who had now risen to her feet. 'Hamish is still a prisoner in Forfar is he no', Meg?'

'No he's no', ye silly auld fule. He got oot this mornin'. In fact, he arrived back here afore ye were up. Wha' is it that wants him?' and the person addressed as Meg appeared in the doorway holding aloft a candle.

'My name is Macrae,' Lora answered, almost trembling with fright as the candlelight lit up the debauched faces and unkempt appearance of the two women. It was easy to see they were mother and daughter, and the one looked as evil as the other.

The younger one fixed Lora with a prolonged and insolent stare.

'So ye're wantin' Hamish, are ye? Well, if Hamish is in, he'll be up i' the garret. I'll tak' ye up to his room if ye like, but mind, I'm no' sure he's there.' As she turned to lead the way, she pushed her mother rudely to one side. 'Get oot o' the road, Mither, and let the young leddy past,' she barked.

Lora's heart was thumping almost suffocatingly as she followed the younger woman along a filthy passageway and up a rickety stair to a narrow landing, the floor of which was thick with dust and rat-droppings, while the walls and rafters overhead were festooned with cobwebs. The smell of the whole house was revolting, but that didn't seem to bother the two female inhabitants.

'Are ye there, Hamish?' the woman yelled, as she banged with her fist on the nearest door. 'Hamish! Are ye in?' But repeated knockings brought no response. 'Naw! He's no' in,' said the woman at last (stating the obvious). 'What do ye want wi' him onywey?'

Before Lora could reply, there came the sound of voices in the passage below and a man's voice could be heard asking, 'Wha' did she say she was, Granny?'

'That'll be Hamish noo,' said Meg, tilting the candle so that it might shed some light on the stairs, and completely ignoring the candle-grease which dripped on to the floor.

The person who was approaching seemed to have a slight limp, and Lora heard the tap-tap of a walking stick. Meg heard it too and immediately remarked, 'Naw. That's no' Hamish. It's Paddy.' Peering down the stair she yelled, 'Hey! Paddy! D'ye ken whaur Hamish is?'

As the newcomer appeared at the bottom of the stair and the candlelight lit up his features, Lora stepped back involuntarily. although he bore no resemblance whatsoever to either of the two women, his looks were equally uncouth. His face was broad, coarse-skinned and ill-shaven, with a ruddy

41

complexion. His hair was a black tangled mass of oily curls, and he wore a tam o' shanter bonnet perched on the side of his head at an extremely rakish angle. There was a patch over his left eye, while the other eye appeared large and protruding, and his breath was heavy with the smell of alcohol.

'Sure, an' what could *she* be wantin' wi' Hamish, think ye?' the man queried, deliberately ignoring Meg's question. He propped himself against the wall using his stick as support, and rested his drunken gaze on Lora although his conversation was addressed to her companion.

'Never you mind what she wants,' snapped Meg. 'Whaur is Hamish?'

'Sure, I'm thinkin' he'll be after celebratin' in the Gairie, same as ye'd be doin' yersel' if ye'd been inside for thirty days an' just got your release, Meggie, me darlin',' replied Paddy, in a rather quaint mixture of local dialect and Irish brogue.

'An' what has he got to be celebratin' wi? Tell me that,' demanded Meg. 'The auld devil owes me mair than three months' rent! An' I suppose that's whaur *you've* been as weel – drinkin' i' the Gairie wi' him! Aye, an' footin' the bill nae doobt!' she added scathingly.

'Sure, an' ye know me better than that now, Meggie,' Paddy teased. 'How many times have ye been after tellin' me I'm just a "chip o' the ould block" – as greedy as sin? Naw, naw! I had nothing whatever to do wi' the payin'. Hamish, the bold boy, jist put it doon on the slate. He was after tellin' the landlord he'd be gettin' a loan from *you*, no less!' and Paddy winked wickedly at Lora, as he waited to see the effect of this latter remark.

'Oh was he indeed?' exclaimed Meg, wrathfully. 'We'll see aboot *that*, though. Jist you get awa' back to the inn an' tell the auld devil he's wanted immediately.'

'No, please don't bother,' interrupted Lora. 'I can go to the Gairie Inn myself and speak with Mr MacCrimmon there,' but as she made to depart, the man barred her way.

'Sure, there's no need for ye to be rushin' off like that, m'lady,' he said. 'If ye're a freend o' auld Hamish we'll be real pleased to be entertainin' ye here till he comes back. Isn't that so, Granny?' he added, turning to address the old woman who had followed him along the passage.

'Aye. That's so, Patrick,' she cackled in agreement.

'Thank you, but I can't stay,' said Lora. 'It's getting late, and I wish to see Mr MacCrimmon before I go home.'

'Oh ho! So it's "Mr MacCrimmon", is it?' mocked Paddy. 'Ould Hamish often said he hob-nobbed wi' the gentry, but sure, I niver believed him. It seems I had been wrang.'

At this point Paddy noisily cleared his throat and spat on the floor, much to Lora's disgust. The sight of her recoil amused and emboldened him. He poked at her playfully with his stick.

'And how did ye get acquainted wi' Hamish may I ask?'

'I'm afraid I have never met Mr MacCrimmon,' Lora replied icily.

'Then what is it ye want to speak to him about?'

'The message is private. Now please let me pass.'

'Oh ho! gettin' hoity-toity, are we?' said Paddy making no effort to step aside. 'Well, if ye canna be takin' o' oor hospitality, at least yer ladyship can be crossin' Granny's hand wi' silver afore ye go. Naebody leaves here withoot gettin' Granny McPhee to tell their fortune. Isn't that so, ould wife?'

'Aye, that's so, Patrick,' and Granny nodded her head in eager agreement.

'I'm sorry, but I've told you already I'm in a hurry. I can have my fortune told some other day,' said Lora, inwardly shrinking from the very idea of that dirty old woman even as much as touching her.

But Paddy was adamant.

'Sure, ye'll be stayin' right where ye are, till ye've crossed Granny's hand wi' silver,' he persisted, and at this point, Meg added her weight to the argument.

Lora realised there was no other alternative but to give in. So she took a silver coin from her purse and dropped it into Granny's dirt-engrained hand. Then she held out her own hand with as good a grace as possible. Meg moved nearer with the candle, and the old woman seated herself on the stairs and peered into Lora's out-stretched palm. For a moment she remained in silent concentration, then she began muttering under her breath and shaking her head.

'That's no' like *you*, Granny. What ails ye this time?' queried Paddy.

'I've never seen onything like this in a' my born days,' declared the old woman in a hoarse whisper. 'There's a lot here I just canna fathom, but I believe ye've had a warnin', Missie, an' ye'd do weel to pay attention to it. As far as I can see, ye're a heidstrong hussie so ye'll be determined to tak' your ain thrawn way. Mark my words though, ye're treadin' a slippery path. I can see ye're becomin' involved wi' men ye ken nothing aboot – baith dark men an' fair men. Aye, an' some that pose as loyal freends may be naught but traitors, for I see fightin', an' bloodshed, an' death. This foolhardy adventure ye've embarked on may weel end in disaster. I canna foretell the final ootcome. It's fair beyond me, but I see ye on a journey, and the sound o' the sea is in my ears.'

'And the message to Hamish?' queried Paddy.

'Aye, what aboot the message? Tell us aboot *it*, Mither,' Meg added encouragingly.

But Lora had had enough. Panic seized her, at the thought of what the uncanny powers of this witchlike woman might yet reveal of her dangerous secret if she stayed one minute more.

With scant ceremony she snatched her hand free from the woman's grasp and pushed Paddy aside. Gathering up her skirts she dashed along the passage and out of the house, fervently hoping she had seen the last of Mistress Crichton's horrible lodging-house and its three dreadful inhabitants.

IV . . . AND NIGHT

In her headlong dash to escape from the lodging-house, Lora soon found herself completely lost in the maze of closes and pends that made up the Crofthead. It was like a rabbit-warren, and the dirt and smell of the whole place was indescribable. Horses and cows, pigs and goats, hens and geese had all fouled the ground, and there were also dung-heaps at almost every doorway. In the gathering dusk the amount of vermin had multiplied, and the unearthly squeals and screeches of rat fights and cat fights were hair-raising to say the least.

Holding her skirts as high as was decently possible, Lora kept running. Twice she traversed pends which had no exit and she was forced to retrace her steps, haunted by the thought that someone with a limp was hard on her heels. There were plenty of people in the area, but after her recent experience Lora was afraid to talk to any of them. At last, however, she emerged on to a steep incline which she recognised as the Tannage Brae, and from there she soon worked out the quickest way back to the Tolbooth.

Shaken though she had been by the unpleasant episode of the lodging-house, Lora was nonetheless determined to continue the search for Hamish MacCrimmon. Accordingly, she headed once more for that part of the Burial Wynd where the Gairie Inn was located.

The front door of the inn opened directly on to the wynd, and, as she approached, Lora could see a group of men dressed in red tunics standing in the pool of light shed by a lantern above the door. The men were English Dragoons, and they were deep in conversation with a civilian.

'An informer!' was the thought that flashed through Lora's mind, and she withdrew into the shadows until the group had entered the inn. To attract the attention of the military was the last thing she wanted at that moment so she looked around for another entrance. A narrow pend led down the side of the building to a backyard where a young man was sweeping the cobbles with a stable besom. He looked a pleasant sort of person, so Lora stepped over and spoke to him.

'Excuse me, please,' she said, 'but do you know if a Mr Hamish MacCrimmon is at the inn, by any chance?'

The young man stopped sweeping. He appeared surprised at what she was asking, but he answered civilly enough.

'Aye. Come to think o' it, Miss, I did see Hamish comin' inbye. He must be back i' the toon again. We hadna seen him for a while. If ye want him ye'll likely find him drinkin' i' the kitchen. Jist step in at the door there, and go richt alang the passage to the far end. The noise'll guide ye!' he added with a friendly grin.

Lora listened to the loud voices, coarse laughter, and general ribaldry which echoed along the passage, and she hesitated. 'It does sound a bit noisy,' she remarked, after a pause. 'I'm afraid it would be quite impossible to talk privately to anyone in there, and I have an important message to give to Mr MacCrimmon. Unfortunately I don't even know what the man looks like. I wonder if you would be kind enough to ask Mr MacCrimmon to come out here and talk with me?'

'Och, aye, I'll sune dae that, Miss. If Hamish is in there I'll sune fetch him oot,' and the young man propped his broom against the wall and disappeared inside, whistling a jaunty Scottish air.

Now that she was about to meet the real Hamish MacCrimmon, Lora felt decidedly nervous. The idea of dealing with another 'rough diamond' like Paddy made her feel quite weak at the knees. Then there was also the possibility that Hamish might be too inebriated to understand what was wanted of him. Or, again, he might be unwilling to co-operate. Lora was so preoccupied with those worrying thoughts that she failed to notice a shadowy figure emerge stealthily from the narrow pend and silently conceal himself behind a stack of beer barrels quite near to where she was standing.

After what seemed an eternity, Lora heard the sound of voices approaching along the passage, and the young man hailed her from the doorway.

'Here's the man ye were wantin', Miss, but I'd a bit o' a job persuadin' him to come oot. I jist aboot had to drag him here by the hair o' his heid! Eh, Hamish?' and he stepped aside to reveal his companion – a half-starved-looking individual, fairly tall, but with a decided stoop, and a general 'down-at-the-heel' appearance. In fact, the man was a perfect example of a 'down-and-out'.

Lora stared at him in dismay. So this was the person she'd been searching for – the man on whom so much was now to depend!

Before she had time to say anything, a man and woman, heading for the back door of the inn, recognised Hamish. With a 'Whaur ha'e ye been a' this time, man?' they stopped to make conversation, thus giving Lora a chance to observe Hamish more closely.

She judged him to be about fifty, and he was so thin his clothes hung on him as if on a coathanger. His hair and moustache had been black, but were now well mixed with grey, and he was balding on top. When talking to people he held his head down, as if to avoid looking directly at them, and his hang-dog expression, and general air of dejection, gave Lora the impression that he had completely lost his self-respect. He didn't look like an evil person, however – more like a weak-willed man who had fallen into bad company.

When the couple moved on, the young man turned to Hamish.

'This is the young lady that wanted to see ye, Hamish,' he said. 'Now if ye'll excuse me, Miss, I'll be gettin' on wi' my work.'

'Thank you very much for your help,' said Lora appreciatively. She tried to press a coin into his hand, but he would have none of it.

'Naw, Naw! Thanks a' the same, Miss. I dinna want ony reward. It was nae bother,' and the lad waved the money aside. Picking up his broom he went off into the stable, leaving Lora and Hamish alone together.

'That was a very obliging fellow,' Lora remarked.

'Aye. He's the innkeeper's son. But what exactly do *you* want wi' me? I've never seen ye in my life afore, to my knowledge,' and Hamish glared under his brows at Lora.

'I have a message for you from a Dugald Lindsay. Does that name mean anything to you?' Lora asked.

'Did ye say *Dugald* Lindsay? Captain Dugald himsel'?' queried Hamish, unbelievingly.

Lora nodded assent, and was amazed to see a sudden change in the man's whole demeanour. His head came erect, his eyes brightened, and the melancholy look momentarily vanished from his face. Self-confidence seemed to flow back into his being. In that moment Lora caught a glimpse of the Hamish MacCrimmon that once had been.

'So, the Captain's still alive!' he was saying excitedly. 'I was sure he must be deid! Is he back here then? In this country?'

'No. *He* is not in this country, but his son is quite near here. Dugald Lindsay wants you to do something for his son. Would you be willing?' asked Lora, watching the man's reactions closely.

'You would not go unrewarded,' she added, sensing that the extra incentive of money might sway the balance.

'But what could the likes o' me do to help his son?' asked Hamish dully, as if his present miserable circumstances had once more swamped him.

46

'There *is* something you can do. I have a letter for you from Dugald Lindsay. Can you read?' and Lora produced the letter and held it out to him.

Hamish shook his head. 'The Captain tried to learn me to read but I didna mak' much of it.'

'Then I'll read the letter to you,' said Lora. 'Do you think it would be safe to read it aloud here, or should we find a more private place perhaps?' and she peered rather uncertainly into the gathering gloom.

'Och, there's naebody here but oorsel's,' said Hamish glancing round the yard. If ye stand under the licht there, ye should see to read.'

So they moved into the small pool of light under the lantern by the door, and Lora read the letter aloud, keeping her voice as low as possible.

Hamish listened without comment until she had finished.

'Aye,' he said, 'I mind the place well, and I havena' forgotten the secret o' the Tower either, but it's a risky business tryin' to help Jacobites nowadays, I'm thinkin'.'

'You were a fugitive rebel yourself once,' Lora reminded him, 'and Captain Dugald Lindsay didn't seem to think you were a coward then,' she added, somewhat scathingly.

'Neither I am a coward, Miss!' Hamish answered indignantly, glaring resentfully at Lora, 'but the toon is fair swarmin' wi' Redcoats, and so will the glens be afore very lang.'

'Exactly. That is why we need your help desperately,' Lora pointed out. 'Surely you wouldn't want to fail your friend's only son! Come with me now – this very night,' she urged.

'I canna do that!' objected Hamish. 'I've just accepted my "arles" from a fairmer, and if I dinna put in an appearance at his place in the mornin' I'll ha'e the law efter me again.'

'You mean you've made a bargain with a farmer at the feeing market?'

'Aye. I accepted his shillin' so I canna let him doon, or I'll be in trouble.'

'But if you don't come now, Angus Lindsay's life may be at stake,' Lora protested, alarmed at the possible consequences of delay.

'I canna help that. I'm *no' free* to come,' argued Hamish doggedly.

Lora thought for a moment. 'If I give you the money to return to the farmer, will you come then?' she asked.

'Aye, well – I could try that I suppose,' Hamish agreed rather grudgingly, 'but he'll no' be very weel pleased. I'll need to see if I can get somebody else that would tak' the job in my place.'

'Do that, then, please, Hamish,' Lora begged, as she took a shilling from her purse and handed it to him. 'You know where to come – your uncle's house.'

'Aye, I gathered it was Linnochmore. The only snag is, my boots are worn through, Miss. They'd never do for walkin' as far as Clova. Could ye spare me enough to buy anither pair?'

47

'I don't know if I have enough money with me,' said Lora peering into her purse. 'How much is a pair of boots? I'm afraid I'll just have to give you what I have left, and if it's not enough you can tell the cobbler to send the bill for the remainder to Miss Lora Macrae, The Milton, Glen Clova.'

'Is that whaur ye bide?' asked Hamish with interest. 'Lord Ogilvy had the big hoose himsel' in my day. I ken the place well.'

'Yes, I suppose you do. Now, we'll expect to see you at Linnochmore by tomorrow night,' Lora emphasised. 'You'll be well paid for your help, but, remember, you must tell no one about this – no one at all. Complete secrecy is essential.'

'Och, I ken that, Miss. Ye can depend on me.'

'And you promise faithfully to come to Linnochmore tomorrow night?' Lora insisted yet again.

'Aye, I promise to come as quick as I can,' he answered doggedly.

'Well, here is the money for your boots.' But, as Lora turned away, she saw Hamish re-enter the inn, and she thought ruefully of her silver pieces and the new boots.

Night had fallen by this time. Normally, Lora would have been afraid to go out alone in the town after dark, but the feeling of elation at having achieved her objective had driven everything else from her mind. Pulling the hood of her cloak well down, she stepped out briskly in the direction of the hostelry where her pony was stabled. As she made what speed she could along the busy High Street she noticed Miss MacLaggan the dressmaker approaching. Fortunately, at the opportune moment, another person attracted that lady's attention and Lora was able to slip past with only a brief acknowledgement.

A narrow close between two buildings provided a short cut from the main street to the backyard of the hostelry. Lora was about halfway through this close when a party of Redcoats came tramping down in single file, with much laughter and jest. Lora flattened herself against the wall to let them pass. Seeing her standing there, one of the soldiers – a youngish man – stopped and confronted her.

''Tis late for a young lady like you to be out alone on the street,' he said, somewhat gruffly (for he had obviously been drinking). 'What d'you say to my seeing you safely home?'

This was received by a burst of laughter from his companions.

''Twould be out of the frying pan into the fire, and no mistake,' chuckled a big burly one. 'Don't you be listening to him, Miss, I'm his superior. Let *me* be your escort,' and he pushed the younger man aside, and extended his arm to Lora with a mock bow.

'Thank you, but I haven't far to go. If you will kindly let me proceed,' said Lora, with dignity, ignoring the proffered arm, and drawing her cloak more closely around her as she made to pass. But the soldier stood firm, and barred her way.

'Not so hasty, Miss,' he said, laying hold of her arm, 'and remember you're speaking to a member of the Duke of Cumberland's army when you're speaking to me. We expect to be treated with a full measure of respect by the likes of you. Just you bear in mind we're your conquerors, and we're here to keep the barbaric Scots in order. That includes your humble self, if you didn't know it.'

Lora's heart was thumping, but, at the man's words, a picture of the scene she had witnessed during the afternoon flashed through her mind, and the indomitable spirit of the Highlander in her asserted itself.

'Let go of my arm this very minute,' she commanded, but the soldier's grip only tightened.

'Say "Sir", when you address me, you little spitfire,' he snarled.

'Never!' cried Lora, and with a quick movement of her right hand she dealt him a resounding slap on the cheek.

Taken by surprise, the man stepped back a pace, and Lora wrenched herself free. But, as she made to run off, he seized hold of her cloak and pulled her back. The sudden jerk caused the hood of her cloak to fall back from her brow, and the light from the lantern, which illuminated the narrow close, revealed her wealth of auburn hair, her finely-moulded features, and flawless complexion. There was a general gasp of surprise from the soldiers.

'By gum! She's a beauty,' remarked one, moving nearer.

'Aye. She be a thoroughbred an' no mistake,' added another.

As Lora continued to struggle against her captor, the men laughed and teased him.

'That filly could take a bit o' breakin' in, Tom! D'ye think you're fit?'

'You've met your match this time, Tommy me boy,' and similar comments.

'I never yet met the wench I couldn't tame,' panted Lora's assailant as she turned and twisted in his grasp. Then with a sudden deft movement, he pinioned both her arms behind her back. She was entirely at his mercy!

'Now, what have you to say for yourself, you little vixen?' he taunted. 'Are you prepared to pay my price willingly, or shall I exact my own fee?' and his whisky-laden breath was hot on Lora's face.

'Let me go!' she demanded. I have no money to give you.'

'’Tain't money I'm after, fair maid. I ain't a greedy man, not I. Give me but a few kisses from those rosy lips and I may decide to set you free.'

'Let me go!' cried Lora again, averting her face.

'Is that your final answer?' asked her captor. 'Then I shall have the pleasure of helping myself, eh?'

Lora began to struggle again, first one way then another but she was no match for the stalwart Redcoat. Her strength was beginning to fail and she felt like a rat in a trap. Then, suddenly, there came the sound of running feet. The soldiers nearby were thrust aside, and someone grabbed Lora's assailant by the shoulder, while a clenched fist hit a smashing blow on the side of his face. Lora was abruptly released, so abruptly, in fact, that she fell back against the wall and remained there, quite dazed and breathless, in the midst of the hubbub that had now arisen.

Gradually it became clear that her assailant and another man were engaged in a hand-to-hand fight. As she watched them pitching to and fro it occurred to her that the other person was familiar. Then with a shock, the truth dawned – it was none other than Paul Reynolds! Fear for Paul's safety now clutched at Lora's heart. How could he ever be a match for all those soldiers. They would surely kill him!

In actual fact Lora's worries were quiet unnecessary. Although Paul lacked the weight and strength of his opponent, he was, nevertheless, an able-bodied young man, and had been trained to give a good account of himself in all such situations. To tackle the group of Redcoats alone would have been impossible, but at the first sound of a fight he had no shortage of supporters. Men and youths came running from the street eager to 'have a go' at the English soldiers, especially after the happenings of the afternoon. Tempers were running high, and this was an excellent chance to get revenge on their oppressors.

Soon the narrow close was jammed with a mass of struggling humanity which spilled over into the street. At the sound of the fray, the back door of the hostelry had been slammed shut, likewise the window shutters. As a result, the only light on the scene now came from the lantern at the end of the close. Seeing a possible way to end the fracas, someone threw a well-aimed stone at the lantern, which smashed to smithereens, showering the noisy crowd below with fragments of broken glass. The scene was plunged into semi-darkness. A minute later Lora felt a tug at her arm and Paul's voice sounded in her ear.

'Quick, Lora! This way! We've no time to lose!' and he pulled her free of the crowd and propelled her towards the innyard.

Terror lent wings to Lora's feet. With Paul still gripping her arm, she ran as she had never run before.

Paul guided her towards the far corner of the yard.

'Nero's tethered over here,' he explained as they ran. 'Where's your pony?'

'In the stable across St Malcolm's Wynd.'

'Good. Up you go on Nero, and I'll collect your horse. You'll have to sit astride, I'm afraid. There's nothing else for it.'

Lora made no fuss. This was certainly not the time to quibble over such niceties! Gathering up her skirts she put her foot in the stirrup, and Paul hoisted her up. As he did so, Lora thought momentarily of the unladylike display of pantaloons and petticoats, and blessed the dimness of the yard.

Quickly Paul untethered the horse and handed Lora the reins.

'Off you go, boy,' he cried, giving the animal a slap on the hindquarters which caused it to rear up. Any less experienced rider would definitely have been unseated, but Lora was familiar with the ways of the big horse. As its forefeet clattered down on the cobbles again, she bent low over the saddle in preparation for a rapid exit under the archway leading to St Malcolm's Wynd.

Paul ran alongside shouting instructions.

'Go by The Roods, Lora! The army is camped out the Kinnordy road. Don't wait for me! Good luck!'

Then she was off at the full gallop, along the wynd and up the steep brae known as The Roods which led northwards out of the town.

It was a long hard pull. As they neared the summit, the big round harvest moon was just appearing above the Hill Wood and there, silhouetted against its orange glow, Lora caught sight of the gibbet. Strategically placed, on the north side of the rough track which led from The Roods to the Hill Common, it loomed above the little township as an ominous warning to all wrongdoers. The contrivance creaked eerily in the wind, and Lora could see the limp form of some miserable wretch suspended thereon. No doubt the victim had been convicted of sheep stealing, or cattle rustling, during the time of the fair, and had suffered the supreme penalty of the law-breaker. Lora shivered, and averted her gaze.

Once over the brow of the hill, the powerful horse made good progress. The road was still busy, as farm carts rumbled on their homeward way over the rough track, and groups of pedestrians plodded wearily back towards the glens. Lora easily overtook them all. Nevertheless, in contrast to the morning, and despite her willing mount, it now seemed a long hard ride, with many weary miles between Kirriemuir and The Milton of Clova. As they journeyed along, Lora's mind was in a turmoil, reliving the happenings of that eventful day, and worrying about the possible outcome. When at last they rode down past the little kirk of Clova, she felt she had never been so glad to see the gateway to her home.

The stableboy came sleepily from his loft at the sound of the stallion's hoofs on the cobbles of the yard, and Lora was only too thankful to hand the horse over to his care. The boy's face registered surprise at seeing Lora with Nero, but he was too well trained to ask questions. On her way to the house, Lora heard another horse approaching and was relieved to see it was Paul on Rufus.

'I didn't expect to see you for sometime yet. You've done well, Paul,' she called to him.

'Yes, very well. Of course your pony was really fresh. By the way, I don't have your side-saddle, Lora. It was no use to me, so I grabbed the first one I could find. We can exchange it for yours next time someone's in town. I just hope the groom doesn't land in trouble!'

'Did anyone follow you, Paul?' asked Lora anxiously.

'I don't think so. Probably no one even noticed we'd gone. The fight was continuing fast and furious when I rode out.'

Loyal had been watching and waiting patiently for his mistress and came dashing to the door to meet her, followed by an anxious Elsie.

'My, I *am* glad to see ye, Miss Lora,' she exclaimed in relief. 'Is Mr Paul with ye?'

'Yes. He's at the stables.'

'Well, I thank God ye're both safe and sound. I forgot it was the Mucklie week until quite late in the afternoon. I was just about to send the stable lad to look for ye when Mr Paul arrived back from Braedounie. He was so concerned about ye, he wouldna' even wait for a bite to eat. He must be starvin' o' hunger. Indeed, I suppose ye both are. Never mind, I've a hot rabbit stew all ready for ye, and the table's drawn up close to the fire in the hall so ye'll soon get warmed up.'

In no time Elsie was back with the tempting dish.

'Will I bide and serve for ye, Miss Lora?' she asked.

'No, thank you, Elsie. I'll manage. Just you get off to bed. You have such early mornings! Good-night, and thank you for waiting up for us.'

As Paul closed and barred the outside door, Loyal dashed off to greet him, while Lora busied herself dishing up the food. It was only when she passed Paul his plate that she noticed his swollen and bloodstained face.

'Paul!' she gasped, 'You're hurt!'

'It's only a scratch, Lora,' he assured her.

'Nevertheless, I'd better go and get water to bathe your face. Your eye is badly swollen,' she pointed out.

'Nonsense. Sit down and let's have our supper. I'm positively ravenous. I'll bathe my face later,' said Paul, brushing her concern aside, and seating himself at the table without more ado.

There was little conversation while they ate, and both did ample justice to the excellent fare. It was Lora who finally broke the silence.

'Thank you for what you did for me tonight, Paul. I'm very grateful,' she said quietly.

'Forget it,' Paul replied, 'but you were crazy to go into Kirriemuir alone during a Muckle Market.'

'I didn't remember about the Mucklie. It just seemed a good day to go in for my dress fitting.'

Paul looked her straight in the eye.

'Are you sure that was the real reason for your visit, Lora?'

'What do you mean, Paul?' she asked, with an innocent air.

'You know very well what I mean. What about the lodging-house?'

'The lodging-house?' Lora repeated, vaguely.

'Yes. After you left the dressmaker you went to a lodging-house in the Crofthead looking for a Hamish MacCrimmon, did you not?'

'Who told you that, Paul?'

'The dressmaker's assistant told me that you were enquiring about a gentleman of that name and she directed you to that place.'

Lora ran her tongue around dry lips.

'And did you follow me there too?' she asked.

'No. As a matter of fact I didn't have to. The dressmaker came in as I was talking with her assistant, and she said she had just seen you hieing in the direction of the inn where the horses from The Milton were normally stabled. I immediately hurried in that direction and found you reclining in the arms of the English army – no less! I must admit,' he added with a twinkle, '*that* incident rather astonished me, after your so very recent declaration of adherence to the Jacobite cause!'

'Paul! How dare you! You know very well I wasn't reclining in that horrible man's arms. He waylaid me. As a matter of fact I slapped his face, but he overpowered me.'

It was Paul's turn to be amazed. 'You mean to say you had the audacity to slap the face of an English soldier, and you all alone against four of them? I must say, Lora, you have the courage of ten men, but it's a blessing for you I happened along when I did. Now, I know you have absolutely no intention of telling me the truth about why you were in Kirriemuir today, and perhaps it would be better if you didn't tell me, but I have reason to believe that you are becoming involved in something which may well prove too big for you to handle.'

'What possible reason can you have to say such a thing?' queried Lora, in little more than a whisper.

'I have *this* reason,' and Paul took an object from his pocket and laid it on the table in front of her.

Lora felt the colour drain from her face. It was a white cockade!

'Where did you get that?' she gasped.

'I found it this morning out on the hillside, where one of your rebel friends dropped it last night, no doubt.'

'What do you mean – *my* rebel friends?'

'I mean exactly what I say. Do you remember when Loyal left you, just as you were skirting the trees on the north side of the garden? Well, it was to me he came. I saw you pass. You were leading the pony, and one man – obviously a wounded or ailing member of the rebel army – was being supported on the pony's back by another kilted rebel. You simply cannot deny it.'

'So you were spying on me!' Lora accused angrily.

'No. I was not spying. I was enjoying a quiet smoke in the garden by moonlight.'

'And I suppose you were spying on me earlier yesterday evening as well?' demanded Lora wrathfully, throwing caution to the winds.

'Earlier in the evening?' Paul paused to think. 'Whereabouts?'

'On the hillside.'

'But I wasn't on the hillside yesterday evening. Great heavens! Lora! Don't tell me someone else has also seen you with those Jacobite rebels! Have you ever stopped to think what the consequences of all this may be? Are those men close friends of yours? Are they local men perhaps?'

'That is my concern,' retorted Lora sharply.

'Well, all I can say is, they must mean a very great deal to you when you are prepared to risk so much for their sakes.'

'You couldn't possibly understand, Paul. You have no Highland blood in you. Indeed, you are a Lowlander. How then could you understand the spirit of the clans, or the strength of loyalty between Highlanders?'

'Are you trying to tell me that Highlanders have a monopoly on loyalty?' asked Paul, his voice heavy with sarcasm.

'No. I'm sorry if I gave you that impression. It's just . . .' but here Paul interrupted.

'My dear Lora, don't try to explain further. Loyalty is loyalty the world over, and genuine loyalty is an admirable quality, but in loyalty, as in other things, one has to get one's priorities right – especially where danger to one's family and friends is concerned. You would also do well to remember that many Scots did not favour the Jacobite cause. So, besides the English soldiery, there could be other enemies on your very doorstep. And as for your crazy idea of calling your dog "Loyal Highlander" so that you have to cry "Loyal" wherever you go, while most loyal Jacobites are trying to make themselves as inconspicuous as possible! Words fail me! Maybe you imagine you are making a brave gesture of clan loyalty, but, in fact, you are only being stupid. However, if you are still determined to go your own way, then the blood be upon your own head. But, I am warning you now, I shall take whatever steps I may consider necessary to protect Aunt Gwyneth and Susan from the consequences of your foolhardiness.'

So saying, Paul walked across the hall and proceeded upstairs to his room without a further glance in Lora's direction.

Lora remained where she was for a time, thinking of the sad plight she was in. So much had happened in the space of little more than twenty-four hours, with so many frightening complications. Now, to make matters worse, Paul had discovered her dangerous secret. And, in that, alas, he was not alone. There was also the mystery spy on the hillside. And what of Hamish MacCrimmon? Could his integrity really be relied upon?

As Lora climbed the stairs to bed she realised how utterly exhausted she was, both mentally and physically. More than anything, she longed for sleep – a deep sleep that would blot out all her newly-acquired worries – yet she feared that those same worries might well condemn her to the torment of a restless night.

Sometime later, still lying wide awake in her big four-poster bed staring into the darkness, Lora's thoughts turned once more to Paul. As she recalled how Elsie had described his genuine concern for her safety, and the speed with which he had set off to look for her, Lora felt a surge of happiness, and a strange new emotion began to stir within her. Carefully she went back over every detail of Paul's brave fight to rescue her from the clutches of the Redcoats. In her mind, at that witching hour of midnight, the whole affair began to don such an aura of romance that Lora's imagination ran riot. Gradually the harsh realities of the day receded, in the face of such pleasant imaginings. All the built-up tensions began to evaporate. Before she had quite realised it, Lora's wish had been granted – she was sound asleep.

V UNEXPECTED COMPLICATIONS

On waking the next morning Lora's thoughts immediately returned to the point at which she had fallen asleep and she found that a little of the magic still lingered. Viewed in the pale light of day, however, Paul's protective behaviour towards her began to assume less romantic proportions. Given the same circumstances, she knew very well he would have done exactly the same for any other female.

'In my own mind I'm exaggerating the whole episode out of all proportion,' she chided herself. 'And Paul of all people! I must have gone crazy!' And she buried her head in the pillow from sheer embarrassment.

Looking back over the years, Lora could not recall one instance when Paul had evinced any particular interest in her. To Susan and herself he had shown exactly the same measure of brotherly affection at all times. Perhaps he had enjoyed teasing her that little bit more than Susan. Now, alas! all she seemed to arouse in him now was irritation and even anger.

'So the quicker you put any such romantic notions out of your silly head the better, Miss Lora Macrae,' she said firmly, addressing herself in the mirror as she completed her toilet. 'From now on, let common sense prevail!'

By the time Lora went down to the dining-room, Paul had breakfasted and gone, for which, under the circumstances, she was thankful. As she ate her solitary breakfast one of the servant girls came to say that a gentleman wished to speak with her at the front door.

'At the front door?' queried Lora, thinking that the gentleman in question was probably Hamish MacCrimmon from Kirriemuir whom she would have thought more likely to have gone to the servants' entrance. 'Did he give his name?'

'No he didna, Miss. Will I go back an' ask his name?'

'No. Don't bother, Lizzie. I'm ready to go down now, anyway.'

When Lora reached the outside door she found her caller's back confronting her. He was standing at his horse's head looking down the glen. Tall and erect, he had a distinctly military bearing, but even from his back view, Lora knew at once that he was a stranger to her.

'Good morning!' she hailed him. 'You wished to talk with me, I believe?'

At the sound of her voice the man turned quickly, and Lora was shocked to see an otherwise handsome young face marred by an ugly scar which ran diagonally across his left cheek from the corner of his mouth to his eye. The skin was so badly puckered that his mouth was pulled to one side, giving the impression of a perpetual grimace.

For a moment the young man stood in complete silence. It was as if he were deliberately watching her reaction to his disfigurement. Then ignoring her question entirely, he blurted out, 'I *am* an ugly devil, amn't I?'

Sensing the man's acute self-consciousness, Lora paid no heed to his remark. She continued to look enquiringly at him and asked quietly, 'What did you wish to talk to me about?'

With an obvious effort, the man pulled himself together.

'I beg your pardon,' he said. 'Please forgive my rudeness. I am Dr Elliott's assistant. My name is Maxwell, and you, I believe, are Miss Macrae. You called on Dr Elliott yesterday about a man with an injured leg. Isn't that so?'

'Yes, that is correct,' Lora replied. 'But I understood Dr Elliott was to come himself.'

'I can assure you Dr Elliott is on his way here, but he had to see another patient at Cortachy, so he sent me on ahead. He told me to call here and you would show me where to go. Does the man live nearby?'

'Yes. The cottage is up on the hillside. Wait till I fetch my cloak and I'll take you there.'

As they climbed the path to Linnochmore they talked about the weather and the glen, while Lora's mind worked feverishly, trying to decide how best to cope with this unexpected situation. How much should be said, and how much should remain unsaid, as far as this stranger was concerned?

'I think it might be best if I went in alone to begin with,' she suggested, when they reached the cottage. 'We haven't told the patient about the doctor coming, so I think I'd better break the news myself.'

Mrs MacCrimmon was alone in the kitchen, so Lora quickly told her about the new doctor. 'Where's Alistair?' she asked.

'Hamish was goin' out the hill to bring in some peat, so Alistair went to lend a hand,' the old lady told her.

'Well, when they come back, I think we'd better warn Alistair to stay out of sight, if the doctors are still here. I feel it would be wiser to let them believe there's only one rebel. After all, we don't know anything about this new man.'

Angus was inclined to be awkward when told that the doctor had arrived, but accepted the inevitable when Mrs MacCrimmon pointed out that his leg would never get better without skilled attention.

'There's no point in pretending to be dumb on this occasion, of course, Angus,' Lora warned. 'You'll have to answer the doctor's questions. Just say as little as possible.'

Obviously it was much too dark in the box-bed for the doctor to examine the wound, so Angus got up, and the ladies set two chairs as near as possible to the tiny deep-set window. Angus then sat in the shadows, with his leg supported on the other chair, in such a way as to ensure that the maximum of light from the casement might be shed on the injury.

When all was in order, the doctor limped into the room and proceeded to examine the leg, after only the briefest acknowledgement of Lora's introductions. He passed no comment at all, until his examination was completed. Then, fixing Angus with a stony stare, he said, 'This is not a recent injury, of course, and it is plainly a battle wound. I have seen many similar. I don't suppose it ever healed completely?'

'*Non*. It did not heal completely, but I injured it again when I had a bad fall,' Angus replied.

'The real cause of the trouble, of course, is a piece of metal embedded in the flesh near the bone of your leg. That must be removed if your leg is ever to heal properly. Tell me, were you wounded at Culloden?'

'*Oui*. Culloden.' Angus nodded in agreement.

'I was wounded at Prestonpans,' said the doctor. 'I presume you are a Jacobite on the run?'

'*Oui*. A Jacobite,' Angus agreed, rather uneasily.

'Then you must realise that I shall have to report your presence to the authorities.'

This remark was received by a shocked silence.

Lora was the first to speak.

'B-but surely you wouldn't do that to a fellow soldier?' she protested, aghast at the very idea, 'After all, you've just said you were, yourself, wounded in the battle of Prestonpans!'

'Oh yes! I was wounded in the battle all right, but I was a non-combatant – a surgeon in the field. I was brutally attacked while unarmed and rendering aid to the wounded and dying. My wounds were the foul work of a bloodthirsty Jacobite. I was a medical officer in the service of His Royal Majesty, King George.'

There was another stunned silence in the room. Then a voice sounded from the doorway.

'What's that ye're saying to them, Dr Maxwell?'

'I'm warning this Jacobite rebel that all doctors are required to report any rebels they may come across in the course of their duty, Dr Elliott.'

'Hoots, man! Away wi' ye! We're no' here to act as spies for King Geordie, or Prince Charles, or onybody else. We're doctors, and our job is to attend to our patients' ailments. We turn a blind eye and a deaf ear to anything we see, or hear, in the course of our duty, so ye'd better get that straight if ye're to be *my* assistant. May be ye *were* wounded by a bloodthirsty Jacobite, and no doubt ye have cause to be bitter about your cruel injuries, but the war is past, man! And ye needna' try to put out your spite on this unfortunate lad. I hardly think he has been personally responsible for *your* sufferings, and he seems to have had his ain share, so let bygones be bygones.'

As he was speaking, Dr Elliott was divesting himself of his coat. Then, turning to the ladies, he said, 'Good day to ye, Miss Macrae, and to you too Mistress MacCrimmon. I hope I find ye both in good health?' When both had replied in the affirmative he continued, 'Well, now, if ye'll be good enough to fetch us some boiling water and some clean white linen for bandages, Dr Maxwell and I will just have a wee chat as to what can best be done about this young man's injury.'

Mrs MacCrimmon produced a piece of clean linen from a chest in the bedroom. Then Lora and she withdrew to the kitchen. Lora proceeded to tear the cloth into strips suitable for bandages, according to Mrs MacCrimmon's instructions, while the old lady built up the fire and swung the iron sway-bar into position so that the kettle hung suspended above the flame.

'It's lucky I had the kettle near' boilin', she remarked, 'It'll no' take long now. Maybe the doctors could do wi' a hot drink afore they start.'

On being asked, however, Dr Elliott shook his head.

'Naw, naw, Mistress. Thank ye a' the same. We need a steady hand and a cool head for this job. We'll ha'e a wee "dram" after our work's done. Now, if ye'll allow us, we'll borrow your kitchen table. It'll save us workin' on our knees.'

For the next half hour or so, Lora was kept busy in the kitchen stoking up the fire to provide plenty of boiling water, while Mrs MacCrimmon gave what assistance she could to the doctors in the bedroom.

At the first sound of the peat-gatherers' return, Lora dashed outside to warn Alistair to stay out of sight, and the two men decided their best plan would be to return to the peat-moss for another load.

Poor Angus suffered all the probing and cleansing of his wound without a murmur, but was 'a bit the worse of the wear' by the end of his ordeal, and needed a 'dram' to revive him.

'Ye'll need to rest that leg for a few days,' said Dr Elliott, 'but the wound should heal now, with the expert care of Mistress MacCrimmon. Ye couldna be in better hands, laddie. Ye certainly landed in the right place.' Turning to Mrs MacCrimmon he added, 'I hardly think we'll need to come back, but if ye have any cause for anxiety, Mistress, just send a messenger to Kirriemuir and one or other o' us will certainly come. Dr Maxwell's my nephew, by the way – my sister's son. He's been a great help to me these last few weeks and he's keeping me up to date wi' the various new developments in medical matters.'

Back in the kitchen, while the doctors drank their 'drams' and partook of Mrs MacCrimmon's bannocks and scones, the old doctor chatted amicably, but the young one remained sullen and withdrawn. He sat with his injured cheek averted, as if still trying vainly to hide his disfigurement. Lora felt sorry for him and she did her best to draw him into the conversation, without much success. After several rebuffs, she gave up, and left him to brood in silence.

As the doctors were leaving the house, Lora heard Angus calling from the bedroom, and she and Dr Elliott turned back.

Angus was sitting up in the box-bed.

'*Merci beaucoup*, Doctor, for all you have done for me,' he said. 'I do not know your fee, but I hope this may be sufficient to recompense you and your assistant,' and he held out two golden guineas.

Dr Elliott walked over to the bed. Taking Angus's hand in both of his, he closed the young man's fingers over the money.

'Thank you, but in your case there is no fee,' he said. 'I am glad to ha'e been of service to ye, and ye may need a' the money ye've got, son. My young brother was "out" in the 'fifteen rebellion so I've some idea o' the trials ye may have to face. And a guinea in your pocket may well be your best friend. Goodbye now, Angus, and Godspeed!'

As the doctor passed Lora, he gave her arm a reassuring pat.

'Don't worry about him,' he said kindly. 'He'll soon be back on his feet now, and able to fend for himself. By the way, I'm sorry if my nephew appeared rude to ye, Miss Macrae, but his wounds have left him wi' a personality disorder which is proving more difficult to cure than any physical injury. Aye, lass,' he added, with a shake of his head, 'such are the fortunes of war!'

Lora helped Mrs MacCrimmon to tidy up. Then, after a brief word with Angus, she hurried off home.

It was past the midday mealtime when she reached The Milton and Elsie informed her that Paul had just left on a business visit to the port of Leith, near Edinburgh, and would possibly be away most of the week. This piece of news ought to have pleased Lora, but somehow, she could only feel a bewildering sense of disappointment. Perhaps it was because she had made up her mind to apologise and to try to heal the rift between Paul and herself. Even a few days' delay might make it that bit more difficult, if not impossible.

In the evening Lora went back to Linnochmore, hoping against hope that Hamish MacCrimmon from Kirriemuir would now be at his uncle's house, but there, alas, she was also due for a disappointment.

'Did ye no' manage to unearth that wayward nephew o' mine, Miss Lora?' Old Hamish enquired.

'Oh yes, I found him,' and Lora briefly described what had transpired between her and Hamish's namesake. 'I understood he was to come here sometime today,' she concluded. 'I just hope he keeps his word.'

'Well at one time ye could've depended on him, but now, as I said afore, I ha'e my doobts,' and Hamish shook his head sadly.

Lora also had her doubts, and she dreaded the thought of having to make another visit to the hateful lodging-house.

Thus began a week of anxiety for Lora and her friends at Linnochmore. As each day came and went, their hopes began to fade. Lora's daytime walks with Loyal now consisted of regular tramps along the hillsides overlooking the road from Kirriemuir. This way she managed to keep the road under almost constant surveillance and so did her best to avoid their being caught unawares by the arrival of Redcoats in the glen. From time to time during the week they heard snippets of news about continuing trouble between the Duke of Cumberland's troops and the citizens of Kirriemuir and this gave them a measure of relief. As long as there was trouble in the township the troops would be concentrated there, and search parties in the glens would be left in abeyance. The only real cheer during this time of waiting was the astonishingly rapid improvement in Angus's health. As his leg-trouble cleared up, so his appetite increased, and his spirits rose. It was now almost impossible to imagine him as the hollow-eyed Angus of scarcely a week before.

Lora continued to carry food regularly to Linnochmore under cover of darkness. In the evenings spent at the cottage she enjoyed long chats with her protégés and learned something of their past, and of how they became associated with the rebel army.

'My wife and I adhered strongly to the Jacobite cause, as did our people before us,' Alistair explained, 'and in my early youth I had been given a good military education in France. We talked the matter over and agreed that I should offer my services to the Prince. The Highland army was advancing towards Edinburgh, by this time, so I rode north and enlisted as a "Gentleman Volunteer", using a false name to guard against any possible reprisals on my wife and child.

'Right from the start there was a great shortage of horses in the Prince's army, but, having my own mount, I proved useful as a scout, reconnoîtring and bringing in military intelligence during the long advances and retreats. At Falkirk I fought as a cavalryman with the Royal Scots, under the command of Lord John Drummond. Unfortunately, my horse had been sadly overworked. It was completely worn out, and collapsed – like so many more – on the long march north to Culloden. There were no replacements to be had, so I attached myself to an infantry regiment, and ended the campaign fighting as a kilted foot-soldier on the field of Culloden.'

Angus's tale was not dissimilar. He had come from France with Lord John Drummond's Royal Scots (French) Detachment, under whose command he also had fought at the Battle of Falkirk.

After various exciting adventures he – like all the other dismounted cavalrymen – had ended in the rôle of a foot-soldier, fighting alongside Alistair on Drumossie Moor.

'Unlike Alistair, I never had any desire to follow a military career,' he told Lora. 'It was my father's idea entirely. Now I have had enough of military matters to last me the rest of my days. My future hopes lie in the peaceful pursuits of painting and sculpture.'

One morning, towards the end of the week, as Lora was stabling her horse after an early-morning reconnaisance, her attention was drawn by the unusual sound of a heated argument in the kitchen quarters. Elsie's voice could be heard raised in anger, while tearful protests came from the unfortunate girl who was the object of her wrath.

'Gracious me! I wonder what's gone wrong over there,' Lora remarked to the stable boy.

'Sounds as if Elsie's readin' the Riot Act this mornin',' said the lad, with a grin. 'Somebody's catchin' it! Thank goodness it's no' me!'

Lora laughed and agreed with the boy as she led her horse into the stall. When she re-emerged, all was back to normal and she had quite forgotten the incident. Later, however, as she made her way back to the house, she met Annie Shaw, one of the maids, heading for the stables. The girl was obviously very distressed and was weeping copiously.

'What's wrong, Annie?' Lora asked, and was answered by a further flood of tears.

When the girl had pulled herself together, Lora asked again what had happened. Between outbursts of weeping she learned that Elsie had accused Annie of stealing.

'But I didna do it, Miss Lora, really I didn't.'

'What was it Elsie thought you had stolen?' Lora asked kindly.

'She said she'd been watchin' every nicht for about a week, and she knew fine I was carryin' awa' baskets o' food from the larder.'

'From the larder?' Lora gasped as she realised the full import of Annie's words.

'Aye. She said the stuff was disappearin' at an awfu' rate, and it wasna Lizzie or Jess, she was sure o' that, so it was bound to be me. I said I didna do it, but she wouldna' listen. She said I was to leave the house at once, and I've to get the stable lad to pick up my kist. I'll never get anither job, Miss Lora,' she sobbed. 'I'll be branded as a thief, and naebody wants to employ a thief, but I never stole onything in my life, and that's the truth,' and Annie's words ended in a wail of despair.

Lora put an arm round the girl's shoulder.

'Stop crying, Annie,' she soothed, 'and don't upset yourself further. Come back to the house with me and I'll have a talk with Elsie,' and Lora began to propel Annie back the way she had come.

'She'll no' listen to ye, Miss. I can tell ye that afore ye start. She's determined I'm a thief.'

'Well I'll just have to convince her otherwise, because, you see, Annie, it was *I* who took the food from the larder.'

'You!' exclaimed Annie in shocked surprise.

'Yes. I needed food for an ailing friend. Of course I ought really to have told Elsie before I took anything from the larder. However, we'll soon put the matter right.'

Elsie was nowhere to be seen when Lora and Annie arrived in the kitchen, but Jess was able to tell them she had gone up to the dining-room to polish silver.

'Well now, Annie,' said Lora, 'I want you to go straight to your room and stay there until we send for you. I'm sorry you've had this upset but please stop crying. There's no need to worry any more.'

Lora was really full of remorse at the trouble she had caused among the servants. If only she had confided in Elsie at the very beginning! Anyway, the time had now come to make a clean breast of the whole affair. In view of the morning's upheaval in the kitchen, she realised she would have to be very diplomatic in her approach.

To Lora's relief, Elsie was quite alone in the dining-room. It was a golden opportunity, and Lora grasped it with both hands.

'Elsie,' she said urgently, 'I've a secret to tell you. Have you time to listen?'

The housekeeper smiled. So many times, throughout the years, she had played the rôle of confidante to Lora.

'Of course, Miss Lora. When did I ever refuse to listen to one of your secrets?' she asked. 'Sit ye down and ye can tell me while I'm cleanin' the cutlery.'

So Lora sat down beside her and poured out the story of how she had met Alistair on the hillside; of Angus's relationship to the Lindsays of Clova; and the letter to Hamish MacCrimmon. She also admitted the real reason for her journey to Kirriemuir; and spoke of how they hoped, when danger threatened, the fugitives would soon be able to hide in the secret chamber in the Peel Tower as Angus's father had done in 1715. Finally she explained that she had been taking food from the larder, and that she had met Annie and had learned of the trouble she had unwittingly brought upon the girl's head.

Elsie listened in shocked silence until Lora had completed her tale. When she spoke, her first thought was for Annie.

'Poor lassie! And to think I branded her as a thief! Thank goodness you met her and brought her back, Miss Lora! As regards your efforts to help the rebels, I hardly ken what to say. It's a terrible risk ye're takin'. And yet, what else could ye do under the circumstances? D'ye know, Miss Lora, I well remember the time when Dugald Lindsay, alang wi' Hamish MacCrimmon and David McInnes, ran the hills here, after the 'fifteen rebellion, and I never knew until this minute that they hid in The Peel. In fact, I never

even knew there was a secret room there. I was little more than a lassie –
for it's thirty years ago – and I always believed that the three men had found
shelter in the "Hole o' Weems" or under "the Laird's Stane". That shows ye
how a secret can be kept among glen folk, and your secret'll be safe wi' me.'

'I never doubted that,' Lora assured her. 'I suppose I was really afraid
you might try to stop me doing what I wanted to do. That's why I didn't
tell you before. But we'll need your help yet, Elsie, as regards food and
blankets.'

'I'll certainly do all I can in that line, Miss Lora, but heaven help us a',
if your stepmother ever finds oot! What did ye tell Annie, by the way?'

'I told her I had taken the food for an ailing friend.'

'We'll continue wi' the story then. The lassies in the kitchen must never
guess what's goin' on. I think the MacCrimmons have been very brave to
give the lads shelter, and we must stand by them. I just hope and pray all
will go well wi' your plans, and that the two young men will get safely out
o' the country.'

'Thank you, Elsie. So do I. I feel much better, now that I've told you,
and I'm really sorry about Annie.'

'Yes,' said Elsie ruefully. 'I'd better go and make my peace wi' Annie
right away. Maybe this'll learn me no' to jump to conclusions. Mind you,
I'm glad Annie's still to be here with us. She's the most intelligent o' the
three, and the best worker. But good worker or no', I wouldna tolerate a
thief among the servants. That can lead to no end o' trouble. It was the
fact that Annie was goin' every evenin' to the alehouse to visit her auntie
that made me decide that she was carryin' the stuff there.'

'Is Mrs MacDougall at the alehouse her aunt? I didn't know that.'

'Aye. Widow MacDougall's a sister of Annie's mother. They were both
Stuarts o' Caddam.'

'Then Dougal MacDougall, the deaf-and-dumb boy, must be Annie's
cousin! I felt sure there was someone Annie reminded me of, and that's
who it is! She has the same shape of face as Dougal, and the same mop
of fuzzy hair.'

'Aye. There's a strong family likeness and a strong attachment as well, '
asserted Elsie, 'for Annie spends a lot o' time wi' the poor laddie. He may
be just "Daft Dumby Dougal" to the rest o' the glen dwellers, and even
an object o' mirth to some, but to Annie he's a person in his own right,
and she declares she can get a fair amount o' sense out o' him. Well, I'll
have to get a move on. I've just had a messenger from Logie House to say
that Mrs Macrae's comin' back tomorrow, and she's bringin' a small party
wi' her. They're to be here until Sunday, so maybe ye'd be kind enough to
supervise the makin' up o' the beds and so on, Lora. I'm thinkin' I'll have
my hands full i' the kitchen from now on.'

When Elsie went back to her kitchen Lora rested her head on her hands and
sighed heavily. So many unexpected complications seemed to be crowding in

upon her, and the return of her stepmother would undoubtedly complicate matters still further. If only Hamish MacCrimmon hadn't let them down!

Except for her usual road patrol with Loyal, Lora spent all day lending a hand with the preparations for the guests. Elsie had told her that a basket of food would now be left in readiness for her each evening, and it was certainly a relief not to have to sneak into the larder and remove the food by stealth. Nevertheless, Lora's heart was heavy as she and Loyal set out on their nightly journey to Linnochmore. What on earth were they to do if Hamish MacCrimmon just didn't come?

As she drew near the cottage, Lora saw Mrs MacCrimmon heading for the byre, with lantern and milking pail.

'Good evening, Mrs MacCrimmon,' she called.

'Oh it's you, Miss Lora. I didna notice ye comin' up the brae. Ye'll never guess! Young Hamish is here at last!'

Lora felt a great wave of relief flow over her.

'That's wonderful news!' she exclaimed. 'When did he arrive?'

'Just about dark, it was. Awa' ye go into the hoose and see for yersel'. The door's aff the sneck, so ye can walk right in. I'll no' be very lang.'

Lora suddenly felt as if she were walking on air, but a rude shock awaited her. The kitchen door was slightly ajar when she stepped into the square of lobby, and she remained rooted to the spot as she gazed into the firelit room. There, seated at the table with Old Hamish and the other three, was someone she had hoped never to see again – Paddy from the lodging-house in the Skinner's Close!

The men were deep in conversation and hadn't heard her enter, so Lora hurriedly withdrew and followed Mrs MacCrimmon to the byre.

The old lady was talking softly to the cow and was just about to seat herself on the milking stool when Lora burst in upon the scene.

'Whatever is that man doing here, Mrs MacCrimmon?' she demanded, without preamble.

'What man, Miss Lora?'

'That Irishman with the patch over his eye.'

'Paddy O'Malley ye mean? Och, he just came along to be company to young Hamish.'

'But how are we to know he can be trusted?'

Mrs MacCrimmon set aside her milking pail and sat down on the stool so that she faced Lora. 'Och, there's no need to worry aboot Paddy,' she said, 'I can tell ye his life's history. We've been acquaint wi' him since he was a wee laddie. His father was Auld Tam Crichton, the packman, and he used to come roond the glen wi' his father. His mother kept the lodgin'-house in those days but she died quite young. After a few years Paddy's father married again, but his second marriage was a disaster. Tam was drinkin' heavily at the time and he'd got into bad company it seems. In fact, his new wife was more or less a woman o' the streets, and she was far younger than

Tam. She was the natural bairn o' a tinker woman – and no' the best kind o' tinker woman either! She and her mother took o'er the lodgin'-hoose, and the auld man had a terrible life wi' the pair o' them. In fact he didna last long. Paddy left Kirrie and went to Ireland to his mother's folk, and he was awa' for years. He was just tellin' us that he only came back to join the Jacobite army and fight for oor rightful king. After he was wounded at Prestonpans he came back to Kirrie and took to bein' a packman like his father afore him. It appears he changed his name to O'Malley – his mother's maiden name – when he was in Ireland, and ye couldna wonder at that. His stepmother had trailed the name o' Crichton through the mire, I can tell ye. But ye needna worry aboot Paddy bein' a traitor, Miss Lora. He has a terrible hatred o' the English, and I'm no surprised at that, considerin' what he suffered at their hands.'

'Well, I'm sorry, but I just don't like the man,' said Lora flatly. 'I met him at the lodging-house when I was looking for Hamish. I *do* wish Hamish had had more sense than bring *him* along! However, he's here now, so I suppose we must make the best of it.'

'Och, once ye get to know Paddy, Miss Lora, ye'll find he's no' such a bad sort. Maybe he'd had a drop too much to drink when you saw him. Drink can alter a buddy entirely, an' that's a fact.'

Lora felt no desire to hurry back to the house now, so she waited until Mrs MacCrimmon had finished the milking, and helped the old lady to carry the pail of milk.

'Good evening, Lora!' said Alistair and Angus, rising with one accord as the ladies entered the kitchen.

'You know Hamish, of course,' Alistair continued. 'Well now, I'd better explain – we've decided to refer to him as Hamish and to his uncle as "Old Hamish" from now on, to prevent any confusion in the future. By the way, I don't suppose you've met Hamish's friend Paddy O'Malley?'

'Yes,' Lora replied rather dryly. 'We've met.'

At this point Paddy rose and addressed himself to Lora.

'Sure an' begorra, I must be beggin' your pardon, Miss Macrae. I'm afraid I was after celebratin' at the market, and was in a rumbustious mood when we met last week. I hope ye'll be forgivin' me now for any offence I may have caused ye.'

Lora was saved the necessity of a reply by Mrs MacCrimmon joining in the conversation at this point.

'Miss Lora was just sayin' she'd met ye at the lodgin'-house, Paddy, but I'm surprised she hasna seen ye in the glen durin' the past year.'

'Sure now, Mistress MacCrimmon, an' ye wouldn't be thinkin' I'd be callin' at the front door of The Milton, would ye? Ye'd hardly be expectin' the foine ladies to be buyin' ribbons and laces from ould Paddy's pack, would ye now? It's the servant lasses that I do business with at the mansion houses. So it's the back door for Paddy, every time.'

'Ye havena been in Clova for a while though, have ye, Paddy? We were beginnin' to think ye'd forgotten about us,' said Mrs MacCrimmon.

'Sure I was up in Glen Clova lately, Mistress, but I didna quite get the length o' Linnochmore. I was after plannin' a trip up Glen Prosen this week but I took the chance o' Hamish's company and came here instead. Sure a cratur's hardly safe travellin' around the countryside on his own at the present time. God bless the ould days, that's what I say. We'll never see the likes o' them again. Mind you, it's safer I am to be out o' Kirrie though, and that's a fact. With those damn troopers – pardon my language – ridin' roughshod o'er a' body, there's no' room for a cripple-dick like me in those narrow streets. Aye,' he continued, indicating the patch over his eye, and looking down at his lame leg, 'them be my battle legacies from the English butchers. "The divil take the lot o' them" says I. Right here an' now, I swear to God, I'm willing to do all I can to help any man to outwit the crafty Redcoats!'

'*Vive la Liberté*! Well spoken, Paddy!' cried Angus, obviously impressed by the Irishman's defiant outburst. 'You have come to the right place! Alistair and I may well need all the help we can muster if we are to get out of Scotland alive.'

'Begorra then, I'm your man,' vowed Paddy, 'an' the divil take the lavin's!'

Lora had to admit, however grudgingly, that this Paddy O'Malley with his unruly curls brushed into shape, clean shaven, and sober, was a very different person from the Paddy she had met at the lodging-house. It seemed her judgement of him had been a trifle too hasty.

Hamish MacCrimmon had taken no part whatever in the conversation. He just sat staring into the fire.

'Why have you been so long in coming?' Lora asked him.

'I couldna help it. I came as quick as I could. The farmer wouldna' let me break my bargain and I didna find anybody willin' to take my place until yesterday.'

'You won't have been to the old castle yet?'

'No. I'll leave that until daylight. A lantern up on the hillside micht attract attention. But, mind, you lads,' he added, turning to address the other men, 'naebody comes up to the castle wi' me. I go there on my own. The secret o' the hidden chamber is mine, and I swore on the Bible that I'd guard that secret. It was handed down to me by my father, and from his father afore that. Aye. As loyal servants o' the Lindsays the secret has been in the MacCrimmon family for generations. It passes from the eldest son to *his* eldest son, right down the line. Isn't that so, Uncle Hamish?'

'Aye. I've heard it said that that was the rule,' Old Hamish agreed.

'And, another thing,' the younger man continued, 'we MacCrimmons can only open the secret chamber for the use o' a true descendant o' the Ancient Hoose o' Lindsay. If we violate our trust, it is said a curse will be laid upon our family for evermore. I've kept my oath, and I'll open the chamber for young Angus, but my secret I share wi' naebody.'

'Mother-o'-God, man!' exclaimed Paddy, 'and what will be happenin' at all, if you depart this life an' ye havena begat a son?'

'That remains to be seen,' replied Hamish calmly.

'But how will Alistair and Angus get out of the place if they can't open it?' queried Lora.

'It's impossible to get out the way they got in unless I'm there to open it for them,' Hamish answered stubbornly. 'Their only exit would be by the underground passage.'

'And where does the underground passage have its exit?' asked Alistair.

'It leads out on to the hillside.'

'But if the enemy discovered the entrance to that passage, then Alistair and Angus could be trapped,' Lora pointed out.

'The chance o' that happenin' is very unlikely. In fact, I'd go as far as to say it's well-nigh impossible,' said Hamish. 'Few, if any, in the glen, are aware o' its existence, and I'd reckon it to be one o' the best concealed entrances to any escape-passage that was ever hollowed oot o' a hillside.'

'Sounds as if we'll be safe there,' remarked Alistair, 'but I hope our stay will be short. We'd like to get away from here before the Redcoats come prowling around, and also before the winter sets in. If any of you gentlemen can think of a means of escape we'd be more than grateful, for we cannot forget the danger our continued presence means for those who have sheltered us. Our enemies would have no mercy.'

'Sure, an' ye niver said truer words,' declared Paddy.

'Well, I must be going,' said Lora. 'I'll do my best to come again tomorrow night, but my stepmother returns tomorrow with a houseful of guests, so I may have difficulty getting away. I shall have to get blankets to you somehow, though, for I'm sure it will be cold, and probably damp, in the old castle.'

'Of course there's no need for them to move out just yet,' Mrs MacCrimmon reminded her.

'No. There's certainly no immediate danger,' Lora agreed. 'Good-night then, everyone,' and, with Loyal bounding ahead, she hurried down the stony path to The Milton.

Mrs Macrae and Susan arrived early the following afternoon, followed by the carriages of their guests. From then on, Lora had little time to let her thoughts stray to the cottage at Linnochmore. Susan was bubbling over with excitement, and eager to tell Lora all about the wonderful time she had had, while Mrs Macrae was adamant that her stepdaughter should play her full part in the entertaining of guests in her own home, whether or not she chose to join in the general social round.

In a way, Lora was thankful for the presence of the visitors. At least it postponed the stormy interview that was sure to come regarding her unfortunate lapse of memory over the Lednathie invitation.

Towards evening Mrs Macrae despatched Susan with a request that the gardener – who was also the local musician – should attend at the Mansion House with his violin, as she had invited a party of gentlemen from Kirriemuir to join them for dinner, and the guests might wish to indulge in some dancing after the meal.

Lora heard of this arrangement with mixed feelings. She couldn't decide whether this would prove helpful or unhelpful towards her planned visit to Linnochmore. Nevertheless, she was determined to get there somehow. She just couldn't rest until she heard how things had gone with Hamish at the Peel Tower.

While she was in her room dressing for the evening, Lora became aware of a number of horses approaching at a brisk canter.

'Aunt Gwyneth's male friends no doubt,' she said to herself, without much interest.

As she glanced from her unshuttered window she could see a party of horsemen swinging into the carriageway. In the gathering dusk she could just make out the leading rider. It was Paul Reynolds mounted on his big black charger, Nero. At the sight of his tall familiar figure, so erect in the saddle, Lora's heart began to beat a little faster, but her pleasure turned to horror as his companions came into view. They were all soldiers – soldiers in red tunics!

VI DEAR ENEMY

Paul's parting words of the previous week flashed through Lora's mind. Surely he hadn't betrayed Alistair and Angus to the English!

'How could he! How could he!' she whispered aloud, as she clutched the windowsill, unable to move, her mind in a turmoil.

Then, gradually, she became aware of voices at the entrance door and Mrs Macrae's cultured tones floated up from the hallway. She was bidding her guests welcome. So these English army officers were her guests after all – the party of gentlemen from Kirriemuir to whom she had referred!

Lora heaved a great sigh of relief, and sank down on the window-seat to still the trembling of her limbs. By degrees, as she recovered from the shock and near-panic of the last few minutes, another emotion engulfed her. The idea of entertaining those soldiers of the English army – the butchers of the Jacobites – filled her with revulsion.

'I shan't go down at all,' she decided, 'I shall plead a headache and remain in my room.' But, even as this idea formed in her mind, so also did the image of Paul's derisive smile. No plea of a headache would fool him. The real reason for her absence would be perfectly clear to him and he would mock her for her cowardice. So once again Lora's unquenchable Highland spirit came to her aid.

'He may laugh,' she said to herself, between tight lips, 'but never will he be able to say that a Macrae has shown the white feather!'

Casting aside the demure dress which she had previously decided to wear,

70

Lora now went to her hanging closet and selected a dress more suited to her mood of defiance. She chose a beautiful sea-green evening gown which her stepmother had brought back to her from one of her visits to the capital. Lora had relegated the dress to the back of the closet as being too sophisticated for any function she was likely to attend. Daringly low cut, its minute waist was emphasised by the width of the voluminous skirt. There was no denying, it was a stylish dress, and Lora decided it was right for this occasion.

With all possible haste, lest her resolution should fail her at the last minute, Lora slipped the dress over her head, fixed the innumerable buttons and bows and arranged the folds of the bodice. Then she fetched out her jewel case. A family heirloom, inherited from her mother, and comprising a magnificent diamond necklace, with matching earrings and bracelet, appeared to be the right choice to enhance the gown. Once these were carefully fastened, and a stray lock of hair brushed into place, Lora surveyed herself in the full-length mirror. Her eyes opened wide in amazement. Never had she imagined she could look like this! The person standing there seemed to be a complete stranger. And, indeed, it was little wonder she felt gratified by her reflection, for her clear skin, pink and white complexion, and red-gold hair, all combined with the sea-green dress and sparkling jewels to create a striking picture.

Holding her head high, to disguise the nervousness within, Lora swept down the stairs to where the company had gathered in the hall. As she descended the last few steps, every face seemed to be turned towards her. Lora was conscious of her stepmother's look of amazement, and of the approving glances of the male members of the company, but, most of all, she was aware of Paul's eyes upon her. Moving confidently forward to shake hands with the new arrivals, smiling and making suitable comments to each, as her stepmother made the introductions, Lora espied a somewhat grudging look of admiration in the smouldering depths of Paul's dark eyes. When he realised she was looking at him, he quickly averted his gaze, but not before Lora had experienced a delicious thrill of triumph.

Lora's partner at table was Lieutenant Lennox Bullard, one of the Dragoons – a young fair-haired giant, very English, very handsome, and an able conversationalist. His gentlemanly air and friendly approach soon dispelled Lora's preconceived ideas of the hardhearted and ruthless English soldiery. Her determination to dislike all Redcoats on sight was no proof against the natural charm of Lieutenant Bullard, and his youthful high spirits were very infectious. In no time at all the two young people were laughing and chatting like old friends, and Lora began to feel more at ease than she had done at any time since the fateful meeting on the hillside. Indeed, she was surprised to find herself actually enjoying this Redcoat's company without any feeling of guilt whatsoever.

Paul's seat at the table was several places away, and on the opposite side from Lora, but she was near enough to see that his face still bore evidence of the previous week's fracas. There was a slight swelling below one eye,

71

and a discoloured bruise along the jawline, besides various partially-healed cuts and grazes on cheeks and brow. Evidently he had already managed to explain away the marks, for no one referred to them, and Lora had certainly no wish to have the matter under discussion.

All through the meal, Paul kept up an animated conversation with his partner – a very attractive, dark-haired, olive-skinned girl called Maria, whom Lora had met for the first time only that afternoon, but with whom Paul appeared to be on very familiar terms. He didn't even glance once in Lora's direction.

After dinner, the ladies withdrew to the library. When the gentlemen joined them there, Mrs Macrae requested Paul and Maria to entertain the company with a song. Paul had a very good voice, but it was soon apparent that Maria was a truly talented singer, and an accomplished musician. She supplied the accompaniment on the spinet, and their clear young voices combined beautifully to produce a fine rendering of 'Drink to me only with thine eyes'. This was certainly not the first time they had sung that particular song together. To Lora, watching in the background, they appeared to be quite oblivious of the audience and were simply pouring out their hearts to each other with every word of the love-song.

As the last notes died away, Lora suddenly, and quite involuntarily, heaved a long drawn-out sigh.

Susan, who was standing just in front of Lora, turned in unfeigned surprise. ''*Tis* rather heart-rending, isn't it?' she remarked, with an impish grin. 'I've heard Paul and Maria sing that song before, and they know how to pile on the pathos, but I didn't expect *you* to be affected in that way, Lora. Up to now you have never been the least bit romantically inclined. Surely Lieutenant Bullard has had a lightning effect upon your emotions!'

Lora decided to ignore Susan's teasing remarks.

'Do you know Maria well, Susan?' she asked, instead.

'No. I couldn't claim to know her well,' Susan replied. 'I understand she lives in Italy most of the time, but when she is in this country, her home is near Leith. Paul has brought her to dinner parties at our Edinburgh house on several occasions. It's my opinion,' (and here Susan dropped her voice to a whisper) 'Mamma would dearly love to see them betrothed. Maria is reputed to be very wealthy as well as talented, you see,' she explained, with a twinkle. 'Between you and me, I think I could give Mamma a piece of news that would gladden her heart,' Susan continued.

'In what way?' Lora asked.

Susan glanced around to make sure no one was listening.

'If I tell you, Lora, you must promise not to say a word to anyone else, because I'm sure Paul would be furious if he thought I knew this.'

'I promise I shan't say a word,' Lora vowed.

'Well it happened this way. When Paul came home to Edinburgh after his last long trip, Maria was at our house to welcome him. He must have got a message to her that he was on his way, and he arrived just before dinner. It was a lovely moonlight night – very romantic! – and after the meal I went to sit on the window-seat in the alcove off the drawing-room, you know where I mean. I was viewing the nightlife in the Canongate when Paul and Maria wandered into the room. They didn't notice me sitting there. I suppose they had eyes only for each other. They were talking away in Italian, as they often do, and of course I didn't know one word they said. Anyway, after a bit, Paul took a small jewellery-box from his pocket and presented it to Maria. When she opened it she went into ecstasies over the contents. It contained a diamond ring. I know, because she took it out of the box and held it up to the light. The jewel was a solitaire – a really magnificent one, for it sparkled tremendously. Alas, a sudden commotion in the street drew my attention and I missed seeing Paul place the ring on her finger. Next thing I knew, Maria had unfastened the long gold chain which was hanging round her neck and had attached the ring to the chain. When she replaced the chain, the ring was concealed inside the bodice of her dress. Paul fastened the chain at the back of her neck. Then he kissed her, and they went off arm in arm. Perhaps it is the custom in Italy to wear one's engagement ring next to one's heart – I just don't know. Of course there is the possibility that for some reason Paul and Maria wish their betrothal to remain a secret meantime. But I'm sure if I had a dazzling ring like that, I'd want to wear it on my finger where everyone would see it and know I was betrothed. Wouldn't you, Lora?'

'Yes. I think I would,' Lora agreed.

Susan's tale had, in fact, provided the spur Lora needed to shake herself free of any lingering romantic ideas concerning Paul. In spite of a twinge of regret that the new-found magic in her life had so quickly been terminated, common sense told her to be thankful that her foolish imaginings had been nipped in the bud before they got out of hand. Had she not laughed at Susan's various disastrous ventures into the realms of romance, and vowed never to wear *her* heart on her sleeve for any man? Well, now was the time to prove it!

So Lora resolutely pushed the matter to the back of her mind. She joked with Susan about her mother's matchmaking tendencies and chatted pleasantly with others of the guests. By the time Lennox came to claim her as his partner for the first dance she had her feelings well under control and was smiling happily.

When Lora and Lennox reached the ballroom, Paul and Maria were already dancing. From then on, Paul partnered Maria repeatedly. Lora herself had no lack of partners but she had hoped Paul might at least spare her one dance. She felt hurt at the way he deliberately ignored her. So, to hide her disappointment, she engaged in a mild flirtation with Lennox Bullard. Lennox was a competent dancer, and, as Lora and he whirled round the room, she became aware that Paul was watching them. Lora smiled a greeting, but Paul's only acknowledgement was to raise a questioning eyebrow. Then he directed his attention elsewhere.

After a succession of energetic reels and schottisches, Lieutenant Bullard, unaccustomed to the intricacies of Scottish country dancing, mopped his brow and suggested they sit out the next dance. Lora readily agreed.

'We can sit in the window-seat in the library,' she suggested. So they slipped away as soon as the next dance was announced.

'Have you ever been in Scotland before?' Lora asked, when they were comfortably seated.

'No. This is my first visit,' Lennox replied. 'I only came to Scotland with the army. Although Lennox is a Scottish name I have no Scottish ancestry. My parents had a friend called Lennox and they liked the name so they decided to call me Lennox too. As you may guess, my name has given rise to various comments during this campaign.'

'Did you fight at Culloden?' Lora felt forced to ask.

'I did,' Lennox answered, 'but let's not talk about that. I'd rather the memory of it was erased from my mind forever. By the way, a detachment from our Company is being posted in Glen Clova very soon. Now that I've met you, I think I'll put in for that posting. It may only be for a day or two but at least we might contrive to meet occasionally if I happen to be off duty.'

'But why should Clova need troops at all? We're a peace-loving community in this glen,' Lora pointed out.

'Perhaps I ought not to tell you this,' said Lennox, 'but there has been talk of rebels being sighted in Glen Clova.'

'Rebels!' exclaimed Lora in consternation, 'W-who s-saw r-rebels . . . ?' and her voice tailed off as she realised the full implication of Lennox's words.

'Oh, please don't upset yourself, Lora! A few rebels here and there means little. There won't be a blood-bath or anything of that nature. We know the likeliest place to look, and we'll soon ferret them out, never fear,' Lennox assured her confidently, and he slipped a protective arm around her shoulder.

'But where have the rebels been seen, and who has seen them?' queried Lora, still somewhat dazed.

'I'm afraid I can't supply the answer to either of your questions. We get reports of that nature all the time. Some are genuine, some are not. Personally I dislike informers. Often an entirely unfounded report can bring down a whole load of trouble on innocent people for no reason whatever, except sheer jealousy, or spite. That sort of behaviour, in my opinion, is despicable.'

'Highlanders don't do that sort of thing,' protested Lora. 'Clansmen are loyal to each other.'

'Yes. I've noticed that about members of clans and I admire their loyalty. They'd die before they'd betray their fellows, but things are different in cities and towns, I'm afraid. They're a mixed bunch there.'

'But how could anyone in Kirriemuir, for instance, pass on information about rebels up here?'

'It's difficult to say. Information can come from a variety of sources. Sometimes doctors who are called to attend to battle wounds are against the rebellion so they feel obliged to report the case. Or, perchance, someone who knows where rebels are lurking may unwittingly divulge the secret in an alehouse. Strong drink loosens the tongue, and our spies circulate in those places for that very reason. Then, of course, there's always the type that can be bribed to "spill the beans".'

'Which of those sources supplied the information this time?' Lora queried, anxious to know the answer, yet dreading it.

'I don't know where or whom it came from. You must remember, I wasn't even interested in what was happening in Glen Clova – until this evening that's to say!' and Lennox smiled down at her. 'From now on, Glen Clova will be the most important place on the map of Scotland as far as I'm concerned.'

Lora tried to smile back but it was a rather wan effort, and Lennox became concerned at the sudden change in her.

'You've gone very pale, Lora,' he said. 'How stupid of me to alarm you with tales about rebels!'

'You haven't alarmed me in the least,' Lora assured him.

'Are you cold then? I thought I felt you shiver a moment ago,' and Lennox took one of Lora's hands in his.

'I'm beginning to cool down after the exertion of the dance but I wasn't aware that I shivered. I'm certainly not cold,' said Lora, not even troubling to withdraw her hand. 'When do you think the soldiers will be coming here?'

'Very soon now, I should think. Probably tomorrow.'

'As soon as that?'

'If it hadn't been for the unrest in Forfar and Kirriemuir we'd have had men here last week. The Commanding Officer is my uncle – you met him tonight – and I must say he never puts off time. All reports are promptly and thoroughly investigated, and he misses nothing. Carelessness just isn't tolerated. We call him "Hawkeye", and he seldom makes a mistake. He has what one could call "unerring judgement".'

'He must take some living up to, that uncle of yours. Is he more lenient with you than with the others, perhaps?'

'No,' said Lennox, rather ruefully, 'he expects a higher standard from me than from any of the others.'

At that point a voice hailed them from the doorway.

'My! My! How serious we are! Where are all the happy smiles now? I was just wondering where the pair of you had got to! Sorry to interrupt your little *tête-à-tête* of course.'

Lora's mind had been so intent on gleaning news from the Lieutenant that she hadn't heard Paul's approach. The hint of amusement in his voice, and the mocking eyes under the dark brows made her suddenly aware of the fact that she and Lieutenant Bullard were still holding hands, while the Lieutenant's other arm encircled her shoulders. Hastily Lora withdrew her hand and stood up, blushing to the roots of her hair, and painfully aware that nothing was lost on Paul.

'Were you wanting me?' she asked, as calmly as possible.

'No. It was Lennox I wanted,' Paul replied.

'In that case, I shall leave you together,' said Lora quietly, and she withdrew, closing the door behind her.

A Scottish reel was in progress. Everyone seemed to be up on the floor, and Lora saw this as the ideal opportunity. Without more ado she sped down the entrance stair, grabbed her cloak, and headed for the kitchen quarters.

Loyal had been relegated to the kitchen for this evening, and he rose eagerly to greet her. As she bent to fondle her pet, Elsie appeared.

'I thought you might not manage away from your guests, Miss Lora, so I took the basket up to Linnochmore mysel', and I carried up a pair o' blankets too in case they were needin' them. I didna go in, but I gathered from Mrs MacCrimmon that the lads were still wi' her at Linnochmore.'

'Thank you, Elsie. That was very kind of you to take up the food, and blankets as well. O, I do hope Hamish has remembered the secret of the hidden chamber! Otherwise I don't know what will happen. I've just heard that someone has reported the rebels, and the Redcoats are coming to search the glen tomorrow. The night is getting late but I must go up to Linnochmore at once and warn them.'

'Will you take another pair o' blankets wi' you then, Miss Lora? I have them handy.'

'Thank you! Yes, I'll take them, Elsie.'

With the blankets a rather bulky bundle under her cloak, Lora let herself out by the back way. As she stepped outside she fancied she smelt tobacco smoke. She quickly drew back, cautioning Loyal to stay beside her. Listening intently she thought she heard footsteps receding down the side of the house and she waited a few moments more. Then Loyal and she hurried on their way.

Linnochmore was in complete darkness. The shutters were closed, and the door was barred, but the occupants were not abed, for Lora's knock was answered almost immediately by Mrs MacCrimmon.

'Who is it?' the old lady enquired rather timorously.

'It's me, Mrs MacCrimmon, – Lora,' and the bar was quickly withdrawn.

'Guid sakes, lassie. Ye're late on the road! We didna expect ye. Elsie MacLennan fetched up the things earlier on, ye see,' Mrs MacCrimmon explained, as she held open the kitchen door.

In spite of the lateness of the hour the men were still sitting round the fire, except for Old Hamish who was snoring away in his box-bed. Relief showed on every face as they realised who the caller was.

'*Mon Dieu!* Miss Lora, you did give us a fright,' exclaimed Angus who was nearest the door. 'And you are in a ballgown! Is something wrong?'

'Yes. I've just heard that the Redcoats are coming to search the glen tomorrow! My stepmother is entertaining some English officers at The Milton and I got that piece of news from one of them.'

'Does that mean somebody has reported rebels in the glen?' asked Hamish, shocked out of his normal morose silence.

'Well, you *could* say that,' replied Lora fixing him with a somewhat accusing eye, 'but I think it's much more likely our secret was overheard in an inn, or alehouse, in Kirriemuir.'

'They certainly didna' hear it from me, then,' protested Hamish, his hackles rising. 'I never said a word aboot rebels to onybody in the toon. An' I only mentioned it to Paddy when we were comin' oot the road yesterday. Isn't that right, Paddy?'

'Sure an' it's the truth he's after tellin' ye,' Paddy assured her.

Lora didn't know whether to believe them or not.

'Have you been able to open the secret chamber?' she asked anxiously of Hamish.

'Aye. I have.'

'Thank goodness for that. I think the English may be here in the morning.'

'Blood-an'-Turf!' expostulated Paddy, 'The divil take the lot o' them! says I. Sure, it's harassed they'll be havin' every last one of us, as it is. There'll be no peace for us nowhere, not even upon the Sabbath day!'

'We'd better move from here early then?' said Alistair addressing himself to Lora.

'Yes. Don't leave it too late, whatever you do,' Lora agreed. 'Now I must go, before they miss me at The Milton.'

'I'll walk a little way with you, if you don't mind, Lora,' said Alistair. 'I could do with a breath of fresh air before I turn in.'

So they left the house together.

'Did Hamish take you up to the Peel Tower, Alistair?' Lora asked as soon as the door was closed behind them.

'Yes. He went up alone first. Then he came back for Angus and me, and took us into the secret room and along the underground passage that leads out on to the hillside.'

'How did you feel about it?'

'Quite frankly, I didn't like it at all. It made me feel almost claustrophobic, but we have to bear in mind that we are fugitives on the run. We are lucky to have faithful friends, and a safe place to go when danger threatens.'

'I only wish we had some definite plan for your escape,' Lora sighed. 'How anything is to be arranged while the glen is swarming with Redcoats, I simply can't imagine.'

'The money to pay for it all has still to be found, of course,' Alistair reminded her. 'I haven't very much, and poor Angus has virtually nothing at all. Unless we find his father's buried hoard, our prospects are bleak.'

'Even though you *do* find plenty of gold pieces Alistair, I'm afraid I wouldn't know how to set about planning an escape route.' said Lora.

'Paddy the Pedlar seems to think he might have some contacts,' observed Alistair.

'Paddy the Pedlar? What possible contacts could he have?'

'One never knows. Pedlars are always on the move, up and down the countryside, and they meet people from all walks of life. You don't seem to like Paddy much, Lora, and I must admit I didn't care for the look of him either, at first, but he grows on one. He has been especially kind and helpful as far as Angus is concerned, so that has helped to change my opinion of him, I suppose. But he also has a naturally cheerful disposition which has proved a benefit to all of us at this time. His fund of amusing stories is endless. Mrs MacCrimmon also appears to be very fond of him, and she has known him all his life, so that, too, is in his favour. Nevertheless, I have warned Angus not to show the letter or the chart to either Hamish or Paddy.'

'I doubt if the letter would mean much to them, Alistair. Hamish can't read, and I don't suppose the Pedlar can either.'

'I wouldn't be too sure about him,' Alistair remarked thoughtfully. 'Paddy's conversation is not without intelligence. In fact, from remarks he has passed, I have got the impression that he has travelled in foreign lands although he has never actually said so. All in all, I have come to the conclusion that he is no ordinary pedlar – at least he is not like any other pedlar I have ever come across. I believe he might well be able to help us, and we are grateful for his friendship.'

'I'd have thought he'd have gone back to Kirriemuir by now. There is nothing for him to do here,' said Lora.

'Oh, he's been going out and about on his pony, peddling his wares as usual. So he's not losing in any way. Besides, he's getting plenty of good food at Linnochmore, thanks to you! and a nice warm bed among the hay in the byre. What more could he want?' grinned Alistair.

'What more, indeed!' echoed Lora. 'It must seem like a palace, after that awful lodging-house in Skinner's Close!'

Lora, by now, had quite forgotten her need for haste, and their walk had slowed to a crawl. Deep in conversation, but keeping their voices low, they moved quietly down the path with Loyal just a little way ahead of them. Although there was no moon visible, the night was fairly clear. It was also very still, and only the occasional bleating of sheep on the slopes of Ben Reid broke the silence. All of a sudden, a startled roe deer darted across the path in front, and vanished into the long grass on the other side. Loyal immediately took up the chase, while Lora and Alistair paused, expecting at any moment to see the reason for the little animal's flight. No other creature appeared, however, and silence reigned as before.

'That's strange,' remarked Lora, looking around her. 'Something must have disturbed that deer.'

As they strained their ears to catch the slightest sound, a movement on the path below attracted Alistair's attention.

'Someone's coming up the path,' he said softly, 'someone tall.'

As Lora peered through the trees the awful truth dawned on her.

'Quick, Alistair! Take cover,' she whispered urgently. 'It may be someone looking for me.'

'With a red tunic?' queried Alistair almost disbelievingly.

'Yes! Get out of sight! Quickly!'

Alistair needed no further bidding, while Lora, without more ado, strode on down the path to meet the newcomer. She had a fair idea it might be Lennox Bullard, and she was right.

'So there you are!' he hailed her. 'What a lucky chance I came this way. Why did you walk out on me like that?'

'I didn't walk out on you. My dog needs an airing last thing at night and I hate to disappoint him. But how did you know to come this way?'

Lennox grinned, 'I must admit, it wasn't just chance, Lora. I went to look for you after Paul had left me, and you were nowhere to be seen. I thought perhaps you'd gone to bed, but your sister Susan went up to your room, and, of course, you weren't there. She remembered that you were in the habit of walking your dog about this time so she suggested I take this path. She gave me directions. But why couldn't you have asked me to accompany you on your walk, pray?'

'You were otherwise engaged, remember,' Lora answered demurely.

'So I was! All right, you're forgiven. But why shouldn't we go for a stroll now? It's really quite a pleasant night.'

'I agree it's a pleasant night, but it's also quite chilly. I think I'd rather return to the house, if you don't mind.'

'Of course! How stupid of me! I'd forgotten you were only wearing a ball dress under your cloak. Come, take my arm. The path is very rough, and those loose stones can be treacherous.'

Lora smiled to herself. If only he knew how familiar she was with every step of the way! What would he think, she wondered, if he knew how many times she had traversed that self-same path during the past week. However, she took the proffered arm and they chatted happily together as they made their way back leisurely to The Milton.

Loyal joined them as they reached the footbridge. Continuing arm-in-arm across the stable yard Lora and Lennox came suddenly face to face with the other officers going to fetch their horses. They were accompanied by Paul Reynolds.

'Oh ho! And where, may I ask, have you two been?' demanded the CO in mock solemnity. 'I must say you young dogs are fast workers nowadays when it comes to courting the fair sex. In my day it took much longer than one short evening to persuade a young lady to go out walking. But perchance the ladies bestow their favours more freely nowadays. There may be something in that. Eh? What?' he boomed. His conversation seemed mainly addressed to Lennox and the other gentlemen, but, as he spoke, his eyes were fixed intently on Lora's face. To her they appeared sharp and cruel eyes that sought to penetrate into her innermost thoughts. She felt a shiver of apprehension run down her spine. No secret would ever be safe from such a man! It was as if those eyes could reach into the furthest recesses of one's mind. He was well-named 'Hawkeye'!

'It's as well you returned when you did, Lieutenant Bullard,' she heard him saying, 'otherwise you'd have had the pleasure of riding to Kirriemuir alone. Pay your respects to your hostess, sir, and fetch your horse at once. We leave immediately.'

Lieutenant Bullard drew himself up respectfully, clicked his heels and saluted.

'Very good sir,' he replied, and, bowing rather apologetically to Lora, he obeyed the orders of his superior and hastened off towards the house to take his leave of Mrs Macrae. Lora was simply left standing, and she was painfully aware of Paul as an interested onlooker. She was also somewhat shaken by the eye-to-eye encounter with Lennox's uncle. Either the man had taken an instant dislike to her, or he thoroughly disapproved of her association with his nephew. 'Probably both, and most likely because I'm Scottish,' Lora said to herself. In any case, she had no intention of being humbled by a Redcoat. Drawing herself up to her full height she looked him calmly in the face and bade him a cool 'Good-night'. After exchanging brief farewells with the other officers, she called Loyal to heel. Then, holding her head high, she walked with a quiet unhurried dignity towards the house.

Lora met Lieutenant Bullard on his way back to the stables and he paused to say, 'Thank you for a very enjoyable evening, Lora dear. I hope to see you again very soon. Please forgive my having to desert you like that.'

'Certainly, I forgive you. You had no alternative,' Lora answered readily, and she held out her hand in a friendly gesture of farewell. Instead of shaking her hand, Lennox bent and kissed it. '*Au revoir,*' he called from the corner of the house, and then he was gone.

'Pity he's a Redcoat,' Lora said to herself, with a sigh. 'I really like that man, but I wouldn't want to have much to do with his uncle!'

Having given Loyal his supper and seen him settled for the night in his usual place by the fire in the hall, Lora rejoined the other guests. She was met by a distinctly frosty look from her stepmother, which was not surprising. Lora knew very well that only the presence of the guests prevented her receiving a severe reprimand for her extended absence, and she thought wryly of the trouble that was building up for her in the very near future.

When Paul returned to the house after seeing off the party of Dragoons, the guests decided to retire to bed. As Lora was about to follow them upstairs Paul called her back.

'Congratulations, Lora!' he said, eyeing her with an amused grin.

'On what, pray?'

'On your cunning strategy this evening. I must say it was cleverly carried out. No one could have guessed – least of all your victim!'

'My victim? What do you mean?'

'You know very well whom and what I mean. Lennox Bullard of course. Who else?'

'Paul! How horrid you can be!' exclaimed Lora, her cheeks flushed with annoyance.

Paul interpreted the flush as a maidenly blush.

'I guessed wrongly then, did I? You are truly attracted to old Lennox. Well I never! Who would have thought it! An Englishman, and a Redcoat into the bargain! Fie! Fie! Lora! You are letting the side down surely!'

Lora would normally have vehemently denied Paul's insinuations but the memory of his behaviour towards her throughout the evening made her change her mind.

'He is very, very charming,' she said slowly and deliberately, as if savouring the memory. 'In fact, I think he is rather special, the English Lieutenant.'

'By Jove! You sound as if you really mean that!' exclaimed Paul looking somewhat puzzled.

'I think I do – in fact I'm sure I *do* mean it,' said Lora, blushing slightly as if her words had even surprised herself. 'But it *is* true. Lennox is very nice. Even if he is a Redcoat! By the way, you seem very familiar with him, Paul. Have you met before somewhere?'

'Yes. As a matter of fact I know Lennox very well. We went to school together. We also did our army training at the same time. Tell me though, Lora, did you manage to get any vital information out of him tonight? I noticed you were plying him with questions when I disturbed you in the library.'

'Really, Paul!' Lora protested angrily, 'you are forever spying on me! I have nothing more to say to you except "good-night",' and, with that, Lora ended the conversation and continued on her way upstairs.

It had been a long day, with many unpleasant surprises, and now another worry would have to be coped with – how to keep the rebels' presence a secret under the very nose of the English army.

The real testing-time was just about to begin.

VII THE NET TIGHTENS

The arrival of the English troops in the glen was heralded by the clang of iron-shod hooves, the jingling of bridles and the tramp of marching feet. To Lora the noise sounded like the knell of doom. With one accord, the Macraes and their guests rose from their Sunday breakfast table and rushed to view the spectacle.

Almost immediately, Susan gave a squeal of delight and waltzed Lora round and round. 'Hurrah!' she cried, 'Lawrie Heathcote is here after all! He said he'd try to get the posting, but he felt sure Lennox Bullard would be favoured, considering his uncle is the Major. I'm sorry, Lora, 'cos I think your Lennox is quite special, but oh, I did *so* want Lawrie to come!'

Lora assured Susan she was pleased for her, and indeed she meant what she said. With Lennox Bullard around in the evenings, life could only have become more complicated as far as she was concerned.

Clova Kirk had no manse at that time and, therefore, no resident minister, but the minister from the parish of Cortachy came to preach in the little kirk every third Sunday. On those occasions the entire household at The Milton, from Mrs Macrae to the humblest servant, attended the Presbyterian church service. All, that is to say, except Paul who was a confirmed Episcopalian. Today Paul had decided to show Maria round Glen Doll while the others were at church, and Lora had seen them ride off up the glen soon after breakfast. Maria looked extremely attractive in her riding habit and seemed to be as competent a horsewoman as she was a musician.

THE NET TIGHTENS

While Lora was dressing for church, a letter was delivered to her room. It was from Lieutenant Bullard. Written in a firm, legible hand it read:

> My dear L,
>
> It is truly with sadness in my heart that I pen these lines to you.
>
> I begged my uncle, almost on bended knee, to allow me to accompany the detachment to Glen Clova, but he was quite adamant. In fact, he told me that he had already approved a transfer for me. Apparently I am soon to take charge of a small Company based near the coast. There is much rebel activity around that area now, and my uncle thinks a young man like me should see more action. So, it would appear my stay in this district may be a short one.
>
> We were all surprised to learn this morning that the Major had decided to return to Clova to take charge of operations there himself. This is all the more surprising because it is such a small-scale search. I can only conclude that the real reason is to further his acquaintance with your stepmother! As you are probably aware, my uncle is a bachelor. So, who knows, I may yet call your stepmother 'Aunt'! What would that make us, I wonder? No time for more. Duty calls, and I must obey. I hope to give this into the hand of Lieutenant Heathcote for safe delivery to you.
>
> I shall never forget our happy evening together.
>
> Adieu, my dear, until we meet again,
>
> Your sincere and sorrowful friend,
>
> LRB

Lora heaved a sigh as she folded the letter. How nice of Lennox to write to her, but then he was that sort of fellow – kind and thoughtful.

Susan came bursting into the bedchamber at that moment to see if Lora was ready to leave for church.

'So you got your *billet-doux* from Lennox! Lawrie brought it here himself, and he and I had a little chat,' she announced happily. 'Did you know that Major Saunders is to be billeted here with us? Mamma invited him to make this his headquarters. The other officer and Lawrie are to be in camp with the men, down in the haugh by the river. Major Saunders was saying he doesn't expect to be in the glen more than a day or two, but it'll be nice to have Lawrie so near, even for a little while. I just wish your Lennox had been with them too, Lora. He's such good fun.'

There was quite a boisterous breeze blowing, as the house-party from The Milton set out to walk the two hundred yards or so to the kirk. It made the ladies glad of their poke bonnets, but it wasn't a cold wind, and there was quite a heat in the sun for the time of year. It was the sort of morning that emphasised the full beauty of the glen, with the hills etched sharply against the clear blue of the sky. All the natural sounds of the countryside were there as usual, but the mill wheel and the forge were silent, as were the harvest fields. It was the Sabbath, and therefore the day of rest.

Five minutes before midday the kirk bell began to ring out across the valley, summoning the parishioners to worship. Its solemn, yet musical, chime fell pleasantly upon the ear. Somehow it seemed to set the seal upon the Sabbath Day, and sought to encourage the little community to keep that day holy. The greetings exchanged in the kirkyard, however, indicated that the thoughts of a large proportion of those worshippers were already centred beyond the Sabbath. 'That's a fine dryin' wind for the stooks'; 'This'll mak' the lambs look weel for the market'; 'Aye, we'll sune get the hairst in, if this weather bides', were typical comments. Even on their one day of rest, the minds of those hard-working people were already occupied with the labour of the morrow. Hardly were they seated in their pews than the effects of their previous six days' labour also became evident, for many were the work-weary heads that nodded in slumber before the minister's lengthy sermon had got properly underway.

Just as the congregation were emerging from the kirk at the close of the service, an army patrol came marching up from the ford. The soldiers were immaculately turned out, and resplendent in their red coats with gold facings. Bringing up the rear, in tattered breeks and tackety boots, his bare, spindly legs completely out of step, was none other than 'the Daft Dumby', Dougal MacDougall. He shouldered a piece of stick in place of a musket, and was obviously enjoying the business of soldiering to the very utmost of his ability. In fact, he almost succeeded in making a mockery of that smart patrol, and the onlookers in the kirkyard were highly amused. On realising that he had such an appreciative audience, Dougal's antics increased. As he strode along, he pulled faces, doffed his cap, and saluted, for the benefit of the younger spectators. Soon old and young alike were convulsed with laughter.

Mrs Macrae and party (being 'the gentry from the Big Hoose') were always given priority in order of exit from the church. They were, therefore, ahead of the main body of worshippers and saw nothing of Dougal's performance. Led by Mrs Macrae they were descending the small slope from the kirk gate to the roadway when the army patrol came swinging into view, and they stopped to let the soldiers pass. At that moment Dougal's eyes alighted on Lora. Flushed with the success of his new rôle of entertainer, he dropped out of the military column, and came marching over to where she stood. With a smart salute, and grinning from ear to ear, he came to a halt in front of her. Then, with chortles of 'O-ooh' and 'E-eeh', he hunched up one shoulder, and peeped coyly at her out of the corner of his eye. Placing a finger to his lips, to denote secrecy, he began rolling his eyes and jerking his head in the direction of the departing soldiers, as if, in some way, the secret concerned them. Finally, he pulled his tam-o'-shanter bonnet down over one eye, winked knowingly at Lora with the other, and commenced to march back and forth before her with an exaggerated air of bravado.

By this time the laughter among the main body of onlookers had died away (after all, one didn't joke at the expense of the gentry) but some of the country girls, about Lora's age, giggled audibly, while Mrs Macrae eyed the charade with obvious distaste. Lora, taken by surprise, could think of nothing to say to Dougal but suddenly Annie Shaw came hurrying forward and seized her cousin by the arm.

'Stop that nonsense, ye daft gowk!' she commanded, and began to drag him off up the road towards his home, scolding him as they went. Dougal, however, continued to look back over his shoulder towards Lora, winking and grinning broadly.

Mrs Macrae now turned indignantly upon Lora.

'Really, Lora!' she exclaimed in exasperation. 'I have never seen such a disgusting display. Whatever was it all about?'

'It certainly wasn't Lora's fault, Mamma,' protested Susan. 'That was just some fanciful game of Dougal's and he just happened to pick on Lora. He could just as easily have picked on you or me.'

Susan's timely interference resolved the matter for the time being, and nothing more was said about the episode, but Lora kept searching in her mind for a possible reason for Dougal's strange behaviour. However, as the guests were leaving in the afternoon there was little chance to brood.

That evening, when Lora went to collect the basket of food from the larder, Elsie opened the kitchen door and beckoned to her.

'I want a word with you, Lora,' she whispered urgently and Lora noticed that she looked carefully to right and left along the corridor before she closed the kitchen door.

'What's wrong, Elsie?' asked Lora.

'I've just been speakin' to Annie Shaw,' said Elsie, in a low voice, 'and I'm very worried. She was tellin' me that, after yon dreadful display o' Dougal MacDougall's at the kirk this mornin', she quizzed Dougal about what made him do it and she got the impression that Dougal had seen you wi' a soldier in the dark one night. Annie's an intelligent lassie, as I've said afore, and she jumped to the conclusion that that might be the reason for you takin' stuff from the larder. She went as far as to suggest that you were maybe carryin' food to the rebel soldiers that were supposed to be hidin' in the glen. I just hope she hasna mentioned any o' this to Lizzie or Jess!'

'What did you say to her, Elsie?'

'I said she'd better no' repeat such nonsense. Knowing her cousin Dougal, he'd probably just imagined the whole thing, and if such a tale reached the ears o' the military it could cause a lot o' trouble. I didna' forget to warn her that she'd be involved if she continued to spread that story withoot any real foundation.'

'Thank you, Elsie,' said Lora gratefully.

'As regards the baskets o' food,' continued Elsie, 'I informed her that I was well aware where they were goin', and that I'd been visitin' the invalid mysel'. I think Annie believed me, and she's the kind o' lassie that'll pay attention.'

Lora thought the matter over for a few minutes.

'Did Annie say if she had any idea where and when Dougal had seen me with a soldier – if indeed he did see me?' she asked.

'No. Annie didna say, but ye'll need to watch out for Dougal now. D'ye mind how he used to hero-worship ye, an' follow ye around when he was a wee laddie?'

'Yes. I do remember that, but I hadn't seen him in the glen for some time. I thought someone said he'd gone to learn to be a cobbler with an uncle of his.'

'Aye, that's right. He went to Forfar to his mother's brother but he came back a few days ago. Poor laddie, he was homesick for the glen, his mother said. He was miserable withoot his pet squirrel, an' his pet hedgehog and such like. The dumb animals mean so much to him, he was really pinin' for them. Of course, the uncle and aunt had difficulty communicatin' wi Dougal, which wouldna' help. He's just a poor soul – more to be pitied than laughed at.'

Lora was much more upset about all this than she cared to admit. It had occurred to her, from what Elsie had said, that Dougal might well have been the spy on the hillside – the dark silhouette on the skyline that had filled her with so much foreboding.

'I suppose I should be glad if that were so,' she said to herself. 'Very few people in the glen would have the faintest idea what he was trying to tell them, and the Redcoats wouldn't be able to get any sense out of him at all.'

On arrival at Linnochmore Lora was informed that Alistair was most anxious to speak with her.

'He said it was urgent, so I'll tak' ye up to The Peel now, if ye like,' Hamish offered. 'It'll be a chance to let ye see exactly where the underground passage comes oot on the hill. I canna bide here much longer and it looks as if it may well be necessary to carry up supplies for a while yet.'

'Have you seen any sign of the Redcoats around Linnochmore?' Lora asked.

'No. There's been no sign o' life here,' Mrs MacCrimmon replied. 'Ye're the first visitor we've had a' day.'

'I'm sorry my visit is to be so short then, and unfortunately, my future visits may be dictated by Major Saunders's presence at The Milton, but I'll come whenever I dare,' Lora assured the old lady, as she and Hamish set off for the old castle.

There was no moon, but the night was starry, and Hamish was now quite familiar with the route. He led the way, and Lora followed closely in his footsteps, with Loyal at her heel. Not a word was spoken, but they made good speed, for both were very sure-footed, and well used to the rough terrain.

'I'll better let ye see where the "chappin' stane" is,' remarked Hamish, when they reached the castle tower.

'The "chappin' stane"? What's that?'

86

'It's this oval-shaped flat stane built into the wa'. Can ye see which I mean? Ye'd better get the feel o' it, since ye'll likely have to find it in the dark. Have ye got it?'

'I think so,' said Lora. 'The stone I'm touching seems to be oval-shaped.'

'Aye. That's it right enough,' said Hamish, after a quick check. 'If ye chap on it wi' anither stane they can hear the noise inside,' and he stooped to demonstrate what he meant. 'We used to use this signal in 1715 and it still works. When Alistair hears the chappin' he'll start crawlin' alang the passage and he'll meet ye at the other end. But mind, it must be the richt stane. Ye could chap on any other stane in the whole Tower and the folk inside would never hear a thing.'

They stopped only long enough to make doubly sure that Lora had got the idea, and could identify the right stone by the feel of it. Then they moved on.

Fortunately the base of the castle was screened from the Glen Doll roadway by a belt of birch trees, and the route to the passage exit was behind those trees. Large boulders of various shapes and sizes had rolled down the hillside over the centuries and it was one of those boulders that Hamish was seeking. Even though he had been to it many times in his youth, he still found it difficult to locate, and the darkness of the night made his task even more difficult. Had Alistair not poked out his head and guided them by a low whistle, they might well have searched half the night.

As they approached the spot, Lora could see that this massive boulder, on its journey down the hillside, had come to rest in such a way that one part of it jutted out about two or three feet above ground like a canopy. Close into the base of the rock, and screened by a combination of coarse grass, heather roots, and blaeberry bushes, there was just enough space for a human body to slip down under this canopy. What Hamish had said was true – the opening was well nigh impossible to find.

After they had exchanged a brief greeting, and Alistair had taken charge of the basket of food, it was decided, for safety's sake, that Lora should join Alistair underground to have their conversation, while Hamish and Loyal kept watch on the hillside.

'There's quite a sizeable cave hollowed out down here at the end of the passage, and we *do* have a candle,' said Alistair.

Getting under the canopy took a bit of ingenuity, to say the least. The rough stone steps leading down into the cave had deteriorated with time, and were awkward and slippery to negotiate. However, with Alistair's help from below, and Hamish's help from above ground, Lora succeeded in making the descent.

'I can see what you mean by feeling claustrophobic,' she said to Alistair with a shudder, as the flickering candle lit up the earthen walls. 'Where's Angus?'

'He remained behind, in the Tower room. One either has to bend double, or crawl on all fours, from here to the Tower, and it isn't easy for him with his injured leg.'

'What was it you wanted to speak to me about? Have you found the gold pieces left by Angus's father?' Lora asked eagerly.

'No we haven't had a proper search yet. I asked to see you because I wanted to warn you, Lora, that someone was spying on you last night.'

'Spying on *me? Where?*'

'Remember the frightened roe deer that crossed the path in front of us last night? Well, after you'd gone on down the path to intercept your Redcoat friend, another fellow, in rather ragged attire, crawled out of the long grass almost exactly where the deer broke cover.'

'He didn't see you, did he, Alistair?'

'No. He didn't even glance in my direction, but he followed you and your friend down the path, keeping at a discreet distance.'

'What did he look like?'

'He was very thin – his legs were like spindles in his boots, and he had a shock of fuzzy hair. That was about all I had time to notice.'

'I know who it must have been – Dougal MacDougall. What you've just told me explains quite a lot,' and Lora went on to tell Alistair about the embarrassing episode at the church gate. 'There is a disappointing side to this too,' she added. 'You see, I had quite made up my mind that Dougal must have been the spy on the hillside, and the idea pleased me – for obvious reasons! Now, alas, that idea has been ruled out. Well, I'd better get away home. The Redcoats encamped in the glen today and the commanding officer is billeted at The Milton. I met him last night and we took an instant dislike to each other, so I certainly don't want to arouse his suspicions.'

Alistair was immediately concerned for Lora's safety. 'We don't need food every night. We can make this last for two or three days, if necessary. Please don't take any more risks for us, Lora. I have been worrying about the old people too. You don't think the Redcoats have any inkling we were staying at Linnochmore, do you?'

'If the report had mentioned Linnochmore they'd have gone there straight away, I should think, and the MacCrimmons hadn't seen anything of Redcoats all day. I expect the house-to-house search will start tomorrow.'

'We shall pray for the safety of all our kind friends,' said Alistair earnestly, as he helped Lora out of the narrow opening.

When Lora arrived back at The Milton she popped into the kitchen to tell Elsie what Alistair had seen of Dougal the previous evening.

'That's fine to know,' said the housekeeper. 'If Annie begins about you an' the rebels again, I can tell her the right way o' the story now.'

Major Saunders was in the library with Mrs Macrae, Susan, and Paul, and they were telling him all about the people of the glen when Lora joined them. After a brief pause, the conversation continued, and this gave Lora a chance to observe the Major. She guessed his age to be about sixty. He was not a particularly robust-looking man. His hair was grey and his thin face seemed rather peaked and tired. Although he had height, he somehow lacked the build one normally associates with military men in positions of authority. Nevertheless, he exuded a definite air of command, and his hawk-like appearance and penetrating eyes sent another shiver of apprehension down Lora's spine.

At that moment Susan's voice cut in on her meditations.

'Oh, by the way, Lora,' she was remarking, 'I thought you said to me the MacCrimmons' niece's husband was deaf. When I was walking past the house yesterday I saw him carrying a pitcher of water from the well. Mrs MacCrimmon called to him from the doorway and he answered at once. In fact, they carried on quite a long-distance conversation.'

For a moment Lora was taken aback by this untimely remark, but she quickly recovered her equanimity and answered quietly, 'The person you probably saw was Old Hamish's nephew, Susan. The niece's husband was definitely hard of hearing.'

'Excuse me, but were those people you speak of actually strangers in the community?' enquired the Major, immediately on the alert.

'No. Of course not. They all originally belong here,' Lora replied.

'Where is their home now?'

'I think they live in Braemar, or somewhere in that direction. Hamish's nephew, of course, comes from Kirriemuir.'

'Are they still residing here?'

'No. The niece and her husband have gone home.'

'How long were they here, and when did they leave?'

'I really couldn't say,' replied Lora evenly. 'I wasn't interested enough to enquire into their affairs.'

'Then I take it that you are still mixing with those people, in spite of all I have said to you on the subject,' Mrs Macrae interrupted rather tartly at this point. 'From now on, Lora, I must insist that you cease to visit those people in their homes, and I must ask you, also, to give up those nightly excursions forthwith. It is unseemly for a young lady like you to go out unaccompanied after nightfall.'

'I am not unaccompanied, Aunt Gwyneth,' Lora protested. 'Loyal is always with me, and I certainly cannot give up taking him for his walk before bedtime.'

'Who is this "Loyal" you speak of?' queried Major Saunders.

'Loyal is my dog, and my loyal companion,' Lora replied. 'No one would dare to lay a hand on me when Loyal is near.'

'I gather this – er – Loyal was not with you the other evening in Kirriemuir, then?'

'What do you mean, sir?'

'I mean your dog wasn't with you that night on which one of my

89

troopers offered to escort you home and got two black eyes for his trouble.'

There was dead silence in the room. One could have heard a pin drop, and Mrs Macrae's face registered a mixture of horror and indignation.

'What is the meaning of this, Lora?' she demanded, 'When were you in Kirriemuir unescorted? I demand an explanation at once.'

But before Lora could say a word, Paul intervened.

'*I* shall explain, Aunt Gwyneth,' he said, 'for I was the person who gave that trooper what he richly deserved.'

'Y-you, Paul?' stammered Mrs Macrae, quite baffled by these revelations.

'Yes. Lora and I were both in Kirriemuir, as it happened, and Lora was walking from her dressmaker to the inn where our horses were stabled. In the narrow pend leading from the Market Square, some troopers deliberately accosted Lora. She asked them to step aside but the leader refused to do so. I arrived on the scene as the man laid hold of her. Naturally, I intervened. A hand-to-hand fight ensued, to which the marks on my face bear testimony. Eventually other people joined in, and it became a proper pitched battle. Did you see anything of the fight, sir?' Paul asked, turning to the Major.

'Yes. I arrived on the scene later. When I enquired as to the cause of the trouble, one of the townspeople said the quarrel arose over a young woman from one of the glens, but no one seemed to know who the young man was who had championed her. I dismissed the matter from my mind, but the trooper concerned happens to be with us on this exercise and he recognised Miss Macrae as he passed the church this morning. I should advise you to have a care, young lady, and you too, Mr Reynolds, for the man is inclined to harbour a grudge. Being a big fellow, and a corporal, he would definitely resent a beating, especially in front of his men. In fact, I am surprised that a young person like yourself was able to cope with him, Mr Reynolds. You must be tougher than you look. Now, you must excuse me, please. We have an early start tomorrow, and I am not as young as I used to be. If you don't mind, Mrs Macrae, I shall retire to bed.' So saying, Major Saunders bowed himself out, and Mrs Macrae hurried after him to ask about breakfast arrangements for the following morning.

Lora had no wish to become involved in an argument with her stepmother, so she also excused herself, took her candle, and hurried upstairs to her room. Sleep was very far from her mind, however, and instead of undressing, she sat down rather wearily on the edge of her bed. With her elbows resting on her knees, and her chin cupped in her hands, she stared forlornly at the flickering candle. Her spirits had reached a low ebb.

Gradually the other members of the household made their way to their respective rooms, and silence reigned in the old house. Some time later the creaking of a floorboard outside her bedroom door roused Lora from her reverie. She knew a moment of real fear as she heard someone fumbling with the door handle. Hastily she looked around for something with which to defend herself against a possible intruder, but a familiar voice sounded through the keyhole. It was Paul. Sheer relief set Lora trembling from head to foot.

'Lora! Are you awake? May I come in?' he asked, in an urgent whisper.

Lora hastily pulled herself together and answered as calmly as possible.

'Yes. Come in, Paul. The door isn't locked.'

Paul opened the door with the greatest of care, and slid silently into the room. Then, like a flash, he swung round, as if expecting someone to be creeping up on him from the rear. He remained peering along the corridor until satisfied that all was well, whereupon he closed the door, almost soundlessly, and turned the key in the lock.

His furtive movements puzzled Lora.

'What is it, Paul? What's wrong?' she asked breathlessly.

'I'm sorry to disturb you at this late hour, Lora,' Paul apologised, 'but I saw a pencil of light under your door, so I guessed you'd still be awake, and I thought this might be the only chance I'd get to talk to you alone. Do you realise you are in grave danger?'

'From Major Saunders?' Lora asked at once.

'Yes. I'm almost certain the Major suspects you of being in some way involved with the Jacobite rebels. He is a very shrewd man, and Susan's unfortunate remarks about the MacCrimmons' relatives weren't lost on him. She may well have put ideas into his head. If that is so, he'll watch you like a hawk from now on.'

'Like a hawk, is an apt description,' Lora agreed ruefully. 'Lennox told me his uncle's nickname in the army is "Hawkeye".'

'Exactly. That's why I was exercising so much care. Where are the rebels meantime, Lora? Are they still in the glen?'

'Yes they are.'

'Not in the cottage at Linnochmore though, I hope?'

'No. they are in a safe hiding place.'

'Yes, but how safe? Remember there's a full-scale search in progress.'

'Nevertheless, I think their present hiding place is quite secure,' said Lora guardedly, determined not to divulge any information on that score.

'Have you been able to arrange an escape route yet?' was Paul's next query.

'No. Unfortunately. Not so far,' Lora sighed.

'In that case, would you like me to try to do something for them?'

'But I thought you didn't hold with the Jacobite cause?' Lora reminded him, in some surprise.

'I don't, but (he paused a moment before continuing) 'I am prepared to do this for the sake of Aunt Gwyneth and Susan, and because of all that The Milton has come to mean to me. If *you* are caught, you know, everyone, and everything here, will suffer.'

These words dispelled any ideas Lora might have had about Paul's concern for *her* safety. She was in no position to stand on her dignity, however, so she swallowed her pride. 'Thank you. We shall be very grateful if you can do something to help,' she said humbly.

'Well now, I am travelling to the port of Dundee tomorrow on business and I shall be there for a few days. Most of my time will be spent on the quayside and it is just possible I may be able to persuade some ship's captain to take the two men aboard. Have they any means at their disposal? In other words, would they be prepared to pay a fair price for the risk involved? Money always tips the balance in cases of this kind, you know.'

'Yes. I realise that. At the moment I don't think they have much between them, but they have the hope of more quite soon. If they can't pay the sum involved, then I shall willingly provide the money myself, so don't let that prove a stumbling block,' replied Lora.

'Were you previously acquainted with those men?' Paul asked next.

'No.'

'Then how exactly did you become involved?'

Lora truthfully described how she had been shouting 'Loyal' over and over again, for the simple pleasure of hearing the word echo through the hills, and how Alistair had come into the wood to investigate. She fully expected Paul to say 'Didn't I warn you?' but, instead, he merely asked 'What are the full names of the men?'

'Angus Lindsay and Alistair Drummond.'

'Have they any local connections? Sometimes that proves helpful.'

'Angus Lindsay is a descendant of the Lindsays of Clova. The old castle was a stronghold of the Lindsays. That was why the rebels fled here after Culloden. Angus's father had instructed him if ever he was in need of help to head for Glen Clova and seek out Hamish MacCrimmon – Old Hamish's nephew. He was batman to Angus's father in 1715,' Lora explained.

'Hamish's nephew was the man you were looking for in Kirriemuir?'

'Yes.'

'I take it you found him, for I heard you tell Susan it was him she had seen at Linnochmore. Is he still there?'

'Yes he is.'

'Good. Could you see him early and ask him to accompany me tomorrow morning? I shall be leaving around seven o'clock. When I have found someone willing to smuggle rebels across to France or the Netherlands, and have sealed the bargain, I shall send MacCrimmon back to arrange the men's journey to Dundee.' Paul paused a moment to think the matter over. 'On second thoughts, Lora, it might be wiser to tell MacCrimmon to set out for Kirriemuir ahead of me. I shall easily catch him up on the way. I don't suppose he has a mount of his own, has he?'

'No, he hasn't, and the MacCrimmons' old mare isn't able for a long journey.'

'In that case, you could let him have one of the horses from our stables.

Remember, he's to leave before me – about a quarter to the hour should be sufficient. Now I must get to bed.'

As Paul turned to go, Lora put a hand on his arm.

'Thank you, Paul, for this, and also for the way you came to my aid in the library tonight. Your timely interference saved a very awkward situation. I am truly grateful.'

For answer, Paul simply placed his hand over hers. No word was spoken but Lora was painfully aware of the hot colour suffusing her cheeks. Thankfully her back was towards the light and she kept her head down and her face averted. Into her mind came the memory of Paul's comforting arms around her on that dreadful day when her father had been killed. How she longed for that same comfort now in the midst of all her troubles.

Paul cleared his throat as if to say something more, but changed his mind. Instead, he gave Lora's hand just one quick reassuring squeeze. Before she had realised it, the door had been opened and closed and Paul was gone – as quickly and as silently as he had come.

While Lora prepared for bed she reflected, rather sadly, on the vagaries of life. Since reaching adulthood and attending parties and balls in the various great houses of the county she had had no lack of male admirers. Indeed, she had virtually taken it for granted that, in the not too distant future, she would meet and fall in love with one of those young gentlemen who would, in due course, ask for her hand in marriage. All very right and proper, with no problems whatever. How very different it was all turning out to be! In the space of two or three days (and quite irrationally, it would seem, considering the life-and-death gamble she was at present involved in) she had allowed herself to become preoccupied with not one but *two* young men, both of whom were equally unsuitable. How could she hope to glean any happiness from a closer relationship with either of them, when one was already betrothed, and the other was an English soldier – the enemy of her countrymen?

Resolutely Lora turned her mind back to the all-important matter of the fugitives and the part she must play in their rescue. She concentrated solely on Paul's visit to her room, and the instructions he had given her regarding the next day's procedure. Yet, strange to say, the person who dominated her dreams that night was not Paul Reynolds. Nor was it a Jacobite rebel. It was a handsome, fair-haired Englishman, with laughing blue eyes *and a scarlet coat!*

Bearing in mind the Major's remark about his intention of making an early start, Lora rose at the crack of dawn to avoid the likelihood of a chance meeting. She also took special precautions to get to the stables without becoming visible from Major Saunders's bedroom window. The stable hands were not astir so she was able to select the pony she wanted, saddle it, and lead it out of the stable without the embarrassment of explanations.

There was no sign of life at Linnochmore, and Lora saw no reason to arouse the MacCrimmons, so she headed for the shed where Hamish and Paddy slept. All was silence there too, but she knocked loudly on the shed door with her fist. The knock must have wakened both men for some whispering ensued. Then Hamish came towards the door.

'Who's there?' he demanded.

'It's me – Lora Macrae. I've a message for you, Hamish.'

At this Hamish opened the door, and Lora beckoned to him to come outside, as her message was for his ears only.

Hastily, and keeping her voice low, she outlined Paul's plan.

'Will you go, Hamish?' she asked anxiously.

'Aye, certainly I'll go, Miss. I'll leave as soon as I've had my porridge.'

'Here's the pony, then,' said Lora, handing him the reins. 'Paul said you should leave about a quarter to seven. Please tell Mrs MacCrimmon I'll be up as usual in the evening, if at all possible,' and, with that, Lora sped back to The Milton.

By that time she was wide awake and had no desire to go back to bed. Instead, she sat down on her window-seat to watch for Hamish. At exactly the appointed time she was pleased to see him go riding by. What she was not so pleased to see was his travelling companion – Paddy O'Malley!

At the entrance to The Milton the riders were stopped by soldiers awaiting the appearance of the Major, but Lora was relieved to see that after only the slightest delay the pair were allowed to proceed on their way. No doubt the Redcoats had recognised them as familiar faces in the Kirriemuir brew-houses.

'I wonder what Paul will say when he sees two of them,' she mused.

With the arrival of the Major, the party of soldiers turned in the direction of Glen Doll. A little later, Paul trotted out of the gate on Nero and headed south for Kirriemuir.

As she watched horse and rider fade to a mere speck in the distance, Lora's lips formed a wordless prayer that, even now, with the scales weighted so heavily against them, their efforts to save the lives of two of the hunted remnants of Prince Charlie's loyal band might yet be crowned with success.

VIII DRAMA OF THE PEAT BOG

For the first two days the Redcoat search was concentrated mainly south of The Milton. When Lora was out walking, or riding, she could see the soldiers spread over the countryside and she heard talk of how all the homesteads on both sides of the glen had been thoroughly searched and the inhabitants interrogated – fortunately, so far, without serious incident.

On the Wednesday morning Lora noticed increased military activity had begun around The Milton. From her window she could see the harvesters being questioned in the fields, and anyone who happened to come around the mill, the smithy, or the alehouse. The soldiers were also systematically searching the cottages, and they penetrated as far as the stables and other outhouses of the mansion house, but no one requested entry into the house itself. When Lora took Rufus for a gallop along the Glen Doll road she could see Redcoats dotted over the mountainsides and combing the woods, but, by midday, a wetting Scotch mist had enshrouded the landscape, and some of the soldiers had had to abandon their project and return to camp.

Since Sunday, Lora had stayed away from Linnochmore and The Peel Tower. She had decided, however, to attempt the journey by midweek as the men's food supply would by then be running low. She was also eager to pass on the good news that Paul was doing something positive about finding an escape route. No doubt, such news would boost Alistair and Angus's morale and give them heart to endure their present miserable living conditions.

The evening mealtime had come and gone without any sign of Major

Saunders. Lora was thankful for his absence, and yet that very absence filled her with a feeling of unease. Perhaps, like the bird of prey, from whence had come his nickname, he was hovering nearby, ready to swoop down whenever she ventured forth! There was also her stepmother to be reckoned with. Mrs Macrae had insisted that she refrain from making her nightly excursions, and her stepmother was quite capable of enforcing her commands.

While Lora sat by her window in the gloaming, thinking of those things, the sound of an approaching carriage reached her ears. Sure enough, a few minutes later, it came bowling up to the front door of The Milton. Lora recognised it as belonging to the Grants of Shielhill, friends of her stepmother, and her heart leapt. Fate was surely playing into her hands! She had only to wait until Aunt Gwyneth and her guests had gone into the library, or into her aunt's sitting-room. Then the coast would be clear.

Draping her cloak round her shoulders she quietly opened her door and tip-toed out on to the landing to listen to what was going on in the hall below. By the number of voices, she gathered there were two ladies in the Shielhill party, and it sounded as if they might well stand there talking all night. Just as it became apparent that they were moving into the library, another sound caught Lora's attention. Someone was riding towards the house. It would be Major Saunders returning! If she moved quickly she might just manage to get out of the way in time! Lora decided to make a bold bid for it, but she was little more than halfway down the stairs when she heard the outside door closing and the Major's purposeful step. Should she run back to her room, or remain where she was and try to look as inconspicuous as possible? She decided on the latter strategy. Nervously she kept within the shadow of the wall, and her heart almost missed a beat as she saw the Major come towards the staircase. He was just about to put his foot on the first step when, mercifully, the library door opened and Mrs Macrae emerged.

'Ah, Major Saunders, I thought it would be you! I'm sorry we had to dine without you, but if you would care to come and talk to my guests for a few minutes, I shall order food to be sent up to the dining-room at once.'

'Please do not trouble yourself, Mrs Macrae,' Lora heard the Major reply, 'I assure you I *have* eaten, and I may be going out again almost immediately.'

Nevertheless, Lora gathered that he had gone into the room to meet the guests – albeit reluctantly – for the voices retreated and she heard the library door close once more. It was now or never, and Lora didn't hesitate. With a quick dash she was across the hall and on her way. Loyal was lying in wait for her, and as soon as she had retrieved the laden basket from the pantry they were on the by now familiar path.

The close mist wrapped them in a world of their own, and the fear of being waylaid faded from Lora's mind as they headed for the castle tower. At first they made good speed but the well-filled basket was heavy. Inevitably Lora's pace slackened. On arrival at the tower, however, she had a short rest while she located the chappin' stane and tapped out the message. Once that had been done, her energy seemed to return and she stepped out with renewed vigour. The footing was treacherous among the rocks and boulders and the ground was marshy in parts, but, guided by a low whistle from Alistair, they were soon at their destination.

'Phew! I couldn't tell you how glad I am to be here!' panted Lora. 'I had imagined so many things going wrong tonight.'

'Isn't Hamish with you?' asked Alistair in surprise as he relieved her of her burden.

'No. I came alone. I'll explain, once I'm in the cave.'

'Your arm must be nearly broken by the weight of this basket,' said Alistair. 'Just wait a moment until I get it safely down the steps. Then my hands will be free to help you.'

Lora didn't enjoy crawling under the rock, among the damp vegetation, and scrambling through the narrow opening, but all went well, and Loyal quickly followed her underground.

'Is Angus ill?' she asked, when she saw that Alistair was alone again.

'No. He's all right. He just turned back to get another candle. He should be here any moment.'

'Well, I'm glad to be able to tell you, at long last, that something is being done about arranging an escape route,' and Lora went on to tell Alistair about Paul's involvement, and the reason for Hamish's absence.

While they were talking, Angus appeared from the darkness of the passage to be given a warm welcome from Loyal, with whom the young man was a great favourite.

'*Bonsoir, mademoiselle,*' he hailed Lora, when he had finished petting the dog. 'It's a pleasure to see you again,' and he grasped her hand in both of his. 'Has Alistair been telling you our good news?'

'No. I haven't had time yet,' said Alistair. 'I've been too busy listening to Lora's news,' and he hastily outlined Paul's plan.

Angus listened intently.

'*C'est magnifique!*' he exclaimed, turning to Lora, 'and our news links up well with yours, for we have found the *Louis d'ors* and the golden guineas which my father hid here in 1715! If your friend can obtain a passage for us, we shall now have ample means to pay for all favours bestowed *en route.*'

'I'm so glad you've found the gold, Angus. That will certainly make things much easier for you. I understand it is very costly to buy the kind of help you will require to get out of this country,' said Lora.

'One can't wonder at that,' Alistair hastened to point out. 'After all, whoever helps us to escape, risks putting his own neck in a noose.'

'Was the treasure difficult to find?' Lora enquired.

Angus smiled. '*Mais oui!* I think it would be true to say that it was carefully and cleverly concealed,' he said, 'but the chart was very accurate, and the booty was undoubtedly worth searching for. Look!' He held aloft a leather pouch which was obviously filled to capacity with coins.

'Perhaps Dame Fortune has decided to smile on us after all,' said Lora appreciatively. 'Now that we have exchanged our good news, I must be off, for I have reason to believe that Major Saunders views me with suspicion,' and she briefly described the happenings of the night before, which finally led to Paul's offer of help.

'As long as the Redcoats are in the glen you mustn't come back here at all,' said Alistair emphatically. 'With the CO under the same roof, it is madness to think of you carrying out basketfuls of food to us, and it is little we need at the moment, in any case, for we have no exercise to give us an appetite. I beg of you, Lora, do not risk another visit meantime. To tell you the truth I am very, very worried about the dangerous position our presence has already put you in.'

Angus echoed his concern.

'Please don't reproach yourselves,' Lora begged. 'Remember, I chose to help you of my own free will, knowing full well the risks involved and, truly, I do not regret my decision. What I fear most is that I may be followed, and your hiding place discovered. Then all would indeed be lost. I think there is little to fear tonight in that respect, for it is very misty. But I shall only come now when I feel it is safe to do so. I just hope and pray that it won't be long before Hamish returns to lead you to freedom. Please don't come outside at all tonight, Alistair. Let me leave entirely alone.'

So saying, Lora picked up the empty basket and signed to Loyal to precede her out of the cave.

The hills were still enshrouded in mist, and Loyal was nowhere to be seen by the time Lora had crawled out from under the canopy of rock. As she stood peering nervously around, unsure whether or not to risk whistling to the dog, a weird sound, coming from behind the boulder, caught her attention and caused her to glance fearfully over her shoulder. What she saw, literally made her hair stand on end. Something, or someone, was rising as if out of the ground, pointing directly at her, and making strange utterances. For a moment she wondered if the apparition was the devil himself, commonly referred to in the glen as 'Auld Nick'. Lora stifled a scream. Then, in a flash, recognition came to her. It was Dougal MacDougall!

Relief flooded over Lora, but it was short-lived when she realised Dougal wasn't actually pointing at her, but beyond her. He was trying frantically to draw her attention to something among the trees, and as she followed his pointing finger, she saw a hazy figure move stealthily out from behind a tree. At the same time there came a chorus of barking from Loyal, who had apparently been stalking the same figure.

'Get away, you brute,' came a harsh, angry voice, and there was a sound like the cut and thrust of a sword. The dog gave a yelp but continued to stand firm, barking and snarling as before.

DRAMA OF THE PEAT BOG

Lora had been rooted to the spot with terror, but concern for the safety of her pet galvanised her into action.

'Loyal! Loyal! come here!' she called urgently.

In answer to her command, Loyal began to move back towards her, still facing his quarry who was now also moving in Lora's direction. As the approaching figure became more visible through the mist, Lora's worst fears were realised. It was none other than Major Saunders! Had it not been for Dougal's timely warning, she would have walked straight into the Major's clutches.

'So! Miss Macrae!' she heard him saying, 'I have caught you redhanded, complete with the food-supply basket! Your little game is up now, and I declare you my prisoner. You have no hope of escape, so you might as well show me where the rebels are. If you don't, we shall damn well smoke them out.'

Without uttering one word, Lora simply took to her heels and fled. Loyal, delighted with this turn of events, and thinking the whole thing some kind of game, bounded on ahead of her, while Major Saunders immediately took up the chase.

Lora didn't look back, but she heard a heavy thud behind her, followed by some angry words from the Major, and she guessed that Dougal and he had, in some way, collided. Alas, the delay was but a short one. Soon there came the sound of footsteps in swift pursuit, and Lora had visions of those long military legs rapidly closing the gap.

The desperate need for escape drove everything else out of Lora's mind, and she sped on without giving a thought to the direction she was taking. The rocky terrain of the hillside proved difficult footing, but, somehow, she managed to remain upright, resolutely dodging hither and thither among the rocks and boulders in an effort to shake off her pursuer.

Once off the hill and on to the more level moorland, she was spurred on to even greater efforts until, to her dismay, she began to feel her feet sinking into black mud. Then the awful truth dawned on her. She was running headlong into a peat bog – a treacherous bog where one false step could mean a slow, sucking death, in the grip of an even more relentless enemy!

Lora shuddered at the mere thought of becoming prey to the bog, but she dare not turn back now, for she could actually hear the Major's heavy breathing. He was hard on her heels! Undoubtedly she was between the devil and the deep sea, but, whereas the bog held only danger to herself, capture now by Major Saunders might mean death to her and all who had assisted in concealing the rebels. She had heard of the terrible ways by which the Redcoats extorted information from their captives, and she feared she might not have the strength to withstand such torture and remain silent. There was no alternative! She must go on into the bog!

Loyal was moving ahead, picking his way with great care. He seemed a fairly reliable guide, so Lora followed in his wake. Every now and then she knew a moment of terror when she made a false step and felt the sucking power of the morass. Somehow she always managed to drag her foot clear, but she hadn't gone far before she had lost both of her shoes, and her stockinged feet were clogged with thick black slime. Beads of sweat stood out on Lora's brow, and so engrossed was she by this new peril that the threat presented by Major Saunders gradually became of secondary importance. So much so, that when she heard a cry for help the full significance did not immediately register on her mind. Then a louder, more insistent appeal brought Loyal, and Lora both, to a halt.

'Help! He-e-elp!' There was no mistaking it – Major Saunders had fallen victim to the peat bog! Lora hesitated. Should she go to his aid, or leave him to his fate? After all, he was her enemy. By saving him, might she not be signing her own death warrant and that of many more? Yet, even before the cry was repeated, Lora knew she must turn back. To ignore that beseeching cry from a fellow human being would surely mean that it would haunt her for the rest of her days.

'Hold on! I'm coming,' she cried, and, with Loyal once more leading the way, she began to retrace her steps.

By the time she came within sight of the Major, the bog had already got a tight hold of him. It was clear his predicament was becoming critical. What could she do? Her strength alone would be no match to that of the bog, and even to venture near the man might spell disaster for herself. Vaguely she remembered having seen some wooden spars a little way back. Possibly the remains of some cart that had got bogged down, and had had to be abandoned. She peered anxiously around. Yes! There they were, beside that wooden post!

As she went to retrieve the spars, Lora noticed that there was also a coil of rope round the post, a grim reminder of some previous rescue attempt at the self-same spot. Quickly she unwound the rope, fervently hoping that it wouldn't be rotten with age. She tested her strength on it and it held. So far, so good! Grasping the coil of rope in her hand she picked her way towards the Major.

'I'm going to throw the rope. Do you think you can catch it?' she cried.

'I think so,' came the reply, but the rope fell short.

Lora pulled it back and tried again. Three times she tried without success, and each time the effort of trying to reach the rope merely caused the Major to sink further into the bog.

Lora decided that the only way to make sure the rope reached the man would be to get closer to him herself. The spars were black with age but she selected the one which looked strongest, and it certainly resisted her efforts to break it. Armed with this spar she advanced gingerly over the squelching bog as far as she dared. Carefully she placed the spar so that it rested on two rocky mounds. Then she returned for another spar and repeated the process. Keeping a tight hold on the rope she then edged her way out along the wooden platform.

'Are you ready?' she called. Taking careful aim she threw the rope with all her strength, and this time it fell within the Major's grasp.

'Got it,' he panted. 'Do you think it will take my weight?'

'We'll just have to try it,' Lora called back. 'Tie it round your waist.'

When he pronounced himself ready, Lora braced herself and began to pull.

'I'm moving,' panted the Major, but even as he said the words, Lora's strength gave out and she had to relinquish her hold on the rope until she recovered her breath. It was quite clear she would never succeed alone.

Then she thought of Loyal. He always enjoyed a tug-of-war, and he was a powerful animal.

'Come here, Loyal,' she ordered, and the big dog obeyed her command, advancing gingerly, with ears down, and tail wagging uncertainly. The problem now was to get the dog to understand exactly what was required of him. Alas, the animal had hardly set foot on the makeshift platform than Lora noticed one of the boards was sagging with the extra weight, and both she and Loyal had to make a quick move back to firmer ground. It was then that she observed Dougal MacDougall standing a little way off. He must have seen what she was trying to do, yet he was making no attempt to lend a hand.

Lora signed frantically to him to come and join her, but Dougal shook his head vigorously and waved her appeal aside. He was grinning from ear to ear, and seemed delighted at the Major's predicament. Placing his hands in front of him, with palms down, and jerking his head in the direction of the Major, he made repeated gestures of pressing downwards. His actions spoke louder than words.

'Push him further in,' was the unmistakable message.

With Dougal in that frame of mind, Lora knew it was a waste of time to keep begging him for help, and time was what they hadn't got, so she turned her attention back to Loyal. The big dog was most anxious to please, and readily applied himself to the unusual task. Grasping the rope firmly between his teeth, he entered into the spirit of the thing with great vim and vigour.

'Come on, Loyal! Good dog! Good dog!' cried Lora encouragingly. With the extra power of Loyal's strength added to her own, it seemed that the peat bog might just decide to yield up its prey. Full of renewed hope, Lora redoubled her efforts, but at the crucial moment, the rope snapped. Lora and Loyal both landed in a heap, while the speed at which Major Saunders had been sinking was accelerated by the sudden jerk. Dougal MacDougall, on the sidelines, was convulsed with laughter at this débâcle, and indulged his merriment to the full. By this time the Major, whose military calm had stood him in good stead throughout his ordeal, had really begun to show signs of cracking under the strain. Lora too, had practically reached the point of despair. However, a quick check on the rope showed that there was still sufficient length, without the faulty piece, so the battle commenced once more.

It was now or never! With many words of encouragement from his mistress, Loyal again applied himself to the task. The big dog seemed to sense the need for an all-out effort, but Lora's own strength was beginning to fail. Then, with his usual unpredictable change of mind, Dougal suddenly decided to lend a hand after all. His decision weighed the balance in their favour. Success was in sight!

By winding the rope round the post, Lora made sure that each little bit gained was securely held. After what seemed an eternity, Major Saunders was at last within reach of the wooden spars.

'Take care you don't move the spars,' Lora called anxiously, as she picked her way forward to help, but this time all went well. The Major freed one leg completely, then the other, and at last, with Lora's help, he crawled towards safety.

Back on solid ground, rescuers and rescued alike threw themselves down on to the heather in a state of exhaustion.

After a time the Major spoke.

'I owe my life to you, Miss Macrae,' he said humbly. ''Tis the worst experience I have ever had,' and he shuddered as he looked towards the menacing bog.

'I could never have saved you without the help of Dougal and Loyal, of course,' Lora reminded him.

'I realise that, but the dog could have done nothing alone, and the deaf mute had no intention at all of trying to save me. It is to you I owe my thanks.'

The Major's voice gradually faded away and there was silence except for his laboured breathing. Lora glanced at him once or twice and thought now how ill he looked.

'Are you all right, Major Saunders?' she asked. 'I think perhaps we had better get you back to the house, in case you catch a chill.'

'Let me rest just a little longer,' he replied, without opening his eyes. 'I shall be better in a little while. The army physician warned me against strenuous exercise of any kind. I see now he was right.'

He lapsed into silence once more, but after another short break he spoke again.

'You realise, don't you, Miss Macrae, that I now have a fair idea of the location of the rebel hideout? Had it not been for the mist I should have pin-pointed the spot exactly, for I was hot on your trail. The one moment you seemed to be just ahead of me, and the next you had 'gone to earth' like a fox.'

'B-but how did you manage to follow me at all?' queried Lora.

'Ah, that was simple. You thought, no doubt, that I hadn't seen you on the staircase but I have very sharp eyes, Miss Macrae. Unfortunately, your stepmother chose that moment to ask me to join her friends. I guessed, however, you would make a dash across the hall when we were in the library, so I excused myself almost immediately and I was in time to hear the door to the kitchen quarters close behind you. What you didn't know was that I had also seen you last Saturday evening setting off with a bulky bundle under your cloak. I actually saw you emerge from the servants' entrance on that occasion.'

Lora pondered for a moment. 'I remember. I smelled smoking, and I thought I heard footsteps,' she said at last.

'Yes. I was enjoying a breath of fresh air and a quiet smoke while the dancing was in progress. You opened the door and seemed to sense my presence, for you drew back. I didn't follow you then, of course, but I made a mental note of the direction you took. One might say I 'smelt a rat'! So tonight I let myself out at the front door and ran up the side of the house to try to intercept you. You had already vanished into the mist, but I heard your footsteps and followed.'

'And what do you intend to do now?' Lora asked, between dry lips.

'I must ensure that the rebels are not allowed to escape. It is my duty as a soldier, and I have never failed in my duty. Perhaps you do not realise the full significance of your own involvement in this affair, Miss Macrae. You have been actively engaged in helping enemies of the realm to evade capture – a serious offence – and the Duke of Cumberland is ruthless as far as rebel Highlanders and their accomplices are concerned. We are instructed to show no mercy. However, out of gratitude to you for saving my life, I shall allow myself to divert the course of justice in one respect.'

'And what is that?' asked Lora.

'I shall refrain from disclosing your part in concealing the rebels. Your name will never be mentioned by me in connection with this affair, and my written reports will bear no reference to any accomplice. I shall, of course, be relinquishing my command forthwith, for I now realise I am not a well man. The army physician has advised me several times to give up for my health's sake, and it is obvious to me now that I am no longer fit to fulfil the duties of an officer of His Majesty's armed forces. Therefore I must go. This will be my final duty concerning the rebellion.'

'But if you are leaving the army, why must you report the matter at all?' Lora asked, clinging to a slim thread of hope.

'Because it is my duty to pass on all relevant information to my successor. That is why.' With those words the Major sank down among the heather again, and closed his eyes. The effort of carrying on a prolonged conversation had exhausted him.

As they lay there in silence on the misty moorland, Lora's mind was working feverishly, trying to plan some course of action that might yet save the day for the rebels. Once Major Saunders was safely back in his room at The Milton she would go to Alistair and Angus and warn them to leave at once. By morning light they could be back across the hills into Glen Esk. Perhaps there would be no real refuge for them there either, but at least it would be better than remaining where they were, only to be dragged from their hiding place to face a firing squad, or a hangman's noose.

A moan from the Major brought her back to the present.

'Major Saunders,' she said urgently, 'we cannot continue to stay here. The ground is damp and the night is growing colder. We shall all suffer ill effects if we remain any longer. Do you think you might be able to walk a bit now?'

The Major opened his eyes and nodded agreement, so Lora struggled to her feet. It was only then she realised how stiff and cold she had actually become.

Dougal also showed signs of stiffness when he rose, and it took their combined efforts to get the Major up on his feet at all. The moon, by now, was beginning to penetrate the mist, so Lora was able to pin-point their exact position, and she had little difficulty deciding the quickest way back to the house.

Their progress through the heather was very slow, and they had covered but a short distance when, without warning, the Major collapsed. Lora dropped on her knees beside him. At first she thought he was dead, but she felt his pulse and it was faintly beating. Even so, if his life was to be saved, she realised they must get help at once. To send Dougal to The Milton would, of course, be useless. The only answer was to go herself.

Taking off her cloak, Lora wrapped it round the Major and signed to Dougal to stay beside him. Then, gathering up her skirts, she made a headlong dash for home, followed by the faithful Loyal.

The loose stones and heather roots of the narrow sheep tracks cut into Lora's stockinged feet, tearing her stockings and bruising her toes until they bled, but she ran on, scarcely even aware of the discomfort. Once on the cart road from Glen Doll to Clova the footing was better, but she was very tired and it was still hard going. She had no idea what time it was; so much had happened since she had set out for the castle and the cave, but she fancied the night must be far advanced. When at last she came in sight of The Milton, and saw that the servants' quarters were in darkness, her fears were confirmed.

On trying the front door, Lora found it had been left unbarred, which seemed to signify that someone was still about, but the fire in the hall was out, and there was no one to be seen. A pencil of light showed beneath her stepmother's sitting-room door, however. As Lora hurried towards it, the door was thrown open by that lady herself.

'Wherever have you been until this time of night, Lora Macrae?' she demanded, fixing Lora with an accusing eye, but her expression changed to one of horror at sight of Lora's shoeless feet, the torn and blood-stained stockings, and the heavily mud-caked clothes. Mrs Macrae's hand flew to her mouth as if to suppress a scream. It was only then that Lora realised the spectacle she must present, but there was no time for explanations.

'I'm sorry if I upset you, Aunt Gwyneth,' she said, 'but help is urgently needed for Major Saunders. He got stuck in a peat bog and he has completely collapsed. I'm afraid he is very ill indeed.'

'Major Saunders in a peat bog?' gasped Mrs Macrae, as yet uncomprehending. 'Stuck in the bog, did you say?'

'No! No! We pulled him out of the bog, but the shock has been too much for him. He is lying unconscious out on the moor. We must get help for him without delay. I shall go and call the Major's batman and the stable lads, and get them to go out and bring him back. If you will rouse Elsie and tell her to put warming-pans into the Major's bed, and light a fire in his room. He will be frozen stiff with cold.'

Still in her stockinged feet, Lora ran to the loft above the stables where the Major's batman had been accommodated with the young grooms. They were all fast asleep, but eventually she managed to wake them and explain briefly what had happened. Then she returned to the house for a pair of shoes and another cloak.

Elsie had already assumed command at The Milton and she insisted that Lora should have a hot drink before going out again. So Lora obediently gulped down a glass of hot milk, while she gave Elsie a short résumé of the happenings of the evening, and described the drama of the peat bog.

'Dear knows how a' this is to end,' said Elsie shaking her head.

As soon as the men had the horses harnessed into a suitable conveyance the rescue party set out, and Lora led them back the way she had come.

The Major lay where she had left him, with Dougal sound asleep by his side. It took a good deal of shaking to rouse Dougal, but no amount of shaking would have roused the Major. He was deeply unconscious, and was quite unaware of being lifted into the haycart, or of the rough, jolting journey back across the moor. Lora by this time was thoroughly worn out, and it was with a sigh of relief she saw once more the lights of The Milton.

Mrs Macrae, with great presence of mind, had sent a messenger to the camp to notify Major Saunders's second-in-command. He, in turn, had despatched one of the Dragoons posthaste to Kirriemuir to fetch the army physician. So, once the Major was safely in bed, nothing more could be done until the arrival of the medical officer.

Lora was glad to discard her mud-caked garments and to have Elsie bathe and bandage her aching feet. Yet, although she was thankful to crawl into bed and rest her weary limbs, sleep would not come to her. She lay tossing and turning, reliving the ordeal of the peat bog. For the moment, at least, there was one consolation – as long as the Major remained unconscious, Alistair and Angus were in no immediate danger. If only Paul could provide a means of escape before the damning evidence could be divulged!

Around daybreak the medical officer arrived. Lora heard his horse coming up the glen. Then she heard the officer being shown up to the Major's room. Later she heard him go downstairs again.

For a little while afterwards Lora lay still, but she was wide awake, and it was daylight. She decided to get up.

It wasn't until she put her feet on the floor that she discovered just how painful and swollen they were. Her arms, too, were full of aches and pains.

'If this continues, I shall be good for nothing, just creaking around like an old woman,' she said to herself miserably, and rather resentfully. Every movement actually did cause a stab of pain, and a resultant fit of depression seemed about to descend upon Lora. She was staring out of the window, feeling thoroughly sorry for herself, when two men on horseback came into view. They were riding up the glen at a leisurely pace, and something familiar about the pair made her look closer. As she did so her depression vanished as if by magic. It was Hamish MacCrimmon and Paddy O'Malley heading for Linnochmore! That was all the cure Lora needed! She completed her toilet at record speed, and dressed herself quickly, in spite of stiff muscles. Once she had found a pair of shoes that were bearable, there was no holding her back.

Despite the early hour, Mrs Macrae was standing in the hall. She was in conversation with a Redcoat army officer whom she introduced to Lora as Captain Owen, the medical officer.

'How is Major Saunders?' Lora inquired.

'He is rather poorly, I'm afraid,' Captain Owen replied. 'He has had a stroke, and his condition gives me much cause for concern. He recovered consciousness for a short time, just after I arrived, but it is difficult to assess his chances of full recovery at this stage. There appears to be a considerable degree of paralysis. I believe you are the young lady to whom Major Saunders owes his life.'

'Did Major Saunders tell you that himself?' Lora asked.

'No, he did not. At the moment Major Saunders has lost the power of speech. Your mother has just been telling me that you were responsible for the successful rescue. Why Major Saunders was foolish enough to go out alone on those hills in the dark, especially when the mist was down, I just cannot understand. It was most unlike him to do anything so rash. Have you any idea what could have possibly induced him to go out there alone, Miss Macrae?'

'No. I was out with my dog when I heard the Major's cries for help,' and Lora glanced at her stepmother to see how she was taking this piece of information. As luck would have it, Elsie appeared at that moment with a letter which had just arrived for her mistress by special messenger, so Mrs Macrae's attention was diverted. The Captain then excused himself to return to his patient, and Lora made good her escape.

'My, I'm real glad to see ye again, Miss Lora,' exclaimed Mrs MacCrimmon when Lora arrived at Linnochmore. 'We've missed your company of an evenin'.'

'I, too, have missed our meetings,' said Lora, 'But I was afraid to risk a visit. How did the Redcoats treat you when they called?'

'Och, they made a thorough search, but Hamish is so deaf they got exasperated and gave up askin' him questions. As for me, I spoke in the broad Scots tongue and they couldna understand a word I was sayin', so they didna bide here lang.'

Hamish and the pedlar were already seated at the table, with brose caups and horn spoons, enjoying a breakfast of porridge and milk.

'How did things go in Dundee, Hamish?' Lora asked, after exchanging a greeting with Old Hamish.

'A'thing went well, Miss Lora. Mr Reynolds sune got it a' fixed up to his satisfaction. We've to run the gauntlet o' the Redcoat patrol here first thing the morn's mornin', for we've to be at the tollhouse in the Pass o' Lumley at sundown. Mr Reynolds will be there to meet the lads, and escort them to Dundee. He's to see them safely aboard the vessel himsel'. He wouldna like to trust anybody else, he said.'

'That's wonderful news!' cried Lora, her eyes sparkling with pleasure, 'and it's just come in the nick of time, for the net is tightening,' and she went on to relate the happenings of the previous night.

Both Hamish and the Irishman were a bit shaken by her news.

'By jove! That was a near thing!' remarked Hamish. 'If the Major had found the entrance to the passage the lads were done for.'

'Sure, it's mad that ye were, to be pullin' him out o' the bog at all,' said Paddy in exasperation. 'Ye should've shoved the Redcoat divil further in, as ye should! Better for the lot of us if he'd never lived to tell the tale. For a' his fine promises, he could be the means of us all swingin' from the gallows yet. That's what some folk call strategy, ye know – sayin' one thing, an' doin' the very opposite.'

Lora was rather perturbed by the pedlar's remarks, but fate seemed inclined to be kind after all.

Over breakfast at The Milton, the army physician announced that he had decided to have Major Saunders removed to Kirriemuir without delay. He also told the ladies that the Major's detachment of troops was being recalled to Kirriemuir. If necessary, another detachment would take its place within the next few days but the general opinion among the men was that the rebels had got out of the area and there was no further need for a military presence. This piece of information was thankfully received by Lora.

Up to the time of his departure Major Saunders had remained paralysed and quite unable to speak. That knowledge – sad though it might be for the Major and his relatives – was also a relief to Lora. So much depended on his remaining silent for just a little longer!

IX 'FECHTIN', AN' BLOODSHED, AN' DEATH!

From her window, Lora kept a close watch on all that was happening around the army camp. She saw the tents being taken down one by one. Then, before mid-morning, she saw the troops move off in the direction of Kirriemuir. She wasted no time in conveying the glad tidings to the cottage.

Hamish, a positive thinker now, who seemed to have regained much of his self-respect and self-confidence during his trip to Dundee, decided at once to fetch Alistair and Angus from the tower.

'It'll gie' them a chance to get accustomed to the daylicht again, and to get a comfortable nicht's sleep afore we set oot,' he said. 'By the way, Miss Lora, I got instructions from Mr Reynolds to tell ye to get another two horses from the stables for Alistair and Angus to ride.'

'When do you expect to leave tomorrow?' Lora asked.

'As soon as it's daylicht. If the Redcoats had still been here we'd have had to try an' creep past in the dark, but we'll make quicker progress by the licht o' day. We'll ride across country, as the crow flies. That way we'll manage to bypass Kirrie and the villages like Glamis, Roundyhill, and Charleston. Paddy there, is weel aquaint wi' a' the drove roads and cattle raikes atween here and Dundee so we'll need to rely on his guidance to get the benefit o' a' the short cuts, for we must be at the Pass o' Lumley at the trysted hoor. A lot may depend on it.'

'Sure, and I'll not be lettin' ye down, Hamish,' the Irishman assured him.

'I'll fetch the horses up as soon as it's clear enough to see,' Lora promised. I can make the excuse that a neighbour needs the use of them for a few days. At this rate I'll soon have the stables emptied. The stable lads will be thinking I'm supplying a horse dealer!'

'As lang as they dinna think you've turned into a horse thief yersel' it'll no' be so bad!' Hamish laughed. Lora looked at him appreciatively. This was the Hamish MacCrimmon that Captain Dugald Lindsay had known.

When Alistair and Angus were once more installed at Linnochmore, Lora brought them up to date with all that had happened since she had left them at the cave exit the previous evening. They were shocked to learn of her hair-raising adventures.

'And to think we were so near, and yet we knew nothing of what was happening and could do nothing to help you! That Dougal MacDougall of whom you speak was truly a friend in need,' Alistair remarked.

'Yes. If it hadn't been for him I'd have been trapped, and you also,' said Lora.

'Then we must see that he is suitably rewarded,' said Angus.

The first thing that met Lora's eyes on her return to The Milton was a pile of luggage stacked near the front entrance door. Evidently her stepmother and Susan were to be off on their travels again.

'Have you decided to "follow the drum", Susan?' Lora teased.

'Why do you say that?'

'Well, when you came home you were accompanied by Dragoons. Now I have just seen the army march off down the glen and here you are hard on their heels. What else can I think?'

'It's not like that at all, silly! As a matter of fact we've been invited to a ball in Forfar tonight. You too, Lora.'

'It's the first I've heard of it. When did we get the invitation and from whom?'

'Major Saunders spoke to us about it, and then Captain Owen invited Mamma this morning. At first she wasn't keen to go, but she received a letter, which apparently changed her mind, and we're leaving after the midday meal. We're not coming back here after the ball. Mamma has decided to go on to Edinburgh, so we are to stay overnight with friends near Kirriemuir. You don't have to come to Edinburgh if you don't want to, but do, *please*, come to the ball! I'm sure it'll be fun. Everyone who's anyone will be there, and you're sure to meet Lieutenant Bullard again. It's too good a chance to miss, Lora! Those English officers are such wonderful dancers!'

'I hardly think my dancing would be up to standard,' said Lora ruefully. 'I feel stiff and sore all over, and I don't think I could bear to put on my dancing slippers at the moment.'

'I'm sorry, I quite forgot about your poor feet,' said Susan with real concern. 'Are they very badly swollen?'

'No, they aren't too bad. As you can see, I am able to wear my walking shoes but I am very tired, Susan. I think I'd rather stay at home and have a rest.'

'Of course! I quite understand, Lora. I think you were terribly brave to do what you did for Major Saunders, and I just hope he appreciates the fact that you saved his life. No wonder you're tired! Even though he's thin he would be tremendously heavy, for the bog would be pulling against you as well. Ugh! The very sight of a peat bog gives me the creeps,' and Susan shuddered at the thought of it.

The meal was served early to suit the travellers. As soon as they had eaten, the carriage drew up at the door. The luggage was stowed away, last-minute instructions were given to Elsie and Lora, and then they were off. Lora waved them goodbye from the doorway, as long as she could see Susan's fluttering handkerchief, but it was with a sigh of relief that she returned to the peace and tranquillity of the silent house.

By now Lora was feeling the combined effects of physical exhaustion and lack of sleep. The day had also become quite humid and oppressive, which added to her feeling of general fatigue. She decided to spend the afternoon in bed.

No one disturbed her, and she slept until evening, when she rose and had a meal in the kitchen with Elsie. Loyal had to be content with a shorter walk than usual, and then Lora went straight back to bed, for she was most anxious to be up in time next morning and have the horses delivered to Linnochmore by first light.

The fear of oversleeping and delaying the men's departure weighed so heavily on her mind that Lora spent a very restless night. She was up, and dressed, well in advance of daylight. In fact, she had the horses tethered at the cottage door awaiting their riders by the crack of dawn.

Alistair and Angus were quite overcome with emotion when the time actually came to say goodbye. They couldn't thank the MacCrimmons and Lora enough for all they had done for them.

'We shall never, *never*, forget you,' said Alistair, 'and we thank you all, from the bottom of our hearts.'

'Thanks be to God that you crossed our path when you did, Lora,' said Angus, 'but – God willing! – we shall all meet again one day, when Culloden Moor and its aftermath are only a sad memory. Alistair and I will make a pilgrimage back to Clova, never fear.'

'That's a promise, now,' said old Mrs MacCrimmon, smiling through tears, and she hugged each of the young men as if they were her own sons. The difference in rank and position had vanished in the face of a common danger. As a final gesture, Angus presented the old couple with a substantial share of the golden guineas retrieved from the tower.

'Naw, naw, laddie,' protested Old Hamish. 'Ye owe us nothing, and ye'll maybe need a' the money ye have to get ye safely back to France.'

'This is only your rightful share!' Angus insisted. We have more than enough money now, and you never know what you may need yourselves in the years ahead. Accept these gold pieces, please, with our sincere gratitude, and use them to keep yourselves warm and well-fed in your old age.'

When the young men emerged from the cottage Hamish and Paddy were already mounted and waiting. Old Hamish had something set behind the door. He retrieved the object as he followed the others out, and he carried it across to his nephew.

'Here's somethng that belongs to you, Hamish lad,' said the old man. 'It's been here at Linnochmore since ye left in 1715, but my father must have hidden it in the roof o' the shed and I only discovered it yesterday,' and he handed Hamish a double-edged broadsword – the Highland Claymore.

Hamish was strangely overcome at the sight of the weapon.

'I got it from the Captain himsel',' he said hoarsely, 'and I never thocht I'd see it again. I'd nae idea I'd left it here. Thank ye, Uncle, I'll tak' it wi' me,' and he promptly strapped the sword to his side.

'Sure, I'm thinkin' we could be in for the divil's own day o' rain,' remarked Paddy, observing the heavy clouds that were gathering.

'Aye, I wouldna be surprised if we had a thunderstorm afore the day's oot,' Old Hamish agreed. 'It looked like nothing else the whole day yesterday. I jist hope you lads escape the worst o' it.'

So, with many good wishes for a safe journey, and many thanks for kindnesses received, the little cavalcade moved off – into the unknown.

Old Hamish's predictions, with regard to weather, proved correct. As the day wore on, the skies grew dark and lowering and ominous rumblings could be heard in the distance. Hardly had darkness fallen than the storm broke over Glen Clova with a frightening intensity. The crash of the thunder seemed to rock the very foundations of The Milton, and the forked lightning was so vivid it lit up the whole sky almost incessantly.

Lora stood by the window in the kitchen absolutely enthralled by the spectacle.

'Come away from that window, Miss Lora,' Elsie begged. 'Forked lightnin' is dangerous, and I canna understand how ye would want to look out at it. We'll close the shutters and light the candles and then it'll no' seem so bad.'

Just as she uttered those words there was an extraordinarily vivid flash, accompanied by an ear-splitting crack and a tremendous crash of thunder.

'Good gracious!' exclaimed Elsie, 'something's been struck by lightnin' no' far from here, I'll warrant ye. The storm's very close. If this continues through the night we'll never get a wink o' sleep.'

'I wonder how they've fared at the Pass of Lumley,' mused Lora. 'I do hope this hasn't prevented Alistair and Angus from keeping the tryst with Paul.'

'Och! I dinna think it would be so bad in that direction,' Elsie replied. 'I noticed the sky looked clearer to the south just afore dark.'

The thunderstorm spent itself fairly quickly and ended as abruptly as it had begun. It was followed by a torrential downpour and then a low wind began to moan eerily around the house. By the time Lora went to bed the wind had whipped itself up to gale force, and she thankfully closed her shutters against the fury of the night. As she lay in her big four-poster bed she could hear a succession of rain, sleet, and hailstones, lashing against the window-panes.

Occasionally a tree, dislodged from its moorings, could be heard crashing to the ground, and Lora shivered as she thought of the fugitives battling against the elements. Would they have had to seek shelter *en route*, or would Paul already have got them safely aboard some merchant vessel in the port of Dundee? She offered up a silent prayer for their safety as she drifted off to sleep.

Lora had no idea how long she had slept, but it seemed only like a matter of minutes, when Elsie's voice penetrated her slumbers.

'Wake up, Miss Lora! Wake up!' the housekeeper was saying, as she shook Lora by the shoulder.

'Have I overslept?' asked Lora, somewhat dazed.

'No, you havena' overslept. It's early yet, but the packman was at the back door askin' for ye. Ye're wanted up at Linnochmore it seems.'

'The packman? You mean Paddy O'Malley?' exclaimed Lora, suddenly wide awake.

'Aye. The very same.'

'B-but where had *he* come from? He just left yesterday morning.'

'Well, it appears he's back again.'

'I hope there's nothing wrong. What time is it, Elsie?'

'It's between seven and eight o'clock.'

'All right, thank you, Elsie. I'll get up right away.'

Elsie had breakfast ready, but Lora didn't linger over it. Calling to Loyal she hurried off, anxious to find out why she had been summoned hence.

The storm had blown itself out, but the gale had left a trail of damage in its wake, and the deluge had brought the Brandy Burn foaming down in flood. There was a fine drizzle of rain falling, and the higher peaks were enveloped in mist.

The door at Linnochmore was unlocked, so Lora gave her familiar tap and walked in, with her usual greeting – 'It's me, Mrs MacCrimmon,' but the words died on her lips as she stepped into the earthen-floored kitchen. There, seated by the fire, were Alistair Drummond and Paddy O'Malley!

All the colour drained from Lora's cheeks, and she stood staring at the men as if they were ghosts.

Alistair rose immediately to greet her, but he looked worn and dejected. The pedlar was fast asleep.

'Come and sit down, Lora,' Alistair said, guiding her to the chair he had just vacated. 'I knew you would get a shock when you saw us.'

'FECHTIN', AN' BLOODSHED, AN' DEATH!

'Whatever happened?' asked Lora in a voice scarcely above a whisper.

'We were ambushed in the Pass of Lumley!'

'And Angus and Hamish? Where are they?'

'Angus is through in the bedroom resting, but, I'm sorry to tell you, Hamish is dead.'

'Dead!' exclaimed Lora in horror.

'Yes. When we reached the pass we could see no life at all around the Tollhouse, so Hamish told Angus and me to take cover and he would go down alone and reconnoître the place. He was almost at the house when a number of Redcoats rose up and confronted him. There was no doubt they had been lying in wait for us. Hamish put up a heroic stand. From the outset he made it quite clear he was not to be taken alive, and he used his claymore to good effect. In fact, he felled two Dragoons and at first beat off his attackers, but, in the end, they cut him down. It was the perfect ambush.'

'How awful! Poor Hamish!' gasped Lora. 'And to think it was I who persuaded him – even bullied him – into this! I feel as if I had lured him to his death!' she concluded bitterly.

'Please don't blame yourself, Lora,' began Alistair. 'Whatever will be, will be. Such is destiny, it seems. Hamish died that Angus and I might live – or so it would appear. What is it the Bible says? "Greater love hath no man than this. . . ?"'

'"That a man lay down his life for his friends",' quoted Lora, her voice choked with emotion.

For the next few minutes neither could speak. Only the crackling of the log fire and the heavy breathing of Old Hamish and Paddy O'Malley broke the silence.

'Do you think the Redcoats would know there were more of you, Alistair?' Lora asked at last.

'Yes. I feel sure they would. Whoever knew enough about our movements to report our rendezvous to the military would be able to say how many we were.'

'So they are likely to be searching for you now?'

'Yes. I should think they will be. As it happened we were lucky. The thunderstorm broke at the providential moment and the Redcoats ran for shelter instead of instituting an immediate search. Angus and I crawled back to our horses and got clean away. By great good fortune we met Paddy near Glen Ogilvy and he brought as safely back here.'

'Paddy wasn't with you at the pass then?'

'No. When we left here he took us by the quickest routes to Glen Ogilvy but we thought his presence at the trysting place might complicate matters, so we agreed to part, and he went off to visit some of his customers around the village of Glamis. It was lucky for us we met up with him again. I'm afraid, on such a night, we'd never have found our way back to Glen Clova by ourselves.'

'And Paul – what of him?' Lora asked, with bated breath.

'We saw nothing of him at all. As I said, there was no sign of life until the Redcoats suddenly appeared.'

Fear for Paul's safety clutched at Lora's heart, but she hid her disquiet as best she could, and forced herself to give her whole mind to the present crisis.

'Will you go back to the secret chamber until we see what else can be done?' she suggested bleakly.

'We cannot get into the tower, Lora. The secret died with Hamish,' Alistair reminded her.

'Of course! I had forgotten! But there is always the entrance via the cave on the hillside.'

'Alas, no! We have already been out there this morning but that particular boulder must have been struck by lightning last night. The overhanging projection was sheared off and crashed down into the cave entrance. The secret chamber and the subterranean passage are lost to us forever, I'm afraid.'

Lora was completely stunned by this final disaster.

'What are we to do then?' she asked helplessly.

'Angus and I have decided we must fend for ourselves. We cannot remain here. Our presence is more dangerous than ever now, for all concerned, and we have already cost one life, remember.'

Mrs MacCrimmon, who had been trying to dry some of the men's wet clothes at the fire, spoke up at this point.

'Ye'll need to wait for one more day, Alistair. Angus is dead beat, and ye're no' much better yersel'. My advice is that ye get as much rest and sleep as ye can durin' the next twenty-four hours. Then ye'll be able to see the whole thing in a better licht, and make wiser judgements. Besides, your horses need a rest as weel. Poor brutes, they've had a lang, weary trek.'

'Mrs MacCrimmon is right you know, Alistair,' said Lora, 'and one more day will give us all time to think.'

'I agree, but what we don't know is how much information the enemy now have, regarding Angus and me. They may swoop at any time. We have no place to hide, so look at the risk to your good selves. However, we'll wait until tomorrow morning – God willing!'

Paddy O'Malley had now wakened up, and Lora turned her attention to him.

'Who were the people Paul was dealing with in Dundee, do you know?' she asked the Irishman.

'I know nothing whatever about them, Miss Macrae. Sure, your Mr Reynolds refused even to let me go to Dundee with Hamish and him. I was left in Kirrie until Hamish came back, as it was. And Hamish was after tellin' me nothin' at all about his trip when he did come back. He wasna the same lad at all. I could make nothing o' him. But if ye want *my* opinion,' said Paddy, sullenly, 'it was the Englishman himself that double-crossed the lads at Lumley.'

'What Englishman?' asked Lora.

'Your Mr Reynolds – who else?'

'I'm sure you are quite wrong there, Paddy,' Alistair interrupted. 'After all, if Paul had wanted to betray us he didn't need to go all the way to Dundee. There were Redcoats on the spot in Clova, and the CO was right there in his own home.'

'Sure, if ye were knowin' the English as I do, ye'd be surprised at nothin' concernin' them, and that's a fact,' declared Paddy determinedly. 'They twist every damn thing to suit themselves.'

'I think you forget, my home is in England, and my wife and I were both born there,' Alistair reminded him sharply, 'but we needn't start an argument, for we're never likely to know who the real traitor was, anyway. The fact remains, we are back where we started, and we must concentrate on our next move, instead of wasting our energy quarrelling among ourselves.'

'Well, sure, that's my honest opinion on the culprit and ye'll maybe find that I wasna far wrong,' declared Paddy. He mumbled something more which Lora failed to catch. Then he settled back in his chair and fell sound asleep again.

The thought of Hamish's untimely death weighed heavily upon Lora, as it did upon the others. Sitting by the fireside, Alistair and she, and the two old people, discussed the matter quietly together.

'When Hamish cam' back from Dundee, I was real pleased to see the difference in him,' said Old Hamish. 'He reminded me more o' what he used to be like in his young day . . . Aye,' he added with a sigh, 'it's sad to think he had to be ta'en awa', just when it looked as if he'd turned o'er a new leaf.'

'It's the Lord's will, Hamish,' said the old lady, 'it's the Lord's will,' and she hastily brushed aside a tear, while her husband poked the fire vigorously in an effort to hide his emotion.

'Whatever your nephew may have done in the past,' said Alistair, 'he certainly did not disgrace the name of MacCrimmon yesterday. Though far out-numbered, he stood his ground, and fought like a hero. Man to man he was a match for any of the Redcoats, though he was old enough to be their father. He wielded his claymore with all the traditional skill and courage of the true clansman. You can be proud of your namesake, Hamish. And I say that with complete sincerity.'

No one spoke after that. They just sat gazing into the flickering flames, each lost in his or her own thoughts. And as Lora stared into the fire she saw in her mind's eye a pock-marked face, and heard the uncouth sound of a tinker's harsh voice – 'I see fechtin', an' bloodshed, an' death,' were the words that echoed in Lora's ears. She shivered involuntarily as she rose to her feet.

'I must go now, and let you get some sleep, Alistair,' she said. 'I'll do my best to think of some way out of this new dilemma, and when I come back in the evening I hope I may have some plan to offer. There must surely be someone, somewhere, who can help us! Meanwhile I shall keep a constant lookout for any Redcoats coming up the glen, so you can sleep in peace.'

Once outside the cottage, with no one but Loyal to see her, Lora gave way to her pent-up emotion, and the tears flowed. The fact that she had been instrumental in sending Hamish to his death made her feel utterly wretched, and the fear that misfortune might, in the same way, have befallen Paul, was almost more than she could bear.

'Please God, let Paul come back safe and sound,' she prayed desperately.

X *THE JOURNEY TO HOWLETSDEN*

The pedlar's remarks about Paul had shaken Lora considerably. She felt annoyed with the man for stating his opinion so bluntly, but she had to admit the matter of Paul's non-appearance at the Pass of Lumley was bound to give rise to just such doubts and suspicions.

When the previous report about the rebels had reached the ears of the English, Lora had reckoned it might have come from one of four sources – from the mysterious spy on the hillside; from Paul; from Dr Elliott's assistant; or (most likely of all) from Hamish's careless talk in a brew-house or alehouse in Kirriemuir. This time it was different. The arrangement for the rendezvous at the Lumley tollhouse had been entirely between Paul and Hamish (or so Hamish had believed). Hamish by then was no longer besotted with alcohol, so the chance that he had 'spilt the beans' on this occasion was very remote. That left Paul. Yet in her heart, Lora knew Paul was no traitor. There must have been a third party involved, of whom Hamish was unaware. She felt sure of that. Mayhap there had even been an eavesdropper – a Redcoat spy, perchance. If that were so, had Paul been captured on his way to the rendezvous? Or had he, like poor Hamish, met his death at the hands of the Redcoats?

Lora tortured herself by returning to those questions over and over again without, of course, getting any nearer the answers. Eventually she realised she must exert the power of 'mind over matter', and dismiss the subject from her thoughts completely. Otherwise she would never be able to concentrate on the present important issue of finding a new escape route. In the meantime she could only hope and pray that a messenger from Paul would soon arrive to allay their fears, and explain all.

On seeking out Elsie, Lora found her checking the contents of the linen closet.

'Elsie, could you spare a few minutes to come up to my room?' she begged. 'I have much to tell you, and I am desperately in need of advice, but we must speak privately. You understand?'

'I understand, Miss Lora. I'll follow ye up,' said Elsie, noting Lora's pale face and strained expression.

Lora hurried to her bedroom window and scanned the road on both sides of the glen. As far as she could see there was no sign of any Redcoats. She heaved a sigh of relief. But for how long?

When Elsie joined her, Lora poured out her tale of woe from beginning to end, withholding nothing.

Elsie was a good listener and she also had the wisdom of her years. She was shocked to hear of Hamish's violent death at the hands of the Redcoats, and of Paul's failure to appear at the rendezvous, and she fully realised the dangerous implications to Lora and the MacCrimmons. She hadn't ruled out further developments in the Major Saunders affair either. Even the Major's partial recovery could mean a Redcoat purge unleashed on the glen. To remind Lora of this at such a time seemed unnecessarily cruel, however, so Elsie held her peace.

'It must have been the lightnin' strikin' that rock that we had heard last night, Miss Lora,' she remarked. 'Mind, I said to ye that something had been hit no' very far awa'? The tragedy is that it had to be that particular boulder.'

'Yes. It seems as if everything is against us – even the Lord himself!' said Lora bitterly.

'Now, now, Miss Lora! Ye mustn't say such things,' Elsie chided her. '"God moves in a mysterious way, his wonders to perform,"' she quoted. 'I've heard folk say that everything works oot for the best if ye've patience to wait, and I've seen the proof o' that in my own lifetime, so it may well prove itsel' in your case yet. We'll jist sit here quietly for a wee while and see what plan of action we can think up.'

So Elsie seated herself on Lora's bed, while Lora sat on the window-seat in order to keep her vigil on the glen. They discussed various projects, none of which proved acceptable, but both ladies were determined to find some way out of the dilemma.

'I believe I've got the answer,' Elsie announced at last. 'It has just occurred to me that the best person to turn to would be your father's friend the auld sea Captain – Colin McNair o' Howletsden in Glen Ogil. Do ye mind o' payin' a visit there when ye were a wee lassie?'

'Yes. I remember, but only just. That's a long time ago. How clever of you to think of Captain McNair, Elsie! I must admit such a person never entered my head. Now that you mention it, though, I believe the Captain would help us. I'm sure he would have been my father's first choice, anyway.'

'Aye. I believe he would. Your father thought very highly o' Captain McNair, and I liked him mysel' when he came to The Milton. He was aye very courteous and kindly wi' a' the servants – a real gentleman. Of course, I realise he may not be in favour o' the Jacobites, but I still think he would help ye, Miss Lora, if only for your late father's sake.'

'His connection with ship-owners and seafarers would be an asset anyway,' said Lora. 'He could probably tell us the right people to contact and where to find them quickly, which is what we need now. I couldn't just send Alistair and Angus to Captain McNair's house by themselves, of course. I must go with them. The business of helping rebels is such a delicate matter, I must make the appeal myself.'

'Aye. I think ye're right there, Miss Lora,' Elsie agreed.

'With the likelihood of Redcoats pouncing on us at any moment, there is no time to lose,' Lora decided. 'I shall go to Linnochmore this evening and make plans for an early start tomorrow morning. Thank you, again, Elsie, for solving our immediate problem!'

Lora spent the rest of the day on lookout duty, but nothing untoward occurred. Nor was there any sign of a messenger from Paul.

At Linnochmore in the evening she found Alistair and Angus much better of the day's rest. When she told them of the plan put forward by Elsie they were both very enthusiastic. The thought that there might still be 'a ray of light at the end of the tunnel' cheered the young men immensely.

After some discussion it was decided that Angus should again play the rôle of a female. 'If we are challenged we can pretend to be a bridal party,' Lora suggested. 'You will be the 'groom, Alistair. Angus will be the bride, and I shall be in attendance upon the bride. How does that appeal to you?'

'So be it! I shall be pleased to fit in with any plan,' Angus readily agreed, 'but I cannot say I am looking forward to riding side-saddle!'

'Do ye ken the road, Miss Lora?' asked Mrs MacCrimmon.

'I have a fair idea of it,' Lora replied. 'I have been there before, but not since I was a little girl. However, I can always make sure we're on the right track by asking passers-by and calling at roadside cottages.'

Paddy O'Malley interrupted at this point.

'Sure now, it's meself that knows the road to Glen Ogil,' he said, 'Sure, I know it "like the back of me hand", as ye might say. It'll be no trouble at all for auld Paddy to be escortin' ye to the Howletsden.'

Alistair and Angus were most enthusiastic about accepting Paddy's offer. After all, had he not proved a most reliable guide up to now? So the matter was settled there and then. The Irishman would accompany them.

Lora had hoped to get away reasonably early, so Elsie came to her bedroom to make sure she was awake.

'It's a driech, driech day, Miss Lora,' she greeted her, as she opened the shutters. 'It's a mist to the very door. Ye'll no' have much pleasure in your long ride this mornin', I'm thinkin'.'

'Mist could have its advantages as well as disadvantages for us, I suppose,' said Lora. 'Anyway, beggars can't be choosers, so we'll have to make the best of whatever weather we get.'

Loyal, as usual, watched Lora's every move as she made her preparations for departure, but Elsie advised against taking the dog.

'I think ye should leave Loyal here, Miss Lora,' she counselled. 'It wouldna be wise for you to be callin' his name around the countryside wi' so many Redcoats on the go. Alistair told ye his attention was attracted when he heard ye cry "Loyal", so ye'd better no' risk attractin' the enemy's attention.'

'I dare say you're right, Elsie,' Lora agreed, but she felt a twinge of disappointment at the thought of leaving Loyal behind. 'I know he's happy with you though, Elsie, so I'll leave him in your care,' she said reluctantly. 'Perhaps you could get one of the girls to exercise him if you're too busy.'

Elsie promised to look after the dog, so Lora took a fond farewell of both. 'My two best friends,' she said, as she hugged each in turn.

The plans for an early departure were effectively upset when Paddy O'Malley discovered that his pony was needing shod.

'If ye ask me it's jist an excuse to get doon to the alehoose again to see that wumman MacDougall,' said Old Hamish, in disgust.

'I didn't know he was specially friendly with Mrs MacDougall,' said Lora, with surprise.

'Och aye, Paddy has been freendly wi' Mistress MacDougall for a lang time, and he's been goin' there an awfu' lot lately,' supplied Mrs MacCrimmon. 'I'm beginnin' to think he's courtin',' she added with a smile. 'Of course, he has a great work wi' her poor dumb laddie, Dougal. In fact, I've heard folk say Paddy O'Malley understands Dougal better than his ain mither does. Paddy may be a bit o' a rough diamond, but he has his guid points, like a'body else.'

Alistair, for some unknown reason, seemed particularly annoyed at the delay. 'If he wanted to see his lady friend he could have gone there last night,' he declared, in high dudgeon. 'We shall wait another ten minutes and no more. If the pedlar isn't here by that time, I suggest we leave without him.'

Lora had never seen Alistair so piqued. In spite of all their various setbacks Alistair had remained calm and good-natured. She guessed there must be some other cause for Alistair's annoyance with the packman. After all, only the previous evening he had seemed specially keen that the pedlar should accompany them.

'Probably some rude remark of Paddy's had upset Alistair,' Lora reflected, for was not she herself still smarting from the Irishman's disparaging remarks about Paul?

They were just on the point of putting Alistair's threat into action when the offending pedlar appeared. He was in a particularly jovial mood and it was very obvious he had been sampling the widow MacDougall's special brew, for his breath was heavy with the smell of intoxicating liquor.

Once again the rebels took a fond farewell of the old couple.

'If anything goes wrong,' said Mrs MacCrimmon, 'just come back to Linnochmore. Ye'll always be welcome here, ye know that – both o' ye.'

As Elsie had said, it was a driech day. A Scotch mist was falling, in the form of a fine wetting rain, and an equally unpleasant icy breeze drove the wet and cold into the somewhat dispirited travellers.

The track down the glen was akin to the bed of a burn. It was badly rutted, and water ran into the ruts, forming into great pools which concealed the treacherous boulders and loose slippery stones underneath. The ponies were sure-footed but, nevertheless, progress was considerably slowed down by the atrocious road conditions. As they proceeded further down the valley the effects of the recent storm became more apparent. Acres of the flat land around the farms of Whitehillocks, Braeminzion, and Clachnabrain lay under a sea of water where the river South Esk had overflowed its banks.

'Just think of the poor tenant farmers and their families,' remarked Lora feelingly as she beheld the scene of desolation. 'Year in, year out, they toil in their fields, literally "working life out to keep life in". Now, in one night, they face utter ruin and starvation.'

Certainly the flood water had left a trail of disaster in its wake. The golden stooks, which had so recently been viewed by their owners with so much satisfaction, were no longer to be seen. Sheaves of grain, swept down from the upland farms, were piled against dykes, fences, and trees, and the carcasses of sheep, also the unfortunate victims of the elements, now lay scattered around like pitiful heaps of sodden wool.

Lora was a little anxious about the Gella Ford which they had to cross. However, with a degree of extra care, all four negotiated the crossing without mishap. At the market muir of Cullow they paused for a short rest. While the horses ate from their nosebags, Lora produced the bannocks which Elsie had packed into her saddlebag for the men. There was also a flagon of milk, but, with rain dripping from nose and chin, and cold wet fingers that could scarcely even hold the flagon, there was little pleasure in the picnic. Paddy O'Malley went on ahead from there, on the pretext of gleaning what information he could about possible Redcoat activities in the area.

Like Clova, the wooded district of Dykehead had also suffered considerably from the gale. Some stately giants had been laid low and had fallen across the track, making detours necessary, but the bedraggled ponies, and their riders, plodded stolidly on.

As they wound their way down the muddy road and under the dripping trees which surrounded the picturesque hamlet of Cortachy, with its castle, its church, and its bridge over the South Esk, Paddy temporarily rejoined them. At the sight of the local inn, however, he made off again, declaring, rightly or wrongly, that this was the best place to get the news.

'Just another excuse to imbibe some more ale, if you ask me,' remarked Alistair in exasperation, as the pedlar spurred his pony towards the inn door.

'*Mon Dieu*, and who could blame him on such a day!' exclaimed Angus.

Alistair looked around with interest as they approached the castle gate.

'So this would be where our friend Lord Ogilvy grew up,' he mused. 'I wonder where he is now, poor fellow.'

'God knows! But there is one thing certain,' remarked Angus with a rueful grin, 'He couldn't be much more uncomfortable than I am, posing as your bride, and sitting on this wretched side-saddle, drenched to the skin!'

Immediately after Cortachy they came to the steep incline known as the Cossacks Brae. Here they dismounted and trudged alongside their ponies. The weather had, if anything, deteriorated, and the mist had intensified, so that visibility was now very poor. They were afraid to forge too far ahead in case they should lose contact with the pedlar, but Lora was becoming increasingly doubtful as to the likelihood of their reaching their destination before nightfall.

They were nearing the tiny hamlet of Memus before Paddy caught up with them, only to leave them again when he noticed a tinkers' encampment conveniently placed beside an alehouse. His already over-rosy countenance beamed at sight of the tents.

'Some freends o' mine,' he explained, 'Sure, I'll need to be havin' a wee word wi' them, if ye'll excuse me. Just you take the road that branches off to the left up there, an' I'll soon join ye. Ye'll better mind ye'll be on the main road to the cathedral city o' Brechin then, so keep your eyes skinned for Redcoats.'

The road on which they now found themselves was fairly straight, with drystane dykes on both sides and scarcely a tree to be seen. In fact, to the weary trio, it was a monotonous road that seemed never-ending. When they came to a crossroads they stopped and waited for Paddy O'Malley.

'Don't you think we'd have been quicker by Glen Quiech?' Lora asked the pedlar, when he finally appeared. 'I can't see us getting to Howletsden now before nightfall.'

'Sure, an' that's why I'm after bringin' ye this way,' he replied. 'We'll be gettin' a night's lodgin' at the Chance Inn, so we will.'

'But we don't want to go to an inn. We want to get to Howletsden,' exclaimed Lora in annoyance.

'Well, that may be, but, sure, ye have no choice, an' the Chance Inn is a decent place, so it is. Ye'll get a clean bed and a good supper, what more could ye be wantin'? The landlord's an auld acquaintance o' mine, an' begorra, his gude wife's one o' my best customers,' announced Paddy, as if that were all the recommendation anyone could require.

Lora had the feeling that Paddy had deliberately planned the day so that they would be bound to stay the night at this inn. 'He has manoeuvred the whole journey just for his own benefit,' she said to herself. She felt decidedly uneasy at the thought of spending the night at some third-rate alehouse, but she was thoroughly tired out and had no idea how many miles lay between them and Howletsden. Alistair and Angus were also weary of the journey, so it was decided unanimously to seek a night's lodging at the inn.

Lora's misgivings remained, but when at last they turned a corner and she saw the dark outline of the building huddled by the roadside with the welcoming glow from its windows, she realised how wonderful it would be just to feel warm again, and to forget the misery of that cold wet night.

'I'll go in alone and ask about accommodation,' she said as they dismounted.

'What an appetising aroma of roasting pork!' remarked Alistair, sniffing appreciatively as the smell of cooking wafted towards them through the open door.

'*Délicieux!*' exclaimed Angus, licking his lips. 'Agree to any terms, Lora, please. I'm ravenous!'

The kindly welcome accorded to her by the landlord and his wife did much to allay Lora's fears. The inn had little sleeping accommodation to offer, but they had one bedroom, which they said the bride and 'groom could have right away, and they would prepare another room for Lora herself while she was having supper. An ostler was called to take charge of the horses, and Alistair and Angus joined Lora in the kitchen of the inn which served also as dining-room and drinking parlour. The innkeeper's wife invited them to sit at a bare, but well-scrubbed, table, while she took their wet cloaks and spread them over a wooden settle to dry in front of the fire.

There was no pomp or ceremony, but the meal was quickly served, the food was well cooked, and the portions were generous. Paddy O'Malley had left them to join an acquaintance of his on the far side of the room, so the three ate their meal more or less in silence. When they had finished, Alistair ordered hot toddy to be brought to their room and then he and Angus retired to bed without further delay.

'I have *your* bed to make up yet, Miss,' said the innkeeper's wife. 'If ye'll just take a seat by the fire I'll be as quick as I can.'

'Thank you,' said Lora. 'We enjoyed our supper, and now I'll be glad to have a seat by the fire. I don't know when I was so thankful to see a fire!' So saying, she crossed the room and seated herself in the chimney corner beside the blazing logs, keeping as far as possible from the drinking fraternity. Gradually, the warmth pervaded her whole body, bringing the circulation back into her chilled limbs, and causing her to feel drowsy.

As she nodded there in the glow of the fire, Lora caught the distant sound of hoofbeats. She listened attentively. They were definitely heading in the direction of the inn, not one or two horses but a whole troop! Fear clutched at Lora's heart. How awful if Alistair and Angus had come all this way, only to be caught at a roadside inn!

The ominous sound drew nearer, and even the drinkers ceased their noisy chatter to listen.

'Sounds as if we're to ha'e a visit o' the Redcoats,' someone remarked.

Lora kept hoping against hope that the soldiers would continue on their way, but her hopes were in vain. With a jangle of bridles, and a clatter of hooves, the troop came to a halt on the roadway outside. Then there came an insistent knocking on the inn door, followed by a loud voice demanding, 'Open up, in the name of King George!' This command sent the landlord scurrying to obey, while several of the drinkers rose and slipped quietly away by a back entrance. Lora remained where she was, striving to appear calm and unconcerned.

Scarcely had the door been unbarred than the room seemed to be filled to overflowing with Redcoat Dragoons, but, thankfully, it was not an organised search of the premises. The soldiers were all clamouring to be served with hot ale or hot toddy, and the landlord and his wife and three daughters were kept busy fetching and carrying to their demanding customers.

Paddy O'Malley had remained seated, when the soldiers first entered. He was in Lora's direct line of vision, and, as she looked at him, she sensed a definite air of tension. She could see that he was covertly watching a group of three men – a sergeant and two corporals. Paddy had a side view of the men, and from the expression on his face it became apparent to Lora that he had recognised one, or even all, of the group. He seemed decidedly ill at ease and anxious to avoid being noticed. A spark from the fire momemtarily drew Lora's attention. When she looked again, Paddy had gone from the room.

Lora rendered herself as inconspicuous as possible by keeping well within the shadow of the chimneypiece, and, luckily for her, the fire had burned low. Her presence went completely unnoticed until one of the soldiers decided he was cold.

'For God's sake, throw on some logs and give us a heat!' he called out. As someone complied with his request, and tossed some tinder-dry wood on the fire, the flames leapt up the chimney and the dimly lit room was transformed into a blaze of light.

When the blaze was at its peak, Lora heard an exclamation of surprise. Then someone spoke her name. Glancing nervously in the direction of the speaker she found herself looking into the familiar face of none other than Lennox Bullard!

'Miss Macrae? Lora? I'm not dreaming am I?' exclaimed Lennox in sheer amazement, as he strode towards her. 'What a stroke of luck! But what on earth are you doing here, alone, in a place like this?'

'I'm not altogether alone,' Lora replied. 'I'm travelling with two companions. We feared the mist and darkness combined might cause us to lose our way, so we decided to put up here for the night. My friends have gone to bed and I have to wait until a room is prepared for me. The inn isn't much to look at, but it's quite clean, as far as I can see, and the food is palatable.'

'Well I just can't tell you how pleased I am to see you,' said Lennox, seating himself in the ingle beside her. 'I haven't been able to get you out of my mind since our happy evening at The Milton, and I was disappointed you didn't manage to come to the ball in Forfar the other night. I danced several times with your sister Susan and she was telling me all about your brave rescue of my uncle from the peat bog. By the way, how are your poor feet? Susan said you ran all the way home to get help, although you had lost your shoes in the bog. She said your feet were so bruised and swollen as a result, you couldn't get on your dancing shoes. Is that right?'

'Yes it is,' laughed Lora, 'But my feet soon recovered. Thank goodness!'

'If I had known, I'd have come and carried you off to the ball myself. I'd have been delighted to have sat out every dance with you, Lora, truly I would.'

Lennox's almost boyish pleasure at meeting her again, cheered Lora tremendously.

'How is Major Saunders?' she asked.

'He is still very poorly, I'm afraid. The power of speech hasn't returned so far, and he is paralysed completely on his right side. I haven't visited him, but my mother happened to be in Scotland staying with friends and she travelled to Forfar when she received word of his illness. She said she would rather he passed away now, than that he should live on as a helpless invalid.'

'That would be dreadful for him, and for all concerned,' Lora agreed.

'And what about my good friend Paul. Where is *he* at the moment?' asked Lennox.

'He is away on shipping business. I'm afraid I don't know where.'

'It was a pity Paul had to leave the army,' remarked Lennox. 'He really loved the life, you know, and he was well suited to it. I have often wished he had been at my side throughout this campaign, I can tell you. He was a born leader, and never afraid to take risks. He was also amazingly resourceful in the most awkward situation. I'm sure he'd have got quick promotion if he'd stayed in the army. As it is, I am told he undertakes quite daring assignments, on behalf of His Majesty's Government, in some of the foreign countries he visits in the course of his shipping business.'

This latter piece of news was a surprise to Lora, and she felt a twinge of conscience at the thought of how she had taunted Paul about being afraid for his own skin. No wonder he had reacted angrily! How she wished she could have confided in Lennox and got his opinion on Paul's failure to put in an appearance at the trysting place! Lennox's unstinted praise of Paul's abilities to look after himself had rekindled her waning hopes, however, and given her fresh heart. So she cast aside her mood of despondency and did her best to appear quite happy and carefree as she and Lennox chatted together in the firelight.

'Are you by any chance travelling in the same direction as we are, Lora?' he asked at length. 'Is there perhaps a hope of our meeting again soon?'

'I think that is very unlikely,' Lora replied warily. 'We came out of our way to get to this inn. Where exactly are *you* bound for, Lennox?'

'We are making for the coast. The rebels are coming down from the hills now, before the onset of winter, and as was to be expected, they are converging on the East Coast ports in the hope of bribing shipping merchants or sea captains to smuggle them out. It is our duty to see they don't succeed.'

'Where are you to be stationed?' pursued Lora.

'I don't know exactly, but we shall be patrolling quite a stretch of coastline, I understand. Tonight we ride only as far as Brechin. We shall receive our orders there.'

The wag-at-the-wa' clock chimed the hour of nine o'clock, and Lennox signalled a message to his sergeant. He glanced around to make sure no one was within earshot. Then he moved nearer to Lora and took one of her hands in his.

'This may not be the best place to exchange confidences,' he remarked, with a grin, 'but "time waits for no man" and it has always appeared to me that that saying applies most of all to members of His Majesty's Forces. Anyway, I feel fate must have taken a hand in bringing us together tonight, so I'm putting my cards on the table. I want you to know, in spite of our short acquaintance, I have grown very fond of you, Lora. Please tell me truthfully, is there already someone special in your life?'

'If you mean do I have a lover, then the answer is "No",' Lora answered quietly. 'I did care for someone. Unfortunately he is already betrothed,' she added, blushing profusely.

'For your sake, I am sorry about that, Lora,' said Lennox sympathetically. 'It must be a miserable experience to love someone who can give no love in return. But, if it is any comfort to you, *I* shall be waiting, should you ever feel inclined to turn in my direction. By the way, I told my mother all about you, and about what you did for my uncle, and she would very much like to meet you and thank you in person. She extends a warm invitation to you to come south with me on my next furlough, in the spring of the year. We live in Gloucestershire, in a beautiful part of the country.' He paused, 'I feel I should tell you now, Lora, that I am seriously considering leaving the army.'

'But you have just been promoted to Captain, haven't you?'

'Yes. I am pleased I have earned promotion, but my parents wish me to take over the management of our estate, and I shall probably relinquish my commission before the end of next year. So you see, Lora, our chance of many more meetings in Scotland is unlikely. But I'm sure you'd love Gloucestershire,' he added, 'and if you came south with me for a week or two it would give us an opportunity to get to know each other better. Please say you'll come!'

To have anyone as handsome and dashing as Captain Lennox Bullard so openly declaring his affections was definitely a flattering experience and Lora was already more than a little attracted to him. The only stumbling block was the fact that he was a Redcoat. But had he not just said he was soon to be leaving the army? Besides, a holiday in Lennox's company would be very enjoyable and need not necessarily lead to anything conclusive. Lora made up her mind there and then.

'Thank you,' she answered. 'It was very kind of your mother to ask me. I have never been south of the border and I'd like very much to visit your home in Gloucestershire.'

Lennox's face lit up. 'I thought for one awful moment you were to turn the invitation down,' he exclaimed. 'But that's a promise now, Lora. My mother will be sending you a proper invitation. Then, as soon as I know when my furlough is due, I shall get a message to you, and I shall come to Glen Clova and fetch you. I shall ask my elder sister to act as chaperone. She is particularly anxious to meet you so she'll be delighted.'

Just then a bugle sounded outside, and the room began to empty.

'That's the call to "boot and saddle",' announced the Captain somewhat ruefully, as he got to his feet. 'I wish I could have sat here beside you all through the night, but duty calls! *Au revooir*, dearest Lora. Take good care of yourself, and think of me sometimes, as I shall undoubtedly think of you.' He bent to kiss the hand Lora had extended in farewell. Then he gave a smart salute. 'Don't forget our mutual promise,' were his parting words, and, with his usual charming smile, he followed the laughing, jostling, troopers out of the inn.

Lora remained where she was, marvelling at the coincidence that had brought Lennox and her together at that wayside inn in the midst of nowhere. The chance meeting had done wonders towards boosting her morale, and she smiled happily as she sat gazing into the flickering fire, lost in day-dreams. Gradually, however, her mind returned to more sombre matters. As she thought of the false image she had deliberately presented to Lennox she became overwhelmed by feelings of guilt and apprehension.

It was quite a relief when the innkeeper's wife announced, 'That's your bed ready now, Miss. I've put in a warming pan, and it's a feather bed, so ye shouldna be cauld. Here's your candle. I hope ye sleep weel, Miss. Good-night to ye, now.'

'Good-night, and thank you,' Lora replied.

The bed proved to be very comfortable and she slept the sleep of exhaustion right through to daybreak, when she was awakened by a cock crowing near her bedroom window. As soon as she awoke, however, the feeling of foreboding once more engulfed her and she made a silent prayer that their journey might not end in disaster.

About seven o'clock there was a sharp knock on the door and a voice announced a ewer of hot water for washing. Lora rose at once, so she was dressed and ready when the call came that breakfast was being served.

Steaming hot porridge and bowls of milk were set out on the bare table, and her three companions were gathered together by the fireplace while they waited for her to join them. Lora smiled as she noted how convincingly Angus was carrying out the rôle of the shy bride. She also noted, with satisfaction, that the men were observing the precaution of talking in undertones, even though there was no one else in the room.

'Sure, I'll be lavin' ye now,' said Paddy. 'I've had my breakfast and I'll be on my way to Ferryden. I'm acquaint wi' the fisherfolk there, and I do a lot o' business wi' them, ye see. Some o' the friends I met at Memus are headin' for there as well, so we'll a' meet and have a real jollification. My very first job, of course, will be to see if I can fix up something for you two gentlemen. I'll come back to the Howletsden posthaste if I manage to contact the man I want. Sure, ye know ye can depend on ould Paddy.'

'*Merci beaucoup!*' Angus replied, appreciatively, 'and we shall be very willing to pay for any services rendered or expenses incurred. Indeed, I can let you have some money now if you wish.'

Paddy smiled happily at this suggestion.

'Sure now, I might just be needin' some money – as an extra incentive to persuade my friends to be makin' a special effort, as ye might say. 'Tis a risky job we'll be after askin' them to do, an' no mistake.'

'*Mais oui*,' agreed Angus. 'We fully understand the danger,' and he took two or three gold pieces from a pocket in his gown and handed them to Paddy.

'I thought you were to take us all the way to Howletsden,' Lora reminded the pedlar. 'That was the arrangement.'

'Sure, an' ye'll be managin' fine without me now, so ye will,' Paddy replied. 'Just you double back to the Daneside crossroads an' turn to your right there. Ye'll see St Ernan's Seat in front o' ye, wi' its cairn o' stanes on the riggin', an' ye canna go wrong. Keep right up the glen to the top o' the Goynd Brae. A wee bittie further on, the road swings to the right an' there's a ford across the Noran. Cross the ford, keep straight ahead, an' sure ye canna miss the Howletsden.'

When Paddy had taken his leave of them, the other three proceeded with their breakfast and decided to be on their way immediately afterwards.

Alistair went in search of the landlord to settle the bill for their night's lodging, while Angus and Lora returned to their rooms to collect their baggage. Lora was just making a final check when Angus suddenly burst in upon her.

'Lora! Lora! *Mon Dieu!* My pouch with all the money has vanished! I left it in a drawer while we were at breakfast.'

'Do you mean it's been stolen?' gasped Lora.

'*Oui! Oui!* Stolen! Every gold piece is gone! *Mon Dieu!* Whatever shall we do?' and he sat down on the bed and buried his head in his hands.

A moment later, Alistair appeared in the doorway. He came in quickly and closed the door.

'For heaven's sake, keep your voices down!' he commanded. 'I heard you from the other end of the passageway. What's gone wrong?'

'Someone has stolen the leather pouch with all Angus's money,' Lora answered bleakly.

'I thought that would happen! And the someone is that damned thief of a pedlar.'

'Paddy O'Malley?' exclaimed Angus and Lora together, in shocked surprise. 'Surely not!'

'Yes. But don't worry. He has got the pouch but not the gold pieces. I saw to that,' and Alistair drew a money bag from his pocket and dropped it into Angus's lap. 'That's your gold intact, Angus. I knew Paddy O'Malley was after it. He came into our room at Linnochmore the night before last. You were fast asleep, and I feigned sleep. I had a pretty good idea what he was after though, and when he seemed to be getting too near his goal I challenged him. He made the excuse he was looking for his pipe, but I guessed he'd try again for the gold, so I decided to take evasive action.'

'*Merci! Merci beaucoup*, Alistair,' said Angus gratefully. 'I just can't thank you enough. I thought our last hope had gone.'

Angus was as white as a ghost, obviously suffering from the shock of his devastating discovery.

'Stay where you are and I'll get you some brandy. Will you have a little too, Lora?' Alistair offered.

'No thank you. Not for me, but I do think Angus could do with a reviver.'

'Well, please remember to keep your voices down. We can't afford to attract attention,' Alistair reminded them.

When Angus had recovered sufficiently they set out on the last lap of their journey.

'I wonder if the pedlar has discovered yet that he has been duped,' mused Angus as they reached the crossroads at the Daneside, and turned towards the Glen of Ogil.

'I should think he'll be very angry indeed,' said Lora. 'What did you put in the leather pouch, Alistair?' she asked with interest.

'I enlisted Old Hamish's help and we made the bag up to about the same weight with pebbles and buttons and anything suitable that we could find. Then we put a few copper coins on top. I was sorry you gave O'Malley these gold pieces this morning, Angus, for I don't think he ever had any intention of trying to help us. His eye was on your pouch of gold. That was the only reason he stuck with us. Now I suppose he may well try to do us real harm, for he is the type to seek revenge, if thwarted. However, since we can do nothing about it, I suggest we try to forget about the pedlar. We are well rid of him.'

While they rode along, Lora told her companions about the happenings of the night before, of her meeting with Captain Bullard, and of what he had said regarding the rebels.

'We heard the arrival of the Dragoons,' said Alistair, 'and we hastened to get into bed in the hope that, if they were searching the inn, they would respect the privacy of a honeymoon couple! I must admit it was a relief when they departed without incident. As regards your friend's comments about the East Coast ports, it is what one would expect at the moment, Lora. We shall just have to take our chance with the rest.'

The mist of the night before had cleared considerably, and although the sky was dull, the air was fresh after the rain. As they made their way by the banks of the River Noran they remarked on its exceptionally clear waters and admired the glorious autumn foliage of the well-wooded Den of Ogil. The ponies had been well fed and rested, so they made good progress, and about noon they rode down into the leafy den from which the hunting lodge of Howletsden derived its name.

'I think I'd better go to the house alone first of all, and explain everything to Captain McNair,' said Lora, beginning to feel decidedly nervous at the thought of requesting help for Jacobite rebels from someone whom she could scarcely even remember.

'Yes. I agree. That would be the best approach,' said Alistair. 'We shall remain out here on the roadway. Let me help you to dismount, and I'll take charge of your pony.'

So Lora dismounted and walked up the short carriageway. She knocked loudly on the heavy oak door to be greeted by a clamour of dogs barking somewhere within the house. After a short delay the door was opened by a rather bent and decrepit old manservant, who looked more like a ghillie, or a shepherd, than a member of the household staff. His face was sharp-featured, weather-beaten and wrinkled, and he wore a well-worn tam o' shanter bonnet on his head.

'Good morning,' said Lora. 'I am Lora Macrae from The Milton of Glen Clova, and I wish to speak with Captain McNair, if you please.'

'Captain McNair is no' at hame, Miss. He left me in charge o' his premises during his absence. Ye may state your business to me, as the Captain's deputy,' he added, with a touch of pride.

'Will the Captain be long away?' Lora asked.

'Captain McNair didna' say exactly how lang he would be. What is it ye want wi' him, pray?'

'I wanted to speak with Captain McNair privately. I need his advice and help.'

'What kind o' advice, and in what way do ye need help?' queried the old man, eyeing Lora warily.

'I have two friends with me. It is for them I need advice and help.'

'Aye, but what *kind* o' help?' the man persisted.

'They are Jacobites,' Lora suddenly blurted out, in desperation.

The old man's eyes nearly popped out of his head.

'Jacobites?' he expostulated. 'Jacobites did ye say? Well, the answer, as far as I'm concerned, is "No Entry"! Captain McNair left me in charge o' his hoose. Good God, wumman! Would ye ha'e it burned doon afore he comes back? Naw, naw, *I'm* in charge here, an' I'll bid ye good day.'

With that, the aged retainer stepped smartly back inside and shut the door, quietly but firmly, in Lora's face.

XI THE SOUND OF THE SEA

Lora was completely shattered. An absolute rejection was something she had never envisaged. For a few moments she stood uncertainly on the doorstep. Then she turned and began to retrace her steps towards the gate. 'Where now? Where now?' she asked herself bleakly.

She was about halfway down the driveway when the door was thrown open and a lady's voice called after her, 'Wait a moment, please!'

Lora turned to see a tall silver-haired lady hurrying towards her, closely followed by the protesting manservant.

'I'm sorry you got such a poor reception,' the lady was saying. 'Please accept my apologies. Jamie is just a little over-zealous in his rôle of protector and I was upstairs when you arrived. It was just by chance I looked out of my window and saw you walking away. I am Mrs McNair. I understand you wished to speak with my husband. Could I be of any help?'

She looked keenly at Lora as she approached.

'Have I already met you somewhere?' she asked. 'You appear vaguely familiar. Should I know you perhaps?'

'I am Lora Macrae from The Milton of Clova,' Lora replied.

'Why then, I *do* know you. How do you do, my dear?' said Mrs McNair, grasping Lora's hand. 'Your late father was my husband's very dear friend. You were but a child when we last met so I may be forgiven for not recognising you. If I may say so, you have blossomed into a very attractive young lady. How did you get here, Lora? By carriage?'

'No, I rode on horseback.'

'Not alone, surely?'

'No. I have two companions with me. They are out on the roadway.'

'Then tell them to come in, Lora my dear. I shall be pleased to meet them.'

Here Jamie hurriedly intervened.

'Ye canna bring them in here, Ma'am,' he protested. 'They're Jacobites!'

At the mention of the word 'Jacobites', the colour seemed to drain from Mrs McNair's face, and she clutched her breast.

'Is it true what Jamie is saying? Are your friends Jacobites?' she asked of Lora.

'Yes.'

'They fought at Culloden?'

'Yes. They are fugitives. We came to ask Captain McNair if he could help us to find someone who could give them a passage to France or the Netherlands.'

'Perhaps I could think of someone to help. Bring your friends in, Lora. We can talk more comfortably by the fire,' said Mrs McNair, obviously making an effort to regain her composure.

Jamie, however, was not to be beaten.

'It's madness to bring Jacobites into the hoose, Ma'am. If the Redcoats find rebels here the place'll be burned doon aboot our ears. Jist think, Ma'am! An' the Maister no' at hame!' Poor Jamie was quite distraught.

'You know very well, Jamie, if Captain McNair had been at home he would have invited Miss Macrae and her friends to partake of our hospitality, and that is what I am doing now!' said Mrs McNair firmly. 'Please ask your companions to come in, Lora. They are welcome.'

Lora needed no further bidding. She turned and ran down the carriageway to where Alistair and Angus were waiting out of sight of the house, on the other side of the high boundary wall.

Lora hastily explained to their hostess about Angus's disguise as a bride, and when the introductions had been made, Mrs McNair turned to the disapproving Jamie.

'Please go and tell Maggie to prepare food for three extra guests, and get young Ian from the stables to attend to the horses,' she requested. Then she led Lora and the other two into a small oak-panelled parlour and closed the door.

Hardly was the door closed than she turned eagerly to Alistair and Angus. 'Tell me, what regiment were you in?' she asked.

'We were with Lord John Drummond's detachment,' Alistair replied.

'Oh!' said Mrs McNair, rather flatly.

'Are you against Jacobitism?' Lora felt forced to ask.

'I'm afraid I was neither for, nor against,' replied her hostess. 'I had heard the uprising described as "a wicked and unnatural rebellion", and I was sad to think of the bloodshed and the loss of young lives on both sides, but my interest ended there. Then, out of the blue, our younger son rode home one day and announced that he was to fight for Prince Charlie. He was training to become a Writer to the Signet in Edinburgh, and we pointed out to him the damage he might do his career but the thrill of adventure had seized hold of him. From the day he left, we have heard nothing of him,' she said sadly. 'We know not whether he be alive or dead,' and with that Mrs McNair dissolved into floods of tears.

For a few moments the young people could think of nothing to say, and there was an awkward silence while Mrs McNair strove to control her grief.

'I *do* beg your pardon,' she said at last. 'It isn't often I break down.'

'You don't know what regiment your son was with?' Alistair asked.

'When he left he spoke of joining Lord Ogilvy's regiment, but, as I said, we have heard nothing.'

'Remember, *madame*, "no news may be good news",' Angus consoled her.

'We thought that might be so, at first, but as the weeks passed we became more and more anxious. My elder son was home from the sea during the summer, and he went north to Inverness to see what he could find out, but his enquiries revealed nothing. In desperation, my husband went off himself, about three weeks ago, and I have heard nothing at all from him during that time. I am almost at the end of my tether,' and the poor woman seemed on the point of breaking down again.

'There is always the possibility that your son is lying low somewhere, just as we have been doing,' Alistair suggested.

'*Mais, oui*, and it may be that your husband, with his sea-going connection, is also staying under cover while he makes the necessary arrangements for your son's escape,' Angus added.

'O how I hope that you may be right!' exclaimed Mrs McNair, drying her eyes.

'If your son was actually with Lord Ogilvy's regiment, all may yet be well,' said Lora. 'Lord Ogilvy and some of his men escaped over the hills to Clova and we now believe that Lord Ogilvy was safely smuggled out of the country quite soon afterwards. Perhaps your son went with him.'

'No. My husband went to see the Earl of Airlie and he was able to confirm that our son was not among those who reached Clova.'

'Do not give up hope, *s'il vous plaît*, dear lady,' said Angus. 'It was every man for himself after the battle. We all took our separate ways, and your son may have been sheltered by kind people, just as we have been.'

Over the meal, Alistair and Angus described to their hostess their journeyings from Culloden to Clova, and also the many catastrophies that had befallen them. The fact that they had survived during nearly five months 'on the run' did much to cheer her. Lora and she had also a great deal of family news to exchange, so the day passed quickly for all four.

In case of any surprise raids by Redcoats, a room was prepared for 'the newly-weds' from which a quick getaway could be made if the need arose. Mrs McNair had been able to think of a possible contact for them in Montrose and she planned to send one of her 'grooms, with a message to the merchant concerned, the following day. So the men retired to bed, and Mrs McNair and Lora lingered on, talking quietly together by the light of the fire.

Every now and then Lora could hear the long-drawn-out 'tu-whit-tu-whoo' of an owl, in the darkness of the den.

'It's easy to see how this place got its name,' she remarked with a smile. 'It's the den of the owls and no mistake.'

'Yes. Some people think the owl's cry is eerie, but I have grown to like it,' replied her hostess. 'I must admit, I would miss the owls if they left the den.'

Just then, there came a distant angry screech which was taken up by other owls until the house seemed to be surrounded by their weird, hair-raising cries. Mrs McNair paused to listen.

'Something unusual has disturbed them,' she announced. 'Someone must be approaching. Can you hear anything, Lora?'

Lora shook her head, but, even as she did so, there came the distant rhythmic sound of hoofbeats. 'Yes, I do hear something,' she said, rather breathlessly. 'I'm sure someone is riding towards the house, and they are riding fast.'

Both ladies rose to their feet, saying nothing, but listening intently. Exchanging anxious glances, they waited, with bated breath, as they heard the horses coming along the road at a hard gallop, and then turning into the driveway. A moment later a loud knocking on the outside door echoed through the hall, followed by the dogs' barking and the sound of Jamie's shuffling steps as he proceeded to answer the summons.

It was impossible for the ladies to hear the conversation which ensued, but the door of the sitting-room was opened quite suddenly and unceremoniously by Jamie, and there, on the threshold, stood Paul Reynolds!

Lora got such a shock her legs could scarcely hold her up. Her mind was in a whirl. Instead of expressing joy at his safe return she simply exclaimed, 'Paul! What are *you* doing here?'

'What do you mean, what am *I* doing here?' Paul demanded indignantly. 'If you want to know, I'm here on your behalf. To warn you of a traitor in your midst.'

'A traitor!' Lora repeated. 'But who?'

'Your pedlar companion – that's who.'

'But you failed us yourself, Paul! Why didn't you keep the tryst at Lumley?' asked Lora accusingly, for this was still the thought uppermost in her mind.

'I didn't fail anyone,' returned Paul sharply. 'It was impossible for me to keep the tryst myself but I sent another man in my place and the poor fellow narrowly escaped with his life. Your rebels were betrayed by the pedlar. But for Hamish's gallant sacrifice they'd all have perished. Indirectly, Hamish also saved my deputy. He saw the skirmish with the Redcoats and made good his escape.'

'The pedlar said it was you who had betrayed them,' Lora blurted out.

'Me? Surely you didn't believe that, Lora!'

'I didn't want to believe it, Paul. Truly I didn't. But I understood that the arrangements for the rendezvous were entirely between you and Hamish – that no one else knew the time or place.'

'So, from that, you decided that I had done the foul deed! Well, I'm certainly not flattered by your opinion of me!'

'But why didn't you send a messenger to explain things to us, Paul? I hoped against hope that you would. When no word came, I must admit my faith in you wavered.'

'As a matter of fact I knew nothing at all about the ambush until late last night when I returned to Dundee. I had to make an urgent journey to Leith at the weekend,' Paul explained.

'So you went to see your lady friend in Leith instead of keeping the tryst!' Lora accused rashly.

It was Paul's turn to be astounded.

'How dare you! My lady friend indeed! If you want to know, one of my merchant vessels in the Firth of Forth was badly damaged by the storm and several of the crew were washed overboard. It was imperative that I should go there immediately. I had no other alternative but to send a substitute to the Pass of Lumley. Surely you don't think I would put a pleasure trip before a matter involving the lives of men!' he expostulated, his cheeks flushed with annoyance.

'Forgive me, Paul! I ought not to have said that,' Lora apologised. 'But how did you know where to find us?'

'I rode up to Clova this morning and Elsie told me where you'd gone. She gave me the necessary directions and I came on straight away. I realised there was no time to lose.'

'And how did you find out the traitor was Paddy O'Malley?'

'There is quite a long story attached to that. I may tell you some day. In the meantime let us just say I ferreted out the information. Where is he now, by the way? Is he here?'

'No. He left us this morning to go to Ferryden to meet some friends of his.'

'But he knows you and the others are here?'

'Yes.'

'Then I advise you to get away as soon as possible. Have you any other plans as regards the rebels?'

'No. Not so far. We hoped Captain McNair might help us, but he is not at home.'

At this point, Mrs McNair, who had slipped out of the room at the beginning of the conversation, taking a reluctant Jamie with her, now reappeared to say that food and drink were ready for the latecomer.

'Please forgive me, Mrs McNair, for failing to introduce Paul to you whenever he arrived,' Lora apologised. 'You must have thought me very rude, but I was quite put out by his sudden appearance. This is Paul Reynolds. You may recall the name. Paul is my stepmother's stepson by her first marriage.'

'How do you do, Mr Reynolds,' said Mrs McNair. 'I remember Lora's father speaking of you, but I don't think you and I ever met.'

While Paul ate, Mrs McNair and Lora talked with him, and he explained to their hostess the reason for his urgent ride. She, in turn, spoke of her worries over her son. Lora also told them about the pedlar's attempted theft of Angus's gold pieces.

'The fact that O'Malley's plan was foiled will make him more vindictive than ever,' declared Paul. 'The rebels cannot remain long here, for O'Malley will undoubtedly denounce them again.'

'Have you any hope of finding a way out for the two boys?' asked Mrs McNair.

'I am actively involved in my late father's shipping business,' Paul replied, 'so I have contacts here and there. I have also a very good friend among the fishing community of Aberbrothock. I think I shall appeal to him to provide a safe hiding place for Alistair and Angus while we investigate possible channels. I had already found a Captain willing to take them on a ship sailing from Dundee, but of course it had to leave without them. It is becoming increasingly difficult to arrange escape routes. The ports are swarming with Redcoat spies, and of course the fishing boats are confined to harbour meantime by order of the government.'

'You look very tired, Paul,' said Mrs McNair at last. 'I think you had better rest here tonight. Your horse has been attended to, so there is no need to worry on that score. It will be well fed and comfortable in our stables, and it will be fresh for tomorrow.'

'Thank you Mrs McNair. I *am* very tired, I must confess. I shall be very glad to accept your hospitality for tonight and I can leave early tomorrow morning. Is there perhaps someone in your household who could direct me as to the quickest route to Aberbrothock? I am not familiar with this part of the country.'

'Jamie will be able to help you. In his youth he was a drover, and walked with cattle and sheep to the various trysts up and down the country. He will know all the hill tracks, drove roads, and cattle raikes, which afford short cuts. My husband has a considerable collection of maps of the countryside, so Jamie and you can study them tomorrow morning.'

Paul and Jamie were already poring over the maps when the others assembled for breakfast next morning and Angus, with his artistic talents, was immediately 'roped in' to making two sketches of the recommended route.

The old man's enthusiasm was almost amusing. He made it quite plain that he couldn't wait to be rid of the uninvited guests. And who, under the circumstances, could blame him?

'I think you people had better remain here another night, Lora, if Mrs McNair is willing to have you,' Paul advised. 'That would give me time to organise things in Aberbrothock. From what you said about the money the pedlar got from Angus, I've been thinking it is very unlikely O'Malley will make any move against you until he has spent that money. He'll be too busy sampling the products of the local whisky stills and the brew-houses meanwhile to bother about retaliation. That will come later when the money is done. I suggest you set out tomorrow morning and keep going at as steady a pace as possible, taking care to keep a keen look-out for any Redcoat patrols, especially where you have to traverse main roads. I shall be waiting for you at Bishoploch where you join the Forfar-Arbroath turnpike. By then I'll have decided where you're to stay, and the safest way to get there.'

Lora promised to take every precaution *en route*. She would have been happier to have been making the journey with Paul, but she realised the necessity for him to go on ahead.

Mrs McNair had already arranged for some food to be packed for Paul, so, as soon as he had breakfasted, his horse was brought from the stables and he was up and off.

The main topic of conversation after Paul had left Howletsden was the falsity of Paddy O'Malley.

'How dreadful to think he could deliberately send his friend Hamish to his death,' said Lora.

'I don't think he had really expected Hamish to be caught in the ambush, of course,' remarked Alistair. 'That was meant for us. He had probably thought Hamish would let Angus and me go forward to the Tollhouse by ourselves. Come to think of it, when we met the pedlar on the road back to Glamis he seemed genuinely surprised to see us, and he was clearly shocked when we told him Hamish was dead.'

'Perhaps so, but might it not be that he was surprised to think we had escaped the ambush which he himself had deliberately arranged for us?' suggested Angus.

'That could be, of course,' Alistair agreed, 'and he was probably on his way to collect the reward for his services, plus a share of the spoils from your leather pouch.'

'I wasn't happy about the pedlar from the very start,' confessed Lora, 'but the MacCrimmons were so sure of his sincerity they made me feel ashamed of my distrust.'

'I must admit, I liked him,' Angus declared. 'He was very entertaining.'

After a further day of rest and another comfortable night, Alistair and

Angus were ready for anything when they met Lora at the breakfast table the following morning. Lora herself had been greatly cheered by the knowledge that Paul was in no way a traitor. So, despite the dangers still besetting them, she also felt wonderfully bright and confident as they prepared for departure.

Having thanked Mrs McNair for her kindness and hospitality, and having expressed their sincere hopes that her worries about her son would soon be happily resolved, they bade her goodbye and rode out from the gateway of Howletsden.

It was a beautiful autumn morning. The rain-washed sky was high and blue, flecked by a few fleecy clouds. Rooks were wheeling and cawing overhead, and the countryside was a kaleidoscope of colour. The horses were fresh and raring to go, and the travellers were young and full of the *joie-de-vivre*. On such a day, amid such pastoral beauty, it was almost impossible to imagine that, for those three young people, danger, and even death, could be lurking round the very next bend in the road.

Their way led eastwards by Auchlochie, then down through the Fern Den and over the Noran Water at the Wellford. They by passed the sleepy little village of Tannadice, and headed for the ford over the South Esk at Finavon.

'It's like meeting an old friend,' Lora remarked, as they approached the river.

The South Esk had meandered by Cortachy, Inverquharity, Justinhaugh, and Tannadice. Now, vastly increased by its many tributaries, it flowed majestically on its way, via Brechin, to its ultimate resting place in the German Ocean at Montrose.

Having crossed the ford, the trio headed along the narrow track that led through the wooded policies surrounding the old castle of Finavon, and began the long tortuous climb over the shoulder of Finavon Hill with its famous hill-fort, steeped in antiquity. Looking back, as the path wound higher and higher, the view towards the Grampian peaks became quite breathtaking. So they paused for a short rest, and ate some of the food which Mrs McNair had given them, while they enthused over the glorious panorama – a panorama that included a wide sweep of the beautiful Valley of Strathmore and the Braes of Angus.

At the crest of the slope the track dipped sharply down the other side of the hill towards the ancient hamlet of Aberlemno, set in the typical chequer-board pattern of an Angus farming landscape, and boasting a unique collection of Pictish sculptured stones. Had they been on a pleasure trip, the scenery alone would have created absolute enjoyment for all three. As it was, they had to keep a constant vigil for possible danger. They also had to make an effort to maintain a steady pace, so there was simply no time to stand and stare.

In the early morning the only people to be seen were farm-workers going about their daily tasks, or Highland drovers on the move with flocks of sheep or herds of cattle. As the day wore on, however, and they drew nearer to the main highways, so also did the traffic increase in variety. Luckily they saw no sign of English military patrols. For safety's sake they made no conversation with anyone they met, Lora and Alistair merely exchanging the time of day with other travellers, and Angus saying nothing at all. Even between themselves there was little talk, except when covering open ground where there was definitely no risk of eavesdroppers.

Leaving Aberlemno they continued over by Turin and were descending a drove road towards the Forfar-Montrose highway when Lora's pony suddenly went lame. A quick examination revealed that a shoe had come loose.

An old man, leading a cow, was climbing the path towards them so Lora approached him.

'Can you tell me, please, where the nearest smithy is,' she asked.

'Aye. There's a smiddy alang the road in the Pickerton direction,' the man replied, turning to point the way with his stick. 'It's jist aff the road a wee bittie – roond the back o' the alehoose yonder.'

Lora thanked him for the information and joined the other two. Studying the sketch of their route she decided she had better go to the smithy alone.

'You two will be better not to hang about on the main road,' she said. 'I think it would be safer if you turned off down the side road towards Guthrie now, and I'll soon catch up, once Rufus's shoe is fixed.'

As Lora led her pony up the cart track from the main road to the smiddy, she could see a group of tinkers gathered round the alehouse door. By the noise they were making, it was quite obvious that they had already had plenty to drink, and Lora felt decidedly nervous at the thought of passing so rowdy a gang. One woman was singing a bawdy ballad, and all the company were joining lustily in the chorus. So Lora kept the pony between herself and them, and hurried past while they were concentrating on their vocal abilities.

The tinker's cart was at the smithy and the smith was busy mending one of the shafts. He was very sympathetic when Lora explained about Rufus's mishap.

'Well, by the soond o' things the tinks'll no' be needin' their cairty for a while yet,' he said with a broad grin, 'so I'll attend to your horsie right away, Miss.'

Glancing toward the main road in the course of his work, he paused and shaded his eyes with his hand.

'Looks as if we're gettin' another visit o' the military,' he remarked.

Lora turned and followed the direction of his gaze, and the colour drained from her cheeks. Sure enough, a small contingent of Redcoats were marching up from the highway towards the alehouse.

'I doobt the sodjers are some like the tinks. They're dry!' quipped the smith. 'We'll see some fun noo, I'm thinkin', if that lot clash. Well, Miss, there's your horsie as guid as new. He's a fine-lookin' beastie. I wouldna mind bein' the owner o' that ane.'

Lora thanked the man for his prompt attention, and willingly paid him for his services.

'Ye'd best lead your horsie past that lot,' he advised Lora as she was preparing to mount. 'Those tinker dogs are the devil-an'-a' for nippin' the horses' heels.'

Lora took the smith's advice and set off leading Rufus. The old tinker woman was still singing – or skirling – at the pitch of her aged voice, with the entire company joining in the chorus as before, and Lora hoped again to slip past unnoticed. Alas, one of the mongrel dogs was stalking a hen, which grew more flustered at the approach of the horse. With much cackling and squawking it flew almost under Rufus's chin. The pony reared and gave a frightened whinny, and the dog rushed in to the attack, just as the blacksmith had warned Lora it would. Rufus lashed out with his hind legs and the bawdy ballad came to an abrupt end, as the tinkers scattered in all directions. Lora held tightly to the pony's bridle and did her best to quieten the nervous animal. Between swearing men, screaming women and children, barking dogs, and squawking poultry, the din which had so suddenly arisen around her was indescribable. It was as if all hell had been let loose.

One tinker, decidedly unsteady on his feet, aimed a kick at the offending dog, lost his balance and fell against another of the gang who was sitting on an upturned bucket. Amidst a volley of oaths, the two men rolled in the dust. Next moment they were kicking and punching each other like mortal enemies. Some of the other men pitched in too, and then the women joined the fray. Even the aged songstress cast aside her jug of ale and hobbled in to do battle.

The smell of unwashed bodies and filthy garments (bearing the additional clinging aroma of wood smoke from the camp-fire) mingled with the over-powering odour of beer, ale, or whisky-laden breath to produce a truly nauseating stench. Lora was by now practically surrounded by a mass of battling tinkers, while the Redcoat soldiers were cheering and shouting encouragement to the combatants from the doorway of the alehouse. It was a hair-raising experience to say the least of it.

How to get clear of this tinkers' brawl was the uppermost thought in Lora's mind. As she sought desperately for a way out, a claw-like hand descended upon her shoulder, and she was dragged forcibly round to face someone she had fervently hoped she would never set eyes on again – Granny McPhee of the Skinner's Close!

For a full moment, Lora stared blankly into that never-to-be-forgotten, pock-marked countenance, before the old woman spoke.

'I thocht it was you, Miss High-an'-Mighty!' she exclaimed. 'Ye didna think ye'd be meetin' Granny so sune again. Did ye now?' and she leered up into Lora's face.

With Rufus to cope with, Lora could only give half her attention to the old tinker. The horse was really frightened and she knew, if she let him go, it would be the last she would see of him, but the old woman clung to her arm in spite of all Lora's efforts to shrug her off.

'I've been hearin' aboot you from Paddy, so I have, and it seems I wasna far wrang aboot you. He was tellin' me ye've been up to some monkey-business wi' Jacobites. Let me see your palm again, ye little hussy.'

'Leave me alone,' cried Lora, 'and get back, or you'll get hurt. Can't you see my horse is scared?'

But, in spite of her warning, Granny McPhee held tight. Between the nervous, struggling horse, and the tinker clinging like a leech, Lora felt she would be literally torn apart. At the crucial moment one of the soldiers decided enough was enough. Lora caught the flash of a red sleeve beside her and a strong hand grabbed Granny's arm.

'Leave her alone! Let her go at once, you old witch! D'you hear me?' came the voice of a man used to command.

Granny retaliated with a string of oaths, but her hold on Lora slackened as she turned her wrathful attention on her assailant.

At the same time a voice shouted, 'Tak' yer hands aff Granny!' and a burly-looking tinker threw himself upon the Redcoat. Another trooper rushed forward to intervene, and for a moment Lora and this second soldier came face to face. Lora recognised him immediately. It was the soldier who had waylaid her that night in Kirriemuir.

The man recognised Lora also. He had just opened his mouth to address her when one of the tinkers hit him a crashing blow on the side of the head with a stick. By now the tinkers had abandoned their personal quarrels in the face of the common enemy. Men and women alike, wielding whatever weapon they could lay their hands on, dashed into the fray in defence of Granny, while the Redcoat Dragoons showed no less determination to champion their comrades.

This was the chance Lora had been looking for, and she seized it with both hands. Pulling Rufus clear of the fraças, she flung herself into the saddle. The terrified horse needed no encouragement. It galloped down the lane and out along the highway as if pursued by demons, and Lora's backward glance assured her that neither Dragoons nor tinkers had even noticed her departure.

Alistair and Angus were very relieved to see her. They had pulled into a wood not far from the main highway.

'We decided to take cover and wait for you, rather than go on by ourselves,' Alistair explained, 'so we saw the Dragoons pass by, and we heard the dreadful din that followed. It was like the noise of a battlefield, without the muskets and the cannonfire. What happened?'

Lora explained about the clash between the two parties.

'*Mon Dieu!*' exclaimed Angus, 'it is a blessing I persuaded our friend here to stay where he was. He was determined to come after you.'

'Thank goodness you didn't, Alistair,' said Lora. 'That would've been disastrous,' and she told them about her meeting with Granny McPhee, and the very same Dragoon who had previously accosted her.

'What a dreadful experience for you, Lora,' said Alistair, noting the look of strain on her face and the pallor of her cheeks.

'Yes. It was a case of "twixt the devil and the deep sea" with that horrid tinker woman and the equally horrid Dragoon. When you come to think of it, though, they actually saved me from each other!'

'I'm afraid you've had some bad moments since your befriended us, Lora,' Alistair remarked.

'Never mind! As long as we get you safely out of the country it'll be worth it all,' Lora smiled. 'Now we must get on our way, and put as wide a distance as possible between ourselves and all those dreadful people.'

Having passed the old Castle of Guthrie, with the tiny hamlet of the same name clustered around its gates, they hastened down past Pitmuies and on by the parish of Idvies. They looked rather apprehensively at the gallows, erected on a hillock not far from the castle of Gardyne, but thankfully, there was no poor departed sinner hanging thereon.

The drove roads and bridle-paths, chosen for them by Jamie of Howletsden, had provided considerable short cuts and by late afternoon they were approaching Bishoploch.

With the memory of Hamish's untimely death still very much in mind, all three scanned the roadway ahead with some trepidation, but Paul was there waiting as arranged. After only the briefest of greetings, they all moved out along the turnpike towards Aberbrothock.

'I'm glad to be able to tell you that I managed to contact my old friend Davie Spinks,' said Paul, as they rode along. 'He was my constant companion when I spent boyhood holidays in Aberbrothock and I knew if I could find him we'd have someone dependable to help us – someone we could really trust. Davie is a deep-sea fisherman. He married recently, and he and his wife Kitty have a fisher's cottage out near the cliffs. We're to go to their house now, and you're to stay with them, Lora, but Davie thinks it would be better if Alistair and Angus went straight into hiding in one of the smugglers' caves at Carlinheugh Bay.'

'We'll be only too pleased to do anything you wish,' Alistair assured him. 'Angus and I would like you to know how grateful we are for all the trouble you have gone to on our behalf, Paul.'

Paul shrugged.

'Lora is the one to thank,' he replied. 'I must admit I have no Jacobite leanings myself. Come to think of it, though, after this amount of involvement I can hardly claim to be a loyal citizen of King George either,' he added with a rueful smile.

Dusk was falling by the time they reached the outskirts of Aberbrothock, and, to Lora's surprise, Paul led them boldly through the town. Although it was growing dark there seemed to be quite a number of people abroad, and Paul appeared to be familiar with many of them, including Redcoats.

'I thought at first we might have to make a detour by Saint Vigeans tonight,' he said, 'but I met Lennox Bullard today and he took me to the officers' mess to meet some of his friends. As it happened I knew most of them already, so I've more or less got the "freedom" of the town now, as one might say. I won't have to dodge army patrols all the time, and that will be a great help. Meantime I'm making my headquarters in the house of a shipping merchant – a friend of mine – down near the harbour. He's out of the country at the moment, but his old housekeeper is there to cook meals for me, so it's all very convenient. I can come and go as I please, without anyone asking awkward questions.'

Davie Spinks had his home beyond the town. It was at the end of a row of fisher cottages nestling in the lee of the sea braes, and facing out over a stretch of grass, and a shingle beach, towards the open sea. Just north of the group of cottages the beach came to an end and the cliffs began. As the travellers drew near, the moon was rising, giving an air of romance and mystery to a scene which immediately fired Lora's imagination with thoughts of secret coves, and rocky shores, and smugglers. She felt a thrill of excitement.

Paul hardly had time to knock on the door of the cottage when it was opened by Davie himself. 'I was watchin' an' listenin' for ye,' he said. 'Just put the horses into the shed. We have neither a horse nor a cow, so there'll be room for them a'.'

A few of the neighbours in the adjoining cottages had evinced some interest when they heard the horses arriving, but when they realised the riders were friends of Davie's they withdrew and closed their doors. Obviously they respected one another's privacy and didn't indulge in spying or eavesdropping on their own kind.

Davie was immensely tall, with a massive frame and a pleasant countenance. He actually towered above the other three men, none of whom was small in stature. His ready smile and firm handshake endeared him to Lora right away and one glance was enough to tell her that this was a friend worth having.

The tiny thatched cottage, with its thick stone walls, had a whitewashed interior and a low, raftered ceiling. The living-room was dimly lit by a ship's lantern and it was sparsely furnished but, even in the poor light, Lora could see that the room was spick and span in every way.

Davie's wife Kitty, rosy-cheeked and open-faced like her husband, was overcome with shyness at first, but soon rose to the occasion and set forth a hearty supper for their guests. Indeed, Lora was amazed at the abundance of food on the table. Kitty must have read her thoughts, for she whispered in Lora's ear, 'We havena as much as this to eat as a rule. It's thanks to Mr Reynolds.'

Everyone enjoyed a hearty meal and expressed their appreciation, but there was no lingering at the table. As soon as they had finished eating, Davie stood up and took his cap from its hook on one of the rafters.

'The moon'll be up now, lads, so it's time we made tracks for the cave. There's quite a lang walk in front o' ye yet.'

Angus once again changed into male attire. Then, laden with blankets, which Paul had provided, the men set off on foot, Paul going along merely for company to Davie on the way back.

Left to themselves, Kitty and Lora set about washing the crockery and generally tidying up after the meal.

Now that she had overcome her initial shyness, Kitty had plenty to say and she was full of praise for Paul.

'Mr Reynolds is a real gentleman. Davie spoke to me aboot him when we were first walkin' oot together. He said Mr Reynolds was the best pal he ever had. Though his father was a wealthy ship-owner, wi' braw hooses in Leith and Aberbrothock, Mr Reynolds was never a snob and Davie said he was feart o' nothing. He was aye prepared to do his full share whatever they were at.'

'I understand Davie is a deep-sea fisherman now,' said Lora.

'Aye, that's his trade but meantime he has a job as a farm-worker,' Kitty replied. 'Since the rebellion, the authorities have stopped the fishin' boats leavin' the harbour, in case they might help Jacobites to escape, ye see,' she explained. 'The fisherfolk here are sufferin' terrible hardship as a result o' that law. Some o' the families are more or less starvin'. Davie was acquaint wi' the farmer at East Seaton. He used to help him wi' the spring plantin' work and at the hairst. That's how he got this job. I had a steady job mysel' guttin' fish at the harbour, and then sellin' it roond the doors, but wi' the fishin' fleet idle, there was no work for me either. However, I've got work as a charwoman. It's just as hard as the fish guttin' but it's warmer work because I'm inside a' the time. I'd like to get back to the fish guttin' though. I enjoy the sing-songs and the laughs we have while we're workin'. Scrubbin' and polishin' on your own is a lonely job.'

Both girls were dozing by the fire when Davie and Paul returned.

'Would ye no' bide here for the night, Paul,' Davie suggested. 'Ye'd be more than welcome.'

'I know that, thank you,' Paul answered, 'but I have someone calling at the house early tomorrow morning and it's important that I should be there. I believe he might have the answer to our present problem and the sooner that problem is solved the better for all concerned.'

'Nae doobt aboot that,' Davie agreed, 'but the lads'll be safe enough where they are for a day or two. They should be comfortable enough too, wi' a' the blankets you got for them. There's plenty o' driftwood if they do need a fire, and there's a freshwater spring nearby. That's one o' the reasons I chose the Dark Cave.'

'Miss Lora and me'll take a hot meal oot to the lads in the evenin',' said Kitty. 'We've aye plenty o' meal and milk since Davie started work at East Seaton. That's part o' his wages, and we're very willing to share what we have.'

'We know you'll look after them, Kitty,' said Paul appreciatively, 'and we're truly grateful to Davie and you for your help.'

The long journey on horseback, combined with the change of air, had made Lora very drowsy and the hour was getting late. As soon as Paul had gone, Kitty suggested Lora should get off to bed and she readily acquiesced. It was a new experience for her to sleep in a box-bed, and the room was very small compared with her bedroom at The Milton. Indeed, it was little bigger than her hanging closet. Apart from the built-in bed, the room contained only a plain wooden kitchen chair and a home-made chest-of-drawers, with a 'cloutie' rug on the stone-flagged floor. Nevertheless, it was scrupulously clean and fresh. A variety of grasses from the sea-meadows had been placed in a jar on the oak chest and an interesting hand-carved plaque of scenes from the Bible hung above the bed. Somehow the spartan simplicity of it all lent the room a unique charm of its own.

For a little while Lora lay awake looking through the tiny, deep-set window to where the moon sailed serenely overhead amid a maze of stars. From a distance there came the long-drawn-out, mournful call of a sea-bird, and the waves lapped softly over the pebbly beach. As she listened to those unfamiliar sounds, the tinker's prophetic words returned to her . . . 'I see you on a journey, and the sound of the sea is in my ears.'

'She must be a witch,' Lora murmured, sleepily, 'but she unwittingly saved me from a Redcoat interrogation today. I guess it was lucky for me she was at Pickerton.'

Whether that guess would prove right or wrong, time alone would tell.

XII THE CURTAIN FALLS

Lora woke to the subdued voices of Davie and Kitty as they went about their early morning tasks in the adjoining kitchen. It was little more than daylight, but Lora felt wide awake and ready to rise. Before beginning to dress herself, she opened the tiny casement as wide as possible that she might absorb to the full the fascinating sights and sounds of the seashore at daybreak.

'Good mornin', Miss Lora. You're early on the go,' Kitty greeted her, when she entered the kitchen. 'I thocht we wouldna' be seein' *you* till dinnertime.'

'Since Alistair and Angus came into my life I've been late abed and up with the lark,' Lora replied with a smile. 'It has become a way of life to me, in fact. I doubt if I shall ever enjoy a long lie again!'

Kitty had the porridge pot hanging from the sway-bar, with a brisk fire of driftwood underneath, so it was no time before they were tucking into the Scottish staple diet of porridge and milk.

Immediately he had finished, Davie rose, laced up his tackety boots, and strode off to his work in the fields.

'Leave the crockery for me to wash up, Kitty,' said Lora. 'Then I'll feed and exercise the horses. When do you come back from work?'

'I'll be back aboot noon,' Kitty replied.

'And what about Davie?'

'Sometimes Davie comes back for his dinner and sometimes he doesna'. It depends where he's workin'.'

147

'Tell me what it is you have for your midday meal and I'll get it ready for you,' Lora offered.

'I made nettle soup yesterday to last for a few days. It'll just need reheated, and we like boiled tatties in the soup,' said Kitty and she showed Lora where both commodities were kept.

Lora's first task was to clean out the stable. She saw nothing of the next-door neighbours so she presumed they had gone off to work like Davie and Kitty. About mid-morning, however, Davie's grandfather, who lived in a similar cottage nearby, wandered round to see what she was doing. The old man made himself known to her and lent a hand with the work but he asked no questions. Minding one's own business was evidently the accepted code of behaviour around these parts.

When the stable was cleaned to her satisfaction, Lora exercised each horse in turn. The gallops along the seashore were as enjoyable to her as to the horses, for the sea air was invigorating, and the horses loved to splash through the briny, and cavort over the shingly beach.

'If only Loyal were here to share in the fun!' Lora sighed, and she was seized by a sudden nostalgic longing for her faithful canine companion.

Back at the cottage, Lora set about stoking up the fire to boil the potatoes and heat the soup. Then she set the table and had everything in readiness by the time Kitty returned.

Davie arrived just as they were about to sit down at table.

'I'm workin' in the field across the brae there,' he explained 'and I felt like a plate o' Kitty's nettle kail.'

They had hardly begun to the meal when Kitty exclaimed, 'Oh, wait till ye hear this, Miss Lora! A queer thing happened this forenune. An auld tinkie wifie cam' to Mrs Smith's door, sellin' heather besoms an' things, and she asked the Mistress if by any chance a Miss Lora Macrae had come to bide in the neighbourhood lately. Mrs Smith hasna been lang in Aberbrothock hersel', so she said she hadna heard o' anybody by that name. I was scrubbin' the lobby, so Mrs Smith turned to me and asked if I could supply the information the woman wanted. I asked the tinkie where this Miss Macrae hailed from and she said "Glen Clova". Then I asked if this Miss Macrae was a tinker like hersel'. She said, "No, Miss Macrae is gentry from the Big Hoose." At that I told her I was jist a puir fisher lass and it wasna likely that I would come in contact wi' gentry o' that kind. But I said if she would describe the young lady I would keep a lookoot for her. Mind ye, her description was accurate. I would easy have recognised ye, Miss Lora.'

'What a blessing you didn't say you knew me!' exclaimed Lora.

'Naw! I had mair sense than that. Forbye, I didna think you'd have much in common wi' yon kind o' woman. I doubted if ye'd even ken her.'

'But I *do* know her,' said Lora, and she went on to describe her meeting with Granny McPhee and her daughter, and Paddy O'Malley, at the lodging-house in the Skinner's Close. She also described her further encounter with Granny McPhee at Pickerton the previous day.

'If ye hadna said the tinks had a fecht wi' the Redcoats at Pickerton I'd have said they were spyin' for the English,' asserted Davie. 'Some o' them would sell their souls to get money for drink, ye know. And I dinna like the sound o' that pedlar ye've been associatin' wi' either. Ye'd better no' venture into the toon, Miss Lora.'

'No. I realise that. But I just can't help wondering what evil they are planning,' said Lora, uneasily.

'Och! worryin' gets ye nowhere. We can consider oorsel's lucky we've had this early warnin' and we'll just have to keep a sharp look-out from now on. Well, I'll have to go,' and, with that, Davie took his cap down off the hook and went away back to his work.

While Lora washed up, Kitty boiled more potatoes and heated the remainder of the soup to take to Alistair and Angus. She put these into heated bowls, wrapped up some bannocks, and filled a flagon with milk. Then she put everything into two of her fish creels.

'Shall we take one of the ponies to carry the food?' Lora suggested.

'Naw, Naw. We'll manage fine between us, an' we'll attract less attention that way.'

'Are we likely to meet many people, then?' asked Lora.

'I hope no',' Kitty replied, wrapping her fishwife shawl round her head and shoulders, 'but one never knows. Better to be safe than sorry.'

There was a fresh breeze blowing off the sea as the girls followed the winding path along the clifftop, and Lora looked around with lively interest at the awesome rock formations, the rich red sandstone of the cliffs, and the blue-green waters of the German Ocean with their frothy edgings of white foam. It was a colourful and impressive sight.

Kitty pointed out landmarks such as 'The Needles E'e; the 'Mermaid's Kirk'; and 'The Mariner's Grave'; all of which intrigued Lora immensely.

Further on she was shown a dangerous-looking hole in the roof of a cave, known locally as 'the Blow-hole'.

'Ye should see it when there's a storm,' said Kitty. 'The water spouts up through that hole as if from a whale – hence its name. And that's "Dickmont's Den" doon there,' she added, as they skirted an exceptionally deep rocky inlet. 'There's naebody around at the moment but I can tell ye it'll be a hive o' smuggler activity after dark.'

'Does Davie take any part in the smuggling?' Lora asked.

'Och aye, sometimes. Near a' the men do a bit o' smugglin' occasionally, but Davie has nothing to do wi' the Dickmont's Den lot. They're professionals – a ruthless gang of law-breakers.'

Every twist of the path revealed some fresh item of interest, and a tremendously impressive stack of rock caught Lora's eye.

'That's "The De'il's Heid",' Kitty supplied. 'It's a very special landmark. Ye're no' likely to forget that ane.'

'It is certainly shaped like a head,' Lora agreed, considering it carefully, 'a rather grotesque head. It's well named, I think.'

Besides the wild and picturesque coastline, the variety of birdlife was amazing. Lora recognised the calls of peewits, oyster-catchers and curlews, while Kitty pointed out cormorants, puffins, kittiwakes, and a variety of gulls, besides the occasional fulmar and guillemot.

'This is absolutely wonderful,' Lora enthused. 'I thought nothing could compare with the hills and the glens but I have to admit now – the coast has its charms! I wish I were on a pleasure visit instead of a life-or-death mission.'

The path, or 'Limpet roadie' as Kitty called it – from the clifftop down to the beach at Carlinheugh Bay – was extremely steep and rather difficult to negotiate, but they supported each other, and, with a good deal of nervous giggling, they at last slithered down to the stony shingle.

'Ye can see the entrance to the Dark Cave at the far end o' the bay, yonder,' Kitty pointed out. The Light Cave is to the right of it. If ye bear in mind the various landmarks ye've seen on the way here, and try to memorise exactly where the path comes down to the bay, ye should manage to find your way on your own, Miss Lora.'

During the long walk from the cottage they had seen various people fishing, collecting driftwood, mussel-gathering, and the like, but nothing to worry them at all or even to remind them of the need for caution. It came as something of a shock, therefore, on approaching the mouth of the Dark Cave, to hear a warning voice.

'Quick! Run girls!' Alistair called urgently.

Lora and Kitty gathered up their skirts with one accord, and sprinted the last few yards over rocks and boulders into the darkness of the cave.

'What is it?' they gasped in alarm. 'Redcoats?'

'No. Not yet. But there's every sign they're coming fast! Look!' and Alistair pointed back the way they had come. Two men had just appeared through the headland from the neighbouring inlet. They were racing along the beach and there was little doubt they were running for their lives.

Sure enough, a moment later a small party of red-coated riders appeared in hot pursuit.

'Where have they come from?' queried Lora. 'I didn't see them come down the path.'

'They'd come through the rock archway called "The Castle Gate", between the adjoinin' bay and Carlinheugh,' Kitty answered.

'Are they heading for this cave, do you think?' asked Lora.

'*Non.* I do not think so,' said Angus, shaking his head. 'I reckon it will be the Light Cave they will be making for. It is the easiest way through this headland.'

150

THE CURTAIN FALLS

The grassy braes and the sandy beach were relatively easy for the fugitives to traverse, but, when these ended, the shingle and wet rocks, covered with slippery seaweed, were exceedingly treacherous. The men slithered and stumbled among the rock pools as the race became a desperate struggle for survival.

By this time the elder of the two men was showing definite signs of tiring, and the onlookers heard him call out to his younger companion.

'Dinna wait for me, Donald. Keep going.'

The young man hesitated, evidently loath to desert his friend, but the older man – the only one carrying a gun – commanded him to go.

'Think o' your wife and bairns, man,' he cried. 'For God's sake run, while there's still time! I'll cover for ye!'

With that, the older man flung himself down behind an outcrop of rock and levelled his musket at the approaching Redcoats.

'I wish we could've done something to help,' exclaimed Alistair agitatedly. 'He'll never hold them.'

Meanwhile, the young man redoubled his efforts to escape, while the Dragoons spurred their horses in pursuit. The man behind the rock fired his musket and the nearest soldier fell from his horse and lay still. Two of his companions immediately swerved aside to deal with the sniper, while the third leapt from his horse, and continued the man-hunt on foot, over the slippery tangle-covered rocks.

From his hiding place behind the rock the man fired again, slightly wounding another Dragoon. Then he turned and took careful aim at the soldier who was pursuing his young friend Donald. Alas! He had run out of ammunition, or the musket trigger had jammed, for no sound came. Without hesitation the sniper leapt to his feet, shouting the war-cry of his clan. Wielding his musket like a cudgel, and plainly determined to fight to the last, he rushed straight at the enemy who were closing in on him. Both soldiers fired their muskets and the man fell face-down on the shingle. One of the Dragoons then dismounted, turned their victim over with his foot, relieved him of his few possessions, and left him where he lay.

The Redcoat who had been shot from his horse seemed lifeless also, but his comrades picked him up and strapped him across his saddle.

In the meantime, gunfire could be heard through the headland. A little later, the fourth Redcoat came back with his prisoner secured. The young Donald had been wounded, for a dark red bloodstain was spreading across his left shoulder. Nevertheless, his captor prodded him along relentlessly, with the muzzle of the musket stuck in his back.

The Redcoats held a brief consultation. Then they bound their prisoner's arms to his sides with a piece of rope wound round his body. The rope was then attached to his captor's saddle. When the Dragoons rode off, back the way they had come, the poor unfortunate Donald was dragged along behind them. Steadily growing weaker from pain, exhaustion, and the loss of blood, he stumbled and fell repeatedly but he made no plea for mercy and was shown none. His plight was pitiful to behold.

The four onlookers in the cave remained in horrified silence until the party of troopers and their captive had disappeared through the headland at the far end of the bay. Lora, in fact, was feeling quite faint.

'How dreadful!' she whispered, covering her face with her hands.

Kitty put a reassuring arm round Lora's shoulder, although she too was visibly shaken and drained of colour.

'Poor devils!' expostulated Alistair. 'All the way from Culloden to end up like that!' and he hastened out to examine the body on the beach. He returned shaking his head. 'Unfortunately I have no spade with which to dig a grave,' he said regretfully, 'but you and I can consign his body to the sea at high tide, Angus. Poor fellow! He'll have to be content with a sailor's grave now, but it's my guess he may well be the luckier of the two.'

'Seeing is believing!' said Angus shaking his head sadly. 'How could one human being be so cruel to another?'

'It might as easily have been you two,' Lora remarked dully, and Alistair nodded agreement.

'Yes. We've been surprisingly lucky so far. They've been searching the beaches and caves twice today already, but they didn't penetrate far into this cave.'

'I don't wonder at that,' and Lora shuddered as she looked into the eerie darkness. 'It's a place for witches and warlocks, I'd say.'

'You're right there,' Kitty agreed. 'Carlinheugh means "Witch's cliff" and that queer-shaped rock inside the cave is "the Devil's Armchair" while "the Devil's Anvil" is nearby. Evidently our ancestors thought the devil had had a hand in shapin' the cliffs and the caves around here. But come on, lads,' she added matter-of-factly, 'you'd better have your soup and tatties while they're still warm,' and she uncovered the creels and handed over the contents.

As soon as they had finished the soup, Kitty rose and collected the empties.

'Davie'll be in needin' his supper afore it's ready,' she said. 'We'd better go. Miss Lora'll bring your next supply o' nourishment. I have to work the whole day, but she'll easy find her road now.'

'Yes. I'll come tomorrow afternoon,' Lora promised. 'Take care of yourselves and don't take any risks.'

The homeward journey was in complete contrast to the outward one. Both girls were silent and subdued, for both were suffering from the shock of the bloodthirsty scene they had witnessed on the beach. The very real dangers of the venture they were involved in had been brought home to them with a vengeance.

When they described the incident to Davie he said at once, 'I think I ken the twa lads ye mean. They've been hidin' in the Seaton woods for a week or twa. Somebody from the Big Hoose has been carryin' food to them. Puir beggars! What an end!'

Lora woke the next morning to find the cottage enveloped in a thick sea-fog. Visibility was down to a few yards.

'Ye'll manage to exercise the horses this mornin' withoot the risk o' bein' spied on, Miss Lora,' said Davie as he left for his work. 'That fog's like a blanket, and I doubt if it'll lift afore nicht.'

Kitty went off soon after her husband, and Lora decided to exercise the horses at once, before the army patrols were likely to be on the move. Somehow she felt on edge today, and it was a relief when the stable work was done and the horses fed and back in their stalls. Even in the house Lora's feeling of unease persisted. The gruesome happenings of the day before kept recurring in her mind and the silence became almost oppressive. It was as if she were cut off from the rest of the world, cocooned in an impenetrable chilly web of sea-fog. She busied herself with household tasks but the eeriness remained, and then it was that she heard a vaguely familiar step approaching the house. Someone with a limp was coming nearer and nearer and she heard the tap-tap of a walking stick. Lora hastened to the kitchen window and her worst fears were realised. It was Paddy O'Malley!

With great presence of mind Lora swiftly locked and barred the door and stood close against the wall where she couldn't be seen by anyone looking in through the window. She held her breath as the pedlar tapped on the door. When he received no answer he knocked louder and became ever more insistent. Then Lora heard him shuffling along to the window. He tried the catch but it held, despite his attempts to force it, so he moved on to try the bedroom windows. Fortunately they were also closed to keep out the penetrating fog. Finally he returned to the door, hammering on it this time with his stick and shouting angrily.

'Open that door, or begorra, I'll break it down, that I will. Sure it's meself that knows ye're in there.'

Lora's heart was beating like a sledgehammer. Then, above the din, she heard another voice.

'Hey! You! Clear out o' there or I'll shoot ye.'

It was Davie's grandfather. Lora crept to the window and peeped out. The old man was armed with an ancient blunderbuss and was determinedly confronting the pedlar.

'I'll give ye five minutes to clear off,' he warned.

The pedlar seemed rather uncertain how to deal with the situation. He could easily have coped with the old man, but the blunderbuss was another matter. In the end he evidently decided that discretion was the better part of valour. He began to move off, shouting abuse and threats of revenge, but Davie's grandfather never wavered. Keeping the gun pointing at Paddy's head he followed him along the track. Before turning back the old man issued a final warning.

'If I as much as see ye headin' in this direction again I'll blaw your brains oot. So ye'll better keep your distance.'

Coming so soon after the alarming experience of the day before Lora felt quite drained of strength and almost fit to weep, but the old man returned later to see that she was all right.

'There's no need for you to worry, lass,' he reassured her. 'Davie asked me to keep an eye on ye, and I'll do that, never you fear.'

Davie and Kitty arrived almost simultaneously at midday and Kitty was full of excitement.

'I've good news an' bad news for ye the day, Miss Lora,' she announced. 'First the good news – your "freends" the tinks were hustled awa' by the military this mornin'. I watched the whole thing, so there's no need for ye to worry aboot them for a day or twa at least. I felt like cryin' "hurray!" '

Davie wasn't as elated as Kitty by this piece of news.

'The Redcoats'll be wantin' information from the tinks,' he said, 'and that auld dame'll realise that her knowledge, aboot Alistair and Angus and you, would be worth tellin' to the enemy, Miss Lora.'

'It looks as if my being here is to be a danger to you two as well,' said Lora, with real concern.

'That may be,' Davie agreed, 'but we were well aware o' the danger when we decided to become involved, so the blame lies entirely wi' ourselves. We'll just have to hope that Paul gets the lads safely on board ship afore the bubble bursts.'

'You said you also had *bad* news, Kitty,' Lora reminded her, with some trepidation. 'After hearing the "good" news I tremble to think what the "bad" news will consist of!'

'The bad news is that the pedlar ye spoke aboot is here in Aberbrothock, an' he's makin' inquiries aboot ye, the same as the tinks were. I went into the bakehouse on my way to work this mornin' and this cripple mannie, wi' a stick, and a patch coverin' one eye, was in there. I heard him askin' if they'd seen or heard o' a Miss Macrae havin' lately arrived in the toon.'

'Someone must've been able to supply him with information then,' said Lora. 'The pedlar was here this forenoon.'

'What!' exclaimed Davie 'Ye mean he was here at the hoose? Did he see ye, Miss Lora?'

'He came to the door, but luckily I heard him approaching and had the door barred. He was very aggressive, and your grandfather heard him banging and shouting. The pedlar left when the old man threatened him with a musket.'

Despite the gravity of the situation, Davie had to laugh.

'That auld blunderbuss has been worth its weight in gold to Grandy these last thirty years,' he grinned. 'It's his treasured memento o' the 1715 rebellion. An' the funny bit is, his ammunition is a' done lang ago. He couldna fire a shot though he wanted to.'

When the other two had left for work, Lora set about doing some household chores to keep her mind occupied. As she was fetching a pitcher of water from the well she saw Davie hurrying towards the house.

'Is there something wrong, Davie?' she asked anxiously.

'No. It's really good news this time,' he assured her, as soon as they were safely within the house. 'I was workin' up in a field beside the Auchmithie road when I heard a horse comin' at the full gallop. It was Paul. He saw me and stopped to tell me that he'd got things fixed up wi' the Captain o' a wine vessel from France. It's returnin' wi' a cargo of lobsters from Montrose and it wasna due to sail for another day. However, the Captain decided to take advantage o' the fog and set sail now. The ship'll drop anchor in Carlinheugh Bay, and I've to row the lads oot. It's ideal weather for an escape job, since we're unlikely to be spotted from the coast. I jist hope the fog doesna lift afore the task's completed. Where's Kitty?'

'Kitty had to work this afternoon, remember,' Lora reminded him.

'Dash it! So she did! I'd forgotten aboot that,' exclaimed Davie with a worried frown. 'I'll need to get word to the lads somehow, but right now I'll need to get back to the field an' unyoke the horses. Then I'll need to fetch the boat.'

'And where has Paul gone now?' asked Lora.

'Into Aberbrothock.'

'Let me go and tell Alistair and Angus the good news, then,' Lora offered eagerly. 'I know the way now, and I'd like to bid them farewell.'

Davie hesitated, but there was no alternative.

'Ye'll need to be careful to keep strictly to the path, Miss Lora,' he warned. 'The cliffs can be treacherous in this weather. Tell the lads to keep a constant watch, and be ready to wade oot whenever they see or hear my boat offshore. Take them some cheese and bannocks and a flagon o' milk to keep them goin'. Ye should have plenty o' time to get oot there an' back afore the next Redcoat patrol. They're timed fairly regular and I saw them returnin' to barracks as I crossed the field.'

Lora promised to pay attention to all Davie's instructions and immediately he'd gone she set about packing a basket with food. Before she left the house, she concealed the basket under her cloak. Then she checked to see that no one was around.

The fog was very close, and Lora was thankful for this as she hurried across the sea braes towards the cliff path, but the world seemed literally to end at the edge of the cliff. She could hear the sound of the waves far below, and the sea-birds wheeling and calling, but her view was limited to a few yards. Lora shuddered a little and drew her cloak more closely around her. The landmarks which Kitty had named were now completely hidden, and the need for caution and concentration was very evident. She met no one at all, and at times the journey seemed endless. Indeed, she began to fear that she had missed the path down to Carlinheugh Bay. However, her judgement proved correct. She located the exact spot, a fact which added considerably to her confidence. With care, the descent to the beach was safely completed and soon she was skirting the bay and heading for the Dark Cave.

There was no sign of life at the cave entrance so Lora ventured a little way inside and called. 'Anyone there?'. The call reverberated round the walls but there was no reply. For a panic-stricken moment she imagined they had been captured. Then she gave her piercing whistle. This time, to her great relief, there was an answering call and the two men came hurrying out to meet her.

'We didn't think it was quite time to man our lookout posts,' said Alistair apologetically, 'but there was no mistaking that whistle!'

'I *am* early,' Lora agreed, 'but I've got wonderful news! Paul has arranged for a ship to pick you up this very afternoon!'

For a moment both men were speechless.

'I cannot believe it,' gasped Angus, shaking his head.

'It seems unbelievable to me too,' Alistair echoed, but his eyes sparkled with excitement. 'Are we bound for France or the Low Countries?'

'For France. It's a wine boat returning from Montrose with a cargo of lobsters. It is to anchor off the bay, and Davie is to row you out. He asked me to tell you to keep a close watch and to be ready to wade out as soon as he gets far enough inshore.'

Lora then produced the food, but both men were too excited to eat.

'We'll drink the milk now and take the food with us,' Alistair suggested.

'So it is definitely *au revoir* this time,' mused Angus. After all our wanderings it is difficult to comprehend that deliverance is truly at hand at last.'

'It seems like years since we crossed the hills of Clova,' said Alistair, 'and how fortunate for us that you happened to cry "Loyal" when I was within earshot. In fact, Angus and I both think the words "To Cry Loyal" could well be your personal motto, Lora, for your loyalty to us through all our subsequent trials and tribulations has been truly magnificent. We owe our lives to you, and we know it.'

They talked together for a little longer as if trying to postpone the actual moment of parting, but Lora was mindful of Davie's warning.

'I really must go,' she said, replacing the flagon in the basket. 'I just hope and pray the fog doesn't lift until you are safely aboard,' and the men echoed her words, for, in the minds of all three there remained the tragic spectacle enacted before their very eyes only the day before. They were well aware that danger was ever-present, even in this hour of delivery.

'*Un moment, s'il vous plaît!*' said Angus as Lora turned to leave. 'We have had this prepared in readiness for this very occasion. It is a pouch with a share of the golden guineas which we want you to divide amongst all the kind friends who played a part in our escape story. As you know, we gave the MacCrimmons some of the gold pieces, but there is also Dougal who deserved to be rewarded; your housekeeper Elsie; Davie and Kitty, and the doctor who refused his fee. Perchance there are others of whom we are not even aware. Please see that each is suitably rewarded.'

'I'm sure none of them will want a reward, but if that is your wish it will be done accordingly. I shall hand over the money personally,' Lora promised, as she placed the pouch of gold pieces in the basket beside the flagon.

'Meanwhile, you will have to be content with the old leather pouch as your keepsake, Lora,' said Alistair, with a smile. 'It has travelled with me through the whole campaign, but as Angus and I have now pooled our resources, one pouch will suffice.'

'I shall never part with your pouch, Alistair, as long as I shall live. It will always be there to remind me that our great adventure together wasn't just a dream,' Lora declared solemnly.

At this point Angus interrupted.

'*Voilà*,' he exclaimed excitedly, 'here is another keepsake for you, Lora,' and he produced from his pocket a piece of folded paper. 'I had intended to let it remain a secret yet awhile, but now I would like you to have a keepsake from me also – to keep beside Alistair's leather pouch,' he added, obviously anxious not to be outdone by his friend.

'What is it?' Lora queried, as she carefully unfolded the slip of paper.

'See! I have designed a personal crest and a badge for you using the words "To Cry Loyal" as your very own motto,' Angus explained eagerly.

'That's wonderful, Angus!' Lora enthused with obvious delight. 'Where did you manage to get the materials?'

'You will recall that I made copies of the plan of our route from Howletsden. Well, I asked Mrs McNair if I could have the quill pen and some paper and ink, and she kindly agreed. That reminds me, Lora. I should like you to buy a gift for Madame McNair for all her kindness to us. The drawings on that paper are very sketchy, you understand, but when I return to Paris I shall do proper detailed drawings. Then I shall get the crest carved from wood, and the badge made of silver, especially for you.'

Lora was absolutely thrilled. 'Thank you a thousand times,' she cried and she planted a spontaneous kiss on his cheek. 'I shall look forward to getting the finished articles, but, meanwhile, I promise you, I shall treasure those sketches,' and before picking up her basket again, Lora tucked the piece of paper carefully away in the bodice of her gown.

At the cave entrance Alistair and Angus bade Lora goodbye. Each in turn clasped her close and kissed her on both cheeks.

'May God be with you,' Lora whispered, in a voice that trembled with emotion, and tears trickled down her cheeks as she walked away. After a few yards she turned to give a final wave, only to find that the sea-fog had already rendered their parting complete.

Picking her way over the damp slippery stones and pebbles of the beach, and through the wet grass of the sea-meadows, Lora meditated on the difference in atmosphere created by blue skies and sunshine. Where beauty had reigned yesterday, everything now appeared weird and frightening, and she was very conscious of her solitary state in that awesome, fog-enshrouded place. The waves dashing against the rocks seemed cruel and relentless. The cries of the sea-birds sounded like wails of despair, while the grotesquely-shaped rocks, dark chasm-like cave-entrances, and treacherous-looking cliffs towering overhead combined together to form what appeared to be an evil, menacing, presence around her. She heaved a sigh of relief when she reached the narrow, winding pathway leading up from the beach. But she soon found that the ascent was to be just as difficult as the descent, owing to the slithery condition of the ground.

Intent on keeping a foothold, Lora was concentrating on one step at a time. She had almost reached the top of the cliff, and was pulling herself up by a tussock of grass, when, without warning, a strong hand reached down and seized her arm in a vice-like grip.

Lora opened her mouth to scream, but the shock had been so great that no sound came. The next moment she was being dragged roughly forward and upwards, and deposited bodily on the grassy bank at the top of the cliff. . . .

Paul, in the meantime, had hardly arrived at his Aberbrothock residence when the old housekeeper announced that a military gentleman wished to speak with him.

'Send him in please, Mrs Cargill,' said Paul, and he was delighted to see the visitor was none other than his old pal, Lennox Bullard.

'It's good to see you again, Lennox,' Paul welcomed him. 'Sit ye down and we'll enjoy a glass of claret together. I've been rushing about all day so I could do with both the drink and the rest.'

'I'm afraid I haven't much time to spare at the moment,' said Captain Bullard as he accepted the proffered drink. 'I've come to see you because I'm worried about your stepsister Lora.'

'Worried about Lora? Why, pray?'

'Well, as you have probably noticed, there are quite a number of vagrants and tinkers around Arbroath at the moment. We've been having trouble between some of them and our men, so I ordered one batch to be brought in for questioning. I decided to have a private word with them myself and find out just what was going on. Tinkers are a great source of information at a time like this anyway. They are always on the move, so they know all that is happening in the countryside, but we also have to watch out for Jacobites masquerading as tinkers. When I was questioning one of the women – a proper evil-looking old wretch she was – she came away with an amazing tale about a Miss Lora Macrae and two Jacobite rebels. One has to bear in mind that tinkers can be awful liars, and this tale seemed so farfetched that I might have been inclined to think the woman had made it up, out of some vindictive desire to do Lora harm, had it not been for one remark. She said she had seen Lora outside an alehouse near Pickerton, on the Forfar to Montrose road, two days ago. As it happened, one of our patrols had clashed with those self-same tinkers at that place and on that very day. One of my troopers had also recognised Lora, and, when *he* was reporting the incident, he mentioned having seen her. He said he thought she'd been having her horse attended to at the forge, and that she'd become involved with the tinkers by accident. The trooper who told me was the one you gave such a hiding in Kirriemuir when he accosted Lora, so he had good reason to remember what she looked like. Tell me, Paul, do you know if Lora has any Jacobite friends – special friends, I mean?'

'She may well have,' Paul replied guardedly. 'After all, she grew up in a Highland glen, the breeding place of Jacobitism.'

'The tinker said she was almost sure Lora was in Aberbrothock. She isn't living here in this house, is she, Paul?'

'No. She certainly isn't staying here. This is the home of a business friend of mine.'

There was a pause. Then Lennox spoke again.

'I've just been thinking,' he said, 'of the meeting I had with Lora at a wayside inn one night last week on the road to Brechin. I was surprised to see her alone in such a place, and said so, but she assured me she was travelling with friends. It never occurred to me that those friends might be Jacobites. If she is in Aberbrothock, and you know where she is lodging, will you seek her out, please, Paul? Tell her to leave the town at once. As far as I know, none of my troopers has heard that tinker's tale, but that old crone won't hold her tongue, especially when she has drink. The last thing I want to do is to arrest Lora, but my present duty is to seek out Jacobites and their accomplices. Should it ever come to a choice between my duty as a soldier and my own personal feelings, then my personal feelings must take second place. You know that, Paul.'

'Yes. I know it,' Paul agreed soberly.

'If Lora's Jacobite friends will give themselves up to me, personally,' continued Lennox, 'I shall do all in my power to see that they are leniently dealt with. Will you tell her that also, please, Paul?'

'When I find Lora I shall tell her all you have said to me, Lennox,' Paul replied quietly, 'and I'm sure Lora will appreciate the true spirit of friendship that has prompted your generous gestures. I shall seek her out without delay, you may depend upon that.'

Captain Bullard paused in the doorway as he was about to leave.

'One more thing, Paul. Please tell Lora that none of this need make any difference between her and me. I shall expect her to keep her promise to me, as I shall keep mine to her,' and, with that, the two men parted.

As Lora pitched forward on to the green sward at the top of the cliff, her assailant also lost his balance and fell partly on top of her. He was breathing heavily, and smelt strongly of alcohol and dirty, sweaty clothes, to which also clung the unmistakable odour of wood smoke. She was at the mercy of a drunken tinker!

Lora struggled to escape from the man's grasp, but he kept a tight hold of her. Then he spoke, and she knew, with a sickening certainty, that she was in the clutches of none other than the wily pedlar, Paddy O'Malley.

'Fine I ken where you've been, an' what ye've been up to,' he declared. Sure, whenever I heard ye were livin' wi' the fisher folk I guessed what the little game would be. I had only to bide my time! An', sure enough! I was just lyin' havin' a rest an' a wee refreshment in the long grass at the other side o' the path when ye went past earlier on. I could've touched your skirts. I was as near as that. An' as soon as ye turned doon the "Limpet roadie" to the beach, I knew ye were headin' for the caves o' Carlinheugh. I had only to lie where I was an' I'd get ye on the way back. It was as simple as that! Sure, ye were after thinkin' ye'd cheated ould Paddy, but, begorra, the O'Malleys are not so easy beat. You an' yer Jacobite friends may learn that to your cost afore this day is oot!'

Lora had no illusions as regards the gravity of the situation. With the knowledge he already had, the pedlar could do untold damage to them all. How dreadful, at this late stage, when success was almost within their grasp! Somehow she had to get free!

The pedlar seemed to read her thoughts, for he gave a sinister-sort-of laugh. With a deft movement he twisted Lora's arm so that she cried out with pain.

'That's just to let ye know that ye needna try any monkey-stuff wi' me,' he warned. 'You're *my* prisoner, an' the sooner ye accept that fact the better for yerself. Sure I'll be keepin' ye here till the next Redcoat patrol comes by. I've no doubt *they'll* be pleased wi' my catch.'

He gave a satisfied chuckle, and produced a whisky flask from his coat pocket. Having slaked his thirst he slobbered a bit and wiped his mouth with the back of his hand.

'Mother o' Gawd,' he remarked, eyeing Lora with an insolent stare, 'Dame Fortune has surely smiled upon Paddy O'Malley this day. Fine I ken how ye've always hated the sight o' me, Miss High-and-Mighty. You were far above the likes o' me. Well, the boot's on the other foot now, so it is. Paddy's the one that'll call the tune from now on,' and he gave Lora's arm such a twist she squealed in agony.

While the pedlar was having another swing from his flask Lora decided to make an effort to get up on her feet. Gritting her teeth against the pain her captor would undoubtedly inflict upon her arm, she made a quick move.

Alas! in spite of his inebriated condition, O'Malley was alert enough to foresee her plan, and able enough to thwart it. In the struggle that ensued, Lora's cloak was wrenched off one shoulder thus revealing the basket which she had so far managed to conceal.

O'Malley's one eye glittered.

'So!' he panted. 'There's the very proof we need! Sure ye canna deny it now. And aidin' and abettin' rebels is punishable by the death penalty. It'll be the gallows for you m'lady, gentry or no' gentry! An' begorra, there's nothing I enjoy more than a hangin'.'

At that moment his eye alighted on the leather pouch in the bottom of the basket. Keeping a tight hold on Lora with one hand he grabbed the pouch with the other. Lora was powerless to stop him.

O'Malley stuffed the leather pouch into his pocket with an air of triumph. Then he had another few mouthfuls from his flask.

'You've got the gold now. What more do you want?' Lora demanded bitterly.

'Sure, I want to see justice done. That's what I want,' he retorted. 'An' I've a score to settle with yon Alistair Drummond. Aye, and wi' Mr Paul Reynolds as weel. I'll no' rest until I see the lot o' ye delivered into the hands o' the Redcoats, an' that's a fact.'

At this point Paddy showed signs of becoming quite amorous. He tightened his hold on Lora and made a clumsy attempt to embrace her, but she fought him off with tooth and nail. Desperation gave her more strength than she had ever imagined she possessed and she redoubled her efforts to get free, while the pedlar puffed and panted and swore at her. As a result, Lora missed the sound of approaching hoofbeats. It was Paddy who first realised someone was coming.

'It's the patrol!' he announced breathlessly. 'Ye might as well give up, here and now.'

For answer Lora made an even more determined effort to get free. This time she actually managed to get up on her feet and summoning all her strength, she threw the basket out over the cliff, complete with the milk flagon.

Paddy O'Malley swore angrily, and hit her with such violence she narrowly missed falling over the cliff edge herself.

'H-elp! H-elp!' Lora screamed, casting caution to the winds. At that moment even Redcoats seemed preferable to remaining in the power of the pedlar. She heard someone reining in a horse. Then, out of the fog a man came running, but it was no Redcoat. It was, in fact, Paul Reynolds.

Relief far outweighed any surprise Lora felt at Paul's unexpected appearance.

'Paul! Help me! Help me!' she screamed at the pitch of her voice, while the pedlar did his best to stifle her cries.

Paul summed up the situation at a glance and he made a beeline for Paddy O'Malley.

'Let her go,' he commanded, and the order was accompanied by a swinging blow to the pedlar's jaw.

O'Malley's hold on Lora's arm slackened and she wrenched herself free. The pedlar staggered from the force of Paul's blow, but managed to keep his feet. He issued a string of foul oaths and lunged back at Paul but his punches were wide of their mark, owing to his state of intoxication. Nevertheless, he put up a good fight, and Lora's heart was in her mouth as she watched the two men battling it out, almost on the edge of the cliff. What O'Malley lacked in skill he made up for in sheer brute force and determination. There was also the danger that Paul might trip, or slip, and be hurled on to the rocks far below. To Lora it was like some dreadful nightmare.

In the midst of the scuffle, three men appeared through the fog. They were running along the path in the Auchmithie direction.

'Hi there, lads! Ye'd better save your energy for fightin' Redcoats. They're hard on our heels,' warned one man as they sped past.

For a moment Paul allowed his concentration to lapse, and in that moment Lora caught the flash of steel. Paddy O'Malley had drawn a knife!

'Look out, Paul!' Lora screamed, as the pedlar prepared to make a dagger thrust. Her warning came just in time to prevent disaster. Paul successfully dodged the blow but almost lost his balance in the process.

The Irishman seemed confident he was now in full command.

'Sure, it's meself that has ye now – the both o' ye,' he cried, brandishing the knife triumphantly. 'The Redcoats will be here any moment, and, begorra, I'll tell them the whole story – as I will. I'll see ye swing from the gibbet yet – the pair o' ye! But right now, I'm warnin' ye, if either o' ye make as much as one move I'll slit yer throat.'

Hardly had he issued the dire warning than Paul made a flying leap. With a piece of brilliant footwork he kicked the knife out of the pedlar's hand and sent it flying through the air.

Lora pounced on the knife almost before it had touched the ground. Without hesitation she turned and threw it as far as she could out over the cliff. Next thing she knew, Paul had hit O'Malley a crashing blow on the chin and the Irishman was flat on his back.

'Have you killed him, Paul?' gasped Lora as she looked at the lifeless form stretched out on the grass.

'No. But he simply had to be silenced at all costs. And just in the nick of time, it seems! Listen! The Dragoons are upon us!'

'What's been happening here?' demanded the young Redcoat officer in charge of the patrol, as he advanced towards them out of the fog. 'I'm afraid I'm the culprit,' said Paul. 'I was on my way to meet my sister and found her being molested by that blackguard of a pedlar. He and I had a fight, and I knocked him unconscious.'

'Hmm. You seem to have done the job very efficiently,' remarked the officer. 'By the way, you and I have met before haven't we?' he asked, looking keenly at Paul. 'Yes we have! I remember now. You're Captain Bullard's friend.'

'Yes. We met in the officers' mess the other night,' Paul agreed, and the two men shook hands. Paul then introduced him to Lora.

'You didn't happen to see three men pass this way, did you?' asked the officer. 'We were hard on their heels but I guess they've given us the slip, thanks to this wretched fog.'

'I certainly did hear running feet but I was too busy dealing with the pedlar to notice which way they went,' Paul replied. 'Anyway, if you've lost those men you have some compensation here. This pedlar is, in fact, a deserter.'

'How do you know that?'

'Something happened recently which raised doubts in my mind regarding this man so I made it my business to investigate his past. I had access to army records and I discovered that his real name was not O'Malley but Crichton. Does that name mean anything to you?'

'Not to me, I'm afraid,' said the officer, shaking his head.

'It does to me, sir, beggin' your pardon,' and a sergeant stepped forward. 'We searched for a Paddy Crichton early last year but he got clean away. It was him that shot and wounded Captain Walker of the Third Battalion. Crichton shot the Captain in the back after receiving a reprimanding. You weren't with our lot at the time, sir, but I thought perhaps you'd heard about it.'

'Yes, come to think of it, I do remember something of *that* incident,' the officer agreed.

'When Crichton was making his getaway somebody took a pot-shot at him,' the sergeant continued. 'We were pretty sure he'd been hit but it was getting dark, I remember, and the search for him had to be called off. In the morning "the bird had flown". Then there came a rumour that Crichton had cleared off to Ireland. Further investigations were made, but no trace was found of him. Eventually I think it was presumed he must have died of gunshot wounds.'

'But how could you really be sure this man is the same Paddy Crichton?' the officer asked doubtfully.

The sergeant meditated for a few minutes.

'I can picture Private Crichton quite clearly in my mind, sir. He had very black, curly hair, similar to this man's and – yes, I remember now. He did have one distinguishing feature – a very bad cast in his left eye.'

With that the sergeant crossed over to Paddy and removed the black patch. The pedlar was coming round by this time. Just as the soldier removed the patch, Paddy opened his eyes thus revealing the tell-tale squint.

'It's him all right, sir. No doubt about that,' the sergeant confirmed.

'A fine piece of detective work all round,' commended the officer.

'I'll give you another bit of advice about that pedlar,' said Paul. 'Don't believe a word he says. He's a born liar.'

'He always was,' the sergeant agreed, with a knowing smile, 'and a thief into the bargain.'

'He is still a thief. He has just stolen my leather pouch,' said Lora, speaking for the first time.

'Oh has he, indeed? We'll soon retrieve that for you, Miss,' and the sergeant quickly produced the pouch from O'Malley's pocket, despite many protestations and dire threats from the still befuddled pedlar.

'Well, we must be off,' said the officer. 'I'm afraid we've lost trace of those other three men but I've the feeling they were smugglers rather than rebels. However, we'll head up through the Seaton Woods and have a look around, just in case they may be lurking about. We can get on to the Auchmithie road from there. Our prisoner will get a "run for his money" I'm thinking.'

'The pedlar has a pony of his own. It must be grazing nearby. I saw it on my way here,' Paul informed him.

'Yes. I saw it too,' confirmed one of the soldiers. So the pony was fetched and Paddy was heaved on to its back, with scant ceremony from his captors. Then with a smart salute to Lora, and grateful thanks to Paul, the officer gave the sign to move off.

'Well, Lady Luck was on our side there!' remarked Paul as the Redcoat patrol disappeared into the fog. 'Had Lennox been in charge the outcome might have been very different. How did you fall into the pedlar's clutches, Lora?'

Lora described how the pedlar had been lying in wait for her as she ascended the steep cliff path leading up from the bay.

'It was a dreadful shock, and I still feel a bit shaken, but otherwise I'm none the worse. What a blessing you arrived before the Redcoats though, Paul! Where were you going?'

'I was looking for you, as a matter of fact. On the way to the cottage I happened to see Davie and he told me you'd gone to the cave so I decided to come and meet you. I have an urgent message for you from your friend Lennox Bullard,' and Paul recounted his interview with Captain Bullard.

'Dear Lennox! How kind of him,' said Lora appreciatively.

'Yes. He is a fine fellow,' Paul agreed, 'but, considering my double rôle in this affair, I can tell you I felt horribly guilty standing there listening to him.'

'I know how you felt,' Lora sympathised. 'I too felt guilty when talking to Lennox. I wonder what he'd think of us if he knew the whole story! Incidentally, I'm glad you were able to expose the pedlar as a deserter. He deserves to suffer for all his double-dealing.'

'It was fortunate for all concerned that Paddy O'Malley set his heart on getting Angus's gold, otherwise he'd have delivered you into enemy hands long before now,' said Paul. 'By the way, in the course of my investigations I also solved the mystery of the spy on the hillside. Do you remember how you accused me? Well, it was Dougal MacDougall.'

'I *had* thought of Dougal,' Lora admitted, 'but how could he possibly report rebels to the English?'

'As it happened Paddy O'Malley was at the MacDougalls' alehouse when Dougal came down off the hill that night. Dougal, no doubt, was full of excitement and the pedlar managed somehow to get the gist of the story out of the poor creature. O'Malley returned hot-foot to Kirriemuir and sold the information to an army informer. For obvious reasons, of course, O'Malley himself had to be wary of any direct contact with the English army! The saddest thing about the whole business was Hamish MacCrimmon's death – a direct victim of the Irishman's greed for gold.'

Paul fell silent for a few minutes. Then he went off to collect his horse which was grazing nearby.

'If you are ready now, Lora, I think we should be moving on. We have tarried here long enough. Are you fit to walk, or would you prefer to ride?'

'I'm quite fit to walk, thank you,' Lora replied. 'O'Malley did me no harm. He kept twisting my arm, which was very painful at the time but left no permanent injury, thank goodness.'

Lora and Paul had walked only a short distance along the cliff path when, to their amazement, the sea-fog suddenly lifted. With one accord they dashed to the edge of the cliff and gazed anxiously out to sea. There, just beyond the bay, the merchant vessel lay at anchor and at that very moment, the little rowing boat with its three passengers was drawing alongside.

Lora fluttered her handkerchief, and Paul waved his arms, in an effort to draw the men's attention, but to no avail. Then, on impulse, Lora pursed up her lips and gave her high-pitched, piercing whistle. The response was immediate. Alistair and Angus turned eagerly towards the cliffs and raised their arms in a triumphant gesture of farewell.

Shortly afterwards the ship weighed anchor and began to sail majestically towards the open sea, while the rowing boat, with Davie at the oars, could be seen pulling back towards the shore.

'Hurrah! We've done it! They're safely aboard,' cried Paul in jubilation, and he and Lora hugged each other with sheer joy and relief.

Then they turned to have a last look at the departing vessel but the fog had closed in again just as suddenly as it had lifted. It was as if a stage curtain had been momentarily raised to receive the final applause and then lowered again upon the last act of the play.

'All's well that ends well,' said Lora thankfully, tears of happiness shining in her eyes, as she and Paul and Nero set off again along the cliff path.

'Yes,' Paul agreed, 'and I'm glad to be able to tell you that one of their companions on board will be Mrs McNair's son. I happened to meet Captain

McNair in Montrose, by mere chance, and he told me he had traced his son who was alive, and unharmed, and in hiding near Montrose.'

'Then he had escaped with others of Lord Ogilvy's regiment after all?' Lora asked eagerly.

'No. It appears that young McNair was not enlisted with that regiment at all. He had met up with Colonel Grant's French Artillery on the way to join the Prince's army. Having had experience as a Writer he was invited to become a clerk to the regiment and remained with the detachment throughout the campaign. To save any possible embarrassment to his family he had enlisted under a false name – hence the difficulty in tracing him.'

'Fortunately, I was able to persuade the captain of the vessel to take on another stowaway. I should think Captain McNair will be well on his way back to Howletsden now with the good news.'

'That's wonderful, Paul! I'm so glad for Captain and Mrs McNair. They are such nice people, and Mrs McNair was so hospitable towards us when we descended upon her as uninvited guests. I'm happy to think that you have, in this way, been able to repay her kindness to us.'

'Well now, the time has come for us to move out of Aberbrothock – and quickly,' said Paul. 'We shall leave for Glen Clova, with all the horses, at first light tomorrow, before those tinkers have a chance to make more trouble for you. After a night's rest at The Milton we shall head for Edinburgh where you'll need to lie low until all this has blown over.'

'Edinburgh!' exclaimed Lora, 'but think what Aunt Gwyneth will say when she hears I've been mixed up with Jacobites! I'd be an embarrassment to her in Edinburgh! She'll never forgive me!'

Paul laughed.

'How little you know of Aunt Gwyneth! No doubt it will surprise you to learn that her recent departure to the capital was for no other reason than to help a Jacobite prisoner, a rather special Jacobite in fact – Lady Margaret Ogilvy!'

'Lady Margaret Ogilvy!' gasped Lora incredulously.

'Yes. Our stepmother and some other ladies have been doing their best to ease Lady Ogilvy's living conditions, and striving to obtain her release from Edinburgh Castle.'

'But I thought . . .' began Lora.

'You thought she'd gone over to the enemy's camp. Didn't you? But Aunt Gwyneth isn't the turncoat she might have appeared to be. She hasn't entirely deserted her old friends. She has been acting a part – a rather dangerous, but highly successful part. Indirectly she also helped you.'

'Helped me? In what way?'

'To escape detection by Lennox. He's no fool, you know. The fact that Aunt Gwyneth welcomed English soldiers to her home and blinded him to your Jacobite activities. But enough of Aunt Gwyneth. From now on I'm going to keep an eye on *you*, young lady.'

'But what will Maria say if you arrive in Edinburgh with me in tow?' Lora felt forced to ask.

'Maria? What has she got to do with it?' queried Paul, quite dumbfounded.

'I t-thought y-you a-and M-Maria w-were . . .' stammered Lora, blushing red with embarrassment.

Paul stared at her. Then, as the truth dawned on him, he threw back his head and laughed.

'What did you think Maria and I were?' he asked. 'Lovers?' He laughed again. 'My dear Lora, if you really want to know, I am Maria's official guardian. I am also her cousin. Our mothers were sisters. Unfortunately, Maria's parents both died when she was a young girl. Her father was an Italian Count, a shipping merchant like my own father, and Maria is soon to marry a Greek shipping merchant. I brought the betrothal ring back to her on my recent return from Greece. Her fiancé gave it to me just before I left for home and he is joining Maria in Leith very soon for the wedding. So, you see, Maria won't mind in the least if you accompany me to Edinburgh,' he finished, with an amused twinkle.

'If I do go to Edinburgh, Loyal must go with me,' Lora announced after a pause. 'He is my faithful companion and I have neglected him much too long already. I just can't go off and desert him again. That would be too cruel.'

'The dog's presence might lead to complications,' observed Paul. 'Besides, he's rather a large dog for a town house, and I should think he'd miss the glen even more than you will. Still, I suppose it could be arranged.'

As they continued on their way to Davie's cottage Paul put an affectionate arm around Lora's shoulders just as he had so often done in days gone by. Then suddenly she remembered her special item of news!

'Oh, by the way, Paul,' she exclaimed excitedly, 'I'm to have my very own motto and crest,' and she withdrew the piece of paper from the bodice of her gown and handed it to him. Paul paused to unfold the paper and study the diagrams.

'This is Angus's handiwork, I see,' he remarked. 'The ideas seem very appropriate, Lora, and I think the award is well deserved. I shall be interested to see the completed work. But tell me,' he enquired, as he handed back the sketches, 'what did Lennox mean by those promises you and he had made to each other. Are you secretly betrothed?'

'No, Lennox's mother wants to meet me, because I rescued her brother from the bog, so she is inviting me down to Gloucestershire. I promised Lennox I would accept the invitation, and he promised he would come to The Milton and fetch me. That is all there is to it.'

'Nevertheless, I think Lennox is in love with you,' said Paul.

Lora blushed.

'Yes, I think perhaps he is – a little,' she agreed.

'And is the feeling mutual?' pursued Paul.

Lora was about to answer in the negative, but something held her back. She thought of Lennox, his charming smile, his lovable nature, his loyalty to her, and she remained silent.

'Well, is it?' Paul persisted.

'I just don't know – I hadn't thought about it,' Lora replied in a small, rather bemused voice.

For a little while after that they walked in a companionable silence, and Lora began to realise that at last the worries and strains of the past few weeks were almost at an end. The rescue had been successfully achieved, and the rift with Paul was healed. There was, of course, this new problem as to whether her affections lay with Paul or Lennox. But that could safely be left for solving in the fullness of time. After all, she probably wouldn't see Lennox again until the spring of the year and Paul would soon be off once more on his travels to foreign lands. Meanwhile it seemed sensible to relax and enjoy the pleasures of the present. The future could look after itself.

'Thank goodness you're back! Am I glad to see you!' Kitty cried, when Lora and Paul arrived at the fisher cottages. 'I was really worried when I came in. Miss Lora was nowhere to be seen, and there was nae sign o' Davie comin' in for his tea.'

Lora and Paul described all that had happened on that eventful afternoon, and Davie appeared on the scene soon afterwards, tired, but jubilant that his part in the rescue had been successfully completed.

Paul left soon after to return to Aberbrothock.

'Be ready before daybreak, Lora,' he said. 'I'll come here for you, because there will be the two extra horses to cope with, and I'd like to be well clear of Aberbrothock before the town comes to life.'

Lora retired early to her room. By the light of a flickering candle she counted all the golden guineas that Angus had put in the leather pouch and decided how many should be given to each of the people whom he had mentioned.

Next morning at breakfast she presented Davie and Kitty with their share. She also left a 'thank you' note in her bedroom and something from herself to recompense them for her board and lodging.

Paul arrived about five o'clock but Lora and Davie had all three horses fed, saddled, and ready to move off, and they were well clear of Aberbrothock before sunrise.

It was a long trek to The Milton of Clova but the further they went from the sea the sunnier the day became, and Lora was happy to be heading for her beloved hills and the reunion with her pet.

Elsie and Loyal gave both the travellers a very warm welcome and it was decided they would spend that night and the following day and night at The Milton before setting out for Edinburgh.

Elsie was anxioius to hear all about the journey to Howletsden and how the trio had been received there by the McNairs. So, on that first evening, Lora recounted every detail of their great adventure, their many trials and tribulations, and the final happy ending to the escape story. Lora then presented the old housekeeper with her share of Angus's golden guineas and Elsie was quite overcome by emotion.

The following day Lora spent much of her time with the MacCrimmons at Linnochmore where she again went over all the tale so that the old couple could follow every step of the way to freedom with the two young men for whom they had risked so much. She spared them the part relating to Paddy O'Malley, however, since the old lady had been so loud in her praises of the pedlar and there seemed no need to disillusion her.

After consultation with Paul and Elsie it was decided to put Dougal McDougall's share in the bank in Kirriemuir where it could be left to grow for him in later years. Paul offered to ride into town, deliver the doctor's share and complete the bank transaction that afternoon. He brought back written proof of the lodgment and this was given to Dougal in the presence of his mother who said she would keep it safely. Both were told that the money was from 'a wellwisher' and the matter was left at that, with no questions asked.

Lora then wrote a letter to Mrs McNair and enclosed her share, with the request that she buy a keepsake from Angus and Alistair with the money. One of the stable boys was instructed to ride to Howletsden the following day with the package.

Only then did Lora have time to do her packing, but, in spite of a late night, she was dressed and ready to set off as soon as they had had breakfast.

They were lucky again, as far as weather was concerned, and they went at an easy pace for Loyal's sake. At the inn where they spent the first night of their journey, Paul met two Redcoat officers with whom he was acquainted. They too were riding to Edinburgh, so, from then on, they made a foursome. Both the young soldiers were high-spirited but well-mannered and Lora found their company very refreshing – Redcoats or no!

On arrival at the Canongate residence Paul found a message awaiting him and announced that he would be leaving the following morning aboard one of his merchant vessels bound for the east. His cousin Maria had, in the end, decided she wished to be married in Italy, the land of her birth, and, by travelling on this particular ship, Paul could be in Naples in time for the wedding ceremony.

'For everyone's sake, Lora, please keep out of Jacobite trouble, from now on,' he advised her. 'Remember, you've done your share for the cause, and can rest on your laurels now. But there is still one request I must make of you.'

'And what might that be?' asked Lora.

'That you rename your dog. There is no need to remind you that we are living in unnatural and dangerous times. To continue to flaunt loyalty to Jacobitism in the face of a conquering army is nothing less than suicidal.

And, remember, in cities especially, walls have ears! Just think how a foolish act of defiance on your part subsequently involved so many others besides yourself in real danger. I beg of you, Lora, please ensure that the same thing could never happen again. One of the soldiers who accompanied us on our ride today heard you calling your dog and said to me "Your sister isn't a Jacobite is she, Paul?" We laughed it off, but his remark made me think.'

Lora listened quietly. Then she gave the matter some earnest thought.

'Agreed!' she said at last. 'Henceforth "Loyal" will be called "Royal". I dare say he'll hardly notice the difference. But that one small word has made a world of difference in *my* life. Just think of all I'd have missed, the people I'd never have met, the places I'd never have seen, if fate hadn't decreed that I was to cry "Loyal!" at that crucial moment on the hillside! Regrets about Hamish will always remain, but as far as my personal involvement was concerned, there are no regrets. I'm glad I was there at the right time to play my part. If necessary I would do it all over again.'

'May God forbid!' was Paul's fervent plea.

Part Two

XIII THE HOUSE OF REID

Life in the city did not appeal to Lora after the free-and-easy ways of the glen. The smoky atmosphere of 'Auld Reekie' made her long for the fresh keen air of the mountains. However, she rode out each day to exercise her pony and her dog, and very soon she found there were many beautiful places in the countryside around the capital.

Then, out of the blue, there came a messenger with a letter for Lora. It bore the seal of a well-known Writer to the Signet, and was written in a very distinguished, if slightly flamboyant, hand. Flushed with excitement, Lora broke open the seal and read:

> To Miss Elenora Cameron Reid Macrae
> of Canongate, Edinburgh and The Milton, Glen Cova, Forfarshire.
> Dear Madam,
> I am favoured with instructions from my client, Miss Emily Reid Riddoch, of The House of Reid, in the district of Lammermuir, to correspond with you on her behalf.
> From enquiries made by this firm it would appear that you are Miss Riddoch's great-niece, and also her nearest living relative. Consequently, the aforesaid lady is considering naming you as the heir to her estate.
> First of all, however, she would wish to make your acquaintance, there having been no association with your branch of the family since the death of your dear mother several years ago. I am requested, therefore, to extend to

you Miss Riddoch's compliments, together with a kind invitation to spend a short holiday at Miss Riddoch's residence in the Lammermuir Hills.

I trust you will favour me with an early reply, so that I may make final arrangements with my client.

I have the honour to be, Madam,

your obedient servant,

James Niven (Writer to the Signet).

Lora realised at once that the lady referred to was her great-aunt – her only living relative – whom she had met very briefly on the day of her mother's funeral. Try as she might, she could not even recall what the lady looked like, but pleasurable anticipation mounted in Lora as she read the letter a second time.

'How lovely to get away to the hills again, Royal,' she whispered aloud. 'That's just what you and I need.'

The Writer's business premises being at no great distance, Lora decided to pay him a personal call and this she did that very afternoon.

A young clerk led Lora up a dimly lit, and very steep, stone staircase to the Writer's room and at first she had great difficulty locating him behind the massive piles of ledgers and tomes which, in some places, were built up almost from floor to ceiling. She found him very pleasant to talk to, however, and he was loud in the praises of her great-aunt.

Lora assured Mr Niven that she was free to go to Lammermuir at any time so he said he would arrange her visit for the following week. Lora then asked for directions.

'No doubt your stepmother's coachman will have some idea of the route to be taken,' said Mr Niven as he pointed out the road to the Lammermuir Hills on a large map of Edinburgh and district which hung on his office wall.

'I shan't be travelling by coach, of course,' said Lora 'I intend to ride all the way.'

'Not alone, surely!' exclaimed Mr Niven, peering over his spectacles, and obviously shocked at the very idea.

'Oh no, not alone. My bodyguard will be with me,' laughed Lora.

'Your bodyguard?'

'Yes. I have a large Deerhound. With him beside me I am quite safe,' she assured him.

So, on a bright November day, with a cool breeze blowing in from the Firth of Forth, Lora headed Rufus south of the city towards the Lammermuir Hills while Royal bounded happily alongside.

Nothing eventful occurred on the journey until Lora was nearing her destination. Riding along the edge of a broad and lengthy strip of woodland which bordered the roadway she heard the sound of a heavy horse and the rumble and creak of a farm cart. Round a bend in the road there came towards her a Clydesdale horse led by a half-starved-looking individual dressed in the tattered remnants of a tartan kilt. The man was tied to the cart by a length of rope, and, trudging alongside the cart were several similarly clad and equally wretched-looking men, all of whom were bound to the vehicle with ropes. Slumped in the cart were two sick, or wounded, comrades, the whole being escorted by two armed Redcoat soldiers. All were footsore and weary – even the escorts – and scarcely gave Lora a glance as they passed by.

Lora had ridden on to the verge and called Royal to heel until the cavalcade had passed, by which time her pony had started to crop the grass. So Lora sat still for a few minutes, following the progress of the weary little band with pitying eyes.

Suddenly, and almost soundlessly, a number of country men armed with staves emerged from the wood and surrounded the group. In a matter of minutes, and without even a shot being fired, the Redcoats were over-powered, the prisoners cut free, and all – including horse and cart – had disappeared into the wood. It was the perfect ambush. Lora went on her way marvelling at the speed and dexterity with which it had been accomplished.

About a mile further on, an old woman was drawing water from a well beside her roadside cottage. Lora paused to ask if she was on the right track for The House of Reid.

'Aye, ye canna miss it,' the woman replied, and she peered closely at Lora. 'But what's a fine-lookin' young lady like you wantin' wi' a place like that? Ye'll find it a gey queer hoose, I'm thinkin', wi' gey queer ongoin's. I declare they turn nicht into day at The Hoose o' Reid nowadays. They dinna even keep the Sabbath day holy – mair shame to them,' and the old woman shook her head to emphasise her disapproval of the residents of The House of Reid.

But, as Lora rode up to the house there seemed little to distinguish it from any other country house of the period. Warmed by the rosy glow of a wintry sunset, it looked stolidly out across the surrounding hills and moorlands as it must have done for many a long day.

Miss Riddoch's welcome was full of warmth and friendliness. A tall, slim, authoritative person, she seemed to Lora to have a fund of energy which belied her years, and her grey hair did nothing to detract from her youthful appearance. She and Lora found much to talk about, so the first evening passed pleasantly for both.

Lora was charmed with the bedroom allotted to her, and Miss Riddoch was pleased to allow Royal to sleep on the fireside rug in the bedroom which delighted both mistress and dog. The feather bed was warm and comfortable and Lora soon drifted into a contented sleep. Something disturbed her slumbers, however, and she raised herself on one arm to listen. It was the sound of iron-shod hoofs on the cobbled yard but that wasn't all. Overhead she could hear the sound of muffled footsteps as if several people were crossing a floor and descending stairs in stockinged feet. A clock in the hall chimed eleven o'clock. It was then that the old woman's words came back to Lora and she decided to investigate.

Cautioning Royal to keep quiet, Lora crept across to the window, opened one of the shutters, and peered down into the dimness of the yard. A sickle moon shed a very frail light for a few moments at a time but was fitfully obscured by a bank of cloud. As Lora's eyes became accustomed to the darkness, however, she found she could just make out the shadowy forms of ponies. Then a door was opened, casting a yellow light upon the scene, and Lora noticed that the ponies had kegs strapped across their backs.

'Their owners must be whisky smugglers,' she mused.

As Lora watched, Miss Riddoch emerged, accompanied by some men, and they held a short consultation. Miss Riddoch seemed to be issuing orders and giving directions, for she pointed and gesticulated several times. Then the men, each leading a laden pony, moved off in single file through the entrance archway. Miss Riddoch watched until all had disappeared from view then she and her henchman returned to the house, closing and bolting the door behind them, and silence reigned once more around the old building.

Lora quietly closed the shutter and scuttled back to bed. She smiled to herself as she thought of Miss Riddoch. That worthy lady wasn't just an ageing member of the local gentry, content to grow old gracefully. No! She believed in creating a bit of excitement in her life, and, at the same time, she probably earned herself a tidy income therefrom.

'Good luck to her!' said Lora as she snuggled back into the warmth of her feather mattress.

In the darkness of the early morning Lora was again aroused by the clatter of iron-shod hoofs on the cobbles. The smuggling foray had apparently been successfully completed, and the ponies were being returned to their stables.

As she dressed, Lora thought about what she had seen and heard the previous night and decided not to mention the subject unless Miss Riddoch did.

During the course of their conversation over breakfast Miss Riddoch asked if Lora had slept well and Lora replied that she was an excellent sleeper and had found the bed most comfortable, and conducive to sound slumber.

Miss Riddoch then tactfully enquired if Lora was for Jacobitism or King George.

'I'm a Jacobite through and through,' Lora replied.

'That makes two of us,' smiled Miss Riddoch. 'Of course I had no close relative 'out' in the 'forty-five, but my fiancé was killed in 1715 fighting for Prince Charlie's father, and I also lost my only brother. However, we must keep such matters to ourselves in times like the present,' and she quickly changed the subject.

Lora spent the afternoon on the moor exercising her pony and her dog. As she was returning to the house at a leisurely pace she saw someone riding quickly towards the arched entrance. Lora's keen eyes noted that the rider

176

was 'a man of the cloth'. He waved a friendly greeting which she readily acknowledged.

Having stabled her pony, Lora decided to go straight to her room rather than interrupt Miss Riddoch's *tête-à-tête* with the minister, but Miss Riddoch opened her sitting-room door and invited Lora to come and meet the gentleman. He was a handsome young man with a pleasant, unassuming manner and a ready smile. Lora liked him at once.

After introducing the two young people, Miss Riddoch addressed the minister.

'This young lady is my great-niece, John, and I am glad to tell you she is, like me, a Jacobite. I propose, therefore, to take her into our confidence, since I intend her to be my successor in The House of Reid. There must be no dark secrets between us.'

Then, turning to Lora, Miss Riddoch explained, 'The Reverend Duncan and I are doing all we can, Lora, to rescue any Jacobites who reach this district. So far, I'm glad to say, we have succeeded beyond our wildest dreams. There is no room for complacency, of course. At any moment things could go drastically wrong. Mr Duncan has called to tell me that he has two more fugitive rebels at the manse. Fortunately we can take them off his hands. Our last batch were safely put aboard a French merchant vessel last night.'

'On my way here, yesterday, I saw some men ambush a Redcoat escort of Jacobite prisoners,' said Lora, and she described what had happened.

Miss Riddoch smiled.

'Our men carried out that rescue. We were alerted that the Redcoats were on the way and the ambush was very successful. All the able-bodied Jacobites were lucky enough to be accommodated on the French vessel last night, along with the others for whom the arrangements had been made. The two wounded men are still in our care, but, fortunately, neither is seriously ill, and they should soon be ready for the journey to freedom. The wood you spoke of is invaluable to us at this time. By the way, John, will Farmer Robb be able to do the necessary again?'

'Yes,' replied the minister. 'I called on him on my way here and he said he'd have a cart passing this way tomorrow, or the next day, and would drop the two men off beside the wood as usual.'

'That will suit us very well. There is no particular hurry. It may take a little time to fix up another escape vessel. The captains demand higher fees every time, and, of course, some of the rebels haven't a penny to their name. Thank goodness for our whisky "still"!' she laughed. 'May it never run dry – or, at least, not until the present emergency is over!'

The minister stayed only long enough to drink a dish of tea with Miss Riddoch and Lora, for the days were getting short, and dusk was falling early.

'Would you care to have a look at our whisky "still", Lora?' Miss Riddoch asked, after he'd gone.

'Yes, indeed I would,' said Lora eagerly. 'I have never seen a whisky "still" but the idea of whisky smuggling has always appealed to me as an exciting adventure.'

'Yes. Well, I suppose to the young in heart it has an air of romance and "derring-do" about it,' agreed Miss Riddoch, 'but I must admit at my age, all the thrill has evaporated. Smuggling whisky at the moment is a matter of necessity for me. It is only to get money to fund our rescue service that I continue, for the risks are great and the gaugers grow ever more vigilant.'

'Is your "still" within these premises?' Lora enquired.

'No. We couldn't risk that. We have it in an old bothy beside a burn – the ideal spot – among the hills. It's about a mile back from the house, in a very secluded place. When we go in daylight we usually take a horse and cart as if we were going to cut peat for the fire. That way we can fetch back kegs under a covering of peat. We just can't be too careful.'

The following day they made a trip to the bothy with the horse and cart accompanied by Old Jake, the handyman, and Royal. Miss Riddoch painstakingly explained each step of the distilling process to Lora who was amazed at all the work required to produce even a small amount of *uisge-beatha*.

'We start off with a sack of barley which we allow to soak in the burn for a day or two,' said Miss Riddoch. 'Then we spread it over the bothy floor and allow it to germinate. That takes about ten days. One soon learns by experience when the barley is ready for the next stage, and after germination it is dried in a lime kiln over a fire of peat to check further growth. Thus the malted barley is produced. It is then put in a tub and boiling water is poured over. Yeast is added to the resulting liquid and it is left to ferment. Known to the smugglers as "wash" this liquid is ready for the "still". But, having gone through the "still" once, it is not yet drinkable. We have to clean all the parts of the still very thoroughly and then repeat the process. Only then do we have "the water of life" – a raw malt whisky.'

'What a lot of labour!' exclaimed Lora. 'But why do you have to be so particular about cleaning the "still" between the two boilings?'

'If we didn't, the second boiling would have a smoked taste which would spoil the malt whisky flavour entirely,' Miss Riddoch explained.

'I must admit I'm quite intrigued by the whole thing,' said Lora, 'and I'd love to take part in the distilling.'

Beginning with small tasks, Lora proved to be an apt pupil. In the coming days she began to take an active part in all the work concerned with the smuggling bothy, thus relieving Aunt Emily (as it was now decided she should call Miss Riddoch) of some of her many duties.

The two rebels, whom the minister was sheltering at the manse, were brought by cart as far as the wood, where Lora had watched the ambush, and eventually reached The House of Reid after dark. There being no immediate danger, the two men were given supper in the kitchen and a heat at the fire before being taken to their place of concealment.

'Come, Lora, and see where we hide our fugitives,' Miss Riddoch invited, and she led the way along a passage on the walls of which hung several impressive full-size portraits of past generations of the Reid family.

About halfway along, Miss Riddoch slid her hand behind one of the oil paintings. With the exertion of a little pressure the painting swung forward, like a door, to reveal a passage and staircase on the other side. The staircase led to a suite of rooms, and Lora realised at once that the muffled footsteps she had heard on her first night had been the Jacobite rebels descending those stairs.

'How ingenious!' exclaimed Lora.

'Yes, isn't it?' agreed Miss Riddoch. 'The House of Reid was well prepared for just such emergencies as we have in Scotland now.'

Lora had been at The House of Reid about ten days when a messenger arrived with a letter from Susan to say that her mother was confined to bed and would be grateful if Lora would return home.

So, on the following day, Lora rode back to Edinburgh, accompanied by the faithful Royal.

'I'm sorry to have to bring you back like this, Lora,' said Aunt Gwyneth, 'but I may be in bed for a week or two yet. I have strained my back in some way, and the doctor says rest is the only cure. As you know, I am in the habit of visiting Lady Margaret Ogilvy at regular intervals and I need someone to deputise for me meantime. Susan is not the right person for this. She means well but she is not discreet enough, and, of course, she has just got engaged to Lieutenant Lawrie Heathcote, a Redcoat Dragoon, so we don't want to cause unnecessary embarrassment there. In any case I'm sure you could handle the matter much more successfully. The other ladies and I have been trying to obtain Lady Margaret's release, but it is like hitting one's head against a stone wall. We are becoming quite desperate.'

Lora was delighted at this opportunity to visit Lady Margaret. The two girls had become quite well acquainted while she was resident at Cortachy and had developed a liking for each other. Armed with a basket of good things from Aunt Gwyneth, she stepped out smartly, and was soon being ushered into Lady Margaret's closely guarded quarters at the castle.

Lady Margaret's serving-maid was in attendance when Lora arrived so the two girls chatted about the weather and so on until the maid took her departure. The poor woman had a peculiar way of walking, and she had hardly closed the door behind her than Lady Margaret rose and gave Lora a demonstration of her mimicing ability, much to Lora's amusement.

'I'm not just being horrid,' said Lady Margaret. 'I'm doing this with a purpose, and I've been practising for weeks. I am determined to escape from

179

this place and the only way I can think of is to impersonate my maid. To do that I must be able to walk exactly as she does.'

As they were talking, Lady Margaret's sister, Miss Barbara Johnston, arrived and the three girls got their heads together to plan the escape.

First of all Lady Margaret was to feign illness. Her sister would then forbid anyone, except the serving maid, to enter her room. Next the maid would have to be persuaded to swap her outer garments with those of her mistress. Arrayed in her maid's clothes Lady Margaret would sally forth under cover of darkness, and hobble her way to freedom.

Lora's part was to remain in waiting at an appointed place and take the escaped prisoner to spend the night at Lora's Canongate home.

'There is no doubt, as soon as your escape is discovered, our home, and the homes of all our friends, will be searched,' said Barbara, with a worried frown.

'I can take Lady Margaret to my great-aunt's house in the Lammermuir Hills,' Lora suggested eagerly. 'She should be safe there until arrangements can be made to smuggle her out of the country.'

'I think that's an excellent idea – if your great-aunt is agreeable,' Barbara enthused. 'I shall try to hold the fort here for as long as possible to give you time to get well away from Edinburgh.'

On the appointed evening everything went according to plan, and Lady Margaret carried off her rôle of serving-maid to perfection as she hobbled past the castle guard. Lora was in her appointed place in plenty of time, but, before Lady Margaret arrived, Lora became aware that someone was watching her from the other side of the street. The lighting was very dim, which was one advantage, but, as the girls moved off, Lora was sure that they were being followed. Accordingly, instead of taking the direct route home, she led the way by devious alleys and closes. Whenever they turned a corner the ladies sprinted down the street as fast as they could in order to shake off their pursuer. As a result, they reached the house and got safely inside with no immediate sign of pursuit from either direction. Lora ran to a window to keep watch but was greatly relieved when no suspicious-looking character appeared and they could breathe freely again. Presumably, whoever it was had abandoned the chase.

Early the next morning Lady Margaret and Lora set off for Lammermuir on horseback, with Royal in joyful attendance. It was a dark cold morning with flakes of snow blowing in the wind but conditions improved as the day wore on and both enjoyed the ride through the pleasant border country.

Miss Riddoch appeared whenever she heard the horses arrive.

'I've brought another fugitive for you to shelter, Aunt Emily,' Lora announced, and she introduced the two ladies and gave a brief explanation of who Lady Margaret was and why she was on the run.

'Lady Margaret will fill in all the details herself when you have time for a chat,' Lora added. 'You will find it all extremely interesting, Aunt Emily. She has had a very exciting time.'

At The House of Reid Lady Margaret was made as comfortable as possible in one of the rooms at the top of the secret stairway. Of the four men already in residence in the adjoining rooms she found that two were already known to her, having held positions of rank in her husband's regiment. So the days of waiting were spent sharing memories of happier times, recounting experiences while on the run, and expressing hopes and plans for the very uncertain future.

Meantime Lady Margaret's sister had carried out her part with skill and courage. She had asked, and had been given, permission to remain beside her sister during her illness and she kept everyone else at bay until she felt sure Lady Margaret would have made good her escape. Barbara Johnston then reported her sister's disappearance and was prepared to accept the consequences. She was ordered to remain where her sister had been imprisoned until a Government enquiry could be made, but was later released.

Lady Margaret escaped on Saturday evening, 21 November 1746, and her friends immediately set about arranging her safe passage to the continent, but winter had set in and conditions at sea were hazardous.

Eventually, about the middle of December a messenger arrived with a letter for Lady Margaret.

'Hurrah! The Captain of a Dutch vessel is to take seventeen of us aboard,' she cried excitedly. 'The ship is sailing from Leith and we have to meet at a fisherman's hut beyond Musselburgh. The ship will make for the adjoining bay and signal for us to go aboard. My friends have managed to get a large boat so that all seventeen of us can be put aboard at the same time. That includes the four men you are sheltering here.'

So the string of ponies with the kegs of *uisge-beatha* were got ready. Lady Margaret was dressed in male attire, as was Lora who accompanied her. Each leading a pony, they set out in darkness with high hopes. It was a long walk but the thought of deliverance at the end kept them all in high spirits.

The fisherman's hut was a well-known landmark so they had no difficulty locating it, but the night was bitterly cold and all the fugitives were glad to get under cover. Lora joined other helpers, at the house of a Jacobite sympathiser nearby, to await developments. The constant fear of betrayal was ever present in all their minds.

Alas! a dreadful storm arose and the merchant vessel, instead of dropping anchor in the bay, was blown out to sea.

This was a dreadful disappointment to all concerned. There was nothing to be done except return to their hideouts as quickly as possible. Lady Margaret returned with Lora to The House of Reid but the four men had met up with army companions and decided to throw in their lot with them. This was on 19 December 1746.

Lady Margaret was still determined to join her husband in France and a merchant friend of the Johnstone family came forward with the proposal that he himself would drive her all the way to Hull. At that time Hull was a busy English port with daily sailings to Rotterdam. So, once more in male attire, Lady Margaret and Lora set off for the appointed meeting place just south of the city.

'This time I shall pose as a young man going away for the good of my health,' laughed Lady Margaret, as she seated herself in their friend's chaise and Lora wrapped travelling rugs around her.

'Thank you so much for your kindness to me, Lora dear. You have been a loyal friend. I shall never forget you. Here's hoping we may meet again in happier times,' and the two girls embraced warmly. Lora wished the venture 'godspeed' and she stood watching until the small carriage had disappeared into the night.

Later Lora heard that Mr Archibald Hart drove Lady Margaret safely to Hull. Unfortunately, as she was boarding a vessel there, she was seized by a military patrol who thought she was the Young Pretender himself. Her escort was equal to the situation, however. He assured the officer in charge that his companion was not a gentleman at all but a young lady of rank who had got into debt as a result of gambling and had, of necessity, to don male disguise and flee the country in order to escape her creditors.

The officer said if it could be proved that the person was, in fact, a lady, he had no desire to embarrass her further. Several females were called in and they testified that the prisoner was indeed a female. She was then allowed to resume her journey, and subsequently rejoined her husband in France.

Lora never saw her again.

It was not until many years later, she learned that Lady Margaret had secretly returned to Scotland during the year 1751 in order that her second child – which she hoped would be a son – might be born in Scotland. At her old home of Auchterhouse, near Dundee, she gave birth to a son who was baptised David after his father. Immediately she was fit to travel Lady Margaret returned to France. She died there in 1757 aged thirty-three years.

Lora had remained at The House of Reid while Lady Ogilvy was in hiding there. Most evenings the girls had spent together but Lora used all the daylight hours for work at the smugglers' bothy. The Revd John Duncan became a frequent visitor at this time and spent many a pleasant hour in Lora's company, much to Miss Riddoch's secret satisfaction.

'Oh, by the way, Lora,' John remarked one day in the course of conversation. 'I met some people from your part of the country at the end of the week.'

'And who might they be, pray?'

'They were tinkers. I was asked to officiate at a tinkers' wedding at the encampment near the village. The bride and groom were middle-aged. Both had been married before and the bride was from Kirriemuir. She told me she had kept a lodging-house in the town. Then I was talking to one of the guests. He had acted as best man to the groom, and he told me that he had been a pedlar in and around the Kirriemuir district. In fact, it was to his father that the bride had been previously married.'

Lora was struck dumb for a few minutes. This was certainly an unpleasant shock!

'I know of those people,' she said at last, speaking as calmly as possible. 'The pedlar came round Glen Clova regularly.'

'Well he has apparently forsaken his Glen Clova customers in favour of life in the big city. His stepmother and her new husband – a Mr McLeerie – have set up a lodging-house in Edinburgh, I understand, and the pedlar is to reside with them and ply his trade from there.'

This was bad news indeed for Lora. She had expected never to see or hear of Paddy O'Malley again, after his being arrested as an army deserter. It seemed impossible that he could have been set free so soon, and yet there was no doubting the identity of those two. They were definitely Paddy O'Malley and his stepmother.

Back into Lora's mind came the memory of the shadowy figure following Lady Ogilvy and herself through the Edinburgh streets. Suddenly she felt convinced that their pursuer had been none other than O'Malley. He must have recognised her as she stood waiting for Lady Margaret. Life, all of a sudden, seemed to have taken on a much more menacing aspect.

Lora and Royal returned to Edinburgh when Lady Ogilvy had gone, and a few days later Royal went missing. No one knew exactly what had happened but it was thought that the street door had been left open and the dog had simply wandered outside.

Winter had now set in with a vengeance, and deep snow and ice rendered the streets extremely treacherous. Nevertheless, Lora searched for her pet unremittingly. Rather than plod through the deep snow she saddled Rufus. He was pretty sure-footed and it was also an advantage to be able to view the streets from the elevated position of the horse's back. Alas! long hours of searching achieved nothing.

On the afternoon of the third day, just about dusk, Rufus unfortunately stumbled. Lora at that moment had turned round in the saddle to peer into one of the narrow vennels and was caught off balance. Next thing she knew she had plunged into a snowdrift.

A woman came running out of a close-mouth and helped Lora to her feet.

'Come inside for a meenute or twa till yet get yer wind back, lass,' she invited, and she called to a man who was shovelling snow to come and hold the horse.

'I really am all right,' Lora protested. 'I haven't hurt myself,' but she was slightly dazed by the fall and the woman was already guiding her into the dark entry.

Somehow the appearance of the woman and the sound of her voice struck a chord in Lora's memory. After a few moments full realisation returned to her! By a strange twist of fate she had landed once more in the company of Paddy O'Malley's stepmother from the Skinner's Close in Kirriemuir!

The woman had left her momentarily to fetch a lighted 'cruisie', and, whenever the light shone on Lora's face she too remembered.

'I ken *you*!' she exclaimed. 'You're the young leddy frae Glen Clova – Auld Hamish's freend! Fancy meetin' *you* again! We bide in Auld Reekie noo. This is oor new lodgin'-hoose, and that's my new man, Rab McLeerie, oot there haudin' your horse.'

'And what about Paddy O'Malley?' Lora heard herself asking.

'Oh, Paddy, the bold boy! He's as large as life. The army picked him up as a deserter, and he got twenty-five lashes for that and for woundin' a superior officer. They were thinkin' o' sendin' him to the colonies, but their boats were a' fu' o' Jacobite prisoners. Paddy was nae further use as a sodjer because o' his cripple leg, but the bold boy offered to work as an informer to the army if they would jist let him ply his trade in and aroond Edinburgh. The army thocht that was a jolly good idea – there's still a lot o' Jacobites on the run, ye ken – so they struck a bargain wi' Paddy and he's jist in his element spyin' on fowk. I mind noo – you were involved wi' Jacobites! Well, ye'll better watch oot! Paddy's had a lot o' success already, and he has nae mercy. If he thinks there's ony dukery-pawkery he jist calls in the Redcoats.'

Lora shivered involuntarily, and the woman thought she was cold.

'Would ye like a wee drappie o' whisky to heat ye up?' she asked.

'No, thank you, I'm perfectly all right,' Lora assured her.

At that moment a shadowy figure appeared in the doorway leading from the inner lobby.

'You left me in the dark when ye took awa' that cruisie,' an indignant voice barked at Lora's companion.

Lora recognised the harsh voice at once. It was Granny from the Skinner's Close!

Granny peered at Lora.

'Is this anither lodger ye've gotten?' she enquired of her daughter.

'No, this young leddy was thrown aff her horse oot there. D'ye no' recognise her, Mither?'

Granny moved forward and looked closely at Lora.

'Of coorse I recognise her,' she exclaimed. 'She's Miss Hoity-Toity frae Glen Clova – Auld Hamish's freend.' Then, addressing Lora, she remarked, 'I never feenished readin' your fortune. Let me ha'e anither look at yer palm,' and she grabbed hold of Lora's right hand before Lora could prevent her.

After a few moments silent meditation the old woman gave a cackle of satisfaction. 'Wait till I see Paddy! This'll interest him, I'm thinkin'. Jacobite rebels are his business noo, and you're up to yer auld tricks, if ye ask me. I see a big hoose and somebody wi' grey hair – a wumman I think. There's somebody else though, somebody wi' a dog-collar. Imagine a man o' the cloth preachin' the gospel and at the same time bein' unfaithful to his King and country! But I see retribution comin' fast so ye'll better heed my warnin', missie. I warned ye aince afore that I saw fechtin' an' bloodshed and death, and, by jove, I see it again, only worse this time, wi' mair corpses.'

Lora had had enough. Pulling her hand away she stood up, withdrew a silver coin from her purse and crossed the woman's hand with silver as she was obviously expected to do. Then she turned towards the door and the younger woman followed her out.

'Thank you for your kindness,' Lora said. 'Here is a token of my gratitude,' and she handed her a silver coin also.

The husband held Rufus until Lora remounted, which merited a further monetary reward, but at last she had left the dingy street behind her and was heading for the Canongate. The lights of home had never seemed more cheering than they did on that wintry evening but her missing pet, and the ominous warnings of that witch-like woman conspired to keep her spirits at a low ebb. Fears for the future began to dominate her thinking, and during the hours of darkness her dreams often became nightmares.

The next day, there being still no sign of Royal, Lora decided to ride to Lammermuir.

'He likes staying there, so perhaps he has gone back,' she said hopefully. But Royal wasn't there either. Lora was becoming desperate. The worry about her pet was putting her off her sleep and off her food.

About a week after Royal had gone amissing Lora had an unexpected visitor in the person of the Revd John Duncan.

'What brings *you* to town, John?' she asked, after she had introduced him to her stepmother and Susan.

'I came to tell you that I think I know where Royal is, Lora.'

'Where?' asked Lora, with bated breath.

'At the tinkers' camp near our village. I saw a big dog – very like Royal – tied to the wheel of a caravan and I asked if they had found the dog. They said the dog belonged to Paddy O'Malley. He had brought it from Edinburgh and left it with them, but they were adamant that the dog's name was "Loyal", not "Royal".'

'"Loyal" was the original name of my dog, but it was considered foolish of me to go around crying "Loyal!" at the present time, so I changed it to "Royal",' Lora explained.

'Then it *will* be your dog, Lora! I'm *so* glad! Will you come back with me and claim it?'

'Yes. Certainly I will,' Lora replied. 'I think it was very kind of you to ride all that way to give me the wonderful news! Thank you so much, John! Truly, I was beginning to give up hope of ever seeing Royal again.'

'Yes. Miss Riddoch told me how upset you were. By the way, I said to your great-aunt that I intended riding into town to give you the good tidings and she invited you to The House of Reid for as long as you can stay. She misses you when you're not there now – in fact, we all do!'

Lora blushed. 'How nice of you to say that! I shall be delighted to stay with Aunt Emily again. I feel very much at home among you all.'

As soon as they had had lunch Lora and John set off.

Riding along the country lanes Lora told John about her chance meeting with O'Malley's stepmother and about the disturbing news she had gleaned regarding Paddy O'Malley. She also told him about the old woman's prophecies and of how her previous predictions had come true. Then she described, as briefly as she could, all that had happened in Glen Clova, Kirriemuir, Glen Ogil, and Aberbrothock, and about the evil part played by the pedlar.

'You seem to have had your full share of adventure, Lora, and here you are involved with Jacobite rebels once again. The pedlar appears to be a dangerous character. We could certainly have done without him poking his nose into our affairs at this time. We shall all have to be extra vigilant from now on. But come, my dear, let us put our worries out of our minds for the present and enjoy the time we have together on this beautiful winter's day amid such ideal scenery.'

So they chatted about many things and both felt supremely happy in the other's company. Even Lora's worry about her beloved pet faded into the background a little. It was an afternoon neither would ever forget, for it forged a special bond between them that nothing could ever take away.

Whenever Lora and John entered the tinkers' camp, Royal proved without a shadow of doubt that he was definitely Lora's dog. His welcome was ecstatic, and the tinkers willingly handed him over.

'They're a decent set of people there,' John remarked as they left the camp. 'In fact, in my experience, most tinkers prove themselves to be trustworthy and dependable if given a fair chance. I can tell you many Jacobites owed their lives to tinkers after Culloden. They rescued, and concealed, dozens of rebels at great personal risk. Indeed, many paid the supreme sacrifice rather than betray their fellow men.'

'Are you a Jacobite, John?' Lora asked.

'No. I'm not,' he replied. 'From the very beginning I thought it was an ill-advised rebellion and would bring disaster upon the Highlands. Prince Charlie had no right to expect so much of his loyal Scottish supporters when he had so little to offer them in return. He had practically no money and no backing from the French. Before Culloden his Highlanders were starving and he had nothing with which to buy food for them.'

'But if you do not approve, then why do you risk so much to help Jacobites?' queried Lora.

'I happened to be an assistant minister in a church near Culloden at the time of the battle and the minister and I went to Drumossie Moor, after the fighting was over, to give what comfort and help we could to the wounded and dying. We were simply appalled at the utter ruthlessness of the Duke of Cumberland and his troops. Any wounded Highlander who couldn't walk off the battlefield was simply "put to the sword" where he lay. I shall never be able to erase from my mind the memory of such cruel senseless slaughter, and I vowed, there and then, that I would do all in my power to help any Jacobite to escape from such merciless killers. When I got my own charge, down here in the Borders, I didn't expect to come across many fugitive rebels but I found that Miss Riddoch was already operating an efficient rescue service and I simply joined forces with her. She is a very brave woman, your great-aunt. I admire her tremendously.'

John accompanied Lora to The House of Reid, and when Miss Riddoch was told about O'Malley, and about the old tinker-woman's prophecies she felt the situation was serious enough to call a meeting of all her helpers.

Old Jake was now the only servant to reside in The House of Reid. All the maids, the cook, the stable boys and the grooms came to work in the mornings and went home at night. Miss Riddoch's nocturnal Jacobite activities had made it necessary for her to alter the running of her household. She had complete faith in all her staff, but she feared the consequences to them if they were found to be living in a house which was harbouring rebels. That was a risk that she herself was willing to take 'but I have no right to impose such danger or others,' she firmly maintained. 'All who participate in our rescue service must do so of their own free will.'

Besides Old Jake and Lora at the meeting there was John, Farmer Robb, Colin the blacksmith, Hector (another local farmer who had lost a son at Culloden) and young Fergus, a farmer's son who had been 'out' in the 'forty-five 'but had quietly returned home and had been overlooked in the rounding-up process.

When Paddy O'Malley was described to the men, Hector said at once, 'I've seen that man hangin' around here lately. He seems on friendly terms wi' auld Mary-Anne down at the cottage. In fact, I thocht he was surely a relative o' hers for I've seen him there several times.'

'I've seen him tae,' said Fergus. 'When I was bringin' the sheep inbye afore the recent storm he was oot near your bothy, Miss Riddoch. You two ladies must have been at the bothy, for the big dog was lyin' at the door I mind. The man was ridin' a piebald pony and he jist went as far as the bothy. When the snaw came on in earnest he turned back.'

'That means the man also knows where our whisky "still" is,' remarked Miss Riddoch with concern. 'This is the worst crisis we've had to face so far.'

Then Lora told them what Mary-Anne at the cottage had said to her about the people at The House of Reid.

Miss Riddoch and the men chuckled when they heard the warning Lora had been given, but the fact didn't escape them that Mary-Anne was probably the person who had initially aroused O'Malley's interest in the inhabitants of the big house and their whisky 'still'.

'She probably told him about your arrival here too, Lora,' said Miss Riddoch.

'Well, if she said I had a large Deerhound with me, O'Malley would know at once who I was. All I can say is "Thank goodness Lady Ogilvy got away safely!" No doubt he's been assisting the army in the matter of her escape from Edinburgh Castle and it may be that that old woman saw Lady Margaret arrive here on horseback with me. Someone was spying on me while I waited for Lady Margaret on the night of her escape from the castle. We managed to shake off that particular spy, but, after I heard that O'Malley was around again, I felt certain that the spy was none other than he. I just hope and pray I haven't been the means of bringing trouble on your head, Aunt Emily.'

'Any trouble that falls on my head, Lora dear, is the result of my own misdeeds and no one else's, so you can put that out of your mind right away,' her aunt assured her.

'Now that we ken for sure that the pedlar's a spy we'll ken how to deal wi' *him*,' said Fergus purposefully.

'Aye. If he was on his own it would be a simple matter, but if he brings Redcoats to back him up we wouldna' stand a chance,' the blacksmith pointed out. 'We havena' the necessary weapons to fight highly trained men.'

'Fortunately we have no Jacobite rebels in our care at the moment,' John observed. 'I just hope there is none waiting for me at the manse tonight.'

While the other men were leaving, John lingered behind with Lora for a few minutes.

'When you take your pony out for its daily exercise, Lora, ride over by the manse and I'll join you for a canter over the moors,' he suggested. 'I have enjoyed our afternoon together so very much I think the pleasure should be repeated as frequently as possible. Don't you?'

'Yes. I enjoyed our journey from Edinburgh too,' Lora agreed, with a happy smile, 'but I shall probably be exercising Rufus in the mornings from now on. Aunt Emily and I have some work to complete at the bothy, so our afternoons will be fully occupied.'

'Mornings would suit me very well, Lora. I shall look out for you tomorrow about nine, shall I?'

'Yes, if the weather is fine I'll be there,' Lora promised, and John kissed her hand before hurrying off to join the others.

So, from then on, Lora's daily routine began with an early-morning gallop on the moors with John and her animal pals – Rufus and Royal. The gallops were exhilarating but the most enjoyable part of the exercise was the journey back when they chatted and laughed together, and slowed their ponies almost to a crawl in order to spin out the time remaining to them for as long as they possibly could.

Gradually Lora began to realise that John had become a very important person in her life. Nowadays she seldom thought about Lennox or Paul.

Her mind was too full of John and the sheer joy she experienced in his company. There was no passing infatuation concerned with this relationship. She realised that she had truly fallen in love with the Rev John Duncan, and John made it crystal clear that her love was reciprocated. In spite of the very real threats of Redcoats and excisemen, life for Lora at that time seemed full of blissful promise.

About two days after Lora had returned to The House of Reid, she and Aunt Emily were completing a satisfactory afternoon's work at the bothy when Aunt Emily happened to glance out of the tiny window.

'My godfathers!' she exclaimed, 'We're done for this time! Here's the gaugers!'

Lora sped to the window and peeped out. In the distance she could see two men on horseback heading towards the bothy. She also noticed that Royal had risen to his feet and was keeping the riders under strict surveillance. As the men drew nearer, Royal's hackles were rising.

'Quick! Aunt Emily! All is not lost,' she cried, 'we can still get the copper kettle and the worm up under the thatch. Royal will delay the men.'

In a frenzy of haste the ladies began to stow away all the incriminating gear. With the strength born of desperation they managed to raise the heavy flagstone in the floor, which acted as a trapdoor, and together they succeeded in pushing tubs and kegs out of sight.

By this time Royal had broken into a furious snarling and barking which was accompanied by a variety of oaths from his victims. The ladies crept to the window to see what was happening.

All their frenzied efforts had been unnecessary. Royal had successfully prevented the men from dismounting, and had finally put the intruders to flight. The big dog continued to attack one of the men as he rode away and no amount of swearing or lashing out with a whip had any effect upon the infuriated animal. Lora recognised the object of Royal's wrath. It was none other than Paddy O'Malley!

'That pedlar must have treated Royal cruelly,' observed Lora. 'I have never seen my dog act so aggressively.'

'I know that particular exciseman is afraid of dogs,' said Miss Riddoch. 'He told me so once when he was on a routine visit to the district, before I became one of the smuggling fraternity. I remember he asked me to shut our dogs in before he would even venture to dismount, and ours were small dogs compared with your Deerhound. He must have been petrified at Royal.'

'What you have just said explains why Paddy O'Malley had lured Royal away,' said Lora. 'That exciseman had told the pedlar of his fear of dogs, and, remember, Fergus said that Royal was lying at the door of the bothy on the day that he saw O'Malley spying around. I've no doubt the pedlar had decided to get Royal out of the way before they came to raid your whisky "still", Aunt Emily. Well I'm glad O'Malley's plan has been thwarted but he will strike again. He's a dangerous man and a cunning one.'

One crisp winter's morning when Lora and John had enjoyed a particularly invigorating gallop over the frozen landscape and were approaching the usual parting of their ways, Lora noticed that John was much quieter than usual.

'What's the matter, John? Something troubling you?' she asked.

'Yes, Lora, there is something.' He hesitated and then continued, 'Sometime before I met you I applied, through my university, to be given a chance to preach the Gospel in foreign parts. I have now been offered a choice of Southern India or Southern Africa.'

'And have you accepted either?'

'Not yet, but I have to make my choice this week.'

Lora felt a pang of dismay.

'And which shall it be?' she asked, in a voice that was little more than a whisper.

'Southern Africa, I think,' John replied. 'The trouble is, since meeting you, I am not so keen to leave my native land.'

'And when will you have to go?'

'Fairly soon, I believe, but I have no set date yet. First of all I may have to meet missionaries who can tell me about the country of my choice and about the people who live there. I shall also have to learn how to set about establishing a mission station or a church in what may prove to be a hostile land.'

'I see,' said Lora slowly. 'I shall miss you,' she added, with a slight tremor in her voice.

They had both dismounted by this time and were standing on a stone bridge which spanned a fast-flowing stream. Leaning on the stone parapet they gazed into the water in silence and, for Lora at least, the beauty of that bright winter's day had faded.

Speech seemed to have forsaken them but, at last John took Lora's hand in his.

'Lora – I wonder, is it – is it possible?' and he stumbled in confusion over the words, 'that you could consider marrying me – and coming with me as my wife?' And the last words came out with a rush. 'You must know by now that I love you more than anyone, or anything, in this world.'

'I love you too, John,' Lora replied, blushing scarlet, 'but I had never thought of leaving Scotland and settling in a foreign land.'

'I realise this must've come as a shock to you, Lora dear, but will you please give the matter some earnest thought and give me your answer as soon as you can? I shall not try to talk you into anything against your better judgement. Your decision will be final.'

John held Lora's hand lingeringly in his. Then he bent and kissed her cheek. Lora felt near to tears as she remounted and set off for The House of Reid. Before she reached her destination, however, her mind was made up. She could never be happy anywhere without John. She must go with him, though it were to the ends of the earth.

In the evening John rode over to The House of Reid and Lora told him what he longed to hear – that she truly loved him and could not bear to be parted from him.

' "Whither thou goest I will go," ' she quoted. ' "Thy people will be my people," ' and John held her close and kissed her repeatedly.

Then together they went to find Miss Riddoch and tell her their wonderful news.

'I don't know what I shall do without you both,' she declared, 'but I am delighted for you. I have always thought you would make the ideal couple and I hope you will have a long and happy life together. I also pray that Southern Africa will be kind to you both and that you will return to spend the autumn of your years at The House of Reid.'

Following O'Malley and the exciseman's visit to the bothy, Miss Riddoch told Lora of a change in her plans.

'Now that the whereabouts of our "still" has been discovered,' she said, 'I've been thinking it would be foolish of us to take further risks meantime. We have used up our present consignment of barley so this is as good a time as any to cease production. There have been no demands on our resources these last few weeks so perhaps the flow of rebels in this area is coming to an end. I suggest we clean out the bothy, so that no tell-tale signs remain, and leave well alone from now on unless it proves necessary at some later date.'

'There is no need for your to go back to the bothy, Aunt Emily. I can clean up for you,' Lora offered. 'If Old Jake brings the horse and cart we can fetch back the kegs that are ready for despatch, and Jake will help me to make certain that all is secure.'

Lora and Jake were very thorough in their work at the bothy and they managed to stack all the kegs in the cart with some peat spread over as camouflage. They were almost finished when they heard a step outside the bothy door and someone talking to the horse which was standing patiently waiting to move off.

It was Fergus.

'By jove! Ye've done a good job here,' he remarked, poking his head round the door and surveying the empty bothy. 'Naebody could tell there had ever been a whisky "still" in here. Ye've done the wise thing to stop for a bit, though. I jist looked in to warn ye that a troop o' Redcoats have pitched their tents near the main road to the village. I had a sniff around and I noticed your freend wi' the piebald pony and anither lad were as thick as thieves wi' the troopers. If ye're to be on the whisky run ye'd better keep your eyes skinned – that's my advice to ye.'

When Lora and Jake arrived back at the house Miss Riddoch hurried out and advised them not to unload the cart.

'The blacksmith was up to say he had a market for all we could supply, but it would need to be delivered tonight. Perhaps the horse and cart would attract less attention than a string of ponies.'

So the cart with its load was left intact and a nosebag of food was fetched out for the horse.

Once safely inside the house Miss Riddoch turned to Lora. Dropping her voice to a mere whisper she said, 'A rebel came here while you were away, Lora. I have never felt so uneasy about any of the men we have sheltered so far. I took the man in but I have grave doubts about his being genuine.'

'Where is he?' Lora asked, in alarm. 'Not in the secret rooms, I hope!'

'No. He's in the kitchen having something to eat. I'd like you to have a look at him and give me your opinion please, Lora.'

Lora made her way to the kitchen as quickly and quietly as possible. The man hadn't heard her approach and, by the glow of the fire and the light of the hanging lamp, she could see him quite clearly from the doorway. She recognised him at once. It was the man who had held her horse when she fell into the snowdrift at the door of the Edinburgh lodging-house – the new husband of Paddy O'Malley's stepmother!

Without hesitation Lora walked into the room and advanced towards the man.

'Good evening!' she greeted him. 'I didn't expect to meet *you* so soon again.'

Taken completely by surprise the man started guiltily and dropped his knife and fork. Then he remained open-mouthed and speechless, staring at Lora.

Miss Riddoch joined them in the kitchen at that moment and Lora turned to address her.

'I thought you said a rebel soldier had come begging food and shelter, Aunt Emily. You have been cruelly tricked. This man is no rebel. I met him quite recently. His name is McLeerie, and he and his wife have a lodging-house in Edinburgh. The Revd John Duncan performed their marriage ceremony some weeks ago at the tinkers' encampment beside the village. Paddy O'Malley was the best man at the wedding. I'm sure you'll recall John's description of the affair.'

Addressing McLeerie again, Lora continued, 'You should be thoroughly ashamed of yourself, Mr McLeerie, playing such a mean trick on a kindhearted lady. If you were in need of a meal you had only to ask and she would willingly have given you one. You didn't need to tell a parcel of lies! I think you should leave this house at once, sir, and never show your face here again.'

So saying, Lora walked to the back door and held it open, while McLeerie grabbed up his Glengarry bonnet and shuffled off without a word.

'That was well handled, Lora. Thank you so much, dear,' said Miss Riddoch gratefully.

'Thank goodness he didn't get any further than the kitchen,' exclaimed Lora. 'In future if you get others coming like that, Aunt Emily, you should blindfold them before they leave the kitchen. No doubt that man's low-down trick was probably thought up by the army. They had encouraged him to persuade you to give him shelter so that they could discover him on the premises and arrest you for aiding and abetting rebels. Did the blacksmith tell you a detachment of Redcoats had arrived in the area again? Fergus called in at the bothy and he told us he saw O'Malley and another man with the English soldiers. McLeerie had been the other man.'

As soon as they had had their evening meal, Lora offered to take the horse and cart to the blacksmith's place. 'Old Jake is tired after the work at the bothy and the walk there and back. He actually complained to me about feeling tired. I have never heard him complain before.'

'I'm not surprised he felt tired,' observed Miss Riddoch. He has always been a hard worker and he has already had his three-score years and ten, you know. Jake resents the infirmities of old age and always maintains he will die in harness. Alas! one has no choice in the matter. It is very good of you to offer your services, Lora, but I don't like the idea of your going alone.'

'Nonsense, Aunt Emily. It is a beautiful night. I shall enjoy the trip and so will Royal. I'll change into male attire since I shall have to stride out alongside the big workhorse. After I have delivered the load I shall pay John a visit at the manse, so don't be worrying yourself if I'm not back by the time you would normally expect me.'

As soon as she was ready, Lora set off with the horse and cart accompanied by Royal. It was a clear, moonlight night with a nip of frost in the air, an ideal night for a smart walk. Lora was looking forward to seeing John and she strode out with a will, humming a cheery little tune. She hadn't gone far when she saw a figure approaching on horseback. It was Colin, the blacksmith. Lora greeted him and he exclaimed in surprise.

'It's you, Miss Lora! I recognised the horse but I couldna' place the slim young man. Where's Jake? I wouldna have thocht they'd let you come on your own. This's no' a job for a woman.'

Lora explained that she had come to save Old Jake the journey.

'I felt sure I could cope, since it was just as far as the smithy and back,' she said.

'But we've to deliver the loads to Haddington!' exclaimed Colin. 'I came to meet Jake to tell him we'd need to alter our route slightly. Did ye ken that the Redcoats have arrived again?'

'Yes. Fergus told us. I should think we have to thank Paddy O'Malley for that. He's up to some of his dirty tricks again, if you ask me.'

'Do you think you'll manage the lang walk to Haddington and back?' queried the smith with some doubt.

'Of course I will,' Lora replied stoutly.

'I have a cart-load of kegs as weel, ye see. My young son is to meet us at the crossroads wi' my load and he'll ride this horse back to the smiddy.'

The boy was waiting, as arranged, and the change-over was quickly effected. Lora and Colin had found plenty to talk about but now there could be no conversation as they had to walk in single file, each leading their horse and cart along the narrow track. Colin went first and Lora found it quite hard going to keep up with the big man's lengthy stride.

At one point Royal gave a low growl and kept pausing to look behind him. Lora fancied she heard a stifled sneeze but she could see nothing although the night was as clear as day.

About half a mile further on, and completely without warning, a gruff voice barked out 'Halt!' At the same time four men appeared from behind a hedge and barred the blacksmith's way forward. Lora recognised two of the men. They were O'Malley and McLeerie. She presumed the other two were excisemen and her heart sank within her. There was no escape!

But Lora had underestimated her companion. Like a flash he produced a thick cudgel out of his cart and confronted his would-be attackers.

'Get out of my way,' he shouted. 'I'll fell the first man that makes a move,' and he brandished his weapon menacingly. With the stature and the brawn of the blacksmith behind it, the cudgel was a very formidable weapon indeed. But there were four to one!

Just at that moment Lora heard a rush of feet behind her and three men dashed forward to join the blacksmith in his stand against his four opponents.

'Take both horses, Miss Lora, and lead them to a safe distance,' the blacksmith directed over his shoulder, without taking his eyes off the four men confronting him.

Lora quickly obeyed. She also called Royal to heel lest he should get in the way, for she could see his eyes were fixed on Paddy O'Malley and his hackles were up.

'Now we'll get this settled once and for all,' bellowed the blacksmith. 'Our lives are no' to be harassed by the likes o' you, so let the best men win. Charge!' he shouted, and the battle began.

The noise reminded Lora of the tinkers' battle with the Redcoats at Pickerton. She couldn't tell friend from foe as the men merged into a struggling mass of humanity. Dreadful thuds, oaths, blood-curdling yells, screams of pain and loud groans echoed on the frosty air as blow was exchanged for blow in quick succession. There was no way of telling which side was winning. Then suddenly two men broke away and began to run. Their two companions continued to fight until they realised the hopelessness of their position, when they also took to their heels and fled, pursued by the blacksmith and his gallant supporters.

'Och, let them go boys! I'm thinking we've given them more than they bargained for,' cried the blacksmith at last. 'Miss Lora and I have a lang trek in front o' us yet so we'll better get on our way. What a blessin' you lads arrived when ye did. I've certainly a lot to thank ye for. How did ye manage to time it so perfectly?'

'We were just keepin' an eye on that pedlar and his partner. We discovered they had been followin' Miss Lora right from the time she left the hoose so we decided to follow them and find oot what they were up to,' young Fergus explained. 'The ither pair joined them near the crossroads where your son was waitin' for ye, Colin. They werena gaugers, as ye probably imagined. They were tinks from the camp. That quartet was meanin' to ha'e a fine haul o' whisky off you folk. Theft was definitely their main object.'

'Well, we've settled their hash for this nicht,' laughed Hector.

'Aye,' agreed Farmer Robb. 'I hardly think they'll be lookin' for another confrontation wi' us for a while. I think we can certainly claim victory in the first round – eh, lads?'

All four men were suffering from black eyes, bleeding noses, cuts or bruises, but fortunately, no broken bones. They treated their injuries lightly and enjoyed a good laugh among themselves about the damage they had inflicted on the other side. Lora and the blacksmith thanked them once again for their timely intervention and then the two parties went their separate ways.

It was a long walk to Haddington but, fortunately, the inn to which they were going was located just off the main road into the town, so they were spared the embarrassment of the horses' iron-shod hoofs, and the lumbering cart wheels, causing a loud clatter on the cobbles and arousing inquisitive inhabitants.

There were plenty of helpers to unload the whisky kegs, so the business was quickly transacted. Then after a hot drink to warm them, Lora and Colin were soon on their way home. Lora, for one, was thankful to be able to sit in the cart instead of having to trudge alongside the horse.

After Lora had set out with the load of whisky kegs, Miss Riddoch went up to her bedroom to close the shutters. Moonlight flooded the room and the view from the window was breathtaking. She decided it would be quite wrong to shut out that beautiful panorama. Instead, she seated herself in an armchair by the window and gazed out across the shimmering, frosty landscape. Peace reigned supreme. Gradually Miss Riddoch began to nod and finally she drifted into a restful sleep.

She had no idea how long she had slept, or whether something had disturbed her slumber, but when she awoke the moon still shone brightly from a cloudless sky and no sound broke the stillness. It was truly a perfect night.

Then, as her gaze lingered on the moorland she became aware of movement. Something was heading in the direction of The House of Reid. It crossed her mind that it might be Lora returning with the horse and cart, but gradually she realised that what she was seeing was a troop of horses, and the riders were dressed in red!

Miss Riddoch remained seated at her window and as horses and men drew nearer she was able to distinguish a piebald pony in the forefront ridden by a man in a dark coat. It was the pedlar – Paddy O'Malley.

Miss Riddoch knew then that this was no friendly visit, and she breathed a prayer of thankfulness that there were no hunted men sheltering in The House of Reid that night.

When a loud knocking sounded on the main door and a harsh voice demanded, 'Open, in the name of the King!' Miss Riddoch rose, lit a candle, and descended the stairs with her normal poise and dignity. She unbolted the door and calmly addressed the troopers.

'Good evening!' she said pleasantly. 'Do you wish to speak with me?'

'Yes, madam, we do. It is for that purpose we have come here,' replied the spokesman, a gruff, rather coarse-looking sergeant.

'Please come in, then,' Miss Riddoch invited, and she led the way to her sitting-room. Three or four of the troopers, together with Paddy O'Malley, followed the burly sergeant into the room. All remained standing.

Miss Riddoch looked enquiringly at the spokesman.

'We believe you have been instrumental in helping Jacobite rebels to evade capture by His Majesty's forces. You must understand that such behaviour is punishable by death,' said the man coldly.

'What possible proof could you have of such an accusation?' queried Miss Riddoch.

The sergeant looked towards Paddy O'Malley.

'From my enquiries in the neighbourhood, sir,' said the pedlar, addressing the sergeant, 'I know for a fact that this woman has been the means of many Jacobites getting through your net. A Lady Margaret Ogilvy escaped from Edinburgh Castle on the twenty-first of November, and, although I was unaware of the escape at that time, I saw and recognised a friend of this woman's waiting in a street not far from the castle. When she was joined by another young lady they dashed off together down a side street. I followed, but my cripple leg prevented my keeping up the necessary speed and they eluded me. I understand, however, that two young ladies arrived here on horseback early the following morning.'

'Is that true?' the sergeant demanded of Miss Riddoch.

'I do not know what he is talking about,' she replied.

'Don't you be too hasty with your denials,' warned the sergeant. 'I think perhaps you do know what he's talking about.'

At that moment a scuffle sounded in the corridor outside and someone was unceremoniously pitched through the open doorway to fall flat on his face on the floor.

It was Old Jake.

Miss Riddoch started forward to help the old man to his feet but the burly sergeant thrust her back.

'Leave him alone,' he barked. 'You're no longer mistress of this house. While I'm here *I'm* in charge.' Then he turned to Old Jake.

'And who may you happen to be?' he demanded.

The old man was out of breath after the harsh treatment he had just received from the troopers. He had struggled to a sitting position but was so breathless he got no further than, 'My name is – my name is . . .'

'Good God!' said the sergeant rudely, 'surely at your age you've learned your own name! And stand up when you're speaking to me,' he added roughly, giving the old man a vicious kick which sent him sprawling once more.

'How can he stand up if *you* continue to kick him down?' demanded Miss Riddoch angrily. 'Have you no respect for old age?'

For answer the sergeant turned and struck her across the mouth with the back of his hand. 'Speak when you're spoken to,' he snarled.

Then turning to two of the troopers he ordered, 'Get him up on his feet,' and Old Jake was dragged upright, only to be struck down again when he failed to understand what the Englishman was saying.

'This is not good enough,' protested Miss Riddoch. 'We demand a measure of respect. After all, you have no proof of any crime having been committed by either of us.'

Paddy O'Malley again interrupted at this point.

'Sure, I'll tell you something else, sergeant,' he said, 'There's a secret door leading to a secret staircase and secret rooms in this house. An auld woman that worked as a servant here long ago told me about them.'

'And whereabouts are they?' asked the sergeant.

'Sure the doorway is hidden behind a portrait, in a hall hung wi' oil paintings, I believe,' said O'Malley, delighted to be the bearer of so much important information.

At this the sergeant seized Miss Riddoch roughly by the arm and pulled her towards the door.

'Show us where all those secrets are or take the consequences,' he ordered, and Miss Riddoch was propelled forward in the wake of Paddy O'Malley, while two troopers dragged Old Jake along, like a sack of coal.

The soldiers immediately began to rip open the canvases and hack the portraits down off the walls. Miss Riddoch could hardly bear to look at such wanton destruction but she had no intention of providing any assistance in their search.

The sergeant was well versed in cruelty, however, and knew exactly how to force her hand.

'Tie him up with his face to the wall,' he ordered, indicating Old Jake.

When this had been done, the sergeant took the point of his sword and ripped the old man's jacket and shirt off his back. Then, tossing his whip to one of the troopers he issued his orders.

'Unless she tells us what we want to know, he will be flogged to death. I will start to count now. Whenever I count to number five apply the whip full strength, repeat at number ten, and so on until we get the results we want.'

'Don't tell them anything, Miss Riddoch,' cried Old Jake. 'Let them do their worst. I'll no' squeal.'

But Miss Riddoch couldn't bear to see such inhuman treatment meted out to her faithful servant and friend.

'Stop!' she cried. 'I will tell you what you want to know, but it will avail you nothing. There are no rebels in this house.'

So saying she stepped forward and manipulated the device that opened the secret door. The sergeant and Paddy O'Malley pushed roughly past her and went to investigate the secret rooms leaving Miss Riddoch and Old Jake in the custody of the troopers.

When they returned, the sergeant ordered both prisoners to have their hands tied behind their backs.

'We have all the proof we need,' he growled. 'Take them outside.'

On her arrival at the manse Lora was disappointed to find that John was not at home, but the housekeeper assured her that he would be back at any moment. 'He told me when to have his meal ready, and he is normally very punctual,' she explained.

But the time passed, and John didn't come.

'I'm afraid I can't wait any longer,' said Lora, at last. 'It's time I was home. Miss Riddoch will be worried about me.' She climbed back into the cart and headed the weary horse in the direction of The House of Reid. It was then that she noticed a rosy glow on the horizon and began to realise that it was a building on fire. With a gasp of horror it dawned on her that it could only be The House of Reid!

All tiredness vanished with the shock of that discovery. Lora jumped out of the cart and began to lead the horse over the moorland track as fast as she could go. She met John while still some distance from the house.

'Oh John! Whatever has happened?' Lora panted.

John dismounted and put his arms around her.

'You must try to be brave, Lora dear,' he said quietly.

'Has something happened to Aunt Emily?' Lora asked in alarm.

'Yes,' John replied sadly. 'I'm sorry to tell you, Lora, but your aunt is dead.'

'Oh no!' Lora cried out in anguish. 'She didn't perish in the fire, did she, John?'

'No, thank goodness for that! Miss Riddoch suffered a violent death, but, at least, it would be mercifully sudden.'

'What do you mean, John?'

'Your Aunt Emily was shot by a Redcoat firing squad, Lora. She and Old Jake died side by side.'

'Oh John, I wish I hadn't gone with the whisky kegs now. I should have been with Aunt Emily. My place was beside her,' wept Lora.

'If you had been with your aunt you couldn't have saved her, Lora. You would have perished along with Jake and her. While mourning for them we must be thankful that you have been spared.'

THE HOUSE OF REID

'Did you see the fire start, John?'

'No. The fire was well alight when I first saw it. I was on my way home from a meeting in Edinburgh and I turned and rode as hard as I could to The House of Reid but I was too late. There was nothing I could do. Quite a few local people had gathered by the time I got there and they gave me the gist of the story. They had also moved the two bodies to a safe distance. Come now, Lora, we will go back to the manse. I must make arrangements to have your aunt's body, and that of Old Jake, brought into the church tonight. Tomorrow, if you wish, we can go to The House of Reid and survey the damage.'

Later, Fergus came to the manse to see Lora and John.

'That pedlar was at the root of the whole tragic business,' he said. 'After our fight on the moor in the evenin', I followed him and his cronies. Three o' them went back to the tinks' camp and remained there but O'Malley collected his horse and made for the Redcoat camp. A party o' them accompanied him to The House o' Reid and I followed at a safe distance. There was nae officer in charge, just a sergeant – a big bully o' a man. Puir Jake suffered some rough treatment at his hands, I can tell ye, but Miss Riddoch stood up to him as best she could. I got near enough to watch through a window but wi' Redcoats at every corner I was at risk o' discovery a' the time and there was nothing I could do to help – unfortunately. When Miss Riddoch and Jake were brought outside, the sergeant accused them o' helpin' rebels to escape and demanded they tell wha else was involved but they would divulge nothing, in spite o' the pressures put upon them. They were staunch to the last. Eventually they had to face a firing squad, while Paddy O'Malley calmly looked on. Truly, I could've torn yon pedlar limb from limb! The Redcoats then set fire to the hoose and marched off, but O'Malley was set to plunder so he remained behind and went into the hoose on the side furthest from the fire. He had nae idea I was around but I waited my chance. I armed mysel' wi' a whip from the stable and I can tell ye I thrashed him within an inch o' his life. He begged for mercy but I locked him in a room and left him to perish in the flames. He had cost a lot o' lives, that damned spy o' a pedlar, but he got his just desserts in the end. I saw to that.'

'And what of all the ponies and the dogs?' asked Lora, dreading the answer and thinking sadly of poor Rufus.

'That was something I *did* manage to do,' replied Fergus. 'I set them a' free. The gamekeeper arrived on the scene and some o' the stable lads, so they rounded up the livestock and took charge o' them. Ye've nothing to worry aboot there, Miss Lora.'

The next few days were a nightmare of grief to Lora.

John held a service for Miss Riddoch in the village church and she was laid to rest in the churchyard where several generations of Reids already lay buried. The service for Old Jake was held immediately afterwards and he too was interred in the churchyard.

The House of Reid had been practically burned to the ground. Of the thick stone walls there remained but a blackened shell, round which the wintry winds moaned drearily.

But life had to go on, and their worries were far from over.

Lora returned to Edinburgh a few days later, accompanied by John and her stepmother was delighted at the engagement, especially when she learned that John was descended from a well-known Border family and was the younger son of a baronet. Mrs Macrae was eager to begin preparations for a society wedding, but Lora was adamant.

'I wish to be married in Clova Kirk,' she insisted, 'and, out of respect for Aunt Emily, I wish to have a quiet wedding.'

On the day that John and Lora arrived in Edinburgh Lora received one pleasant surprise. Paul sailed into Leith unexpectedly! So to him was assigned the rôle of giving away the bride. With Susan acting as bridesmaid, and Mrs Macrae receiving the guests, it was exactly the family wedding that Lora had dreamed of. Lora was also proud to introduce John to Paul, and she was happy to note that each seemed to approve of the other.

'I think you've picked a winner, Lora,' Paul told her when they were alone together, 'but I wonder how poor Lennox will take the news.'

'There was no definite arrangement between Lennox and me, you must remember, Paul,' Lora protested. 'I have written to Lennox to tell him that I will not now be able to keep my part of our bargain and accept his mother's invitation to visit Gloucestershire. Have you any idea where Lennox is stationed meantime, Paul?'

'Yes, I do, and I hope to see him before my next trip abroad. I shall deliver your letter to him personally, Lora. Then I can provide my broad shoulder for him to weep upon,' Paul teased.

Lora remained in Edinburgh when John returned to Lammermuir to finalise arrangements for handing over the charge to his successor.

Two days later Fergus appeared at the Macrae residence in the Canongate.

'I'm afraid I have more bad news for ye, Miss Lora,' he announced, without preamble, when he was shown into the room where Paul and she were talking about her forthcoming sea voyage.

'What sort of bad news, Fergus?' Lora asked, with a sinking heart.

'The minister was arrested by that bully o' a Redcoat sergeant – O'Malley's crony – last nicht.'

'John arrested, did you say?' gasped Lora, the colour draining from her cheeks.

'Aye. The housekeeper brought word to me that he had been arrested on suspicion of helping Jacobites to escape.'

'But what possible proof could they have?'

'They have nae real proof. Only the words o' yon auld tink – the pedlar's relation – that's supposed to ha'e the gift o' the second sicht. I think ye ken wha I mean.'

'Yes, I do know who you mean,' said Lora, bleakly. 'She hinted to me that she knew there was a minister involved in the rescue of Jacobites.'

Paul interrupted at this point.

'But surely no one could be arrested on the evidence of a fortune-teller alone,' he protested. 'Was your fiancé a Jacobite, Lora?'

'No, he was not,' and Lora repeated to Paul and Fergus what John had told her about his views on the subject, and his feelings after seeing the Duke of Cumberland's men massacring the wounded Highlanders on the battlefield of Culloden.

'I think you'd better sit down and tell me all that has been going on during my absence, Lora,' said Paul soberly.

So Lora began at the beginning and told the whole story in detail.

Paul was shocked to learn of Paddy O'Malley's quick release from custody although he had to admit the pedlar would be the ideal spy and would prove invaluable in the hunt for Jacobites and Jacobites' friends.

'So, in spite of my warnings you became involved with Jacobites just the moment my back was turned, Lora,' Paul chided her, 'but, under the circumstances, you were hardly to be blamed. Well, it isn't the easiest of tasks to extricate Jacobite prisoners from the clutches of the English army but, fortunately, I may just happen to have some leverage which I could use on this occasion. We'll see. Where did you say John was taken, Fergus?'

'To the Redcoat camp near our village but when I passed this morning there was some sign of their breakin' camp. Probably preparin' to march back to Edinburgh wi' their prisoner. I suppose the Reverend John Duncan, bein' a parish minister, would be considered quite a catch.'

'Certainly he is a public figure,' agreed Paul, 'and they seem to enjoy making an example of such people wherever possible. I think we must move quickly, and it might be an advantage if you were to come with me, Fergus.'

Fergus was surprised at the deference shown to Paul at the English army headquarters in Edinburgh Castle and he didn't try to conceal his amazement.

'I trained as an army officer and I still serve my country by performing special duties when visiting foreign ports,' Paul whispered, on the side, by way of explanation.

Unfortunately, the commanding officer whom Paul had hoped to contact had gone off duty for the day and had left the premises.

'That prisoner you speak of is being brought here later in the day,' the officer in charge explained. 'I think perhaps you'd better call back early tomorrow. Those cases are usually very quickly dealt with. If they get to this length they are generally assumed to be guilty already.'

Fergus couldn't remain overnight. He had work to do at home and this was their lambing season on the farm so they were specially busy.

'I am very grateful to you for coming all this way to let us know what had happened to John,' said Lora.

'I just hope something can be done to get him set free,' Fergus replied. 'It's dreadful to think folk can be arrested on the word o' a spey-wife.'

The remaining hours of that day dragged past for Lora and sleep deserted her at night. Next day she begged Paul to let her accompany him to the castle so that she might see John, if only for a minute, but Paul dismissed the suggestion at once.

'Considering your part in Lady Ogilvy's escape, and your close association with Miss Riddoch, my advice to you is to keep well out of this, Lora,' he warned her. 'You never know who might recall your face, and very little could tip the balance the wrong way for John.'

When Paul returned from the castle he was alone.

'Did you see John?' Lora asked dejectedly.

'I saw him but that was all. I didn't get a chance to speak to him. However, I put forward as good an argument as I could. I told them my sister was betrothed to the Reverend John Duncan and they took a note of all I said and promised to give it due consideration. I'm thinking it's a blessing Fergus put an end to Paddy O'Malley when he did, otherwise the mere mention of your name would have given the pedlar the chance to convict you too, and John would certainly have been doomed. Indeed, it's possible O'Malley would have had us all incarcerated in the castle before he was finished.'

Lora had no heart for dress-fitting or wedding plans. It was as much as she could do to go out and exercise Rufus and Royal. Each day seemed endless, and the few days that elapsed before Paul was summoned to appear again at the castle were more like weeks.

While Paul was gone Lora hovered near the window but dusk had fallen and the shutters had been closed before the door knocker sounded through the hall and at last she was in John's arms.

'We are not out of the wood yet,' Paul warned. 'I'd advise you to get clear of the city before first light tomorrow, John, and do not linger in Lammermuir either. Just stay long enough to do the essentials. Then head for Glen Clova. There were several in that court-room who were determined to have your blood, minister or no. I must say you put up a good defence on your own behalf, though. You really spoke well.'

'It would all have been in vain,' John replied, 'if you hadn't used your influence. I thank you from the bottom of my heart, Paul.'

Lora rose early to see John off before dawn. She clung to him as if she would never let him go.

'Please try to be at Glen Clova tomorrow night, John,' she begged. 'I shall worry about you until you are with me again.'

'We must put our trust in the Lord, Lora dear,' he whispered, as they parted, 'I shall come as soon as I can.'

When John had gone, Lora didn't return to bed. Instead she hurried to complete her packing, and the rest of the household were also astir early, to prepare for their journey north. Fortunately, the sun shone, and the roads were clear of snow so they made good progress, stopping only to change horses, and to partake of food, at wayside hostelries.

John did not appear before dark the following night. It was well into the next afternoon before Lora caught sight of him riding up the glen and galloped off eagerly to meet him.

All at The Milton were anxious to hear how things had gone with John so he gave an account of the happenings of the past three days while they were gathered round the table for their evening meal.

'On my way to the manse I saw Fergus. He told me that he and the others concerned were all keeping a sharp look-out for trouble, but since none of the English soldiers had returned to the area there had been no need to worry unduly. No Jacobites had put in an appearance either, which, under the circumstances, was a blessing. I was able to see my successor comfortably settled at the manse, and I also introduced him to several of his new parishioners. Then, having said my 'goodbyes', I was riding off down the drive when a voice hailed me from the bushes. It was an old tinker fellow with whom I had become quite friendly during my ministry there. He was a decent old man – well-spoken and quite well-read – not the usual tinker-type. Thinking he wanted to bid me farewell, I dismounted and held out my hand, but, before he would speak, he looked around warily, came as close as he could to me, and lowered his voice.

"Whatever ye do, keep clear o' Edinburgh, Minister," he warned. "Paddy O'Malley's relations have been trying to stir up trouble. They've reported that Miss Lora Macrae was helping Jacobites to escape, and that you were also involved. There are warrants out for her arrest and your rearrest. I spent a night at the McLeeries' lodging-house so I can swear to the truth o' the information. If the Redcoats come here I'll see that they're put off the scent. In which direction will I send them, sir?"

"Say we have both gone to the west coast, Hamish. Thank you for your timely warning, old friend, and here's something to buy yourself a wee dram," I said, and with that I leapt into the saddle and I didn't put off until I reached here. We shall have to sail from Dundee to London now, Lora. Instead of a dignified departure from Edinburgh, with friends waving, as befits "a man of the cloth" and his lady, we shall be slinking off like all the other refugees.'

'Well if that sort of departure was good enough for so many of our friends, it's good enough for us,' laughed Lora.

In spite of the alarming news, everyone at The Milton was determined to make the wedding as happy an occasion as possible. The next day Lora took John to meet all her friends in the glen. It was also a last farewell, for Mrs Macrae had decided against renewal of the lease of The Milton. Edinburgh was to be her sole place of residence from then on. So, for Lora, another chapter was about to close.

Sunshine heralded the great day and the glen was arrayed in all its early spring beauty. As the wedding bells pealed out from the little church among the hills Lora's heart was filled with thankfulness that John had been spared to her. Whatever dangers the future might hold, they would face them together, side by side, as man and wife.

Just before they left for the ceremony, a far-travelled package was delivered to Lora. It had come all the way from France.

'For me? From France?' Lora asked in a puzzled voice.

Then she remembered!

'I know what it'll be,' she exclaimed. 'My personal crest and badge from Angus. What a wonderful wedding gift! It's so beautifully packed I don't think I'll open it before we leave,' and John approved of her decision, for time was getting short.

Everyone combined to make the wedding breakfast as jolly an occasion as possible, although all knew the final parting was imminent.

Lora, John and Royal were to be driven to Dundee by Mrs Macrae's coachman, and Paul had decided to avail himself of a lift, so he helped to keep up their spirits during the journey.

It was dark before they reached the quayside and Lora's heart was in her mouth as she watched the Redcoats' close inspection of all passengers. The port seemed literally to be swarming with English soldiers and she wondered nervously if John's name and hers had been added to the list of wanted persons. Luckily, Paul recognised one of the officers, and their friendly exchanges helped to ease the tension. Nevertheless, Lora heaved a sigh of relief when they were finally allowed to go aboard.

Paul had advised them not to hang around on deck but to go below immediately, and remain in their cabin until the ship had put to sea. He helped them to stow away their luggage, then wished them *bon voyage*, and the final farewell was over.

On the long sea voyage from the port of London to Capetown, Lora opened Angus's package. Besides the beautifully carved shield and the solid silver badge, it contained a long, nostalgic letter.

During their years of exile Lora was to look upon those works of art many times, and read and re-read that lovely long letter, while in memory she relived the stirring adventures of those troublous days in Scotland when to cry 'Loyal!' spelt danger, and the shadow of death was never far away.

EPILOGUE

Lora, John and Royal arrived safely in South Africa. They settled in a beautiful part of the Cape Province, where John established a Scots kirk for the Scottish settlers in the area. They had two children – both boys – and they all grew to love the country of their adoption.

Several times throughout the years, Paul visited them on his way to, or from, the East, and this kept them in touch with home.

After sixteen happy years in the Cape Province, John unfortunately developed Blackwater Fever and died. Lora was devastated by his loss but Paul happened to arrive soon after and he persuaded Lora and her boys to return on his ship to Scotland. Paul had, by this time, married his cousin Maria who had been widowed very early when her first husband was lost at sea.

About a year after Lora's bereavement, Paul succeeded in bringing Lennox and Lora in touch with each other again. Lennox had never married and when he visited Edinburgh he discovered that he was as much in love with Lora as ever.

So, more than twenty years after they had first met, Lora and Lennox were wed. Lora was by that time still only thirty-eight years of age. They settled on Lennox's estate in Gloucestershire and had one child – a daughter.

Lora's boys completed their education in England but they missed the land of sunshine and both eventually returned to South Africa.

Lora never crossed the sea again, but Lennox and she saw the nineteenth century well on its way, and lived happily to a ripe old age.

GLOSSARY

a'body—everybody
afore—before
ain—own
ane—one
arles—money fee paid (to confirm work
   engagement)
auld—old
aye—yes
aye—always
bairns—children
baith—both
besom—broom or brush
bide—stay
boozin'—drinking alcohol
braw—fine
breeks—trousers
buddy—person
brose caup—wooden porridge bowl
canna—cannot
canny—gentle
cairty—small cart
cauld—cold
chappin'—knocking
clachan—a (small) village
claith—cloth
cratur—creature
cruisie—old-time oil lamp with rush
   wick
dae—do
daft gowk—silly fool
deid—dead
de'il—devil
dinna—don't
dominie—schoolmaster
doobts—doubts
dourness—sullen attitude, unfriendliness
driech—wet and miserable
dukery-pawkery—falsity
feart—afraid
fechtin'—fighting
frae—from
fule—fool
garret—attic
gey—rather
gi'e—give
guid—good

hairst—harvest
haudin'—holding
haugh—meadow
heid—head
howe—hollow
jist—just
kail—broth
ken—know
kist—chest or trunk
laddie—boy
lassie—girl
licht—light
mair—more
mind—remember
the morn—tomorrow
nae—no
nicht—night
noo—now
ony—any
oors—ours
oorsels—ourselves
pend—alleyway, cul-de-sac
puir—poor
(cattle) raike—common pasture for
   grazing cattle *en route*
the riggin'—mountain top, hilltop
smiddy—smithy, or forge
sneck—catch (on door or gate)
sodger—soldier
stane—stone
(whisky) still—apparatus for making
   illegal whisky
settled their hash—put an end to their
   plans
ta'en—taken
tatties—potatoes
thocht—thought
thrawn—ill tempered, determined
tink or tinkie—tinker
toon—town
tryst—meeting place, or market
trysted—arranged to meet
twa—two
wa'—wall
weel—well
whaur—where

207

Howletsden

Glen-Ogil

Den of Ogil

Auchlochie

from Glen Clova

R. South Esk

Noran Water

Chance Inn

The Fern

Glen Quiech

Cullow

Wellfot

Dykehead

Cortachy Cas.

Memus

Prosen Water

Tannadice

to Kirriemuir

R. South Esk

Justinhaugh

Finav Cas

Finavon Hill

Sketch of Cliffs at Aberbrothock.

Seaton Den

Auchmithie Rd.

Cliffs

Dark Cave.

Catlinheugh Bay.

path

The De'il's Heid.

path

Cliffs

Dickmont's Den.

The Blowhole.

Cliffs

The Mariner's Grave.

The Mermaid's Kirk.

to Davie's Cottage

The Needle's E'e.

Helen B. McKenzie